For Daisy.
Maybe you could pick mine up once in a while.

EMPIRE OF THE GODS

BOOK I IN THE JACK GIBSON SERIES

BENJAMIN NASH

This is a work of fiction. Names, characters, places, and incidents either are the product of the author's imagination or are used fictitiously. Any resemblance to actual persons, living or dead, events, or locales is entirely coincidental.

First edition November 2021

Editing by Bryony Sutherland
Author photo by Asia Pracz
Cover design by aksaramantra
Typesetting by Julie Springer

ISBN 978-1-7399761-0-1 (paperback)
ISBN 978-1-7399761-1-8 (ebook)

CONTENTS

PROLOGUE

People say they remember where they were when the twin towers fell. Well, it was the same for me when the Pyramids were destroyed. I was at work, listening to Tony Angelos talking about his new slow cooker while wondering which of life's wrong turns had screwed me this badly. The soul-sapping discussion drew to a close when Laura from IT blurted the news out across the office. Trust her to hear it first; she never does any bloody work.

When we weren't being interrupted by anything as mundane as our actual day jobs, everyone spent the afternoon glued to whatever screen they could lay their hands on. Footage was plastered across every news and social media outlet on the planet, so people could vicariously experience the shocking violence of the initial blasts, and gawp at the heart-wrenching stories of human casualties.

Television commentators filled the days that followed discussing and dissecting the blurry images. The advanced nature of the missiles meant fingers were pointed at powerful governments. Some people thought it was a secret test launch gone tragically wrong; others that it was a deliberate attack on the Egyptian State. But if anyone knew the real answer, they were choosing to remain silent.

CHAPTER 1

Two a.m. in the hotel bar and sleep wasn't on the agenda. We were on day four of an eventful team-building week in the Cotswolds. The day's highlights included our poorly constructed raft mirroring the Titanic's maiden voyage and Denzil shouting at Mike during the balloon debate to, 'Get out before I push you out, you bellend!'

We were staying at an old stone manor house called the Naysmere Hotel. Nestled in the heart of the idyllic English countryside, it had looked amazing on the website. In reality, it was a complete dump. With hindsight, our suspicions should have been raised by the number of flares and kipper ties in the hotel photos. Denzil ranted about suing the scumbags for false advertising, but as they still had the same interior furnishings from the pictures, I told him they were probably safe.

We were the last men standing in the hotel bar that Thursday morning. Actually, we were sitting, on account of us being so drunk. The barman was multi-tasking, glued to a TV report about the previous week's missile attacks in Egypt, and attempting to extricate the contents of his left nostril. My grandad once said a refusal to give in no matter the odds was the mark of a great man. Credit where credit's due, the guy persisted with a range of fingers and techniques before securing his quarry.

'I'm going to bed,' I announced, causing Denzil to look at me like I'd just morphed into the barman's bogey.

'What's your problem?' he replied. 'There's free alcohol and no work tomorrow.'

'We've got to be up soon,' I said.

'We've got to be up soon,' he repeated in a baby voice. 'You're twenty-four, not eighty-four!'

I rested my head on my folded arms. 'I'm tired and I'm drunk.'

'Gibby, Gibby, Gibby. Going to bed early still won't get you into Lucy's knickers.'

'Piss off.'

'So, you do fancy the boss then,' he said, laughing.

'I don't,' I protested. But it was true. I liked her so much it hurt.

After singing tunelessly about me wanting to both kiss and marry her, Denzil gave me a sympathetic look. 'You need to let that one go, my friend,' he said. 'She's too professional to cross that line.'

I knew he was right, but hearing it still made me feel hollow inside.

'Besides, you'd need to grow a pair first and tell her how you feel. And let's be honest, mate, that's not really your style.'

'What do you mean?'

'In life's great game of chess, some of us move the pieces and some of us are the pieces.'

'Charming.'

Denzil patted me on the shoulder. 'We're in the midst of a crisis here, my friend. And I'm not talking about that cover-up in Cairo.'

'Not this again,' I mumbled.

'You're ignoring the signs.'

'I'm ignoring you.'

'Incinerating the Pyramids of Giza was no accident. You can't tell me the work experience kid at the Pentagon accidently pressed the wrong button. I'm telling you mate, dark forces are at work as we speak.'

'Yeah, they're called rum and coke.'

Denzil turned to the barman. 'Hey mate? Can you look after our drinks, please?' The man grunted in response as Denzil put an arm around my shoulder and guided me towards the door.

'Where are we going?' I was struggling to walk in a straight line.

'Shh.' Denzil glanced at the disinterested barman, then squeezed me tighter. 'I've got a little something to give you in the toilets,' he said with a creepy wink. It was a disturbing moment.

As we stumbled past the front desk I noticed the receptionist was staring at me. I smiled back in an attempt to disarm her and received a deathly glare for my troubles.

Denzil laughed. 'If looks could kill, Jack Gibson, you'd be six feet under.'

I glanced back and was irritated to see she was still watching me, like a nosey Miss Marple. Once safely inside the sanctity of the men's toilets,

Denzil ushered me into a cubicle and locked the door. He wasn't the thinnest guy around, so it was a bit of a squeeze.

'Well, that's rather delightful,' he said, clocking the previous occupant's deposit. Denzil dropped the loo seat, opened his wallet and removed something small. He started swinging it backwards and forwards in front of my face like the world's worst hypnotist. Following his hand made me want to barf, which forced me to grab his wrist. That's when my brain registered the small plastic bag filled with white powder.

'So, amigo,' he said in a rubbish foreign accent, 'are you ready for a little Colombian adventure?'

'Nice accent, dickwad. I didn't know Colombia was in Sweden.'

Denzil pulled out a bank card and chopped up two lines of coke on top of the cistern. 'Give me a note,' he said, and I passed him a twenty, which he rolled into a neat tube and used to snort one of the lines. He handed it to me as he tilted his head back and sniffed. 'Whoa! Now that is good stuff, Gibby.'

I inserted the note into my nose, pressed a finger over my left nostril and tried to inhale the powder. I was swaying from the copious amount of alcohol I'd consumed, so it was a struggle to line up the tube with the charlie. However, after several failed attempts and a few choice insults from Denzil, I managed to hoover it up. I sniffed several times as I unrolled the banknote, then used my finger to wipe off the residue before shoving it back into my pocket.

Denzil laughed and patted me on the shoulder as I rubbed the chemicals from my finger onto my gums. 'That gear is definitely going to sort you out,' he said.

'What gear would that be then, fellas?' came an authoritative voice from somewhere above our heads.

We looked up and saw a man peering over the top of the cubicle.

'It's the police, lads,' he said. 'Open the door and keep your hands where I can see them.'

My heart sank into my shoes. Mum and Dad were going to bloody kill me.

When my brother died my parents kindly decided to hang the combined weight of their hopes and dreams on the coat hook of my life. They'd expected big things from their decidedly average son and had experienced regular and profound disappointment ever since. Now this moment of stupidity was going to ruin my life once and for all, and the worst thing about it was that I had no one to blame but my pathetic, idiotic self. I was spared from further self-loathing when Denzil bent over and his backside slammed me face first into the toilet door. This resulted in a small nosebleed for me and a loud 'You idiot!' for him. My friend lifted the loo seat and threw the drugs into the pan.

As he reached for the handle, the policeman made a heroic leap into the cubicle. 'Get away from that flush!'

But Denzil was a man possessed.

I'd known Denzil Reid for nineteen years. Yes, that's right, since the very first day of school. Okay, the second, because Jamaica's finest—his words, not mine—wet his pants on the first morning and it put me off going anywhere near him. Neither of us had the best of childhoods and as the years slid by, our damaged souls were pulled together like lost magnets. Now we were inseparable. The guy had even helped me get a job at the same company as him when I left university. Given the length of time we'd spent in each other's company, you might be surprised to learn I'd never seen him in a fight. I mean, I'd watched him run away a few times. I'd even seen him hide in a Grundon bin when Dean Lacey wanted to beat him up for hitting on his sister, Carley. But actually going mano-a-mano? Never.

To be perfectly honest, I didn't see a great deal that morning either. This was mainly because my eyes were streaming like Niagara Falls because that moron almost broke my nose on the door. I'm happy to report, however, that the boy gave a pretty solid account of himself while trying to flush the evidence away. Well, he did alright until the officer pulled Denzil's hoodie up over his head. As my friend was plunged into darkness and for reasons best known to himself, he started screaming, 'Auntie Cedella! Help!' at the top of his voice.

Heavily outgunned, Denzil stopped struggling and the melee drew to a close. That's when I noticed a second police officer shouting and banging on the door. It turns out the average toilet cubicle isn't made for three. You can fit one person in there comfortably, two if you're a parent with a small child, or if you're consuming cocaine with your bestie like my good self. But three? That's too much of a squeeze. I tried to comply with the second crime fighter's request to exit the stall. The issue I faced was the lack of space to actually open the door. This left an unsatisfactory gap to try and wriggle through, a manoeuvre made even more challenging by the eager second officer yanking on my left arm. I was formally introduced to fears for future fatherhood as my bits made contact with the edge of the door. The officer kept on tugging with the persistence of a yappy little dog. When it started to hurt I let out an involuntary 'Ouch', followed by a rather desperate, 'Hang on', and finally a panicked, 'My nuts!'

I was free. I froze as I found myself staring into the face of a female police officer. Then I found myself staring at the wall as she set about throwing me against it. Fortunately, the woman was quite small. If the six-foot-four monster hauling Denzil out of the cubicle had done it, I would have lost most of my front teeth. With her it was more like when your mum gives you a slap for bad behaviour when you're a teenager. I mean the will was certainly there; she just lacked some of the power. Bless her.

By now the line of charlie mixed with a healthy dose of adrenaline had sobered me up and I longed to be back in my drunken haze. Maybe that way I could escape the feeling of being totally and utterly screwed. I watched as Big D was hauled unceremoniously out of the cubicle with his hoodie still over his head. His jeans had slipped down in the ruckus, so he had an offensive portion of arse candy on display.

The police officers ordered us to hold our hands out in front of us as we were presented with every criminal's must-have fashion accessary: a set of handcuffs. I've always believed it's important for one to be on trend. I felt a bit like a delinquent from a cheap reality police show, but without the terrible tracksuit and trainers.

'Right lads,' said the woman. 'What drugs were you taking? Coke? Speed? MDMA?'

I stared at the floor like my eyes had been glued to it and prayed for the grubby tiles to swallow me up.

'We've just caught you in the act,' said the male officer. 'Stop wasting everybody's time and tell us what it is.'

Denzil managed to say 'It wasn't drugs,' but his voice came out like a wimpy five-year-old's. Man, we must have looked like a right pair of wieners.

'So, was it you two gentleman that vandalised the Mercedes?' The female officer's distaste was written all over her judgy face.

'What Mercedes?' replied Denzil.

'The black one in the car park with "Kevin's a cockhead" keyed down one side.' She was standing a little too close for comfort and I was definitely getting guilty-until-proven innocent vibes. 'The receptionist saw someone fitting your description running away,' she continued, turning her condescending gaze on me. Now it made more sense why the receptionist had been staring at me like I was off to murder the entire population of the local village.

I was overtaken by a feeling of immense injustice.

High Tower turned to his partner. 'Are you alright here for a moment? I need to search the stalls.'

'Yeah, no problem,' she replied, turning her attention right back to me. 'You could have done this the easy way,' she said in a patronizing tone. 'You're just making it worse for yourself.'

I was really starting to dislike her, so I decided to focus on the copper heading back into the cubicle to hunt for evidence. I wondered if he'd imagined when signing up for a life of crime-fighting that he'd be fishing for drugs at two-thirty in the morning in a turd-infested fudge pot. When I heard, 'For God's sake!' emanating from the stall, I guessed he'd spied the gargantuan brownie gracing the bottom of the lavatory. I hoped that vision would be enough to deter him from his planned itinerary of jobbie-bobbing, but the sound of a splash indicated Britain's finest must have dived right on in. I had a vision of his crap-covered hand triumphantly raising a bag of coke aloft, like King Arthur pulling Excalibur from the stone. But if the bag had been open when it hit the water, the evidence could already have been washed away.

My mind switched to an image of me in a courtroom with my mum in tears and my dad looking like he wanted to castrate me. I began bargaining with God, promising to be a better person if he'd just let me get away with my misdemeanour. The fact I hadn't seen the inside of a church since I was seven was irrelevant. Desperate times call for desperate measures.

There was a scream. And it was one of the worst I'd ever heard. Even worse than my dad's when Mum accidentally reversed his brand-new car into our garden wall. It was so high-pitched and so full of shock that it sent a shiver racing down my spine. I made eye contact with Denzil, who at least had the decency to look as aghast as I did. Then came a series of loud crashing and banging sounds as the plastic cubicle walls shook like they were in the midst of an earthquake.

'Are you alright in there, Greg?' The policewoman looked spooked, but then I imagined PC Greg was normally the one causing the screams, not making them.

The male officer came flying out of the cubicle and crashed into the wall, forcing Denzil to leap sideways to avoid being flattened. The screaming continued as he did a strange, frantic jig around the interior of the men's toilets. I watched, mesmerised, as he leapt about, screaming, shouting and slapping at his clothes.

Now, while my substance-fuddled brain wasn't fully operational at this point, it was still functioning enough to detect that something was seriously wrong. And that's when I noticed he'd done more than get the foot-long mess on his fingers. It was stuck to his clothes.

How the hell did that happen, I wondered, with no small amount of disgust. Until I saw them, that is. Them being the hundreds of tiny brown legs and the two ruby-red eyes. That was the moment the proverbial penny dropped like a smokestack treated with dynamite. I was looking at a giant brown insect and it was one of the ugliest, creepiest things I had ever laid eyes on.

I stood there frozen, like a guy paired with Medusa at a speed-dating event. The creature writhed about on Greg's clothes, emitting high-pitched squeaking sounds. I winced when it started burrowing down the top of the policeman's trousers. Greg tried grabbing hold of the monstrosity, but whatever the thing was, it was strong enough to fend off a being that was a hundred times its size. The officer's howls roused his partner from her trance and she ran towards him, pulling out her mace spray. I rated the chances of that plan working out as somewhere between overly optimistic and no sodding way.

'Help me,' he shouted, over and over.

The female police officer sprayed the giant bug, but it was already too late and the abomination slipped down the top of his trousers like a child slurping spaghetti. Her next move was to try and undo his belt, but the man was rolling around too much for her to get anywhere near his crotch. I watched in horror as the creature moved around to the back of his trousers.

Greg was grabbing his rear end by this stage, screaming, 'No!' His eyes went as wide as the coffee coasters my Nanny Bertie brought back from Greece last year, and for the briefest of moments he stared right at me, before his eyes glazed over. I watched with mounting alarm as bright red blood flew from his mouth and covered the floor. Then Greg went limp.

'What in the name of God was that?' I shouted at no one in particular.

The second officer threw herself down next to her partner. 'Greg! Hang in there buddy,' she cried, while fighting to undo the man's trousers. Unfortunately, performing this task meant she was too preoccupied to notice the sounds of cracking ceramic toilet bowls and splashing that were coming from the direction of the stalls.

'Er, what's that noise?' Denzil didn't have to wait long for an answer. From under, over and around the cubicle walls, more of the brown creatures appeared. Except this time there were thousands of them.

CHAPTER 2

The giant insects began flooding the men's bathroom like water overwhelming a sinking ship. I shouted at the officer to run, but it was too late. The creatures swarmed all over her, burrowing inside her ears, eyes and clothes. She screamed, allowing at least three to force their way down her throat, tearing her face apart in the process. The memory of it still haunts the dark corridors of mind, by which I mean it gives me a serious case of the willies.

My survival instinct kicked in and I dragged a hyperventilating Denzil to his feet.

'Move!' I screamed, shoving him towards the door.

The floor disappeared under the advance of the writhing, squealing abominations and I was obliged to push my mate out of the toilets with such force that he stumbled and fell. I turned and only just managed to close the door before the creatures thudded against it.

Denzil rolled onto his back. 'What are those things?'

I had no fricking clue, and to be honest, even if I did, right then I was too freaked out to form a sentence.

'What in the blazes are you doing?' shouted the receptionist.

I glanced in almost every direction before realising she was talking to us.

'Officers,' she cried in the direction of the toilet door. 'They're getting away!'

Damn, she was annoying.

There was a loud shriek and I spun around, expecting to see more of the bog bugs cascading down the paisley-carpeted stairs. What I saw instead was our manager, Lucy Chong, leaping down them two at a time. She had a towel wrapped around her head like a turban and another covering her body. They weren't the longest and I swear I got a flash of the box.

'Help!' she screamed in her American accent. 'There's giant earwigs!'

Lucy ploughed straight into me and grabbed hold of my hoodie to stop herself falling over. I made a pathetic 'Oof' noise as the wind was knocked out of me. I maintained some semblance of pride by staying on my feet. But only just.

Lucy's eyes bulged with fear as she shook me and glanced nervously back up the stairs. 'Earwigs,' she repeated. 'There's giant earwigs.'

I told her to calm down, but she carried on shaking me.

'One got into my makeup bag.'

'It's alright,' I told her, in a half-arsed attempt at being comforting.

'I'll have to throw it away,' she continued, sounding manic. 'They crawled out of the goddamn toilet.'

'Please stop shaking me,' I said.

'The toilet!'

'Stop it,' I replied. And that's when I lost it. 'Will you stop bloody shaking me or I'll start shaking you!' It came out with more gusto than intended, but it had the desired effect. Lucy stopped.

Now, under normal circumstances I appreciate it's not considered good form to shout at a woman in distress. But in my defence, I was under the influence, I'd been arrested, I'd seen insects eat two police officers alive and I'd barely escaped with my life. So, I'd say these circumstances were pretty bloody extenuating.

I looked down at my manager clinging to me in that skimpy little towel. Then, for the briefest of moments I forgot all about the crap critters. Lucy was so lovely. She was smart, driven, funny, kind and pretty. My ideal woman. I mean, she was quite old. I wasn't sure of her exact age but she was the wrong side of thirty, although I'd never been averse to an older lady. Sadly, however, my crush on her remained unrequited.

Denzil clambered to his feet. 'This is so messed up,' he said. 'If they're in the downstairs toilets and up in Lucy's room, then this whole place must be riddled.'

Lucy looked down at my hands, then at Denzil's. Her eyes narrowed as she took in her surroundings for the first time. 'Why are you both in handcuffs?'

'They were vandalising cars,' said the receptionist.

'Oh, piss off, Cruella,' said Denzil.

'How dare you!' The receptionist looked appalled. 'I know a pair of criminals when I see them.'

'Just shut your mouth, you big ball bag.'

'Don't be so rude, Denzil,' said Lucy.

But the receptionist wasn't listening. 'Officers?' she cried, scampering towards the men's toilets.

Her trajectory filled me with a sudden surge of dread and I instinctively cried out, 'Don't open it!'

The woman halted at the sound of an agonized scream emanating from the top of the stairs. We turned to see Alison from marketing holding the rear end of a bug that was protruding from her left eye socket. Her hands, cheek and the front of her pale-blue, sheep-patterned pyjamas were covered in blood.

'Help me!' she cried, as it twisted and whipped its body about in the air.

I was struck by a wave of nausea. I tried looking away, but it was already too late. Denzil and Lucy leapt aside as I utilised the contents of my stomach to create some impromptu floor art.

Lucy shrieked as Alison stumbled and fell down the stairs like an unskilled stunt performer. Our colleague came to rest in a crumpled heap at the bottom with her neck bent at a sickening angle. I retched as the bug vanished inside her skull. Then, from distant rooms and corridors throughout the hotel, we heard a grotesque chorus of people crying out in terror and pain.

'Officers!' screamed the receptionist as she twisted and rattled the door handle.

'Don't!' cried Denzil.

But there was no way she was going to listen to a pair of alleged criminals, so we watched in horror as she pressed her shoulder against the door and forced it open.

When Denzil screamed 'Run!' I didn't even bother checking to see if Lucy was with me. There was no pseudo-heroic ladies first malarkey. I was so scared that I turned and ran as fast as my legs would carry me. I skidded as I reached the main door, knocking it open with my outstretched arms. The handcuffs cut into my wrists and the cold night air slapped me around the face like an angry lover. I moved in the style of a panicked gazelle and was at least twenty yards across the car park when Denzil's cries stopped me dead in my tracks.

I looked back to see him helping Lucy navigate the sharp gravel. With every muscle, nerve and sinew in my body screaming at me to get the hell out of there, I forced myself to go back.

'Get on my back,' I shouted, leaning forwards and shoving my bum in Lucy's general direction. With my hands cuffed in front of me I must have looked like a demented skier.

Lucy threw her arms around my neck and jumped on. 'My towel!' she said as it came loose. But right then I was far more concerned about my survival than her decency. So, half choked and with my boss shrieking hysterically in my ear that Denzil would get a 'goddamn smack in the mouth' if he looked at her again, I ran, or should I say, plodded as fast as I could towards my car.

As the hotel was such a dump, there was no way I would have left anything of value in my room. This meant I had my wallet, phone and car keys tucked safely away in the pocket of my jeans. I ran, or more accurately, stumbled and wheezed past several cars until we arrived at my brand-new pride and joy, a Renault Megane RS in metallic black.

The managing director at work had told me not to buy French. 'You should always go German,' he'd advised, unaware that other people's salaries didn't stretch to his Porsche. But as I'd always been a huge fan of pains au chocolats, snogging and Brigitte Bardot, I went for it. And with around 300bhp, a 0-60 speed of under six seconds and a monthly fee I could just about afford, I say *Vive la France.*

It soon dawned on me that the combination of handcuffs and alcohol were going to make driving tricky. The thought of someone else touching my baby nearly made me retch for a second time, but sadly there was no other option.

'Lucy,' I said, 'You need to drive.'

'Okay,' she replied, repositioning the towels. 'Where are the keys?'

'In my left pocket.'

She turned towards Denzil and raised a hand in the air. 'Seriously, Denzil, if you check me out again I swear to God I'll be applying pressure to your face with my fist.'

Denzil mumbled something about not flattering herself.

A scream accompanied by the sound of breaking glass drew our attention, and we turned to see a shadowy figure fall from an upstairs window, landing on the gravel with a spine-chilling crunch. A middle-aged man in socks and Y-fronts raced out of the hotel covered in several of the giant bugs. He ricocheted off a parked car, setting off the alarm, before stumbling away into the darkness. Fear surged inside me and I thrust my groin towards Lucy like a seventies deviant disco dancer while yelling, 'Get the keys!' Lucy shoved her hand into my pocket and deftly removed them, avoiding touching my bits in the process, much to my disappointment.

We were soon racing along dark country roads with me telling Lucy every five seconds to drive carefully and her telling me every five seconds to shut the hell up. She also removed the second towel from her head and placed it across her lap to prevent old perv-alert in the back from seeing too much.

'One of you call the cops,' she said, which illustrated that despite being highly distraught, she was still way more compos mentis than we were. 'And an ambulance,' she added. 'God, I hope Jo and Susan are okay. The authorities need to get those creatures contained.'

'Did you see Alison?' asked Denzil.

'Shut up, mate.' I placed a hand over my mouth.

'Her neck all bent and twisted like that.'

'Please shut up.'

'And that thing eating its way into her head—'

'Be quiet, jackass,' snapped Lucy. 'We all saw it. You don't need to keep going on about it. Now do something useful for once in your life and call the cops.' She put her left hand on my leg. 'Are you alright?'

'Yeah,' I replied. But I really, really wasn't.

It's strange, because if you'd have said to me when I woke up that morning that I'd be spending part of my day with a half-naked Lucy stroking my thigh, I would have thought it was Christmas come early. Right now, however, was a hollow victory. So, I ignored the rubbing and focused on my breathing. Perhaps then I could hold on to whatever was left in my stomach.

Denzil shook his phone, holding it against different windows, while pulling a series of facial expressions suggesting constipation. 'I can't get any reception.'

I spent a few moments wrestling my phone from my pocket. 'Me neither.'

'Jesus Christ,' said Denzil. 'We're in the middle of nowhere. We'd better not break down around here, because with that pretty mouth of yours, Gibby, you'll be in all sorts of trouble.' He chuckled to himself. 'I'm joking, of course. You look more like the weird kid playing the banjo.'

'I play your mum's banjo,' I replied.

'Tell me you didn't just say that, Jack?' said Lucy. 'That's disgusting.'

'I know,' I said. 'It's riddled with crabs.'

Lucy slapped me around the head. 'Don't. Be. So. Gross,' she said, in time with the blows. 'How much have you two had to drink tonight? And don't tell me it's one or two.'

Unfortunately, Lucy had never understood the British drinking culture: namely that a functioning alcoholic back home in San Francisco is known as someone with a social life in the UK.

'Two or three,' replied Denzil.

'Oh my God.' She sounded on the verge of tears. 'It smells like a brewery in here.'

We all went quiet. I'm never good when women get upset. I never know what to say. I once dumped a girl called Julie Smith in a cheap steak restaurant. I thought that being in a public place would afford me some degree of safety. Not so. When I made my announcement, she burst into tears. Massive, loud sobs with stringy snot running all down her face. It was so embarrassing. Our fellow diners stared at me like I was some sort of wife beater. I wouldn't have minded, but I'd only been dating the bunny boiler for three weeks. I felt her being all over Uncle Bob at my cousin's wedding the previous weekend was acceptable grounds for early termination. Still, she exacted her revenge by throwing a vodka and cranberry juice all over my jeans. I had to get the 194 bus home looking like I had serious urinary problems.

The much saner Lucy Chong sniffed a couple of times and appeared to pull herself together, thus saving me from having to say anything. Thank God.

We made a brief stop at the side of the road so Lucy could change into the spare clothes I had in the boot. These comprised a grubby T-shirt, a tracksuit and a pair of wellington boots left over from Monday's activities. I could see she wasn't impressed from the expression on her face. Fair play to the woman, despite looking like she was being force fed-cat sick, she put them on.

'They don't smell so great,' she complained.

'Sorry,' I replied. 'It's the best I can do at the minute.' All my clothes were too big for her small frame, and she looked like a cross between a pig farmer and a rapper with hygiene issues.

We got back into the car and carried on driving through the countryside. It's strange how the rural landscape can look so beautiful by day and so bloody creepy at night.

'I'll keep heading for the motorway,' said Lucy, during another burst of competence. 'Keep checking your phones for a signal.'

As we followed the twisting, turning roads, we began the rather delicate task of explaining to our manager how we'd ended up in handcuffs. We avoided all references to class A drugs and hanging out together in a toilet cubicle. Fortunately, after a lifetime of lying our way out of trouble, we were able to provide a coherent tale of innocent victims, mistaken identity and good old-fashioned wrong place, wrong time. If Lucy didn't know us so well, she would have believed it. Sadly, we were all so engrossed in the tale of our unjust criminality that we didn't notice the crossroads up ahead, or more importantly, the big old car that was racing towards it without any lights on. Well, not until it was too late. I saw the outline of the vehicle about a milli-second before the impact, which was followed by a detached kind of shock and a generous surge of pain. Then the whole universe twisted and spun in slow motion before somebody turned out the lights.

CHAPTER 3

I woke up to find my face squashed against the passenger airbag. For a split second I couldn't remember a thing. Then, like the proverbial tsunami, it all came flooding back. The toilet centipedes, the booze, the drugs and the police.

'Is everyone okay?' asked Lucy.

'I think so,' I replied.

'Am I okay?' asked Denzil. 'Well, let me see. I've been physically assaulted in a toilet; I've been arrested; I've been forced to dump a perfectly good gram of coke; I've been chased by thousands of big, scary murdering centipedes that sprouted as if by magic from a number of toilet bowls; I've witnessed the horrendous deaths of several people; I've got the hangover from hell; and, oh yes, I just received a massive testicle wedgie from my jeans when the car we were escaping in was involved in a serious road accident.'

I waited a few seconds before responding. 'Yeah, but apart from that, are you okay?' Even in the most challenging of times, I think it's important to maintain one's sense of humour.

'Sure,' he replied, adjusting his crotch. 'Apart from that, I'm tip bloody top.'

'Sorry, Denzil,' said Lucy. 'Did you just say "gram of coke"?'

'He said can of coke,' I replied.

'No, Jack, I'm pretty sure he just said "gram of coke".'

'Can of coke.'

'Gram of coke.'

'Can of coke.'

'Just because you keep repeating it, Jack, won't make it true.' Lucy's eyes went wide. 'Oh my God. That's why you were both being arrested. You're drug addicts!'

'We're not drug addicts.'

'I don't believe it.'

'We're not drug addicts,' I repeated.

'You don't use needles, do you?'

'No, because we're not drug addicts.'

Lucy stared intently at nothing in particular. 'Well, that explains why Denzil's project was such a disaster.'

'No,' I replied. 'That's because Denzil's a flipping idiot.'

'Shut it, booty breath,' said Denzil.

'Jesus, Jack.' Lucy shook her head. 'I can't believe this. I literally cannot believe it.'

Ms Chong went quiet and stared out of the window. It's strange how people can view things so differently. I guess that's why there are so many wars. What to Lucy was the most shocking and appalling thing ever, was to Jack Gibson and Denzil Reid an average weekend night out, or night in, talking garbage. But I wasn't in the mood to debate the moral question of recreational drug use with my line manager, particularly when I didn't have a leg to stand on. I decided to borrow from Lucy's country and silently plead the fifth, before making a swift exit.

I unbuckled my seatbelt and pushed the door open with my foot. As I gingerly exited the remains of the most expensive thing I'd ever bought, I was confronted by a scene of utter carnage. My once beautiful car sat in the middle of the road, the left side comprehensively smashed to buggery. Feeling nauseous yet again, I bent over and rustled up a quick pavement pizza, or in this case, a countryside curry. There was a surprising amount left, despite the Stalinesque purges of the night thus far. This time some of it even came out of my nose. It was most unpleasant.

I spat a couple of times and felt sorry for myself. The world around me now smelt of sick. By this point in the proceedings I was hurting all over, although where the hangover ended and the car crash began was hard to say. My eyes followed a trail of debris along the road and off into a field. I could see the assorted detritus culminating several metres away in an SUV lying on its roof. While I knew I should check if anyone was injured, I was terrified of what I might find. But sometimes, walking away just isn't an option. I switched on my phone torch and limped towards the upturned vehicle.

The car windows, or what was left of them, were blacked out, making it difficult to see inside.

'Hello?' I called. 'Is anyone hurt?'

Judging by the state of the car, it was a dumb question, but I needed to say something, right? After several hard yanks on the door handle, a loud 'For Christ's sake' and a John McEnroe-style 'You've *got* to be kidding me', the door flew open. I lost my footing and fell unceremoniously onto my backside. Now I don't know what I'd been expecting to see after the supremely bizarre night I'd just had, but this was not it.

The driver's seat contained a woman with dark hair and olive skin whom I guessed was in her late twenties, covered in a worrying amount of blood. The passenger side was half squashed by the newly concave roof and populated by a weird-looking man in blue face paint. What disturbed me most was that he was dressed like a Pharoah and clutching an ornate golden box. I had an unsettling flashback to a news report showing a parent carrying a dead child away from the rubble of the Pyramids.

As nasty as it may sound, because obviously the poor guy had just been involved in a serious road accident, he looked like a right wally. I decided that if I was ever going to be caught up in another car crash, it would never be while wearing fancy dress.

'Ternion,' whispered the man.

Pissed out of his head as well, I thought. No wonder they bloody hit us. 'Sorry, buddy, what did you say?'

'Ternion,' he repeated. His eyes were closed and his voice came out like a rasping gurgle. He didn't sound like he was in the best shape.

'Try to stay calm,' I said. 'We'll get you an ambulance.' Although how I was going to rustle up one of those without a working phone was anyone's guess. I tried thinking back to the company first aid course I'd attended. I couldn't remember a great deal, apart from snobby Jessica from HR accidentally burping while attempting to resuscitate the CPR dummy, and Denzil having simulated sex with it every time the trainer's back was turned. I now regretted not paying more attention. Why is it things never seem important at the time?

What I did know however, from watching a reality TV show, was that the blue man wasn't the only one of us that needed to keep his composure. My having a meltdown wasn't going to do Papa Smurf here any favours. I needed to remain cool, calm and collected if I was going to help these poor souls.

'What's your name?' I asked.

The man began mumbling, but I couldn't make out what he was saying, which forced me to lean in closer.

'You're going to be okay, my friend,' I said in the tone you reserve for the old and the moronic. 'Just try and stay calm, yeah?' I looked around for my friends. 'Lucy?'

The man started coughing violently.

'Just try to stay calm, okay? Denzil?'

The blue man reached up and grabbed the front of my hoodie, at which point my brain registered that he'd painted his arms and hands blue as well. Full marks for going the whole nine yards with the costume, I thought, hoping none of it would rub off on my top. I was a long way from civilisation and therefore stain remover.

'Ternion,' he repeated.

'What's your name?' I asked again, before shouting once more for my irritatingly absent friends. 'Denzil? Lucy? Will you get the hell over here right now!'

The blue man pulled me towards him. He clearly wanted to say something, but I winced and tried to back away as I got a whiff of his vile breath. Then I realised that the stench was coming from the puke in my nose. But death breath or not, it was still too close for comfort and I was about to back away when the man's mouth dropped open like a big old basking shark and he went as limp as Macbeth's Porter.

I felt an invisible force dragging me towards the ornate golden box. With arms outstretched I reached for it like a mindless zombie. A muffled voice inside my head was telling me it probably wasn't the smartest idea to be opening it, but I couldn't stop myself. As soon as I touched its icy surface I knew I'd messed up. The lid lifted and a brilliant blue light poured out of it, striking me in the face. I could feel my eyes, nose and throat burning as I struggled to breathe. When I screamed, nothing came out. The pain was immense. It felt like an icy, concrete river was being poured into my soul.

Was this it? Was I destined to die in a field in the Cotswolds at only twenty-four? It wasn't quite the passing in my sleep from old age that I'd envisaged. I hadn't even achieved anything noteworthy in my life. No children, no fortune, no diseases cured, no orphanages built and no annoyingly ungrateful cats hissing at me while I rescued them from trees. Hell, I hadn't even assembled the coffee table I'd purchased from IKEA six months prior. I didn't know if the staff at the Pearly Gates had a category for oxygen thieves, but I had a sneaky suspicion I would be on it.

My feet left the ground as I was launched backwards into the air like I'd been caught in a Hollywood bomb blast. Then, for the second time in ten minutes, my conscious mind took a holiday.

I re-entered the physical world to find Lucy and Denzil leaning over me. Nice to see they'd bothered to grace me with their presence.

'Well, you give him mouth-to-mouth if you're so bloody keen,' said Denzil.

'He could be dying,' insisted Lucy.

'Then let's not make his last memory be his best mate trying to slip him the tongue.'

'Fine. I'll do it then.'

I opened my eyes and Lucy let out a gasp. 'Jack! Are you okay?'

'See,' said Denzil, 'he's fine.' His eyes widened. 'Bloody hell!'

My heart sank. 'What is it?'

Denzil flipped me the bird. 'How many fingers am I holding up?'

'Just the one you use to pick your dingleberries.'

'Will you two grow up?' Lucy looked like she wanted to slap us.

They helped me into a sitting position before Denzil picked up the wing mirror that had fallen off my car.

'My poor baby.' I gazed over at the wreck.

'Forget the car,' said Denzil. 'Look at you.'

'What?'

'If stupidity was an illness, you'd be terminal.'

They were looking at me like I was a nine-legged lab rat. 'What?' I examined my face in the mirror. 'Am I bleeding or something?'

'For God's sake,' said Denzil. 'You're such a dumbo. Here's a clue, brain box. What colour were your eyes when you woke up this morning?'

'Brown,' I said. Then I saw them. 'Oh, my good God,' I screeched. 'My eyes have gone blue.'

'Gone blue?' said Denzil. 'You look like the Kwisatz Haderach.'

'The what?' asked Lucy.

'The Kwisatz Haderach.'

'And for those of us with a life, I'll say it again,' Lucy retorted. 'The what?'

'The Kwisatz Haderach. *Dune.* The spice. You know? Blue eyes?'

Lucy stared at him blankly.

'From the spice,' said Denzil.

Lucy shook her head.

'The novel, *Dune*, by Frank Herbert.'

'Remind me why you two don't have girlfriends again?'

'Oh, hold on a second,' said Denzil. 'Let me just stitch my sides back together.'

The memory of the blue light and the strange passenger hit me like the realisation that you've just forgotten your mum's birthday. I stood up as fast as my battered body would allow. 'The blue man!' I almost shouted.

'Woah there, buddy.' Lucy grabbed my arm to stop me from falling over. 'I think you need to sit back down for a bit.'

'No,' I said, swaying like a jelly skyscraper. 'Look behind you. There's a blue man.'

'What are you blabbering on about?' Denzil turned to look at the upside-down car.

Lucy let out a squeal.

'Crap on my face,' said Denzil. 'There's a blue man.'

'Duh!' I hobbled back over to the car. 'There's a woman too, but she's not blue. I think they were on their way back from a fancy-dress party.'

We all stared into the vehicle.

'What the hell is he wearing?' Denzil asked.

'I have no idea,' I replied.

'Right. One of you check for a pulse,' said Lucy. 'They look like they're in pretty bad shape.'

'Calm down, little Miss Manager,' said Denzil. 'We're not at work now.'

Lucy put her hands on her hips. 'Do you want me to sign off your bar expenses or not?' she said, eyebrows raised to the sky.

'Alright, no need to get your knickers in a twist.'

We stood back and waited in silence as Denzil moved in to check the woman's pulse and then the blue man's. He sucked in a mouthful of air like a mechanic about to tell you that your car needs a whole new engine.

'What?' I asked.

'Well, I'm obviously not a doctor.'

'You're kidding me.'

'But I'd definitely say they've taken a trip to destination dead.'

'Their poor families,' said Lucy.

'Let's put Lucy's towels over them,' I suggested.

'Why?' asked Denzil.

'To give them some dignity,' replied Lucy, sounding irritated.

'Well, they don't give a toss, do they?' Denzil appeared confused. 'They're dead.'

'You really are heartless,' stated Lucy.

'Chill out, I'm only saying. But on a side note, Sherlock Holmes, what makes you think they were on their way back from a fancy-dress party?'

'Well, you muppet, why else would he be wearing blue face paint?' I asked.

'Well, *you muppet*, what if it's not blue face paint?'

'I'm sorry?' asked Lucy.

'It's not face paint,' said Denzil.

'Say that again.'

'Okay. It's not face paint.'

'What do you mean it's not face paint?' I asked.

'Jesus!' he snapped. 'You two have got worse hearing than my Grandad Ainsley. I mean it's not frigging face paint.' Denzil stepped to one side. 'Just look at him.'

It's strange how you can miss something that's right in front of you. It could be an interesting building you pass every day on your way to work, or my Nanny Bertie when she accidentally walks into the men's toilets. Then something happens and you turn your head, or security politely escorts you out and you just can't understand how you missed it. Well, this was one of those times.

Now that I really looked at the guy, it was obvious that it wasn't face paint. In fact, the more I stared at the lifeless body, the weirder it became. The man's skin was pale blue, and his head was completely bald. He looked a bit like Captain Jean-Luc Picard if he'd just drowned in a frozen Alaskan lake. He also looked taller than I'd first thought, appearing to no longer fit into the car. I guessed I must have hit my head pretty hard when I fell.

'This is seriously bad,' said Denzil. 'First the pyramids are destroyed and now some weirdo turns up looking like the love child of Dory and Tutankhamun.'

'Don't forget the toilet centipedes,' I added.

'And those monstrosities.' Denzil let out a long sigh. 'You can't tell me it's a coincidence.'

We stood and stared at the silhouettes of the bodies for quite some time, without saying a word. During this bizarre night our dull little worlds had been ripped apart and we had no clue how to deal with it. Absolutely none.

Denzil went back to the car to fetch the towels and Lucy started to cry. The stupid handcuffs meant I couldn't put an arm around her, so I rested my hands on her shoulder. It made me look a bit like a dog begging for treats, which wasn't overly far from the truth.

'Hey, it's going to be alright,' I said, lying through my teeth. The reality was it was a total shambles, but women love hearing that crap, don't they? Lucy turned her body to face me and lifted my arms up, sliding them over her head. I was so surprised I almost pulled away. She rested her face on my neck, held me tight and continued to cry. I could feel her warm, wet tears on my skin. At least I hoped it was tears rather than snot.

I'd wanted to be with Lucy since the first day we met. She was everything I'd ever wanted in a girlfriend and more. To be this close to her now, even as innocently as this, was electric. As we stood there with our bodies pressed together, my heart began to race faster and faster. I was lost in the moment, overwhelmed by the thoughts and emotions it evoked. Her warm skin, her long hair and the gentle rise and fall of her chest that came with each of her soft, shaking sobs. The world around us faded sweetly away and the only things that mattered, or even existed in the universe, were the two of us standing there together, entwined in our perfect embrace.

Then disaster struck. I was getting a boner.

CHAPTER 4

There is nothing in the world that will ruin a platonic moment with a woman faster than getting a massive boner. I was about to be demoted from caring male friend to sex pest. I needed to do something, and I needed to do it fast.

My first attempt at damage limitation was to gently twist my hips, thus preventing little Jack from pressing into Lucy's leg with any degree of force. Annoyingly, she moved her body in perfect harmony with mine and the nightmare stiffy kept on coming. Next, I thought about breaking off the hug and walking away. But I knew that if I stopped suddenly, I'd look like an inconsiderate arse and that strategy was sure to prevent any future physical contact. The situation was getting desperate and I scrambled to think of something to reverse my rapidly depleting fortunes. Then, it came to me in a stomach-churning flash of inspiration. My mum and dad having sex.

Few things on God's green earth are as appalling as the thought of your own mother and father getting down and dirty. I honestly believe that if you surveyed a million people in the street, nine out of ten would rather watch acts of genocide. I dragged kicking and screaming into my mind's eye the image of Harold giving Brenda some X-rated loving. Sure enough, just like the British Expeditionary Force at Dunkirk, the wily fella made a tactical retreat. Cockgate had been successfully averted.

'I hate to ruin the moment,' said Denzil, 'but I really need a number one.'

Lucy sniffed and stepped away from me. 'I could use the restroom too,' she said, wiping the tears from her puffy eyes.

'Alright, we'll all go then,' I said. 'Because there's no way I'm being left here on my own with lady corpse and the dead blue bloke.'

'Lady Corpse would be a good name for a metal band,' Denzil mused.

Lucy shook her head and mumbled something that sounded suspiciously like, 'Bloody moron.'

As dawn broke, we were presented with a beautiful patchwork of rolling green fields and hedges to our left, and thick woodland to our right. We walked far enough into the trees to be hidden from the road. Then Lucy walked even further to make damn sure she was also hidden from us. Getting the little man out while handcuffed proved tricky. But after considerable struggling and no small sense of personal achievement, I was soon watching the steam rising up from my wee as it pattered onto the twigs and leaves covering the woodland floor.

'Ah! Bugger me westward,' said Denzil. 'I needed that slash. I was about to piss all down myself.'

'Thanks for sharing,' I replied. 'That was really touching.'

'Whatever, turkey brain,' he said with a laugh. 'Seriously though, what the hell happened to your eyes? Are you feeling okay?'

I told him about the blue light and how it had felt like it was freezing my soul.

'Well, that definitely isn't good,' he concluded once I'd finished.

'You're a real comfort as always.'

From the direction of the road came the sound of cars screeching to a halt.

'Thank Christ for that,' said Denzil. 'I thought we were going to have to walk out of here.'

'This should be interesting. Trying to explain away the random corpses.'

'Let's just go and see who it is,' Denzil suggested. 'They might have a phone we can use, or give us a lift.'

We made our way back through the trees and were about to step out into the field, when Denzil pulled me to the floor. This caused the handcuffs to cut into my wrists. 'Ow!' I blurted out. 'What the hell was that for?'

'Shh.' Denzil placed a finger to his lips and pointed straight ahead.

I found myself looking through the bushes at four large SUVs and several motorcycles, parked up in the middle of the road next to the remains of my poor little car. Standing around the wreckage in the field were figures in black military combat gear, holding large guns.

What stood out the most however, was the beast man. The guy, if indeed the thing was male, was well over two metres tall and built like a brick out-house. The monstrosity was sporting black clothes like the others, only several sizes bigger. That's where the similarity ended. The creature's head was covered with jet black fur and a matching set of snazzy black horns. His stubby face looked like a cross between a panther and a minotaur, and twice as mean. Just looking at him filled me with a desire to run away, bloody quickly.

'What in the name of Hasselhoff is that?' whispered Denzil.

'Oh, hold on a second,' I replied. 'Let me just look it up in the encyclopaedia of monsters that I've got stuffed down my underpants.'

We watched the creature lift the woman from the wreckage and gently place her onto the ground. Kneeling down, he held his massive hands over her body, closed his eyes and began to chant. A shimmering halo appeared around the edges of the two figures.

'What the hell is that light?' I wondered.

'What light?'

My mouth dropped open like the bow doors on a car ferry as the halo evaporated and the woman got to her feet.

'You told us she was dead,' I whispered.

'But she didn't have a pulse,' Denzil protested. 'On my mother's life she didn't have one.'

'Welcome back, Grand Master,' said the beast in a deep, thundering voice. 'This is a strange place to ask us to meet.'

'Something guided me here,' she said. 'Where is Anattai?'

'He has passed beyond my help.'

The woman looked sad. 'Remove his body from the wreckage before anyone sees his true form.'

'It is being done.'

'And the ark?'

'Empty.'

'Impossible,' she said.

'We heard a scream like the death of a thousand suns and then silence.'

'But who beside the creator goddess could absorb such power?'

'There may still be those who can.'

'That ancient bloodline ended in the Deluge. The stories we discovered of a secret craft bearing them to safety are no more than that.'

'And you are certain of this?'

'I was there. I saw the horror with my own eyes. Nothing survived. We made sure of that.'

'And still you were motivated to prevent others from reading those… 'stories'? The beast man looked thoughtful. 'My people talk of the Ternion seeking out a vessel. And were you not guided to this place?'

The woman searched the sky of flickering stars, as if hoping they could provide some answers. 'If they'd been walking the earth for thirteen thousand years, I think we would have known about it.'

'Perhaps.'

She turned to face the beast. 'Could anyone absorb it? Would they have to be a creature of immense power?'

'In theory. Although it wouldn't end well.'

She looked back at my ruined motorcar. 'If the driver of this vehicle absorbed it, then we need to find them, or the war will be lost.'

'And we need to move quickly,' said the beast, 'because if by some miracle a human did absorb it, it's going to tear them apart.'

'This was my doing,' said the woman.

'What's done cannot be undone,' said the creature, and I felt slightly disturbed that he was quoting Shakespeare. 'Now is the time for action, not remorse.'

A young man with a hipster beard and a physique of which Action Man would have been jealous stepped towards them and bowed his head.

'Grand Master,' he said in a Scottish accent. I had no idea what the title meant, but it sounded important, if a little draconian. 'We should check the plates and scan the road for several miles in each direction.'

'Do we have any Archans available?' asked the woman.

'Not right now,' said the man. 'But I could call them.'

'Do it.'

After a nod from the Scotsman, a female soldier threw what looked like two silver Frisbees into the air. They hovered about ten feet above the ground, then shot off in different directions.

The monster scanned his surroundings and I ducked down as far as I could as his gaze passed over our hiding place.

'The owner's name is Jack Gibson,' said the Scotsman. And I swear to God a little bit of wee came out of me when he said it.

'Listen to me carefully,' called the Grand Master to the assembled soldiers. 'This is the most important mission of your lives. I don't care who you have to bribe, torture or kill. Just bring me Jack Gibson. And try not to damage him too much.'

'We need to find Lucy,' said Denzil. 'Right now.'

CHAPTER 5

Lucy had just finished draining the tank and appeared both surprised and irritated to see us emerging from the woods.

'Why are you morons crawling on the ground?' she asked. 'You do know you're probably lying in fox pee?'

We glanced behind us before getting to our feet.

'Soldiers are chasing us, there's a war and Jack's about to die,' said Denzil.

'I beg your pardon?'

'Okay, torn apart.'

'And there's a talking monster,' I added.

Before Lucy could respond we had spun her around, grabbed an arm each and guided her away from our pursuers.

'We need to get out of here,' I said, as the fear motivated us to start jogging.

'Slow down,' said Lucy.

'And I need to see a doctor. Like right now.'

'Try to stay calm, Jack,' she suggested, as we ducked and weaved through the trees. 'And for God's sake tell me what happened.'

'Jack's going to die if they don't find him,' Denzil panted.

'Well let's find these people then. And quickly.'

'Sod that,' said Denzil.

'This isn't about you, Denzil Reid.'

'I'm not sure I'm overly keen on the idea either.' I proceeded to tell Lucy about the disturbing blue light and the conversation we overhead back at the crash site.

'Oh my.' Lucy chewed her lip. 'How are you feeling?'

'I don't know.'

'You must be feeling something?'

'I honestly don't know!'

'Okay,' said Denzil, trying to sound authoritative. 'I'll take it from here. Right then, Gibby. Imagine you had to tell us exactly how you felt, or you'd be forced to lick your Nanny Bertie's doody hole.'

'Jesus Christ, Denzil,' said Lucy. 'What the hell is wrong with you?'

'Right after she's released the chocolate hostages,' he continued.

'Were you dropped on your head as a child or something?'

'What would you say?' he persisted, in the earnest tone of a TV quiz-master pushing for an answer at the end of a round.

I tried to focus on how my body was feeling, rather than the threat of my nanny's doody hole.

'Oh yes,' he continued. 'And she's eaten a really spicy curry that's given her bubble guts.'

'Goddamn it, Denzil,' said Lucy. 'On what planet is that going to work?'

I thought about this for a couple more seconds before responding. 'I'd say I feel okay.'

'I rest my case, your honour,' declared a smug-sounding Denzil.

Lucy's eyes narrowed.

The sun rose as we made our escape through the countryside. It was difficult moving through the trees over such uneven ground. Lucy and I kept up the pace, but I could tell Denzil was struggling. It was his own fault though. I'd been telling him to come to the gym with me for months.

'Did anyone. Just hear. A strange. Whizzing noise?' he asked in between pants.

'It's the wind rushing past your ears because you're running so damn fast,' replied Lucy.

'Kiss. My. Rear rocket-socket,' he wheezed.

The woods came to an abrupt halt. As we left the shelter of the trees we stopped to stare at the picture postcard world that lay before us. Well, Lucy and I did. Denzil just stood there with his hands on his knees, breathing hard and staring at the ground. The scene was so quaint it could have been a movie set. Emerald-green fields and rolling hills stretched as far as the eye could see. In the distance a pretty village sat nestled in a valley, comprising a jumble of limestone buildings and thatched cottages.

'Is that a farmhouse?' Lucy pointed to our left. 'They might have a land-line we can use to call the cops.'

'Let's hope so,' I replied. 'I'm starting to freak out.'

Lucy placed one of her hands on my forehead and studied my face for a couple of seconds. 'How are you feeling now, sweetie?'

'Bloody awful,' replied Denzil.

'Not you, you cretin. I'm asking Jack.'

'Surprisingly okay.' My spirits soared from her calling me sweetie. 'Keen to get the image of Denzil's "rocket socket" out of my mind, though.'

Conscious I might not have a great deal of time left in this world, we raced towards the farm. A few minutes later we arrived at a large stone cottage, partially covered in vibrant green ivy. Behind it sat a number of honey-coloured stone barns. The house had been given some modern architectural accoutrements that made it look like a show home from a design magazine. If the people who lived here were farmers, then the agricultural industry must have been booming. An old blue van, an expensive SUV and a green military-looking Land Rover sat on the large gravel drive. I knew which one of them I'd rather own. The image of my ruined car flashed through my mind and I cursed under my breath at the memory. As we approached the front of the building, I heard a dog bark and what sounded like raised voices.

'Looks like Farmer Giles is having a domestic,' said Denzil. 'I bet the wife caught him at it with the animals.'

'Why do you have to be so disgusting all the time?' said Lucy.

'These country types are all at it.'

'Only in your disturbed little head.'

'Everyone knows it's a side effect of the mind-control chemicals governments spray on the population from planes. It makes people do loads of weird stuff. Ever heard of chemtrails?'

'Of course I have. They're water vapour. And there's no evidence people are sleeping with farm animals as a result.'

'Actually, I saw a documentary about it,' Denzil persisted.

'Don't lie.'

'I swear to God I did.'

'You don't believe in God.'

'Semantics.'

'Actually, I think BS would be more accurate.'

'Whatever.' Denzil waved her away. 'Anyway, there were these guys in your country who ride horses.'

'A lot of people ride horses in my country,' said Lucy. 'Have you not heard of cowboys?'

'Not like this they don't.'

'Woah!'

'You sounded like a cowboy just then,' said Denzil.

'Okay, you can stop now.' Lucy scowled at him. 'I know exactly where this is going.'

'It was pretty interesting to be honest.'

'I think you might be confusing "interesting" with "repugnant".'

'What's a woman with long hair got to do with it?'

Lucy looked confused, although not as confused as Denzil.

I shook my head. 'That's Rapunzel, you bellend.'

Lucy raised her hand. 'If you don't shut your disgusting mouth right now, I swear to God I'll swing for you.'

'Alright, calm down.' Denzil turned to look at me and raised his eyebrows. 'Someone's been exposed to too many chemtrails.'

Then Lucy hit him. Hard.

Denzil wandered off in a sulk as Lucy and I approached the farmhouse. Judging by the earlier shouting, it wasn't the best time to be knocking on this particular front door. But it was a good half hour since the beast man had casually handed out my death sentence and I was becoming increasingly keen to phone for medical assistance. As I glanced around, my eyes were drawn to a series of large red splotches on the driveway. As Lucy reached up to ring the doorbell, I grabbed her wrist.

'What's wrong?' she asked, her finger hovering over the button.

'Tell me that isn't blood.'

Lucy followed my gaze and then dropped her hand. 'I think it could be,' she whispered.

A woman's scream cut through the early morning haze and my heart leapt like a flea in a circus. Whatever was going on inside that house, it sounded serious.

'We should help her,' I said.

'There's keys in this one.' Denzil peered through the window of the SUV.

I placed a finger over my lips and presented him with my best shut-the-hell-up face.

Lucy stepped forward. 'Let's look through the farmhouse windows and see if we can work out what's going on.'

BANG.

We froze. The sound was so loud and so shocking that I could still hear the echo long after it passed.

'Was that a gun shot?' asked Lucy.

'Let's just get out of here,' I replied.

'Roger that,' she said, as we turned and ran towards Denzil, who was already clambering into the passenger seat of the SUV.

'Get in the car,' he yelled. But we were already on it.

'You need to drive,' I reminded Lucy. I glanced frantically behind me from the back seat and then at Lucy, who was staring at the wheel. 'What's wrong?'

'I'm not sure,' she said.

'About what?' asked Denzil, who sounded just as freaked out as I felt.

'About stealing a car,' she said. 'I don't want to go to prison.'

'Are you kidding me?' Denzil whacked the glovebox with his handcuffs.

I tried to sound as calm as possible as I leant into the front of the car. 'Considering our current predicament, I don't think the usual rules apply, Lucy. Do you?'

'Oh, screw it.' The engine glided effortlessly into life. The tyres scraped on the gravel driveway as she hit the gas. Lucy guided the huge car out of the gate and onto the narrow country lane. I took another nervous glance out of the back window and my heart sank like a brick in a milkshake. A red-haired soldier was racing out of the farmhouse. He stopped, raised a nasty-looking rifle and began shooting at us. Bang, bang, bang came the loud staccato sounds, and *Anthem for Doomed Youth* by Wilfred Owen popped into my brain. The gunfire clearly indicated that the gentleman wasn't happy with our acquisition of the motor vehicle.

'Get down!' I shouted as bullets peppered the back of the SUV and the rear window exploded into a thousand pieces, showering us with fragments of glass. As we flew around a bend in the road, the combination of centrifugal force, smooth leather seats and no seatbelt propelled me headfirst into the door. After a mad scramble I managed to find enough purchase to stop me from slipping about like a newborn giraffe. But it still took another three bends for my testicles to grow back enough to dare to peer out of the remains of the back window. I let out an audible sigh of relief when my brain registered that we were well and truly out of sight.

'Is everyone okay?' asked Denzil.

I touched my chest and felt my adrenaline-filled heart beating insanely fast. 'I think so.'

Lucy's knuckles were white from gripping the steering wheel and her eyes held a wild, manic expression. I turned and placed a hand on her shoulder and she reached up and took hold of my fingers.

'Are you okay?' I asked softly.

'I will be,' she replied in a voice so faint that I could barely hear it over the hum of the engine.

We drove for another mile or so before Denzil broke the silence. 'So, what's the plan, then?'

'I guess a hospital would be a good start,' I replied. 'Then we need to find a police station to report this mess.'

'And you don't think they already know about it?' asked Denzil. 'Of course they bloody do.'

'Who are "they"?'

'The secret forces running the sodding world.'

'This isn't *The X-Files*.'

'I know it's not. That was the Majestic 12 and I'm talking about the New World Order.'

'Jesus Christ, Denzil. There's no totalitarian world government behind this.'

'You need to trust me mate, I know about this stuff. And I'm telling you that someone in charge knows what's going on.'

'Alright then, smart arse. What the hell is going on?'

'Some sort of secret stuff,' said Denzil. 'And you can bet your bottom dollar that the police, the army and the government know all about it.'

'But how?' I replied. 'We're in the middle of goat-sex-nowhere and no one can get a phone signal.'

'We're in the Cotswolds,' said Denzil. 'Not the Desolation Islands.'

'Yes, but if no one has a phone signal—'

'Just because our useless network—who incidentally, I'm switching from when we get out of this mess—has crapped out on us, it doesn't mean they'll all be down.'

'Why not?' I asked. 'This is some seriously crazy shit. And without the networks functioning, how can the emergency services respond? They don't know what they don't know, do they?'

'The military has a network to use when the civilian ones go down,' replied Denzil.

'Says who?' asked Lucy, snapping back into life.

'Oh, do me a favour,' said Denzil. 'Everyone knows that.'

I felt strangely defensive of her. 'Well, I don't.'

'No,' he said. 'But then you are a total nob head.'

'Funny.'

'Either way,' continued Lucy, 'two cops have gone missing. Someone's going to be looking for them.'

'Not if it's part of a plan to take over the world,' replied Denzil.

'Let's just get Jack to a hospital,' said Lucy. 'Unless he's half husky, those eyes are a long way from standard issue.'

'Fine,' I replied. 'But then we really need to make a plan.'

And that's where the conversation came to an abrupt halt.

A combination of speed and not being able to see around most of the bends meant that we didn't notice the other vehicles until it was too late. One moment I was happily perched on the back seat, holding Lucy's hand, and the next I was hugging the dashboard, as Lucy swerved violently, drove through a low stone wall and crashed headlong into a tree. I was busy complaining about the injustice of hitting my head twice in two minutes when we heard men shouting. Before my confused mind could work out what the hell was going on, the door was thrown open and I was dragged out of the car by my left leg. My head bounced off the ground and the wind was comprehensively knocked out of my lungs, like a crystal meth piñata at a rehab clinic's Christmas party.

As such, it took me a couple of seconds to notice the military-grade rifle that had been shoved in my face. A soldier was screaming at me, but in all the noise and confusion I had no clue what he was saying. I raised my cuffed hands and started shouting things like, 'What are you doing?' and 'I've not done anything!' but it didn't do any good. My garbled dialogue was rewarded by being dragged to my feet and pushed up against the back of the car. Denzil cowered beside me as beams of reality burst through the adrenaline clouds, and the soldier's alien words took on human form.

'Turn around,' he commanded, before giving me the roughest body search of my life. It made the ones you get in airports seem very civilised indeed. After he'd satisfied himself by groping my entire body, he shouted, 'Clear!' right in my sodding ear. Some people have no manners. I attempted to move but was struck in the other ear with a rifle butt and pushed back up against the SUV. Being in handcuffs was really placing me at a disadvantage.

I could only watch as Lucy was thrown against the vehicle, face first. A cut opened up above her right eye. Another soldier gave her a rough body search, then placed a gun barrel against her forehead. Her face was a mask of pain and fear and she started to cry.

I knew in that moment I loved her. That may sound pathetic. Jeez, it may even be pathetic considering I'd never so much as kissed the woman, but I didn't care. Seeing her in pain ignited a raging fire inside me that filled the deepest, most lost corners of my soul. For the past two years I'd spent most of my waking life with Lucy. I'd probably seen her more than my friends and family. Well, apart from Denzil, of course, but he's pretty much part of my life's furniture. Lucy Chong was the reason I got out of bed every morning, and more importantly, why I went to work with a huge smile on my face. I mean, let's be honest, it wasn't going to be the job. Just a smile from her was enough to make my heart start racing like Jesse Owens. I thought about her all the time. I thought about her when I saw couples together, or if I was listening to music, even when lying in bed waiting to fall asleep. Some days it had almost driven me insane. Now, seeing her hurting like this filled me with an anger and fear I'd never experienced before. I had to help her, I had to protect her, but what could I do? I was one frightened person in handcuffs against a group of armed soldiers.

I sprang into action. Pushing the soldier away, I placed myself between her and the nefarious attacker.

'Please don't hurt her,' I said in a voice that even baby Thumper would have been embarrassed by. Although I hated myself for it, right then it was all I could manage.

The soldier that had been restraining Lucy stepped so close to me that our noses were almost touching. I noted the smell of stale alcohol on his breath. An image of the Einsatzgruppen throwing back strong liquor to help them murder their way across Eastern Europe flashed through my brain. I tensed my muscles and prepared as best as I could for the inevitable blow.

'Boo!' said the soldier and I jumped out of my skin.

His buddies roared with laughter. It was one of the most humiliating moments of my life.

One of the other men approached Denzil. 'Denzil? Denzil Reid?'

Denzil's expression changed from fear to confusion to an awkward smile.

'It's me,' said the soldier. 'Charles Eze.'

Charles & Eddie's nineties hit, 'Would I like to You?' popped into my head. Despite my fear I calculated he was most likely born before the song was released. I concluded not all parents are 'that' cruel.

'Charles?' asked Denzil tentatively.

'It's alright, fellas.' Charles grinned at me. 'I used to date Denzil's big sister, Audrey.'

The other soldiers watched with deadpan expressions as I helped Lucy sit down. She wasn't in good shape.

'What on earth are you doing here?' asked Denzil.

'We made a last-minute decision to meet a friend en route. He said there'd be something in it for us, if you know what I mean. What's with the handcuffs?'

Denzil looked at his hands. 'We had a misunderstanding with a couple of police officers.'

'I can see that.'

'I don't suppose you've got any bolt cutters? Or a phone?'

'Sorry mate, all the networks are down and we left the base in a hurry. There's some insane stuff going down.'

'The insane stuff wouldn't happen to involve giant centipedes?'

'No,' said Charles, looking troubled. 'A swarm of wasps the size of rugby balls.'

Denzil's mouth fell open. 'No way.'

'Strange creatures have been appearing all over the country. Everything's falling apart.'

'Do you know what's causing it?' I asked.

Charles glanced at me before turning his attention back to Denzil. 'No idea. They don't tell us anything. But pretty soon it's going to be anarchy.'

'Are we at war?' asked Denzil. 'We overheard a group of soldiers talking about it on the way here.'

'What soldiers?' Charles frowned.

'We saw them when we were hiking through the countryside. They said something about a war or something.' Denzil clearly wasn't comfortable telling Charles about the beast man or the Grand Master's resurrection.

Charles softened. 'I don't.' He placed a hand on Denzil's shoulder. 'But my advice is don't trust anyone. The police and the military are falling apart. It's going to be Mad Max country around here soon.'

Denzil nodded.

Lucy's head began to wobble and she looked like she might pass out.

'How's Audrey doing?' asked Charles. I assumed he must also have been drinking because he was acting like they were chatting at a family barbeque and not immersed in this unfolding world of horror.

'Fine,' said Denzil, slowly. 'She's living in Birmingham now.'

'Birmingham?' said Charles, nodding.

'She works for a law firm.'

'Well, she always was destined for greater things.' Charles's grin broadened. 'That's what I liked about her. So, is she married then? Kids?'

The question was so transparent it was borderline embarrassing.

'No kids,' said Denzil. 'Much to Mum's annoyance. And she's just broken up with her boyfriend.'

'Why was that?'

'It turns out he already had a girlfriend and two kids in Spain. So, you can imagine how that went down.'

I looked at the other soldiers. They hadn't moved once during the entire exchange.

'What a scumbag,' said Charles, who sounded decidedly happy about it. 'And how's your mum?'

'She's good, thanks,' replied Denzil. 'She always said she wished you two had stayed together.'

'Jesus Christ,' said a huge soldier with a shaved head and broken nose. 'Do you want to bone him or something?'

Charles turned to look at his colleagues and then back at us. 'You can't stay out here. It's not safe.' He glanced at the SUV. 'We've got orders to head to a base north of here. We need to collect some of the lads en route, but we've got room for one more if you want to come.'

Denzil looked at me and then at Lucy slumped against the vehicle. 'I can't leave my friends,' he said.

'Don't be crazy,' said Charles. 'Things are going to get really bad.'

'Take Lucy,' I said.

'No!' said Lucy.

'Right men, we're leaving,' called one of the soldiers.

Charles turned to Denzil. 'If you're coming, then you need to come right now.'

Denzil looked like he was trying to calculate the square root of a totem pole. 'Take Lucy,' he said.

The other soldiers started climbing into their jeeps.

'We have to go now,' urged Charles.

'You need to go with them, Lucy.' I dragged her to her feet and half carried her towards the jeeps.

'I'm not leaving you.'

Denzil turned to Charles. 'Take her with you,' he said. 'Please.'

'I'm perfectly capable of making a decision for—' Lucy stumbled. Her eyes were closing and she was clearly in a lot of pain.

'Just go,' I repeated. 'Someone needs to look at your head. Besides, one of us being safe is better than none.'

She glared at me defiantly, but then her legs buckled and I had to grab her arm to stop her from collapsing.

'That decides it,' I said.

'Be careful,' she whispered. 'And don't do anything stupid.'

I laughed. 'Me, do something stupid?'

'I need to tell you something,' she said.

'We have to go,' shouted Charles, tucking what looked like a Glock into the front of Denzil's trousers, like a father getting his son ready for an exceptionally violent school trip.

'Tell me later.'

'I'll get help and come back for you,' said Lucy. 'I won't leave you here.'

Charles helped her into one of the jeeps. I was relieved she was going to be safe, but sad to be separated from her. That was until Lucy's vehicle pulled up next to us and Charles leant out of the window.

'There's a base several miles east of here,' he called. 'The location is classified, but if you can find it, I doubt they'll turn you away.'

'Thanks, Charles,' said Denzil.

The jeep started to pull away and Charles had to shout his next words. 'We're meeting our sergeant at a nearby farmhouse. It belongs to his parents. Then we'll get Lucy to safety. I promise.'

I thought of the red-haired soldier emptying his rifle in our general direction. 'Oh God,' I said to Denzil.

'What is it?'

'I think I've just made a horrible mistake.'

CHAPTER 6

We checked the SUV. Even a complete moron could tell it had gone to the great scrapheap in the sky.

'We need to get back to the farmhouse,' I said. 'And quickly. That's where they're taking Lucy.'

The journey, which had seemed so short in the car, felt like an eternity on foot. Along the way Denzil tried reassuring me that Charles was a good guy and Lucy would be in safe hands, but I wasn't so sure.

As the farmhouse came into view my heart sank like a snitch tied to a concrete block. 'The army jeeps have gone,' I said, struggling to catch my breath.

'Just keep going.' Denzil pushed me onwards.

'What if she's in trouble?'

Denzil didn't respond. At the end of the day I couldn't blame him; it was a dumb question.

We stopped at the gate and stared at the silent cottage. The military vehicles hadn't just spirited Lucy away; they'd taken any vague notion we had of being able to help her. Panic and desperation rose up inside my chest.

'What do we do now?'

'We take a look around the back.' Denzil didn't wait for a response, and I ran to keep up with him as he conducted a full loop of the house. The place appeared deserted and I spun around, scanning the empty countryside.

'It doesn't look like they're here.'

'Bollocks,' said Denzil. 'They could have gone anywhere.'

Hopelessness overwhelmed us and we were forced to sit down in defeat at the side of the old building. As we looked out over the fields, a tear ran down my cheek. I'd never felt so useless in my life. Although in my heart of hearts I knew the chances of finding Lucy were about as slim as finding the cure for cancer under the nearest rock, something deep inside me was too stubborn or too stupid to accept it. My mind raced as I tried to come up with a plan.

At some point I realised Denzil was standing up. 'I've got an idea,' he said.

'Please make it a good one.'

'Let's check the house to see if they've left any clues. Maybe we can work out where they went.'

'Holy mackerel, Quincy,' I replied. 'That's a bloody great idea.'

The plan was made easier by the discovery that the front door had been left unlocked. We stepped inside and began our search. I don't know what sort of clues we were hoping to find. Maybe a book of matches with a phone number on it, or a map with a big red X marked next to a destination, but it definitely wasn't two naked, mutilated bodies. We found them in the dining room: a man and a woman in their late sixties. They'd been tied to a couple of Scandinavian-looking chairs and had clearly taken one hell of a beating. A large kitchen knife protruded from the man's gut and several nails had been hammered into both of their shins. Glasses and a moustache had been drawn on the man's face in black marker and a beard and freckles onto the woman's. I'll spare you the state of their genitals. Belts were fastened around their necks and wet towels and an empty bucket sat in the corner of the room. Looking around, I could see a mass of photographs strewn across the floor. It must have taken them a long time to die and I had to wonder if Charles had been a part of it.

Over on the wall, a safe hung open. The painting that I assumed had once covered it lay discarded on the carpet. A familiar wave of nausea hit me at the sight of the tortured corpses. Fortunately, my stomach was beyond empty by this point in the proceedings. So, after a bit of retching and prancing on the spot like a demented horse, I was able to gain mastery over my errant bodily functions.

We stared transfixed by the horror that our brains were struggling to comprehend. My fears for Lucy's safety were magnified tenfold. Worst of all, it was my monumentally stupid idea for her to go with the soldiers. What had I done?

'We need to call the police.' Denzil sounded like he was on the verge of tears.

'I know we do.'

'Like, right now.'

'We'll do it as soon as we can.'

'We have to do it *now*, Jack,' he insisted.

'As soon as we can, I promise.'

'We've got to tell somebody. This isn't right. None of this is right.' Denzil wasn't an emotional guy, but the ocean of trauma we'd swam through in the past few hours would be enough to mess with anybody's head. 'How could anyone do this?' he asked. 'It's sick.'

I turned Denzil away from the corpses and stared directly into his eyes. 'I don't know, buddy. But we need to suck it the hell up so that we can find a way to help Lucy.' I had to shake him so that he peeled his eyes away from the carnage. 'Now let's get focused and start looking for clues, okay?'

Denzil wiped the tears from his eyes.

'Okay?' I repeated.

'Okay,' he replied, 'Let's help Lucy.'

Hanging out with Mr and Mrs Dead wasn't the best thing for Denzil to be doing in his current state, so I steered him towards the door, which is when I heard the groan.

'Jesus,' I said, before pointing out the seriously bloody obvious fact that, 'He's alive!'

We raced over to the man and Denzil loosened the belt around his neck.

'Are you okay, mate?' my friend asked.

The guy's eyes remained shut but his head started to sway from side to side. 'Charlotte,' he mumbled.

'Is *she* Charlotte?' I pointed to the woman with both of my cuffed hands.

The man didn't open his eyes; he was too beaten up. He was making this horrible gurgling sound as he struggled to breathe. I untied him, which was tricky in handcuffs, while Denzil set about removing the belt from the woman's neck. I watched him check for a pulse, but after a couple of seconds he looked at me and shook his head.

'Charlotte?' repeated the man.

Sometimes, the kindest thing you can do for someone is to tell them a white lie. Like the time my mum and dad went on holiday to Turkey. Denzil got so out of his brains on booze and pills that he let Lisa Oldroyd tug him off all over my parent's bedsheets. Unfortunately, he failed to inform me of this fact and I wasn't able to clean up before my parents got home. Harold and Brenda would have been pissed off, not to say freaked out to know that Denzil had been busy showering their sheets with his love-shake. So, to spare them the upset and more importantly to explain away the nasty white marks,

I unselfishly blamed it on Buster, God rest his doggy soul. To be fair, I did feel a bit guilty when my dad announced over dinner one Tuesday evening that we might have to put him down. But after a couple of check-ups and more probing than a mission to Mars, the vet put it down to stress. So, Buster lived to lick his butt another day, although the poor mite was never allowed back into the bedrooms or onto the sofa.

I decided that the best course of action was to spare the guy from any more suffering. So, with the best of intentions and a heavy heart, I took him by the hand and whispered, 'She's safe, my friend. Charlotte's safe.'

The rise and fall of his chest began to slow as he surrendered his grip on life's great ladder. Now, I'm not religious at all, but I still felt it appropriate in the moment to say a simple prayer for him. So, I asked God to take him to another place, a better place, far beyond the pain of our sick, twisted world. Crouched down beside this man that I'd only just met and would never truly know, I shared the last precious moments of his life as he slipped away.

'Everything's okay, my friend. Everything's going to be okay.'

The serenity of the moment was shattered by Denzil shoving me out of the way. 'Don't you bloody die on me now!' he cried while slapping the man around the face and head.

'Denzil?' I shouted. The guy had clearly lost it.

'Where have those soldiers gone?' he demanded. 'They've got Lucy. You have to tell us!'

The man was silent for a couple of seconds and I honestly thought he'd checked out of life's hotel. Then, perhaps because of Denzil's tone, but more likely because he was getting tortured for the second time in what was turning out to be a really crappy day for him, the gentleman jerked back to life.

'Where have they gone? You need to tell us where they've gone!'

The guy grimaced.

'Where have they bloody gone?' screamed Denzil.

'Last,' replied the man, his eyes still shut.

I sprang into action. 'Stop it, Denzil. You're hurting him.'

But Denzil wasn't listening. 'Last what?'

'Boat. Last,' said the man.

'What bloody boat?' Denzil leant in closer. 'Is it the last boat somewhere? You have to tell us. Our friend's in danger.'

'John,' he said.

'Who's John?'

'Stop it, Denzil,' I said.

'North,' said the man.

'North what?' shouted Denzil. He continued to shake the man, but it was no use: the poor chap's spirit upped and left the building.

I dragged Denzil away from the now definitely dead man. 'He's gone,' I said. 'Just calm the hell down, will you?'

Denzil shook me off and took a couple of steps backwards. 'Fat load of good that did us,' he wheezed. 'We'll never find Lucy now.'

'I wouldn't be so sure,' I replied, a thought forming inside my tiny brain.

'You what?'

'Well...' I frowned. 'I think I might know where they're headed. Just think about it for a second.

Denzil adopted the expression of a man trying to pass a grand piano.

'Charles said the base is north of here,' I said. 'What's the furthest John that you know from here?'

'Probably John O'Conner. Remember his family moved to Sydney when we were at school? You can't get further than Sydney.'

I rested my head on the tips of my fingers and took a deep breath. 'You're such a twat. I don't mean a person. Think of places, man. Places!'

'St John's Wood?'

'Further.'

'Erm, St Johnstone?'

'Getting warmer.'

'Don't know.'

'Think Scotland.'

'I just did.'

'Well, think of it again.'

'Bonnie Prince Charlie.'

'I said places, not people.'

'Yes, but that's not a person, is it? It's a song.'

'That's 'The Skye Boat Song', you weirdo.'

'Oh yeah.'

'Let's try this again. What place is the furthest north from here?'

'The North Pole.'

'Were you dropped on your head as a child? Think Britain.'

'Shetland Islands.'

'Oh, my sodding good God.' I slapped myself on the forehead, taking care not to knock myself out with the handcuffs. 'What about John O'Groats? You utter div.'

'I was going to say that next,' he said.

'Whatever.'

'But how does the boat fit in?'

'How about because it's on the coast,' I replied.

Denzil shrugged.

'There's loads of places around there you can catch a ferry from,' I said.

'How do you know that?'

'Because Jenny Hanson and her family got a ferry from near there when they went on holiday to Orkney.'

Denzil grinned. 'The same Jenny Hanson who wanted you to wear a wetsuit during sex, because she had a thing for Special Forces frogmen?'

'Yes.'

'The same Jenny Hanson who liked to hunt for belly button fluff in your navel?'

'Yes.'

'The same Jenny Hanson who got smashed on vodka and threw up all over the present table at your cousin's birthday party?'

'Unfortunately, yes.'

'Well, Gibby, she was a keeper. What went wrong?'

'Ha bloody ha.'

'John O'Groats sounds like a decent guess to me,' said Denzil. 'But why there?'

'Maybe the whole country's like this?' I said. 'And maybe there's a ship that's going to take survivors off the mainland to somewhere safe.'

'The Shetland Islands?'

'Maybe.'

'Guess I'm not such a div after all, then.'

'Debatable.'

Denzil flipped me the bird. 'While that does seem like a plausible suggestion, how are we going to get there? It's not as far as Sydney, but it's still a long way to the north of Scotland.'

I paused. 'How about the old van out the front?'

'Good plan. Let's try and find the keys.'

'We'd best grab some supplies as well,' I added, 'because I'm guessing there won't be too many shops open today.'

'And let's see if we can find a telephone.'

The mention of supplies made me aware of just how incredibly hungry and thirsty I was. The feeling kicked in like a rodeo bull and I knew I had to eat and drink something before I fell over. With Denzil in firm agreement we made our way towards what we hoped was the door to the kitchen. However, upon opening it we realised that we may have a slight issue retrieving supplies, which came in the form of an angry white dog. I'd opened the door maybe six inches when it started snarling and barking like an absolute mother.

My default response was to slam the door shut. The pathetic scream that escaped my mouth would have been embarrassing if it weren't for the fact that Denzil's was even worse.

'They've got a pit bull,' cried Denzil, like he'd just been castrated.

'It's not a pit bull,' I replied.

'Bull crap. Did you see its face?'

'It's not a pit bull.'

'What is it then?'

'It's an English bull terrier.'

'Well, it looks like a sodding pit bull to me.'

'It's not a pit bull.'

'Just because you owned that scabby old fleabag with the fart problem,' said Denzil, 'doesn't make you Mr Crufts.'

'I never owned your mum,' I muttered as I began carefully opening the door.

'Erm, Jack?' asked Denzil.

'What?'

'I was just wondering why you're opening that perfectly robust door again?'

I ignored him and opened it wide enough for the dog to poke its egg-shaped head through. It was one pissed-off beast and it was only too happy to display a rather vicious-looking set of teeth.

'Seriously,' said Denzil over the barking, 'what the hell are you doing?'

'We need to make friends with it.' I tried to sound more confident about the situation than I in fact was.

'Friends?' cried Denzil. 'Have you lost your mind?' He looked at me like I was an extra from *One Flew Over the Cuckoo's Nest*. 'And you've got the cheek to accuse me of being dropped on my head? It wants to rip your bloody face off.'

'How else are we going to get food?' I held out the back of my hand, praying the furry fella didn't decide to rip it off.

The dog continued enthusiastically with its programme of growling and barking.

'Can you stop staring at him, please,' I said calmly. 'You're upsetting him.'

'Seriously, Gibby? Are you actually taking the piss right now? *I'm* upsetting *him*?'

'Shh,' I replied as the dog began to sniff my hand in between barks.

'Sod this for a game of Yahtzee,' said Denzil. 'I'm going to check out the rest of the house.' So off he went, leaving me alone with what now seemed like a pretty scary-looking dog.

As the first American Mr Benjamin Franklin once said, 'He that can have patience can have what he will.' And after a few anxious minutes I found myself sitting on the kitchen floor, eating a stale French loaf and stroking the dog. According to the silver nametag attached to his thick black collar, he was called Ziggy. Despite the dicey introduction, he seemed like a friendly chap. Particularly after I'd fed him a tin of dog food I found in one of the cupboards.

A car horn sounded outside and Ziggy started barking again.

'Shh, buddy,' I said as I gave him a couple of strokes on the top of his head. 'Let's go and see what's going on.'

I walked outside, closely followed by my new canine companion, to be confronted by Denzil standing next to the van. He was toting a rifle in one hand and a massive floppy dildo in the other. Ziggy increased his barking by several decibels as he advanced towards my best friend. Denzil didn't even flinch, he just nonchalantly threw the phallus through the air and cried, 'Fetch!' Ziggy did what any self-respecting pooch would do when presented with something to chase and skidded off across the gravel in hot pursuit.

'What the hell are you doing with that thing?' I asked.

'I couldn't find a stick,' he replied.

'Not the cock, you moron, the gun.'

Denzil reached into his pocket and pulled out a small key, which he threw at me. It bounced off my head and landed on the floor.

I responded with an 'Ouch' even though it didn't actually hurt.

Denzil laughed. 'Nice catch, bonehead.'

'What's this for?' I asked as I bent down to pick it up.

'So, it turns out that the Deads are sex people.'

'*Were* sex people,' I corrected him.

'Okay, *were* sex people. They've got all sorts of bondage stuff upstairs. Some of the equipment you can buy these days is crazy. Did you know that there's a device you can slip inside—'

'Get to the point please, Mr Around The Houses.'

'Seriously though, Gibby, you won't believe what's up there.'

'I'll take your word for it. Now tell me about the key.'

'Well lucky for us they are sex people,' he said. 'Because they've got sets of actual police handcuffs, just like ours.'

That's when I realised that Denzil no longer had any cuffs on.

'Awesome,' I said as I used the key to undo my own set.

'I know, right?' he replied.

'I could hug you right now.' I rubbed the cuts and angry red marks that decorated my wrists. I was sure they were going to leave a few new scars.

'I'd prefer it if you didn't.'

I began stretching my arms out in lots of random directions. 'That feels amazing,' I announced.

Ziggy reappeared and dropped the dildo at Denzil's feet. My friend picked it up and pretended to throw it at me.

'Please don't,' I cried. 'That's been up her fanny.'

'And her ringer.'

'Nice.'

'And his.'

'You can stop now.'

'And probably the neighbour's.'

'Stop means shut the hell up, yeah?'

'Well, I did tell you these country types are all at it.' Denzil threw the rubber penis once again for Ziggy to chase.

'Don't let him put that in his mouth,' I said. 'It's probably covered in all sorts of germs.'

'You mean all sorts of sperms,' said Denzil, laughing.

'Yeah, clever,' I replied dryly. 'What about the gun?'

'Oh yeah. So, I found this bad boy in the top of one of the cupboards and I also found a couple of boxes of bullets. We can both have a weapon now. I reckon they could come in handy if we meet any dodgy people.'

'Yeah, really handy when we don't know how to use them.'

'It's not rocket science. Besides, we used to go to Battle Camp all the time.'

'I don't think paintball counts as actual weapons training, does it?'

'Same difference,' he replied.

'I think it's time to find the phone and call for help.'

'Good luck with that,' replied Denzil. 'The landline in the cottage is dead and I didn't see any smartphones lying about.' He began turning on the spot and staring up at the sky. 'Can you hear that?'

'What?'

'That subtle whizzing sound,' he said. 'I heard it before, when we were running through the woods.'

'Hearing things that don't exist is the first sign of insanity,' I answered supportively.

He raised a hand, signalling for me to stop. 'Just listen.'

Convinced I was watching Denzil undergo a minor mental meltdown, I decided to check out the condition of the old van that we were hoping to drive to Scotland. Walking around the outside, I prodded and kicked the tyres appraisingly, which to be fair didn't seem too bad. It was old and rusty, but it looked like it was still in regular use. I was just about to walk back to where Denzil was doing his imaginary plane spotting when I froze.

Hovering a couple of metres in front of my face was a small silver disc, resembling a UFO for mice. It looked like the ones released by the female soldier at the crash site. As I stood there, an electric green beam shot from the front, lighting up my face and virtually blinding me in the process. The light travelled up and down my body as if it was scanning for something. I felt like an item being swiped through a supermarket checkout.

Denzil called to me from the other side of the van. 'Are you sure you can't hear anything?'

I was almost too afraid to speak or move, so I opted for responding to Denzil in a whisper. 'Denzil? Help!'

'Maybe it's in my head?' he shouted.

'Denzil?'

'God, I hope I haven't got tinnitus.'

'Help!'

'What's schizophrenia?'

'Help me!'

'I think my Grandad Ainsley might have that.'

'*Help!*'

'He's always shitting himself.'

By that point it dawned on me that Denzil wasn't coming to my rescue. I would have to try and save my own sorry self. If I could just make it back to the house, I might stand a fighting chance.

My first thought was to turn on my heels and make a run for it. But then I remembered a nature documentary I'd seen on TV last year. The presenter said the worst thing you can do with a dangerous animal is turn your back on it or try to run away. As counter-intuitive as it may sound, you need to stand your ground. But this wasn't a wild animal and I wasn't sure that logic would translate to this situation.

As the disc moved closer and the green light kept scanning me for God knows what, I began to freak out. One wrong move and I could be dead meat. Then my senses were violently assaulted by an almighty bang and I dropped to the floor as fast as gravity would allow, just as the silver disc exploded in mid-air.

Rolling onto my back, I looked up at a triumphant-looking Denzil, who was holding a smoking rifle. I patted myself down to check I was still in one piece.

Denzil looked down at me. 'I knew it wasn't bloody tinnitus,' he said.

CHAPTER 7

Denzil sifted through the remains of the silver disc with his foot. 'We need to leave.'

'What are you thinking?'

'I'm thinking that silver thing must belong to Mr Monster and his band of merry morons, and they're probably on their way here right now.'

'Oh crap,' I said. 'Let's just grab some food and get out of here.'

Normally it takes me ages to pack. I hate it. Not as much as shopping, but it's certainly up there. It is definitely the worst part of any journey or holiday. Well, that and having Denzil shagging some woman he's just pulled from Luton in the bed next to me, mumbling stuff like, 'Time for the love machine,' and 'You'd best use your whole hand, or I won't feel it.' Funnily enough, the idea of a monster and a shedload of soldiers wanting to remove my brains proved a powerful motivator.

I ran into the house and headed back through to the kitchen. I found a bundle of plastic bags under the sink and started filling them with anything vaguely food-related. Next, I jogged back through the house, grabbing Ziggy's lead from a table in the hallway.

I lifted the telephone receiver and checked for a tone, not that I didn't trust Denzil, of course. I found myself greeted with a depressing silence. Looking up I saw a number of framed photographs belonging to the occupants. There was something familiar about a person in one of the photos. Stepping forward for a closer look, I realised it was the red-haired soldier that had fired at us, proudly clasping a scroll in a University graduation photo. Standing on either side of him were the Deads. I'd heard of dysfunctional families, but this was taking the biscuit. Even if the safe had been stuffed full of valuables, their deaths had been cruel. It must take incredible hatred to torture your own parents. I thought about Lucy at the mercy of the soldiers and my heart sank.

When I entered the dining room the mutt was right where I'd expected him to be, whimpering and rubbing his nose up against the dead woman's leg. I don't know why, but I felt he needed to see them, to help make sense of what was happening. I guess it was a stupid thought, I mean, he was just a dog after all. Bending down, I stroked Ziggy on the back of his head while doing everything humanly possible to avoid looking at the corpses. Excuse the pun, but I was getting sick of constantly throwing my guts up.

'Come on Ziggy,' I said in the kindest tone I could muster, clipping the lead to his collar. 'It's time to go.' That's when I happened to glance at one of the photographs lying on the floor. I knelt down for a closer look and a chill ran down my spine. I now understood why a child would hate their parents that much. But there was no time to dwell on those horrors, we had to get moving. So, I hooked the array of carrier bags over my fingers and started pulling Ziggy away. Reluctantly, but with far less of a struggle than I had expected, Ziggy left behind his old masters and the world he knew, and followed me out to the van. I placed the bags on the ground and opened the door so I could lift the dog up onto the front seat. 'Bloody hell, Ziggy,' I groaned. The furry fella weighed a ton.

Denzil shambled out of the farmhouse laden down by a sports holdall, a quilt and a couple of cushions. He looked from me to Ziggy and then back at me again before shaking his head. 'Something to sleep on,' he said, as he threw his haul into the back of the van.

I gathered up the plastic bags and chucked them on top of the quilt. Grabbing the rest of the stale French loaf, some cheese, a big bag of crisps and a bottle of fizzy water, I slammed the doors shut and went around to the passenger side. Denzil started the engine as I climbed onto the grubby seat and he began scraping the gears in a flustered attempt to find reverse.

'Come on, you piece of crap,' he muttered.

'Navy SEALs,' I said. 'Slow is smooth, smooth is fast.'

Denzil paused, looking like he wanted to give me a slow, smooth punch, then took a deep breath and tried again. This time he achieved his quest to find reverse and we lurched out of the gate and onto the road. Finally, we were in hot pursuit of Lucy. Well, lukewarm pursuit, anyway.

Without satellite navigation, a traditional map or any sodding clue where we were, we decided our best bet was to drive around until we found signs for the M40 motorway. It was a stressful and frustrating plan, as the more we fart-arsed about, the further ahead of us the soldiers, and more importantly,

Lucy, were getting. As we snaked through the idyllic English countryside, past quaint cottages, rolling hills and stone-walled fields, I decided this would be a great place to bring someone for a romantic weekend. I even went as far as noting down the name of a nice hotel that we drove by on my phone. It was oddly comforting to think about life after this nightmare was over. It filled me with hope.

'Are you feeling OK?' asked Denzil. 'It's been hours since your eyes turned blue.'

'I think so,' I said, 'I'm just really worried about Lucy.'

Denzil pushed the van as hard as he could, but despite his best efforts the rust bucket wasn't built for speed. We didn't say much as we drove along, because we were too busy stuffing our faces. The only time we broke the silence was to mention how hungry we were, how concerned for Lucy we were, burp from the fizzy water, or if we approached a fork in the road and needed to decide which direction to take. Despite vomiting a number of times during the previous hours, coupled with a lack of available toothpaste, Denzil seemed happy to share the bottle of water with me. So, I let sleeping dogs lie and kept quiet. I periodically glanced at my phone in the hope that we could call the police, but there was still no signal.

After about ten minutes Denzil's eyes grew wide as wheels.

'What is it?'

'Look,' he said, pointing to our left.

I stared out through the filthy windows at the undulating green fields beyond. It took me a couple of seconds to notice them. Denzil stopped the van and we sat and gawped at a group of strange shapes. The creatures looked a bit like giant sheep. Well, if sheep were created by Doctor Frankenstein, that is. They were comprised of multiple twisted limbs, and raggedy patches of wool were scattered across their big leathery-brown bodies. In places you could see exposed bone and tendons.

'If hell's a farm,' said Denzil, 'then I think we might just be passing it.'

I watched the creatures as they grazed frantically in the field. They looked as if they had never been fed before. 'What do you think they are?'

'God knows. But they're getting through that grass fast enough.'

We watched for a few more seconds. 'Can we go please?' I asked, feeling increasingly uncomfortable about the macabre spectacle before us.

'Amen to that,' said Denzil.

After forty minutes traversing the very beautiful, but very empty country-side, and failing to coax anything but static from the dodgy old radio in the dodgy old van, we passed a sign for the motorway.

'Frigging finally,' shouted Denzil.

I rubbed Ziggy behind the ears and pressed our foreheads together, before whipping my head back to avoid a stinky face lick.

'Be careful you don't catch something from that pit bull,' said Denzil.

'He's not a pit bull,' I replied with a sigh.

'It doesn't matter. You should never let a dog lick your face or touch a cat's bottom.'

'What on earth are you going on about?'

'It's true.'

'And where did you get that public health warning from?'

'My uncle.'

'Your uncle?'

'Yeah, my uncle.'

'Your uncle gave you some seriously weird advice.'

'Yeah, but it doesn't make him wrong.'

'No, but it makes you wrong,' I replied. 'In fact, very wrong if your family felt they had to steer you away from those two delights.'

'Well don't come crying to me when that mutt has given you dengue fever and your penis falls off,' he said.

'Wow! I didn't know that was a symptom of dengue fever. I guess it's a good job you get it from mosquitoes, in places slightly more tropical than the Cotswolds, you total moron.'

'Oh, shut up.'

'Whatever, cat bottom boy.'

I felt a wave of relief as we joined the A40 and passed a sign for the city of Oxford. Finally, a place I recognised.

'This road's going to take us round the top of Oxford to the M40,' Denzil explained. 'From there we can head north.'

'Or we could get to Oxford, find the nearest hospital or police station and get some help.'

'I didn't think of that.' Denzil frowned. 'Sorry mate, I'm not thinking straight at the moment.'

'Don't worry about it.' I patted him on the shoulder. 'The world is a messed-up place today.'

After several minutes we started to see the occasional vehicle. There weren't many of them, but all had one thing in common: they were driving like nutters. Despite maintaining a respectable speed, we were being overtaken by every car on the road. I was actually quite offended when we were passed by a grey-haired pensioner in a beige jacket and driving gloves. The guy had a matching beige car with a panama hat resting on the back shelf. I shot Denzil a 'What the hell are you doing?' look. He gave me the finger. It was a disconcerting feeling to be the slowest people out there. It felt like we were being left behind. I began to pine for my wrecked car. The world and its mother wouldn't be overtaking us if we were driving that little speed machine.

Just then I noticed something flash across my wing mirror. I leant forwards and stared at the reflection, hoping to catch another glimpse of the mystery object. I maintained my vigil for a few more seconds, but whatever it might have been, it was long gone.

'What's wrong?' Denzil asked.

'Nothing…I thought I saw something.'

'What?' he said, sounding worried. 'Another flying disc?'

'No. Well, I don't know what it was. Probably just a red kite or something. After all, you get a lot of those in the skies these days.'

Two seconds later there was a huge thud on the roof, which rather disconcertingly began to buckle. This started Ziggy barking like an absolute lunatic.

'That doesn't sound like a red kite,' shouted Denzil.

A spot of electric green light pierced the dented roof, causing us to scream like extras in a zombie movie.

'It's a tinnitus disc,' Denzil cried.

'Go faster!'

The green dot became a line, then two lines, then three and finally a large rectangle, before a whole section of the roof was lifted off. My jaw dropped like a gigolo's pants as above our heads a huge robotic figure shimmered into existence.

'It's Iron Man!'

Green beams shot from the figure's wrist, severing my seat belt in two places and making me check my crotch was still in one piece. I was then lifted unceremoniously by my right armpit up through the hole in the roof. Ziggy was going ballistic by this stage as Denzil grabbed onto my right leg, and both of us were screaming like our balls hadn't dropped.

'Help!' I yelled.

'I can't hold on!' Denzil clung desperately to me.

'Don't let me go!'

'I'm trying,' he screamed.

But it was too late. The thing lifted me up and out of that seat like I was lighter than air.

Denzil lost his grip both on my leg and the steering wheel, causing the van to swerve violently from side to side. Now, I'm not sure whether you've had the opportunity to be dragged onto the roof of a crappy old van by Robocop at around eighty miles an hour. It's a difficult experience to put into words. Let's just say there's a high probability of damp underwear. Convinced I was about to die, I lay like a wet noodle, staring numbly up at my attacker. Then the shooting began.

It was around that point that things got really weird. Losing interest in me, the robot lifted its eyes skyward as bright green flashes leapt from its wrists. I could see its target way above our heads in the form of a black triangular craft, which I guessed was maybe part of a top-secret military black project like the TR-3B or something. Either way, it wasn't the type of plane I was used to seeing. The robotic figure lifted into the air and started to fly, yes that's right folks, it flew towards the jet. Without conscious thought, but still riddled with fear, I slid along the van and, utilising the newly installed sunroof, dropped back down onto the front seat. I managed to shout, 'Go! Go! Go!' as Denzil pushed the accelerator flat to the floor. He rocked backwards and forwards like a weirdo in an attempt to go faster. This obviously did sod all, but I had to give him ten out of ten for effort.

'Where is it?' shouted Denzil.

'It's fighting a secret jet plane!'

'A what?'

'A secret jet plane.'

Denzil stared at me open-mouthed.

'Don't just sit there catching flies,' I cried. 'Drive, you bellend. Drive!'

I watched the sky through the hole in the roof as the machines engaged in a strange dance, launching an array of coloured lights at one another. Denzil almost drove us off the road as he tried to catch glimpses of the battle. Each traversed the skies at insane speed, turning on a sixpence and performing manoeuvres I would have thought impossible if I hadn't just seen them with my own eyes. The whole episode was so bizarre it didn't look real.

Their deadly engagement edged higher and higher into the sky, before they disappeared into the thick cloud that so often graces this island nation. The blinding balls of light they were firing at one another lit up those clouds like angels having a disco in heaven. Despite the intense fear that threatened to overwhelm me, the scene was both magnificent and beautiful. After a few seconds the clouds faded back to their various shades of white. If anyone had casually glanced skywards in that moment, they would never have known that the inconceivable machines had been there.

After Denzil's frightened babble about Black Triangular UFOs and the Belgian Wave of 1989, he landed back in reality. 'We've got to get off the motorway.'

'What about Lucy?' Torturous images of the soldiers hurting her flew around my head like Iceman chasing a bogey, and I had to fend off the vision of her having nails driven into her legs.

'You want to hang around and wait for Marvin the paranoid android to come back?'

'But we need to find her,' I said. 'She's in danger.'

'No, Jack,' said Denzil. 'Right now, we need to concentrate on staying alive.'

After what seemed like a lifetime of nervous glances skywards, we eventually found an exit from the motorway.

'Get off here,' I said.

'Really?' Denzil's voice was laced with sarcasm. 'I was thinking we should just drive right past it.'

'Alright. You don't need to be a prick about it.'

'Well it's a bloody dumb thing to say,' he snapped.

Our burgeoning argument ended with my heart sinking faster than Jakarta during global warming. It was the same feeling you get right after someone you care about dumps you, only a trillion times worse. Open-mouthed, we stared at the burning remains of the vehicles in which Lucy and the soldiers had been travelling. A swirling mass of raging flame engulfed them, among which I could see a number of cremated bodies hanging out of the vehicle and in the road. I was reminded of that photo of the burned Iraqi soldier propped up on the dashboard of his truck during Operation Desert Storm. The American press refused to publish it, but there was no one here to censor this image now. It was right in front of my eyes for my brain to store away in its database, ready to pop up at any inappropriate moment.

'No, no, no, no, no,' said Denzil. 'Oh my God, Jack. Please let her be okay.'

We pulled up as close as we could and I jumped out of the van and ran towards the flames. The heat was unbearable, forcing me to back away with my arms held over my face. I moved around to the back of the trucks, desperately trying to see inside. I could hear myself saying, 'Maybe she got out?' But all the rear doors were shut and I knew without question that no one could have survived this. I began to shake.

Denzil came over and hugged me. He was trying to speak to me and I think Ziggy may have been barking, but it all seemed so far away, like the noises were coming from the other end of a vast tunnel. All I could do was hope that she hadn't suffered.

'She didn't deserve that,' said Denzil.

I stepped away. My throat was dry and I couldn't speak.

'Do you think it was the robot?' he asked.

My legs betrayed me, and I collapsed to the floor as tears filled my eyes. I honestly didn't care what happened next. Live or die. It didn't seem to matter anymore.

'I never got to tell her how I felt.'

Denzil crouched down beside me, placed his hands on my shoulders and looked me directly in the eyes. 'I know you're hurting right now,' he said. 'I know the bottom has fallen out of your world and you feel terrible. But we have families who care about us, Jack. They'll be worried sick.'

I turned away, but he took my chin in his hands, forcing me to look at him.

'You know they would want us to do everything we can to survive. To get back home to them. We need to survive, Jack. For them. Do you understand?'

I thought of Harold and Brenda. They were a complete pain in the arse, but they loved me unconditionally and I was all they had left. Losing me would destroy my mother. I looked at Denzil and nodded slowly.

'It's time to go,' he said.

We climbed back into the old blue van and drove around the burning wreckage, leaving the A40 and whatever remained of the woman I loved behind us forever.

CHAPTER 8

We drove in silence while I waged an internal war of attrition.

It wasn't like I was new to loss. Thomas's death had cracked the sky and shattered the very earth upon which I walked. There's an infinite intensity to the pain and grief caused by losing your identical twin. The trauma leaves a wound so vast it can never heal. I hadn't celebrated a birthday since I reached eighteen. Leaving for university gave me the opportunity to be permanently unavailable for my parents' unwelcome plans. In the years since graduating, I would mark it by sitting on the old weathered bench in the little copse at the crematorium. I shared my dreams and fears with the birch trees in the hope that Thomas could hear me. I needed him to know that I missed him, and somehow I sensed him, as if a silent part of my brother still lived inside of me.

While Lucy could never fill a void of such magnitude, because no one could, her friendship and kindness had made life bearable again in a way that I no longer thought possible. She was the rainbow following my blackest storm. And for what she gave me, however small, I would be forever grateful. Now she had left me too and I felt like a surfer being pulled underwater by an unstoppable wave of sadness: spinning, crushing and drowning my exhausted soul. The fact I'd never been with her physically didn't make the sensation any less valid, nor the pain any less pronounced.

We drove on without any clear direction or plan, as if we could leave all the hurt behind us, if only we could get far enough away from the burning wreckage. It was dark when we turned down a narrow track and parked up under a dense canopy of trees. We sat there for quite some time before Denzil broke the silence.

'Do you remember the conference in Berlin?'

Several seconds passed before I could bring myself to speak. 'Yes.'

'We were so wasted after all those shots.'

'It was a pretty crazy night.'

'That's an understatement, Gibby,' said Denzil. 'I'm surprised Tony didn't get alcohol poisoning. He must have drunk a whole bottle of whisky.' He smiled. 'And then there was Heidi from Dortmund.'

'Düsseldorf.'

'I don't know why, but German women get me rock hard.'

'Even the ninety-year-olds with STIs?'

'I just love a woman with a foreign accent, Gibby. German, Japanese, Jamaican, Indian, Chinese, Spanish, Australian, Italian, Somalian, American.'

'Please tell me you're not about to list every country on the planet.'

'It's just so goddamn sexy.'

'She was from Düsseldorf, by the way.'

'Well, wherever,' he said. 'I still can't believe she jumped me out the back of the hotel.'

'I still can't believe you didn't use your hotel room,' I replied.

'It was her idea,' he protested. 'Plus, I might have been too drunk to give a monkey's.'

'Classy.'

'But anyway, my point is this—'

'Oh, so you do have one then?'

'Of course I do. Do you remember when Lucy caught us, and didn't report it?'

'She did tear you a new one, though,' I replied. 'I can still hear her shouting about what a disgusting disgrace you were.'

'That was a brutal exchange,' Denzil admitted.

'By exchange do you mean Lucy shouting at you, while you stood there looking like you were about to cry like a baby?'

'Oh, piss off. I thought I was about to lose my job.'

'Not that you listened to any of her advice.'

Denzil smiled. 'Thanks for speaking up for me. I appreciated it. You helped to calm the situation.'

'Well, I was hardly going to leave you hanging.'

'I'm really going to miss her. I know she was always on my case, but I still respected her.'

I raised an eyebrow.

'I did! Honestly.'

I let out a long breath. 'She was incredible.'

'And she was one good-looking woman.'

I smiled. 'And she was one good-looking woman.'

'I never told you this,' he said, 'but she definitely liked you.'

'She was a good friend,' I replied.

'No, numb nuts, I mean, *you know*.'

'What?'

'I mean she wanted to bump bits with you.' He elbowed me in the side.

'Shut up.'

'On my life,' said Denzil, wide-eyed and innocent.

'No, she did not.'

'She so did.'

'Me?' That couldn't be true. Surely I would have seen some sort of sign?

'Why not you, Jack Gibson?' said Denzil. 'You're an amazing guy.'

I watched him out the corner of my eye.

'I mean, you are a massive penis and I hate your guts,' he flashed a cheeky smile, 'but you're amazing nonetheless.'

I frowned.

He elbowed me on the arm. 'Didn't you notice that she was always cock-blocking you on nights out?'

'She never cock-blocked me.'

'Er, yes she did cock-block you, Gibby. You were just too smitten to notice. Anytime a woman went near you, she'd appear from the magical land of nowhere and scare them away.'

Now that he said it, a few things started to click into place. How had I never noticed? I'm not sure if it made me feel better or worse. 'Well, it's a bit late to be telling me this now, isn't it?'

'I suppose it is,' replied Denzil in barely more than a whisper.

I sniffed and wiped my eyes on my sleeve. 'What do we do now, then?'

'Let's just camp here for the night.' He peered into the dark woods. 'The trees should keep us hidden from any prying eyes.'

I opened the door and Ziggy clambered over my lap to escape, presenting me with a faceful of dog derrière in the process. 'Thanks for that,' I said, checking my phone. 'Still no sodding signal.' As I watched Ziggy taking a pee I realised that with everything going on I hadn't given him much thought. After all, he'd lost someone too. As there's no time like the present, unless you're a historian, I decided I would rectify this. I'd bought an assortment of dog food from the farmhouse, so I set about making him happy through the medium of food, which is basically like crack cocaine to dogs.

Despite neither of us being tired, we settled down to sleep in the back of the van. Denzil, Ziggy or possibly both kept passing wind during the night, which made the whole set-up a little on the unpleasant side. However, it was warm and it was dry, so I couldn't complain. I lay there in the darkness unable to sleep, the image of the burning vehicles imprinted on my brain. I was so lost in thoughts of Lucy that I didn't realise Denzil was also awake.

'Jack?' he whispered, almost making me jump out of my skin.

'Yeah?'

'I want to go home.' He sounded upset.

'Me too.'

He let out a long sigh. 'I need to know Mum and Audrey are alright. I'm really worried.' Denzil's family had been through the ringer since his dad passed away. His mum struggled to raise two children on her small salary and she hadn't always had the greatest of boyfriends. I mean, they all started out being charming and suave, buying her presents and taking her for fancy dinners, until the real versions appeared. One guy did some horrific things to my best mate until his mum found out and kicked him to the kerb. The wounds hadn't broken Denzil, but they had left him fiercely protective of his mum and sister, and I'd always admired him for that. The guy can say some stupid stuff and be a complete bloody moron, but if you're one of his people then he's loyal like no one I've ever met. And who doesn't want a friend like that, right?

'We'll set off at first light,' I said. 'I'm sure they're okay. Try not to worry.'

The words were as hollow as I felt, but right then my bank account of practical solutions was very much in the red. I hoped my parents were okay too. Harold and Brenda weren't adventurous types and I wasn't confident they could navigate this type of disaster. My mum struggled to run a bath, let alone away from a hoard of deadly bug monsters, so I prayed it was only a local problem. But either way we needed to get home.

'We have to get you to a doctor first,' said Denzil.

'I'm alright,' I replied. 'If I was going to die, I'm pretty sure it would have happened by now.'

'I agree. But whatever that blue light was, it affected you enough to change your eye colour. That's not normal, Gibby. Let's get you checked out to be on the safe side, shall we?'

I wondered what my parents would make of my new look, if you'll excuse the pun. 'Well, I guess Oxford is the largest place we'll pass on our way home. So let's stop there and try to find a phone and a doctor.'

'Okay.'

We fell silent again. I was bone-tired and my body ached from sleep deprivation mixed with the empty, sick feeling of loss. Eventually, fatigue won the battle and I drifted off into the land of snoozeville.

I found myself standing on a cracked desert plane under a sky of infinite stars. Before me stood a mass of swirling light, stretching hundreds of feet into the air. My cloak whipped and billowed from the winds that emanated from the mesmerising shapes. As I stood there and watched, a circle began to appear at the centre of the chaos. Now I can't say how I knew, but this was definitely some sort of tunnel, although where it led I had no idea. As I moved towards the gateway, the dancing winds became progressively stronger. I was drawn to the hypnotic quality of those circular shapes like a navigator returning home from years at sea. Gritting my teeth, I leant forwards and pushed onwards and into the midst of the stargate.

I awoke to find Ziggy lying next to me on his back with his tackle on full display. His small chest was gently rising and falling and I could feel his warm breath on my face. My bladder was about ready to burst, so I took my aching body off into the trees to resolve the situation. I wobbled about on the spot and yawned as I drained the main vein and tried to work out how long I'd been asleep. I had no idea, but I was so exhausted that I concluded I could sleep for a thousand more years and it still wouldn't be enough.

As my senses returned I became aware of a strange static charge in the air. I zipped up my flies and looked around for the source. I watched open-mouthed as three white lights drifted silently over the tops of the trees. It looked like something out of a crappy UFO documentary. For the first time in my adult life I wondered if Denzil's conspiracy theories may not be so crazy after all. Almost. I wasn't going to take any chances, so I dropped to the ground behind the nearest tree, almost landing in my own whizz.

A ball of orange light fell down through the canopy to the woodland floor. From my hiding place I saw the centre of the orb open up and two giant octopuses with writhing tentacles came pouring out. Despite the shock of what I was seeing, my brain was still functioning enough to estimate their bodies at about a metre in length and their tentacles probably another two. The first octopus was feeling about on the ground with its obnoxious tentacles like a blind person reading Braille. Its obvious intelligence was really creepy. But it was its twin that stole the horror show as it raced up a tree and used its limbs to swing from branch to branch like a seriously screwed-up primate. The speed and agility of the thing was as frightening as the vision was disturbing. As the psycho cephalopods drew closer it dawned on me that while they weren't quite the aliens Denzil had suggested frequented such aircraft, I was trapped.

'Ball fiddlers,' I muttered under my breath as a surge of panic began to rise up inside of my chest. An infant could have found a better hiding place than this. I was standing behind a tree like a wally as two monsters approached. Maybe the summation of the majority of my school teachers, namely that I had bags of untapped potential, was somewhat wide of the mark.

It became painfully obvious that trying to outrun the octopuses would be tantamount to a death sentence. So, I stood there, crapping myself and praying for a smart idea to present itself to my overloaded brain. While I was busy panicking, the beasts were busy getting closer. Five metres, four, then three. I held my breath and stood as still as I could. It was the only option I had. They stopped when they reached my tree and the ground-based monstrosity started groping around near my feet with its tentacles. I was totally and utterly screwed.

The sound of a motorbike engine roared from somewhere off in the distance. The creature froze, listening to the sound. Octopuses can do that, you know? Hear things, I mean. You wouldn't think it, would you? They don't hear as well as squid, not that it's a competition, of course, but they still can. I was surprised that its statocyst would work in the open air. But hey, it didn't matter how they detected the sound, because detect it they did. And thank Christ for that, because after a momentary pause they set off in squidgy pursuit.

I fought hard against the tide of fear that was in danger of dragging me down into a watery grave. This process took a fair amount of self-motivation, but eventually I plucked up the courage to peer around the side of the tree. Mr and Mrs Tickle were nowhere in sight, so I took the opportunity to scamper off through the woods like a frightened squirrel. The exhaustion I'd been feeling barely registered as my body drowned in a fresh burst of adrenaline. When the three white lights re-appeared overhead, I threw myself down behind a bush and prayed they wouldn't notice me. I watched and waited as they moved silently away over the trees, gathering momentum. In the dawn light I could now see they were attached to the underside of a dark triangular craft. I guessed it was the same one that had battled with Iron Man. It was probably a solid guess too, because how many of them do you see flying about on any given day? I wondered whether it was piloted by the octopuses. Surely not. Because let's face it, that would be ridiculous.

I nearly gave Denzil a heart attack when I burst into the back of the van. His expression of panic would have been hilarious if I wasn't petrified myself. I pulled the poor chap to his feet as Ziggy leapt about, barking. As I pushed him into the front seats I was babbling incoherently about squid and ships. Meanwhile, Denzil looked like he'd just been caught by his neighbour fast asleep in bed with the man's wife. The imaginary homewrecker finally snapped into action and turned the rusty vehicle around, and we bounced back out of the trees, along the track and out onto the open road.

Once again, we found ourselves driving aimlessly through the countryside. The roads were empty except for the remains of another road accident. The two cars were complete write-offs and it looked like they'd been there for a while. A roof box on one of the cars had been damaged and clothes were strewn all over the road. Denzil slowed the van down and pulled up alongside the collision. I could see a woman slumped over the steering wheel in one of the vehicles, but there was no one else around.

'Do you want to check if she's okay?' he asked.

'Not really,' I replied. 'But I will.' Sometimes you just have to put yourself in the other person's shoes, right?

Denzil cut the engine and handed me the Glock. I took it reluctantly and approached the wreck. 'Hello?' I called, but she didn't respond. The driver's door was wide open so I leant in and touched the woman's neck. Her skin was ice cold and I couldn't find a pulse. I took a step back and gazed down at the lifeless corpse. I wondered who this lady was. Was there someone out there right now, hoping and praying for news that she was okay? It was just another tragedy that had taken place during the past couple of days, big enough to tear people's entire worlds apart, yet almost non-existent in the machinations of our vast universe. Thinking about it made me feel unsettled, like a helpless particle being blown around on solar winds. I picked up a green jacket I found on the floor and covered her with it, then turned and walked away.

Denzil watched my expression as I climbed back into the van. I shook my head and he sighed and gave a tiny nod in response. He turned the key in the ignition and the engine spluttered and died.

'Well, that doesn't sound good,' I said.

Denzil frowned and tried again.

The engine spluttered and died once more.

'Bollocks,' he said, whacking the steering wheel.

'Not now,' I said with a sinking feeling in my chest.

Denzil took a deep breath. 'Slow is smooth, smooth is fast.' The poor guy clearly hadn't grasped the meaning of the phrase. But he was my best mate, so whatever. Denzil attempted to start the van twice more—slowly, bless him—but unfortunately the rust bucket was adamant it didn't want to play ball. He leant his head back against the chair and closed his eyes momentarily, then turned to face me. 'It looks like we're walking.'

'Whoopy bloody do.'

We grabbed some food from the back of the van and I set off along the road with Ziggy pulling on his lead. It was irritating, but I let him off as he was, after all, just a dog.

'Wait up,' called Denzil.

I turned back and gave him a weary look as he jogged along the road to catch us up.

'I'm not sure it's a good idea to stay on the road,' he said.

'But we might see someone.'

'Exactly,' said Denzil, looking concerned.

I knew he was right, but I was tired and I was hurting. 'For God's sake. It's going to take us forever to get home.'

'Like your mum says, Gibby. Better late than dead.' Denzil realised he'd struck a nerve as soon as he said it. I gave him a filthy look but by some miracle I managed to keep my mouth shut.

With that, we climbed over the picturesque but wobbly stone wall on the side of the road and began crossing a field.

'I'm so bloody tired,' I said.

'I know, mate,' said Denzil sympathetically. 'Me too.'

'Maybe we should stop for a bit?'

'Let's get further away from the van first. There's no point making it easy for those people and their pet monster to find us.'

We walked along in silence for about half an hour. As we crossed the patchwork of fields, I thought about the Hobbits fleeing the Shire with the Black Riders hot on their heels. I concluded that dangerous adventures were a lot more fun when you weren't actually part of them. Despite the myriad of questions I still had about the black triangle, the insane octopuses and the flying robot, it was Lucy that consumed my thoughts. I could sense my attraction morphing into obsession, born from the knowledge that I'd never see her again.

I was torn from my musings by a huge roar overhead. I instinctively threw myself down onto the grass and into something rather unpleasant. Rolling over, I looked up to see a series of jet planes racing across the blue sky.

'Where do you think they're going?' asked Denzil, who'd sensibly remained standing.

'No idea,' I replied. 'But I don't fancy their chances against the black triangle or the robot.'

We watched the jet fighters disappear over the horizon before continuing onwards. It must have been about twenty minutes later that we finally sat down at the edge of some trees to eat. I was so worn out that the first thing I did was lie down on the grass and fall asleep.

I woke up to find Ziggy licking my face. 'Urgh, get off me you, sicko!' I pushed him away. His attention was simultaneously cute and repulsive. Denzil was sitting under a tree with the rifle on his lap and a tin of cold baked beans in his hand. As he consumed them he pulled the appropriate faces.

'How are you feeling?' he asked.

'Like I've just run an underwater marathon in a suit of armour.'

He opened another tin of beans and handed it to me. Under normal circumstances I would have turned my nose up at them, but now I wolfed them down and followed the culinary delight with a warm milk chaser. Then I tipped some dog food onto the grass for Ziggy.

'Have you noticed it?' asked Denzil.

'Noticed what?' I looked around me for a bag for the empty bean can. I'd learnt the country code as a child and old habits die hard.

'The silence.'

'Well, we are in the country,' I replied. 'You're not going to hear much.'

'No, listen.'

I decided to humour him.

'There's no sound at all,' he continued. 'No birds chirping, no insects buzzing, no farm animals, nothing. It's completely silent.'

He was right. It was like God had taken his big old heaven hoover and sucked all the sound out of the world. It was eerie, and made it seem like we were completely alone. Unfortunately, it didn't mean we were.

We sat and listened to the oppressive sound of nothing right up until Ziggy started to growl.

'Don't move,' whispered Denzil.

Naturally, I moved straightaway. As I turned to my left, I noticed I was being watched by a grotesque little excuse of a creature. The freak looked like a bald squirrel but it had torn flesh and ruby-red eyes. The mini minger was displaying a horrific set of razor-sharp teeth. Ziggy started barking and tugging on the lead. When it came to fight or flight I knew exactly which side his bone was buttered. In response to this animalistic show of strength, the demon squirrel started squealing. Its calls were answered immediately by the cries of more creatures somewhere above our heads. Denzil leapt to his feet and cocked the rifle, and we watched as small abominations fell like living raindrops onto the grass all around us. Ziggy barked and leapt about, unsure of where exactly to focus his aggression.

'We're trapped,' I said, picking up the Glock, and we backed further into the trees. 'Ziggy?'

Now whether it was because he was obedient or whether it was because he knew we were ostensibly shagged, he turned and sprinted back to us with the devil squirrels hot on his heels.

Denzil started to fire his rifle and instantly scored two direct hits. Maybe the paintballing had paid off after all? Nevertheless, the other sixty-odd baby beasts just kept on coming.

I opened fire and hit precisely nothing. So much for Battle Camp. I was forced to go old school and throw the bloody thing. It was probably a violation of the country code, but then I don't remember it referencing hand guns. 'Leg it,' shouted Denzil and we turned and ran off through the trees. I scooped up a large stick without breaking my stride. I wasn't sure it was going to be much help in the inevitable battle, but there was nothing else to hand. We tore out the other side of the trees and found ourselves in yet another field. There are a lot of those in the Cotswolds. We ran across the uneven ground despite the risk of sprained ankles and were making good progress. Unfortunately, the devil squirrels were just that bit faster, and we soon realised we had no hope of outrunning them.

'I need to stop,' panted Denzil.

Now the last bloody thing I wanted to do was stop, but I knew they would catch us eventually. So, like Butch and Sundance, it was time to make our last stand. Although I hoped this one would be marginally more successful.

'Come on, then,' I shouted as Jack Cassidy and the Denzil Kid turned around to face their foes. I dropped Ziggy's lead and raised my stick like a baseball bat just as the first wave attacked. Everything became a blur as I swung my makeshift club at anything small, gross and moving. The squirrels went flying into the air upon contact, although somewhat vexingly every time I hit one of the buggers it seemed to get back onto its little monster feet and come at me again. In regards to my teammates, Denzil was using his rifle as a club and Ziggy raced around snapping at anything that got close enough. One squirrel managed to leap onto my foot and then race up my body towards my face with terrifying speed. I only managed to grab its bony tail after it had taken a decent chunk out of my neck. I swung it around and threw it as hard as I could. Rather satisfyingly, it caught one of its butt-ugly friends in the face and they both went rolling off across the grass. Ziggy yelped and I turned to see that he had one of the creatures on his back and another two were climbing up his trailing lead that I'd dropped to the ground in the melee. Denzil pulled the first creature from Ziggy's now bloody fur and dropkicked it away like an angry rugby player. He then set about stamping on the other two as if he was putting out a fire while shouting something that sounded like 'Manky little rats.'

As suddenly as the attack began, it was over. The squirrels stood up on their hind legs like meerkats, listening intently. This was followed by a chorus of shrieks, before they turned and ran back towards the trees.

Denzil and I stared at each other. The guy was seriously out of breath. 'It must be your aftershave, Gibby,' he said, forcing a smile.

I chose to ignore him. 'We need to keep moving. I don't know about you, but I sure as hell don't want to meet whatever it is they're afraid of.'

CHAPTER 9

We hightailed it across a field, through some trees and up a hill. The good news was that the fear subsided, but the bad news was that the pain from the squirrel bite increased. By this point my neck was bleeding and stinging like an angry wasp. After a rather unsatisfactory consultation with Doctor Denzil, the conclusion was that I'd probably live. Ziggy's back appeared to be faring about the same, so we pushed on under the proviso we'd clean our wounds at the first opportunity.

The immense fatigue gradually set in and I felt an overwhelming desire to stop and sit down. Yes something kept me going. After about twenty minutes we arrived at a road, and decided to follow it until we hit civilization. It took over an hour to achieve this, coming in the form of a high stone wall topped with an electric fence. Hardly a metropolis, but Denzil was convinced it belonged to a stately home. So, we followed it for over a mile until a sign on a huge iron gate announced our arrival at Ashbury Hall. His smugness was almost unbearable.

The intricate patterns on the gate made me feel strange: a creepy mix of odd symbols and demonic faces. Whoever wrought that iron into shape had some serious issues.

'Let's knock,' said Denzil, clearly less perturbed by the entrance art than I was.

We approached the gate and Denzil pressed the modern-looking buzzer. After a wait that lasted about as long as it took for us to almost give up, a male voice replied with, 'Yes?'

'Hello,' said Denzil in his best telephone voice. 'My friend and his dog are injured and we'd be super massively grateful if we could use your telephone to call for help, please?'

This generated another long pause followed by a 'Stay there.'

Denzil rolled his eyes, unimpressed by the level of service we were receiving. We stood around like a couple of spare parts until a green 4x4 came cruising towards the gate. It stopped several metres away and two men stepped out who looked unsettlingly like East End gangsters. They carried efficient-looking assault rifles and as they raised their weapons, we raised our hands.

After a few tense minutes of being groped and grilled, the men muttered something about expecting us sooner. We then found ourselves in the back of the 4x4, heading deep into the heart of the estate.

It became clear from the length of time we spent in the car that the manicured grounds were extensive. After rumbling over a number of cattle grids, my mouth dropped open as all manner of exotic animals came into view. Zebras, giraffes, elephants and oryx with their insane horns meandered about in groups. A troop of baboons groomed one another while a flamboyance of flamingos, and yes, that is the collective noun, covered the edge of a lake. It was like Richmond Park on steroids. The road snaked through a large area of ancient woodland, reminiscent of a scene from *Robin Hood* but without the men in tights. After a few hundred yards, beech, oak and chestnut trees gave way to mighty redwoods, beyond which lay Ashbury Hall.

The name really didn't do it justice. There was nothing hall-like about it. It was the biggest palace I'd ever seen. I couldn't believe something as fantastical as this existed in the world and I'd never heard of it, let alone in my own country. Ashbury Hall was a thing of architectural wonderment and made Versailles and Blenheim look like poor cousins. Denzil mumbled something about it costing more than a panther's pubes. I couldn't decide whether that meant panthers were excessively hairy or if Denzil just held their crotch hair in high regard. I loved him, but sometimes I had to wonder.

We pulled up outside the front of the building. No tradesman's entrance for us. Thugs in sunglasses opened the doors and I stepped onto the crunchy gravel. We stood at the foot of a huge stone staircase, leading to an intimidating entrance of jaw-dropping splendour. Giant double doors sat at the far end of a deep porch at least forty feet high and lined with columns. The columns and ceiling were tattooed with intricately carved images depicting serpentine creatures ascending skyward.

Slipping into tourist mode, I stopped to have a quick gawp. The images looked as strange and creepy as the gate art. The moment didn't last long as one of the meat heads pushed me in the back and told me in a deadpan tone to 'Move it.' As I approached the doors I became aware that I looked like a total tramp. I tried brushing some of the dirt from my clothes but had to admit defeat. As the saying goes, you can't polish a turd, which in this case was the sheep turd smeared all down my jeans from the jet plane incident.

One vast door swung open and we stepped into another world, one where my bank balance would be about as useful as a chocolate fireplace. The gargantuan entrance hall was an obscene affair of marble, red carpet and giant statues, some of which had a distinctly unsettling vibe. I wondered if the owner's ancestors had been fans of the High Victorian Gothic style, or just wrong'uns. Large colourful butterflies, more magnificent than any I'd ever seen, flapped through the air around us. I looked up in awe at the glass-domed ceiling decorated with a rotating map of the night sky. My eyes traced the shapes of constellations marked out by small stars. It appeared incredibly real. I watched in awe as a shooting star passed across the scene.

Denzil diverted my attention with an elbow to the ribs. This was fol-lowed by an embarrassingly loud, 'MILF alert,' which reminded me of the times my half-deaf Nanny Bertie talked about people when she thought they couldn't hear, and they always bloody could. I particularly enjoyed it when they made eye contact with me, it was so flipping awkward.

Factually speaking, however, Denzil was correct. A woman approached us with a grace and style that would put most catwalk models to shame. Her hair was as black as the expensive clothes she wore. It was hard to guess her age, but she was definitely the wrong side of forty. Her captivating smile lit up the vast room. When she opened her mouth, the words slid from her blood-red lips like silk. I had the sense that she could get most men to do whatever she wanted, something that made me feel deeply unsettled. I therefore decided to remain not just firm, but ruthless in the face of such overwhelming beauty.

'Good afternoon, gentlemen,' she purred. 'I'm Lady Ashbury.'

'Hello, Lady Ashbury,' we chorused like a couple of virgins. The ruthless thing hadn't got off to the best of starts.

'Call me Beatrice, please,' she said as her eyes lost focus and she began to whisper. 'No space nor time will ever fade, the knowledge shared etern-ally. Watching stars now long since made, with sapphire eyes like solar seas.' Snapping out of her trance she beamed at us again. 'Now then, I believe you're in need of some assistance?'

Our response came in the form of a babbling monologue about broken phones, soldiers and monsters. When we'd finished she threw her head back and laughed.

'How wonderful! But I'm sure there's no government conspiracy: the phone signal is simply shocking in this part of the country.' She flashed me another stunning smile. 'It's why I prefer to spend most of the year in Mayfair. But fortunately for you sweet gentlemen, we have some of the modern essentials, such as a telephone.'

This announcement lifted my spirits.

'But first, we shall tend to those nasty cuts.' Lady Ashbury raised a hand and a servant with a face like a slapped fish came rushing over.

'Ma'am?'

'Ask Doctor Selwood to meet them in the Blue Room.'

'Ma'am.' The servant dutifully scampered away.

Lady Ashbury raised her hand once more and a sullen woman appeared at her side, whom she introduced as Sarah. Lady Ashbury instructed her to take us to the Blue Room. We thanked our host, who smiled and walked away. As she did so, a huge black snake appeared from out of nowhere and fell obediently in step beside her. Well, in slither. Ziggy began growling and pulling at his lead while Denzil fired off an impressive range of expletives. It was such a bizarre scene that my brain didn't register fear until they were long gone and I was left trying to calm down my frightened pooch.

Hearts still racing, we followed Funface to a room decorated from floor to ceiling in pale blue. Denzil decided it would be amusing to ask her why it was called the Blue Room. The ice-cold stare he received in response was truly a thing of wonder. Thankfully, the equally miserable manservant reappeared to break the now awkward silence, and he was accompanied by a grey-haired man sporting a tweed suit.

'Good afternoon, gentlemen,' he said in a jolly tone. 'I'm Doctor Horatio Selwood.'

I liked him immediately. He had a kind face, a bushy beard and a firm handshake. He cleaned up my neck using a number of items from his black leather doctor's bag.

'That should do it,' he announced upon completion.

I smiled and thanked him, but Denzil still looked concerned. 'Does he seem healthy to you?' he asked the doctor.

Doctor Selwood looked surprised by the question. 'Is there something I should know about?'

'No…' Denzil sounded sheepish. 'Well, yes, I mean it's just that yesterday his eyes were brown and now they're bright blue.'

'Have you seen this before?' I asked with no small amount of concern.

'I confess I have not, but Lady Ashbury informs me she has. And she assures me you're quite well, quite well indeed.'

I decided to ask Lady Ashbury about this as soon as possible, along with why she had a bloody great snake following her about like the world's scariest lapdog.

"Does she have any medical qualifications?' asked Denzil.

'She is the wisest person I know. But we can't have you worrying about poor old Jack here, can we?' Doctor Selwood said with a chuckle, before proceeding to give me a full once-over. Fortunately, this involved a blood pressure and heart-rate check rather than a drop and cough. He also took the time to examine Denzil before pronouncing us as, 'Tickety-boo.' God, the guy was posh. He even checked Ziggy out and said that he needed stitches, advising that we leave the dog with him. I felt a bit uncomfortable leaving my canine companion, but as Ziggy didn't look overly bothered I decided that if he was happy, then so was I.

Armed with the comforting knowledge I wasn't about to keel over any second, when sullen Sarah reappeared we followed the miserable woman through a maze of corridors and staircases. I was keen to ask her where we were going, but less keen on the potential response. Instead I decided to take the mature approach and pull faces behind her back, which appeared to entertain Denzil. We were eventually guided into a study that commanded an impressive view of the grounds and told to wait. Then Sarah was gone.

'She clearly loves her job,' I said as the door clicked shut.

But Denzil had other things on his mind. 'How fit is Lady Ashbury?'

I laughed.

'I think I'm in love,' he said. 'And by love, I mean I want to put my willy inside her and wiggle it about a bit.'

'Well, if you just stick it in and wiggle it about a bit then I guess that's why you're single,' I replied.

'Piss off.'

After a discussion about the health and safety risks associated with owning giant snakes, we turned our attention to the room and began exploring.

'Look at all this old shit,' said Denzil, as he spun the antique globe that was sitting on top of the huge wooden desk.

'It really is an incredible place.'

Denzil frowned. 'This is the worst globe ever,' he said. 'I mean, where the hell's "Tharsis Rise" or "The Isidis Basin"?'

'Not sure,' I replied. 'The Middle East maybe?'

The door opened and a dashing male model breezed into the room accompanied by a panda. 'Hello gentlemen,' he said in the poshest voice I'd ever heard. And I mean, this was a whole other level. Forget a plum in his mouth: this dude had the whole damn tree. He also had a handshake that felt like iron. 'I'm Lord Randolph Tarquin Ashbury the third,' he proclaimed like a King of Legend. 'Welcome to my humble abode.' The guy was exceedingly handsome and charismatic as hell. My fantasy about Lady Ashbury leaving her wrinkly old husband to shack up with me vanished like Houdini's elephant. 'Rooms have been prepared for you to freshen up for tonight's party.'

'Party?' I replied, unable to tear my eyes away from the cute killing machine sat by the door scratching its tummy.

'Sebastien,' said Lord Ashbury, 'be a good fellow and wait outside.'

To my utter amazement, the bloody great bear got up and waddled out of the room. It even closed the door.

'Impressive, isn't he?' asked Lord Ashbury. 'Science is more advanced than you'd imagine. World governments have been using genetically modified animals for years.'

Denzil gave me a look that said, 'I told you so.' And like any mature, well-adjusted adult that realises they were wrong, I chose to completely ignore him.

'How do you train it?' he asked.

'Sebastien's brain has been altered to radically increase his intelligence, then it was simply a case of civilising him.'

I wondered if someone had also civilised a couple of octopuses.

'Perhaps they should have called that film *Planet of the Pandas*,' said Denzil.

'Is it safe?' I asked.

'Quite safe,' said Lord Ashbury as he puffed out his chest. 'I consider Sebastien a friend.'

'Does Lady Ashbury's snake qualify as a "friend"?'

'Quite so. You can't tame an ordinary black-necked spitting cobra.'

'That thing's a cobra? It's bloody massive.'

'Its size and pigmentation were enhanced. What Lady Ashbury wants, Lady Ashbury gets.'

The whole thing blew my mind. Denzil clearly felt the same, because when I glanced over at him, he looked like someone had just told him field mice could play the saxophone.

'We have a ball this evening, old sport,' he continued, 'and you two chaps are going to be our guests of honour.'

Denzil said it sounded cool, but I thought it sounded odd. Not as odd as a panda operating a door, but strange none the less. Why would they want a couple of scumbags like us at their party?

'What's the occasion?' asked Denzil.

'Why, to celebrate life, my dear boy,' said Lord Ashbury with a laugh. 'To celebrate life.'

Despite being freaked out by the panda, we couldn't help but join in with the laughter. The man was just so damn likeable.

Lord Ashbury explained his Great Uncle Montague had been part of a secret society of hellraisers back in the 1800s. Their members comprised some of the most rich and powerful men in Britain and they met once a month during the full moon in the underground caves behind the house. He leant towards us, lowering his radio presenter voice as he said, 'Once down there they conducted their dark and dirty business.'

'Ah, that's grubby,' said Denzil, pulling back in disgust. 'That's just unnecessary.'

'Well, they seemed to rather enjoy it,' said Lord Ashbury.

'There really are some mucky people about,' said Denzil. 'Imagine the smell.'

Lord Ashbury looked confused. 'The caves are quite well ventilated.'

'Even so,' continued Denzil. 'You'd think with all their money they could have bought a thunderbox.'

'I'm sorry, old chap. I'm not quite sure that I follow.'

I decided it was time to shift the focus of the conversation. 'What type of secret society was it?'

'Why, a secret one, dear boy.' Lord Ashbury winked and tapped the side of his nose.

'But what did they do?'

'Some things remain an Ashbury family secret, of course, but let's just say hedonism and debauchery.'

Denzil's eyes lit up like a kid who had just met the real Santa Claus. 'Orgies?' he blurted out.

'Sins of the flesh were most certainly on the menu,' replied Lord Ashbury with a look on his face that was too sex offender-esque for my tastes.

'Can I join?' asked Denzil.

The Lord laughed. 'I'm afraid not, old sport. I'm not sure you gentlemen quite fit the membership criteria.'

I guessed these millionaires weren't looking for office workers that dipped into their overdrafts every month.

'I had a threesome once at university,' said Denzil.

'Right.' The Lord raised an eyebrow.

'Did they have names?' I enquired.

'Rosalind and Kelly.'

'Not them, you idiot. The secret society.'

'Ah,' said Lord Ashbury. 'Yes! They called themselves the Brotherhood of the Snake.'

'Bit sexist,' said Denzil.

My mind drifted back to Lucy and I lost interest in the conversation. 'Could we use your telephone please? We really need to call our families to let them know we're okay.'

'Why of course, old sport. I shall organise it post-haste.'

'Thank you.'

Lord Ashbury pulled a cord on the wall and a manservant with thinning grey hair and weaselly eyes appeared in the doorway. 'Ah, Fishman. Be a good chap and take these two gentlemen for a hot meal, then on to their rooms to freshen up.'

'Very good, sir.'

We followed Fishman to a colourful dining room with an immense table. Strange artwork, urns filled with giant feathers and fancy golden cages containing large, exotic birds decorated the room. Above our heads hung a series of grand chandeliers, dangling from an ornate ceiling. Fishman instructed us to sit down at one end of the table.

'Shotgun!' cried Denzil with the desperation of a kid busting for a pee, and took the position at the head of the table.

Fishman left and we found ourselves momentarily alone.

'Lord Ashbury reminds me of Jay Gatsby,' said Denzil, 'with all that "old sport" business.'

'I know,' I agreed.

'So, who would you rather do it with then?'

'I don't think I fancy grinding on Lord Ashbury or Fishman.'

'No, you muppet, Daisy Buchanan or Jordan Baker?'

'Oh!' I replied. 'Jordan Baker.'

'You're such a loser.'

I was about to lay out my argument when a servant appeared with the sort of food you'd expect to see in a five-star restaurant. Fishman came creeping in behind her.

'This is a bottle of Chateau Lafite 1865 from Lord Ashbury's cellar,' he announced, shoving a grubby-looking bottle in my face.

'That's really kind of him,' I said, wishing it was beer.

'The wine is from the Médoc region to the north-west of Bordeaux,' he continued pompously, pouring a small amount into my glass. 'It was owned by the Rothschilds.'

Denzil gave a subtle yawn. He was clearly as underwhelmed as I was.

'The great Baron James Mayer de Rothschild purchased it in 1868,' continued Fishman. 'It was gifted to Lord Ashbury last year.'

'Wow,' I replied, trying to sound enthused.

'This wine is very, very special indeed,' he said in a tone that indicated he thought I was a moron. 'I hope you are able to enjoy it.'

I chose to ignore the dig. Twatman watched me patiently. I hate tasting wine; it's the most uncomfortable moment in a restaurant. If you know wine, then you probably love it. If you don't, then you look more awkward than a farmer caught hanging out the back of a goat. Which is yet another reason why you should never go for dinner on a first date.

I lifted the antique glass, swished the liquid about a bit, had a quick sniff and took a sip of the red fluid. All of a sudden, something quite remarkable happened. Something I could never have expected. As soon as that vintage wine hit my tongue, I knew without a shadow of a doubt that it tasted exactly—and I mean exactly—like a glass of red wine.

'That's incredible,' I said in the most impressed tone I could muster. I didn't mean it, but it seemed to satisfy the pompous twonk. Fishman poured two modest glasses, recorked the bottle, then placed it in a cabinet and left.

'Stingy bastard,' said Denzil, as he retrieved the wine and filled our glasses to the top. Some spilt onto the table and I had to lean forward to take a few quick sips before I could lift the glass. We demolished the food and then downed the rest of the bottle before hiding it at the back of the cupboard.

It actually tasted pretty nice. I decided to keep an eye out for the brand next time I was in the supermarket.

After a brief chat about the merits of Lady Asbury's medical opinion and the blue light, we discussed the bloody great zoo animals that almost turned Denzil's trousers into a latrine.

'I keep telling you, Gibby, the government are up to all sorts of sinister stuff.'

I frowned. 'I get why they'd experiment with animal genetics, but how did these creatures end up as the Ashburys' house pets?'

'Maybe the Ashburys work for the government?'

'And why the hell haven't we heard of this place before? It's the National Trust's wet dream.'

Sarah returned mid-conversation and took us to our rooms. I confess I was starting to feel lightheaded from the alcohol. We dropped Denzil off at 'The Gorgo Suite' and walked up to a door that said, 'The Thamuz Suite.' To say it was grand was an understatement. Like most of Ashbury Hall, I felt like I'd stepped into a fairy tale. I explored, opening and closing any doors or drawers I could find and examining the toiletries. I was busy sniffing the shaving foam, which isn't a euphemism, when there was a loud knock on the main door. I would have answered it but whoever it was entered of their own accord. It was a good job that I wasn't rubbing one out. I hastily exited the en-suite bathroom.

Standing before me was a boy of about twelve or thirteen with a shock of red hair and freckles. A woman in her late twenties had placed a bottle of wine on the table by the window and was carefully pouring a large glass. She was clearly more generous than old Fishman, the bloody bellend.

'I've come for your clothes so they can be laundered,' said the boy. He had an unsettlingly vacant expression.

'Thanks,' I replied. 'Although I don't have any other clothes.'

'There's a dressing gown in the bathroom,' said the woman in the same distant tone as she handed me the wine glass.

'Okay,' I replied. 'Give me two minutes, then.' I took a large gulp of the wine and returned to the bathroom, where I removed the keys, wallet and phone from my pockets before changing into the robe. Feeling a little exposed, although fortified by the wine, I handed my filthy clothes to the boy, who left immediately. The woman headed into the bathroom and started running the bath.

'Thank you,' I said awkwardly. 'That's kind, but you really don't need to do that.' My head was starting to feel fuzzy and I could feel myself beginning to sway a little. I wondered if I'd actually drunk more than I thought.

'Lord Ashbury asked me to run you a bath,' she said. 'Why don't you enjoy a glass of wine?'

The woman guided me into the chair next to the table containing the wine bottle. While keeping my legs well and truly closed to prevent a possible outbreak, I stared out at the beautifully landscaped gardens at the rear of the house. The wine was slipping down far too easily and my cloudy brain wondered if the grounds were the work of Capability Brown.

The woman reappeared, announced my bath was ready and left. The door clicked shut and I found myself alone for the first time since leaving the Naysmere Hotel.

Silence.

I gazed around the room, seeing nothing. Dark thoughts simmered, then swirled in my mind, before taking over completely. I relived the monsters, the violence, the fear and the slaughter. I thought about my family and how desperately I missed them. And then I thought of Lucy. The woman I loved was gone, and worst of all it was I who had sent her to her death.

Whatever had possessed me to force Lucy to go with the soldiers? Rage and grief hit me and I started taking bigger and bigger gulps of the wine, hoping the sudden influx of alcohol would wash away the pain. But all it did was slam me face first into a wall of drunkenness.

Why did I always lose the people I loved? What had I ever done to deserve that? It wasn't fair. The anger started to build up inside like a volcano. Then it erupted.

I stood up, knocking the chair to the floor, and flipped the table over. Fortunately, the wine bottle was empty, otherwise I would have made a right old mess. I charged around the room, shouting and cursing, before tearing off my robe and throwing it into the bathroom. Then, with bum and balls on full display and my todger flapping about like a Jolly Roger in a storm, I pulled the cushions off the small sofa and threw them onto the floor. I kicked them around the bedroom like a demented footballer.

I screamed and charged at the bathroom door, taking a huge swing at it with my fist. But I slipped, overstretched and missed the target, landing in a heap on the floor. And there I lay on those cold ceramic tiles, panting and staring up at the ceiling, tears pooling in my eyes and running into my hair.

Alone and broken, I fell into oblivion.

CHAPTER 10

I awoke to the sound of knocking. Thankfully, the world was no longer spinning like a puppy in a tumble dryer. On the flip side, I felt like I'd just been turned over by Mike Tyson, but I guess you can't have everything.

The discarded bathrobe lay a few feet away, curled up next to my decency. I set about retrieving it, which at that point in time was only possible on all fours. Nipples, bum and boy bits covered, I entered the bedroom to see it was now dark outside. How long had I been asleep? On the upside, my freshly laundered clothes and trainers were waiting in the wardrobe. On the downside, the woman I loved was gone forever.

The knocking morphed into a series of loud bangs and Denzil's dulcet tones drifted into the room.

'Oi? Nob-head? Answer the door.'

'I'm coming. Chill out.' I opened the door to find myself confronted by an annoyingly fresh-faced Denzil.

'You look terrible,' he said.

'Thanks,' I replied. 'I feel it.'

'Did you manage to get some sleep?' Denzil pushed past me.

My minor mental meltdown came flooding back.

'Earth to Jack?' Denzil clicked his fingers in my face.

'Yeah…I think so.'

'Good. Because you'll need all of your strength for the ladies tonight. Time to find me a rich wife.' He began dancing about on the spot.

I felt sick and knew it was from more than just the wine. 'I'd rather sleep,' I told him. No way was I in the mood to party.

There was a knock at the door and I cursed under my breath. I couldn't get a moment's peace in this sodding place.

'It's open,' called Denzil.

A servant entered the room carrying an ornate wooden box. 'Lord Ashbury wondered if you would care for some pre-party entertainment,' he said, before opening the container to reveal a plethora of drugs.

Denzil's mouth opened and closed like a fish on a carpet.

'What's that?' I asked, struggling to believe my eyes.

The servant talked us through the collection of drugs like a sommelier in an upmarket restaurant.

'How much can we have?' asked Denzil as soon as the guy finished his well-executed speech.

'As much as you like, sir,' came the polite response.

'As much as I like?' Denzil stared into the gentleman's eyes as if attempting to read his soul.

'Of course,' replied the man. 'But don't feel the need to rush. There will be plenty more at the party.'

Denzil selected ten grams of coke. It reminded me of our student days when we used to steal all the complimentary sauce sachets from restaurants. 'Holy moly,' he said once the guy had left. 'Can you believe this, Gibby?'

'Not really.' I stared at the drugs, feeling numb.

Convinced this was going to be the best party ever, Denzil chopped up two of the biggest lines you've ever seen on an antique dresser. I wasn't in the mood to partake, but I did it just to try and temporarily erase the memory of Lucy.

The bath the servant had run for me was now stone cold, so I opted for a quick shower before putting on my freshly laundered clothes. It felt amazing to be clean again.

Fishman reappeared from the land of arse-kissing rich people to inform us that Lord and Lady Ashbury were waiting to see their guests, namely us, in the Great Hall. If possible, he looked even more smug than during our previous encounter. It took quite a while to reach the Great Hall as the palace was so damn big. I decided the Ashburys must have some serious wealth. I was impressed they could afford to run a house like this without opening it to the public to generate extra revenue. It was a luxury usually only enjoyed by oligarchs and dictators.

The Great Hall turned out to be the most lavish part of the house thus far. I felt like I'd stepped into a movie. A carnival of elaborate decorations, circus performers and exotic animals lay before us. There were fountains, ice sculptures, famous musicians belting out hits and the ambience was controlled by the most incredible lighting I'd ever seen. I ran my eyes over the scores of well-heeled party guests, noting that the men were all about forty-plus and came in every shape and size, while the women were much younger and uniformly beautiful. I concluded that if money can't buy you happiness, it can sure as hell buy you a beautiful wife.

The huge hall was crammed full of people, but as soon as we walked in, every last one of them turned to stare. I'd never felt so horribly out of place in my whole twenty-four years on this earth. What made it worse was they were all dressed in exquisite costumes or lavish formal attire while we were sporting hoodies, jeans and trainers.

'Well this is nice,' I mumbled.

'Don't take it personally,' replied Denzil. 'They've probably never seen a face as ugly as yours before.'

'You're a dick.'

We were saved from further embarrassment by the divine Lady Ashbury and her terrifying companion, who glided over to welcome us with what appeared to be legitimate enthusiasm. She had the ability to make you feel like the most important person in the world.

'I trust you're feeling suitably rejuvenated,' she said, giving me the faintest of winks.

'Is that thing legal?' asked Denzil, glancing nervously at the sleek black killing machine.

Lady Ashbury stroked the snake's head and smiled like a loving mother. 'You don't have to worry about my beautiful Nahash. I can assure you that you are quite safe.' Despite Lord Ashbury's earlier claims of civility, Denzil still looked a long way from convinced.

'Doctor Selwood told us you've seen people with eyes like mine?' I asked.

'I have indeed,' replied Lady Ashbury, 'You are an extremely rare breed, Jack Gibson.' She paused. 'Rarer than you can imagine.'

'What causes it?'

'It?' she asked. 'You are a silly thing. It's just the pigmentation of your eyes.'

'Well, it never used to be.'

'Of course not. But now you have awakened.'

I wanted to say, 'What do you mean, awakened?' but Denzil got in there first.

'So he won't drop down dead any time soon?'

'Oh, you are adorable. You have my word that Nahash won't hurt you and Jack won't drop down dead any time soon. In fact, quite the opposite.'

I was prevented from questioning her further as Lady Ashbury started introducing us to a stream of people. It turned out the guests came from all corners of the globe. Several faces I recognised from the television. Despite the diversity, there were three things all of them had in common: money, power and an unsettling interest in us. After about fifteen minutes, Lady Ashbury made her excuses and left me speaking to a foreign general in full military regalia. I concluded from the chest full of medals that he must be a great war hero. He seemed like a nice enough chap though, and was keen to tell me about his seventy-four Bentleys. He was halfway through an interesting story about how he'd won the last three national elections with one hundred percent of the votes, when Denzil dragged me away. My friend was on a mission to find the waiter he'd seen walking around with a silver tray covered in lines of coke.

'Well, this is certainly an impressive bunch,' I said, as we cut through the crowds of the great and the good.

'Impressive?' said Denzil. 'These posh twits?'

'What do you mean?'

'Look around you, Gibby. This room is the result of generations of inbreeding.'

'Hardly,' I replied.

'Just like the Habsburgs and their big old flappy jaws. I bet half this lot have an extra toe nestling in their handmade shoes, or a couple of teeth growing out of their elbows.'

'Thanks for that, Charles Darwin. I feel truly enlightened.'

'You know what I mean.'

'I know people can't help the way they're born.'

'All I'm saying, Gibby, is don't let the glitter and the glamour fool you.'

'What are you going on about?'

'Think about it,' he said. 'No one really makes hundreds of millions of pounds through honest to goodness hard work, do they? It's done by exploiting other people.'

'Is it?'

'Of course it is. Then they throw some of the money they didn't really make at a public project like a concert hall or a museum, while all of their rich friends stand around telling them how wonderful they are. Meanwhile, it does bugger all to help the poor homeless people shuffling past the building every day, begging for money.'

'But those projects do a lot of good in the community.'

'Poor people can't eat Mozart,' said Denzil. 'Besides, with all the tax breaks they get, we unknowingly end up paying for part of their wet dreams out of our own pockets.'

I wasn't sure if it was true or not, but decided it was worth looking into when all of this mess was over.

We wandered about until we found the waiter and I reluctantly did another line, but I still couldn't shake off the ghost of Lucy. We grabbed some fancy pants cocktails and went to check out the lounge. It was large and dimly lit, containing a range of chairs and sofas positioned in clusters around low tables. We snaked through the groups of guests until we found an empty table of our own. For the next hour we sat alone, chatting and ordering cocktails and chemicals from the waiting staff. During this time Denzil seemed in no rush to use his newly acquired personal stash.

I was beginning to feel marginally bulletproof when Lord Ashbury approached us, flanked by two size zero women, who in the darkened venue resembled supermodels. It took me a couple of seconds to realise that one of them actually was. I'd seen her in TV advertisements and magazines.

'Hello gentlemen.' Lord Ashbury flashed a smile that wouldn't look out of place in a toothpaste commercial. 'Are you enjoying our modest soiree?' The guy was smoother than a wet sea lion covered in cream.

'Best party ever.' Denzil looked totally wired. His pupils were like dinner plates.

'These two gorgeous creatures are Eva and Marta,' continued Lord Ashbury.

I thought about how Lucy would respond to someone referring to her as a creature. God, I missed her.

'They're dying to meet our two mystery guests.'

Marta the real-life supermodel gave me the cutest of smiles. It was a good job I was so trashed, otherwise I would have frozen like a rabbit in a large set of headlights.

'Ladies,' said Lord Ashbury, placing a hand on each of their backs, 'this is the famous Jack and Denzil.'

'Ladies,' said Denzil with a big cheesy grin.

'I'd like to stay and chat,' said Lord Ashbury, 'But duty calls. Sadly, there really is no rest for the wicked.' He released another blinding smile into the world and walked away.

'Sit down, ladies, sit down.' Denzil patted the space on the sofa next to him. I took that as my cue to move my backside over to the opposite one.

As I stood up, I looked over at the table to my left and saw a young woman dressed in casual clothes, snuggled up with a young guy whose face eclipsed even that of Lord Ashbury. He must have had about four shirt buttons undone and his perfectly chiselled pecs were bursting out of the top. They looked like an odd match, purely because he was so incredibly handsome. But then my attention was drawn to Marta the model, as she sat down next to me in her extremely short dress. Eva placed herself next to Denzil. It transpired that they were both models from Russia, and they were intelligent, charming, captivating, sexy as hell and all over us. I was immediately suspicious. As we laughed and joked, Marta edged progressively closer until she lifted my arm up and placed it around her shoulder. I was pretty trashed by this point and decided I'd stop questioning why the great and the good, or according to Denzil the greedy and the gross, would be excited to have two random gatecrashers at their party, and why a pair of supermodels would fancy Denzil and me. As such, when Marta stuck her tongue down my throat I just went with it. I mean come on, who wouldn't?

I was starting to feel happier again when Eva reached into her clutch and pulled out a small silver box with a snake on it. Inside were a number of blood-red pills.

'Do you fancy having a little fun, baby?' she said to Denzil in her sexy accent.

'Hell, yes.' Denzil's smile stretched from ear to ear.

Eva placed one of the tablets on her tongue, leant forwards and kissed him. She pulled away slowly and handed Denzil his drink. He smiled, took a swig and swallowed the drug.

Marta took identical-looking tablets from her bag and started stroking and kissing my neck. 'Go on, baby, have some fun,' she whispered.

'What is it?' I asked.

'Something to help you relax,' she said. 'Swallow it and we can go upstairs. You'd like that, wouldn't you?'

Now don't get me wrong, on a normal day I would have liked that. In fact, in one way I wanted to go upstairs with her more than anything. But I was still traumatised from losing Lucy and there was a tiny voice somewhere in the deep recesses of my mind telling me something wasn't quite right.

'What's in it?' I asked.

'Would you excuse us for just a moment please, ladies' said Denzil, as he stood up. 'I need to have a quick chat with my friend here.' He put his hand on my back and guided me a few metres away from the table. 'Alright, what's the problem?'

I sighed. 'It doesn't feel right.'

'What doesn't feel right?'

'This. The party, the people. And I don't think now's the best time to be getting completely out of it.'

Denzil laughed. 'Well, I'm already completely out of it.'

'I'm not even sure we should be doing drugs anymore.'

'Are you insane?'

'Well, your Colombian adventure at the Naysmere was hardly a success.'

'You need to stop stressing.'

'I need to call my parents.'

'We can do that later. Just relax, mate.'

I looked around the room. 'You've got to admit this set-up is a bit on the weird spectrum.'

'Don't be a div. It's amazing.'

'Hold on, weren't you the one slating all these people a few minutes ago?'

'I said they were immoral,' he replied, 'not that they couldn't throw a good party.'

'Then you don't find it odd that these rich, successful people are so interested in us?'

'So, your issue is that everyone's being too nice?'

'You know that's not what I mean.'

'Look,' he said, 'just chill out, relax, enjoy yourself. We've been through some truly horrific things over the last couple of days. We nearly died, for God's sake. We deserve some fun.' Denzil flashed a cheeky grin. 'How about I ask the DJ to play 'Bright Eyes' for you? We can have a singalong.'

'Don't be a cock.'

'Oh come on mate, I'm only joking.'

'It doesn't feel right,' I persisted.

Denzil sighed. 'You can't bring her back, mate.'

'Woah!' I replied. 'That's out of order.'

'I'm sorry.' Denzil placed his hands on my shoulders. 'You're right. That was out of line. All I'm saying is that the last day and a half has been an absolute goddamn horror show and we deserve to be happy for a while. Plus, these women are the hottest things I've ever seen.'

I knew I wouldn't be able to persuade Denzil to see it from my point of view when he was this far gone. So, for the time being I decided to let things run.

We returned to our seats and I held out my hand. Marta giggled and handed me a red pill. I lifted my cocktail, opened my mouth, placed the tablet onto my tongue and put the glass to my lips. Taking a large swig, I subtly deposited the pill into the cocktail. I put the drink now containing the pill back down on the table and made a big deal of pretending to swallow it. Denzil clapped while Marta smiled and stroked the back of my neck.

We continued chatting, but it wasn't long before Denzil started to look worryingly spaced out. What the hell were in the pills they'd given us? I felt obliged to try and look just as ruined as my friend, so as not to give the game away. I listened as the women spoke in Russian for a while. I had no clue what they were saying, but it sounded serious. Eventually, they took us by the hands and led us through the party. I kept my eyes half closed and tried not to walk too efficiently. I could have sworn that everyone was staring at us as we passed.

We headed back towards our rooms, and eventually parted company with Eva and Denzil. My friend looked to be in bad shape and I decided that I would need to check up on him later. When we reached my room, Marta pulled a key card from her small clutch bag and opened the door. Seeing her do this made me feel distinctly uneasy, and I decided to put a chair against it during the night to stop any unwelcome visitors.

Marta wasted no time in guiding me across the room and shoving me backwards onto the bed. As I watched her out of my barely open eyes, I decided she was probably the most beautiful thing I'd ever seen. I pushed aside the nagging thought that I'd much rather be with Lucy. But despite the vision of female perfection standing before me, I realised I wasn't emotionally ready to have sex with anyone right now. I wasn't even sure I'd be able to perform.

The model stood there in the dimly lit room and watched me in silence. I decided I should follow the approach of every self-respecting opossum and play dead. Or in this case, play wasted. She wore a strange expression that I couldn't read, but it appeared to contain little emotion.

'Jack?' she said coldly and I made a tactical decision not to respond. 'Are you awake, baby?'

I lay there, engaged in some sort of motionless Mexican stand-off until Marta, satisfied that I was no longer participating in the conscious world, turned and left the room.

As soon as I heard the door click shut I opened my eyes, jumped up and started freaking out. I knew from my balls to my bones that something was seriously wrong. Who were these people? What were they up to? Why were they so interested in us? And why the hell did they have a giant snake and a Panda that understood English?

We needed to leave Ashbury Hall as soon as physically possible. Unfortunately, there wasn't really anywhere to go. Assuming we could get out of the house, navigate the estate and overcome the armed security, the countryside was swarming with killer monsters. On top of that, Denzil was in no fit state to do anything. I'd have to figure this one out for myself.

I concluded my first port of call would be to check on Denzil. I let myself out of my room and crept along the deserted corridor, the whole while feeling massively conspicuous. When I reached his door, I pressed my ear to it and listened, but heard nothing. I waited a few seconds before being brave enough to try the handle. There was a loud click and it opened; the sound almost made me jump out of my skin. I took a deep breath and stepped inside.

The room was empty. I could tell from the imprint on the bedsheets that Denzil had either gotten lucky, or more likely passed out. As I moved closer towards the huge four-poster bed, I trod on his clothes. This concerned me deeply because they looked like they'd been cut off him. Where the hell could he have gone without those? Ignoring the powder, I took the phone and wallet from his jeans pockets and placed them in mine. I had an image of Eva chasing a butt-naked Denzil along a corridor. However, he'd consumed enough drugs and alcohol to floor a horse tonight and so it didn't seem likely he would be that mobile. I didn't have long to ponder his fate however, as angry voices drifted in from the corridor.

'He's not here, ma'am,' said a man who sounded suspiciously like Fishman.

'Well, where is he?' came the harsh response from Lady Ashbury. 'Check his friend's room.'

My heart sank. They were talking about searching Denzil's room and here I was, standing in the middle of it like a lemon. I looked around for somewhere to hide but couldn't see anywhere suitable. I checked the bed, but there was no way I could fit underneath, and it was far too late to try and climb out of the window. I was trapped. I spun on the spot, making an assortment of panicky noises.

Then I saw it. The top of the antique wardrobe. I remembered playing hide and seek as a child at an old estate cottage my family was holidaying at. My dad said we should hide under a table outside the summer house. It was in plain sight, but it was dark and because Dad, Thomas and I stayed perfectly still, my uncle and cousins walked right on by. Good shout, Harold!

It was a long shot, but I had no other choice. I climbed onto the desk next to the wardrobe and hauled myself up onto the large piece of wooden furniture. The door flew open and a man in a long black habit entered the room. It was Fishman. I lay perfectly still, too afraid even to breath. Lady Ashbury breezed in, dressed in a dark robe, and waited while her manservant searched the suite. My heart almost leapt out of my chest when he threw open the wardrobe doors below me.

'He's not here, ma'am,' he said.

'Well, find him!' Lady Ashbury sounded furious. 'And bring him directly to me. The ceremony begins soon and we need a third sacrifice.'

My heart sank through the floor, well, I mean it sank through the wardrobe.

'You don't wish me to take him to the caves, ma'am?' said Fishman.

'Are you questioning me?' asked Lady Ashbury in a tone suggesting that he shouldn't.

'Of course not, ma'am.' Fishman sounded both intimidated and confused.

'And if you don't find him and bring him to me immediately, you will be taking his place!' With that, they were gone.

And so I found myself alone, hunted, in mortal danger, heavily under the influence, and lost somewhere in a giant palace with my best friend about to be sacrificed. This was definitely not the best party ever.

CHAPTER 11

I lay on top of the wardrobe and listened to the silence. Paul and Art were right: it definitely has a sound.

The level of interest these people had displayed in us now became distressingly clear. Powerful, sinister individuals sporting black robes wanted to use us for human sacrifice. I was in a real-life horror film. I mean, why couldn't the super-rich have normal hobbies like everyone else? Surely a photography class or sushi-making course wouldn't be so bad? After all, everyone could use the rule of thirds in their life. Except me, of course. What I needed right now was to find the caves and rescue my friend.

I didn't know where the caves were, so fixing that would be my first task. But even if I did find Denzil, what then? The satanic cult—for that was surely what it was—must have more than three hundred members along with armed security. What could I do in any practical sense to help him? It was hopeless.

I'm ashamed to say that the thought of using the ceremony as a diversion to make a run for it did cross my mind. But that was just the fear talking. I knew from my toes to my nose that if I was in trouble, Denzil would move heaven and earth to save me.

Lucy once asked me on a night out in the local pub why I was friends with him. She said he was holding me back and I should find a more mature social circle, whatever that meant. I knew he acted like a complete cretin, but what people didn't see was that it was a defence mechanism. He really had been through a lot. But that guy was there for me when Thomas died, like no one else was. I could honestly say I loved him like a brother. Admittedly, an annoying and at times extremely embarrassing brother, but a brother nonetheless. So, there would be no leaving Denzil Reid to die on my watch.

I climbed down from the wardrobe, opened the bedroom door and peered into the corridor. The coast was clear. What was a little hazier was the number of people that were looking for me, but I had no other option but to get up and get moving. Time wasn't on my side. I took a deep breath, told myself to grow a pair and stepped out into the open. My heart was pumping like a gigolo at a twenty-four-hour orgy as I jogged through the palace. I prayed no-one would see me as I tried to remember the route back to the ground floor. But it was difficult in such a vast labyrinth of identically decorated corridors.

I was leaning over a banister and contemplating a descent when a large, aging man dressed in a black robe and clutching a snake mask spotted me. I froze like a deer in a freezer.

'Are you lost, old bean?' he asked.

I stared at him.

'Don't worry,' he said, 'I'm running late myself.'

I looked him up and down and a cunning plan formed in my head. Well, maybe not that cunning: it was the oldest trick in the book. I needed a disguise, and this bozo's cloak and mask would do nicely.

I flew into character. 'This place is simply vast,' I said in the plummiest tone I could muster. 'How's a new fellow supposed to find his way around?'

The man gave me a warm smile. 'So, you're an acolyte, are you?'

I nodded.

'Welcome to the family,' he said with a manly handshake. 'I wondered why you didn't have a robe.'

'I don't suppose you'd point me in the right direction?'

'Why of course, my dear boy. Follow me.'

We ignored the stairs and continued along the corridor as the gentleman made small talk. It was mainly some nostalgic claptrap about when he'd had his initiation and complaining he'd missed the party. I wasn't paying much attention to be honest, as my mind was focused firstly on my newly formed plan and then on a table several metres away. Actually, it was on the china vase sitting on top of it. I decided I could use it to strike him on the back of the head and render him unconscious. You see it in all the movies. The trick as I'd observed it was not to hit him too hard.

As we drew alongside the table, I grabbed the china vase and swung it at the back of his head. There was a thud as it made contact with his skull and the man dropped to the floor. Unfortunately, he seemed to have missed the memo, because instead of falling unconscious as per the plan, the idiot started shouting for help.

I had to do something before his cries brought hordes of cult members bearing down on me, so I hit him again. It wasn't the most cerebral of plans, if you'll excuse the pun, but it's all I could think of. Still, he kept shouting, so I was forced to do it again, and again, and again. But the guy just wouldn't shut up. A number of blows bounced harmlessly off his outstretched arms, but I dug in deep and persisted while telling him to shut the hell up. Sadly, he wouldn't listen, but I guess in his defence he was being bludgeoned by a stranger at the time.

I flashed back to watching Lucy driving away with Charles and an anger started to build inside of my chest. Why did she have to die? Why was life so unfair? The anger turned to rage and like a Sith Lord I channelled it into the assault. After a few seconds of my frenzied attack, his cries for help transformed into pleas for mercy. I didn't stop though, I couldn't. I was a man possessed. I kept on hitting and hitting him until he fell silent. I stood there panting and clasping the blood-soaked vase. Then the reality dawned on me. What had I done? I dropped the receptacle and reached down to check his neck for a pulse. Nothing. I tried his wrist, but there was no sign of life there either. That's when I knew that like 'Bohemian Rhapsody', I'd just killed a man.

I dropped to the floor, feeling sick to my stomach. That hadn't been the plan. He was only supposed to pass out like in the movies. I know some people say kill or be killed, them or me, they would have done the same to you, and all of those things; but whether he was part of this diabolical group that wanted to sacrifice me or not, it didn't make me feel any better inside. I knew that I'd crossed a fundamental line and there was no going back. Ever.

I couldn't find a door that was open, so after wrestling the robe from his lifeless body, all I could do was leave him there on full display for any passers-by to stumble across. It was a terrible plan because he could have been discovered at any moment. But there was no other choice and I had to press on.

I felt a bit better after putting on his robe and mask. No one would ever guess who I was with my face and clothes hidden. Well, as long as they didn't look at my trainers. The guy had child-sized feet, so there was no way I'd be squeezing my canoes into his fancy shoes any time soon.

I spent several minutes searching for an exit while my fear for Denzil grew. But my search proved fruitless. I was completely lost and time was running out. How could I help my friend if I couldn't even make it to the caves? It took another couple of minutes to realise it was legitimately hopeless. After cursing extensively I sat down against a wall and rested my masked head on my knees. I was fighting back tears when a series of loud cracking sounds burst through my panic and a shiver ran down my spine.

Looking up I saw the ceiling lights in the corridor exploding one at a time, plunging me into darkness. Frantic, whispering voices danced all around me. Somehow to my left I could make out a small pale boy. I froze.

Thomas.

We watched each other for a few seconds before he raised one of his little white hands and beckoned me towards him. As I got to my feet, he turned and disappeared into the darkness.

I jumped up and gave chase. Most of the bulbs were out in the corridors, so I only caught glimpses of him when he passed momentarily through random patches of light. The whispering whipped and flickered around me the whole time that I ran, but I couldn't make it out.

At last I began gaining on him, which was surprisingly difficult considering he was still a scrawny little kid and I was a fully grown adult. I called out his name, shouted for him to wait. But he kept on running. Just when I thought I was about to catch him, I charged around a corner and found myself standing in the brightly lit entrance hall at the rear of the house. A group of people wearing snake masks and black robes turned to look at me. I span around on the spot, shielding my eyes from the sudden excess of light. As my eyes adjusted, I realised my brother had vanished.

Significantly shaken, I decided to follow my fellow cloak wearers at a distance, hoping they'd lead me to the caves. We exited the building via a huge rear door. Fortunately, no one was paying any attention to another faceless, silent guest, which was fortunate considering my overly dramatic appearance. I knew my plan was working when we left the ornamental gardens at the back of the property and began to follow a gravel path, lined with flaming torches. They had the effect of making the event seem both clichéd and scary as hell. I thought about my strange vision of Thomas. Maybe I'd done more drugs than I thought. It wasn't long before I saw the entrance to the caves, which created a millisecond of elation followed by a terrible sinking feeling.

What was I walking into? Whoever the Brothers of the Snake were, they clearly hadn't been resigned to history like Lord Ashbury had implied. These dickheads were very much alive and kicking, and I was about to face them. I was so scared I could feel my teeth chattering as I reached the entrance. I wanted to run away so badly. But Denzil was down there somewhere and he needed me. I'd already lost Lucy. I wasn't going to stand by and lose Denzil as well.

I tried to control my breathing as I passed through the gate and descended the steep stone steps. They seemed to go on forever. I thought back to my childhood, when I'd climbed the stone steps of Durham Cathedral with Thomas. I remembered thinking we must be ascending to the clouds. We stood on top of that tower under the endless summer sky, laughing and staring out over the city. Hidden inside the innocence of our childhoods, we thought everything would last forever. The knock on the door came less than a year later. It was a rainy Saturday afternoon and I was watching TV. It's strange, but I already knew something was wrong. The police officers said they were sorry. It still hurts to think of him being left alone to die in a ditch after that coward hit him. Was he frightened? Did he call for me?

My heart longed to travel back to that day on top of the cathedral. To hear his laugh, to feel the wind on my face and to be immortal again, unmarked by the cold, hard realities of life. But you can't go back, can you? All you can do is fight to hold on to those fading memories with every ounce of strength that you have, and move forwards one small step at a time.

As I made my slow descent, strange sounds echoed up from the depths. I couldn't make out what they were, but they sure as Shirley didn't sound like anything good. My traitorous brain conjured a plethora of satanic nightmares. Every horror movie I'd watched, every hellish painting I'd looked at, every demonic thing I'd read or heard exploded into my mind's eye. I felt an overwhelming desire to kick the late Hieronymus Bosch square in the nuts, or maybe shove his paint brush up his arse, I couldn't quite decide. I once heard someone say that everyone finds God on their deathbed. While I wasn't quite on mine now, I'd definitely changed into my nightwear, so I started asking him for help. I've actually never been all that religious, but as I was about to walk into a nest of devil worshippers, I decided it might be prudent to get the big fella onside. So, I started to pray, by which I mean I began jabbering things to myself like, 'I'm sorry I'm a massive douche, God, please don't let me die.'

By the time I'd reached the bottom step I realised the sounds I could hear were people chanting. It was horrifically eerie. I arrived in a wide corridor with red torchlight flickering on the walls, giving the distinct impression that I'd descended into the depths of hell itself. The tunnel twisted and turned, so I couldn't see any further than the next few metres. My year eight geography teacher, Mr. Jenkins, who had the dodgiest moustache you'd ever seen, a penchant for cheese and onion sandwiches and standing too close, told us that distances are hard to judge underground. But if I had to guess, I'd say I probably followed the passage for forty or fifty metres before the entrance to a chamber opened up before me.

I entered the vast space to see neat rows of people swaying and chanting. I took up position on the back row and began moving from side to side in an attempt to fit in with the rest of the crowd. I felt like the new guy at a fitness class, turning up late, hiding in the back and trying not to screw up the steps. Everyone was lined up with such precision that it reminded me of another bunch of sickos that was good at standing in neat rows, often in places like Nuremburg. You would probably know them as the Nazis. They were into all sorts of dark, occult stuff. Okay, this was satanic, but it seemed similar. I'm also pretty sure that Hitler used to hump his dogs. I think I read that somewhere, or maybe Denzil told me, I'm not sure. But in television documentaries his dogs are always walking like they've been interfered with. I swear to God, if you can find a documentary film containing footage of Adolf Hitler hanging out with one of his canines, watch it and tell me that German Shephard hasn't faced its own Battle of the Bulge.

The cave ceiling was so high that it was lost in darkness. I guessed it would have taken years to carve out this much space. Thinking back to Denzil's comments at the party, I wondered which poor souls had to do it. At the far end of the chamber the floor was raised like a stage, although whether it had been cut from the rock or someone had assembled a makeshift platform I couldn't say, as it was obscured by the mass of freaks in black cloaks. On top of the stage was a huge statue. The body was that of a person, but the evil-looking head was all snake. Around its neck hung a pentagram and it was illuminated by the sickly orange glow of a giant firepit.

Before this visual monstrosity stood three wooden crosses, each fitted with restraints. The two end ones were empty, but the middle one had a naked woman strapped to it, whom I guessed was a couple of years younger than myself. Her dark hair came down to her shoulders, partially tied back by the ball gag in her mouth. What disturbed me most was how calm she looked. Then it hit me. It was the young woman I'd seen at the party with the super-hot guy with the pecs. I thought about the little red pills Eva and Marta had given us and it became painfully obvious that we weren't the only targets of the evening.

A tall figure appeared from a doorway to the left of the stage sporting an elaborate snake's head mask. If he was trying to look scary, then he'd done an amazing job. The swaying and chanting stepped up a notch at the person's arrival. Then my heart almost punched its way out of my chest as Denzil was dragged into the chamber and tied butt-naked to a cross. Well, he still had his socks and trainers on, but if anything, that was even more humiliating. I looked around the cave at all of the nut jobs swaying and chanting like demented clones. How in the name of Entebbe could I rescue him from this lot?

Now I'm not normally a glass half empty kind of guy, but after making a quick assessment of the situation, my professional opinion was that I was screwed. On the pros list I had the element of surprise: something most attacking commanders would give their mum's right arm for. The cons list, however, was a little busier. Firstly, I was standing at the back of the room with a wall of around three hundred psychopaths to get through. Assuming I overcame that obstacle and reached the stage, I'd still need to untie Denzil without anyone overpowering me. If by some miracle I managed that, then I wouldn't be able to go back the way I came. I needed the door at the side of the stage to be an exit route and not just a dead end. If that wasn't a big enough pile of poo to climb, the guy was completely out of it! That meant I'd have to carry him. How could I outrun a bunch of raving nut jobs with that big lump on my back?

Assuming I made it to the stage, untied him, escaped through the side door and gave everyone the slip while running at two miles an hour, there was the not insignificant issue of armed security to contend with. Oh yes, and at some point during that whole palaver I'd need to find him some clothes, to stave off pneumonia once we were back wandering the monster-infested Cotswolds. I laughed bitterly to myself. I had two hopes of saving Denzil: Bob Hope and no hope. And Bob Hope's dead.

The sinister figure on stage raised his arms and the room fell deathly silent. As soon as he opened his mouth I knew it was that posh plonker, Lord Ashbury.

'Mighty Serpent of Truth,' he cried, and commenced chanting.

The sick congregation joined in with his chanting and I decided I should try to follow suit to avoid looking suspicious. As I didn't know the words, I did what I do at weddings and christenings when they expect you to sing along in church. I mumbled.

'Mistress of Eternity! Noble Ahriman of Persia! Python Of Greece!'

Talk about overly dramatic; it was like a twisted pantomime.

'Wise Serpent of the Hidden Sanctum! Our Goddess Hyrattanti! You Who Challenged the Great Deceiver!'

No one bothered saying the last line. Unaware of this plan, I made a weird mumbling sound. It was like being in a bar and the music cutting out just as you're shouting 'Wank' or something equally as embarrassing.

The people next to me turned to stare.

'Sorry,' I muttered in my plummy voice while patting my chest. 'I've got a bit of wind.'

One person shook their head and another tutted, but it seemed to satisfy them. Thankfully Lord Ashbury started with his insane ranting again.

'You, who gave the gift of knowledge to mankind! We, your humble servants, come together in this place to give praise to your glory through the sacrifice of the chosen.'

Crap. My time was running out. Denzil was about to be sacrificed and I needed to do something. I just didn't know what. I stood there watching and panicking as Lord Ashbury ran his hands all over the woman's body and face. He couldn't have looked more like a creepy sex pest if he'd tried. The poor woman was so out of it that she actually smiled when he touched her. It didn't last long, though. Another cloaked figure walked onto the stage holding a red velvet cushion. Lord Ashbury took hold of a ceremonial knife that had been lying on top of the object and held it above his head.

'Through blood comes tribute! Through tribute comes knowledge! Through knowledge comes power! The blood is power!'

The room filled with the sound of chanting, the words becoming increasingly passionate with each uttering. Lord Ashbury sliced a pentagram into the woman's marble flesh. Well, he tried to. Art clearly wasn't his strong suit. Periodically, he stood back as his assistant tipped water down her front, removing the excess blood. I wanted to stop them so badly, but what could I do? People were dying and I was just standing around like a gormless coward. I had to do something. I had to. But what?

That's when I decided to rush the stage, although I confess that I had some issues trying to get my feet onboard with that little plan. *Move*, I screamed silently at myself. *Go!* But my useless feet remained rooted to the spot. I tried counting down from three to one, but every time I reached zero, nothing happened. Waves of self-loathing washed over me as I watched Lord Ashbury put a hand around her throat and squeeze. The woman kicked and struggled as the chanting reached a crescendo. Then he cut her throat. I swallowed a gasp. You really had to wonder about some people's upbringings.

Two women and a man walked onto the stage wearing the same black robes, except their heads and faces were on display for all to see. It was irritating to realise I'd voted for one of them in the last election.

I'm going to spare you the details of what happened next during the ceremony. I prefer not to think about it. But let's just say it was the most barbaric and grotesque thing I'd ever seen. And it caused a fierce anger to surge inside of my chest, overtaking the fear.

I couldn't comprehend the arrogance of these people. Just because they had more zeros printed on a piece of paper than most didn't mean they had the right to take lives. And like all bullies, they were preying on the weakest and most vulnerable people they could find. I hoped with all my heart that she had some really nasty disease and they got sick and died from it.

After expertly demonstrating how to be subhuman scum, they stood up, were presented with masks of their own and slithered away into the crowd.

My heart pounded and my brain raced. People were committing acts of murder and cannibalism. In the Cotswolds! It was beyond wrong. How could anyone be so evil? I didn't have a great deal of time to ponder that one as Lord Ashbury was already walking over to Denzil. That toffee-nosed arsehole was about to torture and murder my best friend.

I shivered as Lord Ashbury placed the blade onto my friend's chest and prepared to cut. Fear surged inside of me like a collapsing ice cap and I felt a strange connection to the weapon. Then, not only to my surprise, but to the surprise of every Tom, Dick and Harriet in the cave, the object melted away. A confused Lord Ashbury stared at his now empty hands, then he spun around, searching the floor. There were gasps from the crowd and my head began to throb. I felt what later turned out to be blood trickling from my nose. Quickly recovering from the incident, Lord Ashbury put his hands around Denzil's throat and began to squeeze.

I finally sprang into action. I remember saying, 'Oh no you don't, you posh dick' before pushing forwards through the crowd. Getting to the front was surprisingly easy in the end. All I had to do was apologise repeatedly in an upper-class accent, say 'Excuse me' a couple of times and state clearly for the record that I was about to be sick. It turns out that even Devil worshippers don't like to get splattered with stomach stew.

I could hardly believe it as I leapt onto the stage. Nor could the audience, it seemed, because I'd almost untied him when a huge fist connected with my head. This was followed with more blows and numerous hands clawing at me. It was brutal.

I wasn't going down without a fight, though, no sir. Still fuelled by intense rage I struggled and fought like a cornered leopard, but there were too many adversaries and my clothes were pulled from my body while I was punched, kicked and beaten. I felt like a child trying to fight an army of adults. I was howling like a crazy person as they strapped me to a cross and rammed a ball gag into my mouth. At first I shouted and tried to resist, but the force was so great that I was worried my front teeth were going to get knocked out, so I had no other option but to open my mouth and allow the gag to be rammed in. It felt like the sides of my lips were going to tear apart as they tightened the contraption, and it made me think back to the female police office at the Naysmere Hotel.

Lord Ashbury was handed a fresh blade as he leant towards me and whispered in my ear, 'It's the highest of honours to be sacrificed in her name.'

God, I hated him.

'Surrender your worthless soul.'

Now, if I'd been able to speak there would have been a few responses I could have given to that. However, 'Yeah, that sounds like a really great plan mate,' was not one of them. To say I was scared at this point would be an understatement. I was freaking out like I'd never freaked out before.

'You should have taken the pill,' Lord Ashbury murmured before picking up the knife. 'Through blood comes tribute! Through tribute comes knowledge! Through knowledge comes power! The blood is power!'

I watched, eyes bulging out of my head as the knife tip was placed against my chest. Then he started to cut.

As I was sliced like a cheap supermarket birthday cake, I screamed and fought with every ounce of strength I had in a pathetic attempt to break free of my unbreakable bonds. Sadly, for me, but not the manufacturer's reputation, they did exactly what they'd been designed to do. My head throbbed and pulsated as another icy shiver slipped down my spine, but sadly this time the blade remained uncomfortably solid. I was immersed in a universe of pain, unable to focus on anything but its horror. Blinding colours filled my vision and I stepped into a tunnel of light.

I raced through a swirling and twisting tube, travelling faster and faster. Space and time no longer held meaning for me. I was moving through it, outside of it, beyond it. Colours shifted and changed and I could hear a musical humming growing ever louder. My momentum increased exponentially, yet I didn't seem to move at all. Some greater understanding appeared to hang just outside my mind's reach.

A series of loud cracks began to tear the universe apart. I could hear voices crying out in terror and pain. The light from the tunnel grew brighter in unison with the screams until my senses were overloaded. Then, just like the universe that surrounded me, I was torn apart.

CHAPTER 12

I opened my eyes to a scene of utter carnage. Satanists in black cloaks were running and screaming and dying. As the last of the panicked crowd fell to the chamber floor, I could see figures with machine guns moving amongst them. A handsome, well-built man with thick black hair lowered his weapon and undid the straps holding my legs.

'It looks like we arrived in the nick of time, Jack,' he said in a friendly voice. 'That's quite an art project on your chest.' He freed my hands, lowered me to the ground and removed the gag. In all the surrounding chaos, it didn't even register that he knew my name. Another guy was doing the same for Denzil, whom I was part happy, part jealous to see hadn't received a chest tattoo like mine.

'Hager,' called my rescuer, 'see what's through that door.'

'Sir,' replied a second man with scruffy blond hair who was built like a tank.

My chest was absolute agony and tears were running down my face. The black-haired man, whom I guessed was in his mid-thirties, removed a small rucksack from his back and pulled out what looked like a black pen. As soon as he jabbed it into my neck, the pain, the fear and even some of the trauma of my recent violent assault instantly vanished from my body. I could hardly believe it.

Like a fallen Adam, I became shamefully aware of my nakedness. I gathered up my discarded clothes from where they'd been tossed and swiftly got dressed. The neck of my expensive T-shirt had been stretched during my disrobing and the new fit of the garment irritated me. First world problems, I know. Denzil was on his feet now, looking fully compos mentis and asking why he was in the nude. The huge blond soldier with the strange name reappeared from the side entrance. 'There's a tunnel we can use to get out,' he said.

Denzil looked lost. 'Is there a phone or a wallet back there?'

'No,' replied the man.

Denzil swore profusely until I produced them from my pocket. I opted to back away when he tried to hug me, though.

Another soldier with olive skin and a scar down his right cheek had stripped one of the male corpses and threw the clothes at Denzil's feet. 'Put them on,' he ordered.

Denzil swore some more.

'Who are you?' I asked the first gentleman.

'You can call me Antony.'

'Are you the police?' asked Denzil.

The man called Antony gave him a friendly smile and turned away.

We crossed a chamber that was now filled with the eerie moaning of injured and dying cultists. Denzil had to shout over them when stating that he drew the line at wearing the dead man's undies. I made a point of treading on as many wounded satanists' heads, knees and crotches as possible on the way out. It was an immature and morally dubious gesture, but it made me feel better. Hey, they tried to sodding kill us. We followed the eerie tunnel until we reached the stone steps and made our ascension back to the surface. Denzil was cheered along the way by the diamond-encrusted Zippo lighter that he found in the deceased worshipper's trouser pocket. It softened the blow of him currently being dressed like a seventy-year-old fashion-phobe.

'I'm done with drugs,' I announced to Denzil. 'Don't offer them to me again.'

'Me too.'

I raised an eyebrow. 'You think you can stop?'

'Of course I can.'

'How much are you getting through these days? Two grams a week?'

'If it means not waking up strapped to a cross with my dick out, then yes, I can most definitely stop. And have you seen these bloody trousers? Even my Grandad Ainsley wouldn't wear them.'

'They do present a pretty unique look.'

'Where the hell did that soldier find them? In lost bloody property?'

The sense of relief when we left the creepy old caves was immense. After believing with cast-iron certainty that they were going to become the final resting place of Jack Gibson, I was hit by a wave of euphoria. It didn't last long, however, because I knew we were still a long way from being home and dry.

'Stay close,' warned Antony. 'We may face some resistance.'

'I need to find my dog,' I said.

'It will have to stay behind.'

My heart sank. I couldn't leave Ziggy with these dickheads. If they could torture and sacrifice humans, imagine what they would do to an animal? Leaving the furball here was signing his death warrant, but what could I do? There were people with guns on the estate that wanted to kill us, and these soldiers were our only chance of escape. As we walked through the fresh night air I scrambled to think of a canine rescue plan. Unfortunately, the place was a vast maze and I had no idea where to start.

Several loud bangs resounded and I heard something whizz past my ear.

'Move!' shouted one of our rescuers, as they began returning fire.

Not wishing to hang about and get shot, we sprinted across the manicured green lawn towards the side of the house. About twenty metres from the building, three figures materialised from behind some bushes that had been clipped into the shapes of various animals. Barrel flashes lit up the darkness.

'Into the house,' shouted Antony amidst a hail of bullets, and we all made for the door at the rear of the building.

The soldiers paused as we entered, their rifles raised to face any new threats. But the room was empty.

'Keep moving,' said the point man, and we headed towards an internal door at a march. It was like being in a movie, except I wasn't usually about to fill my pants with poop parcels while watching TV. Well, apart from that one time in Bali. But I'd eaten something dodgy at a street market, so that didn't count. Our small group moved from room to room, and the soldiers dispatched anyone brave or stupid enough to get in our way. Despite the sounds of guns popping and cracking all around me, my ears were drawn towards a faint sound to the left. I listened for a couple of seconds before realising it was a dog barking. But not just any dog. It was my dog, Ziggy!

We passed through another door and into a hail of bullets, which immediately forced us back into the previous room.

'I'm hit,' said the soldier with the scar on his face. Weirdly, he sounded like he was making a casual comment about the weather, not that he'd just had a projectile rip into his body.

I had to conclude that these were some seriously tough people. They took up positions on each side of the door as they fought against the larger force of armed guards in the next room. The sound of the gun fight was deafening and I'm not ashamed to say that I had a little panic.

'I can hear Ziggy,' I told Denzil from my position on the floor, and I watched him straining to listen through the crackle of gunfire.

'Well, it definitely sounds like a dog,' he said, 'but how do you know it's Ziggy?'

'I know my own dog. And we can't just leave him here to die.'

'Er, yes we can.'

The gun fire was escalating and I realised that the wealthy elites had brought a lot of protection to the event. 'Jabari,' said Antony, 'see if you can find a way to circumvent the entrance hall.' The soldier to his left with the huge beard nodded, and was gone.

Ziggy continued to bark. It was obvious that no one wanted to rescue him, well, no one except me. And don't get me wrong, I got it, I really did, he was just a dog, but we'd been through so much in the past forty-eight hours that the thought of leaving him behind broke my heart. I knew if I said anything they'd try to stop me, so, without a word I leapt up and ran towards the barking with Denzil and my new comrades shouting at me to come back.

I sprinted down one of the long corridors that traversed the house towards the increasingly loud barking. Without my armed entourage I felt exposed and it made me wonder why I'd decided this was such an excellent idea. Speed became my friend and following the noise, I flew through a door that led into a massive industrial kitchen. Sitting in one corner was a cage containing Ziggy. My heart leapt as soon as I saw him. I guess his did too, as he started howling.

'Hello boy!' I called, while trying to ignore the fact he was currently in the same room they cooked meat.

I saw a flash of something to my left and pitched myself sideways. It was my old chum Fishman, wielding a vicious-looking kitchen knife and an expression of pure hatred. I backed away from him while Ziggy went totally crazy.

'Through the blood comes tribute,' he said.

Oh, for God's sake.

'Through blood comes tribute,' he repeated.

'You don't have to do this,' I said.

'Through tribute comes knowledge.'

I backed into a work surface. There was nowhere left to go.

'Through knowledge comes power,' Fishman cried, his face twisted with rage.

'It's over, Fishman,' I said. 'You don't need to do this.'

He clearly felt that he did. 'For Goddess Hyrattanti!' The manservant leapt towards me, slashing at my face with his knife.

I ducked to the right as the blade whooshed past my head. Then I raced along the edge of the work surface towards the corner of the room with Fishman hot on my heels. I grabbed a large silver tray and swung it around just in time to block his next strike. I aimed my second swing at his head and caught him on the temple with the tray, causing him to cry out in pain or possibly anger, it was hard to tell. I threw the object in his general direction and he was forced to raise his hands to block it.

Seeing my chance, I seized his wrists and we started to wrestle. I soon realised I was in trouble because Fishman was much stronger than me. It was a nasty surprise considering what a scrawny little rake of a man he was. I fought as hard as I could, but my arms quickly tired and I wasn't sure how long I could keep up this level of intensity.

Fishman clearly felt the tide turning as well because his expression became a sneer. 'Goddess Hyrattanti,' he said. 'I, your humble servant, give you this offering—'

'Fuck you!' I managed to spit out by way of response. Okay, so it was more like, 'F-Coo,' but at least I made the effort.

The blade hung a couple of inches in front of my face and Fishman stared into my eyes like he was trying to see into my very being. He twisted the knife and edged it up under my chin.

'Grant me your power!' he cried as the blade pressed into my neck.

My arms shook as the last of my strength began to slip away. I knew in that moment I'd reached the end. I had nothing left. I closed my eyes.

I knew I couldn't win. Panic surged through my veins like electricity as the large knife penetrated my skin. A desperate longing for my mum hit me like a thirty-mile-long train with no breaks. I'd heard of dying soldiers calling for their mothers on battlefields, but I never thought I'd be in that position. It's hard to put into words how I felt in that moment, but my spirit longed to be in the safest, most protected place I'd ever known. Still, some basic human instinct kept me in the fight. I felt cold as I focused everything I had on keeping the blade from entering my face.

The pressure lifted from my neck like a summer sunrise. Opening my eyes, I saw Denzil fighting to pull Fishman away from me. He'd come to my rescue! I could have kissed the guy. And this is exactly why I was friends with the big oaf. By which I mean because he came to my aid and not because I wanted to kiss him. A surge of euphoria hit me, which provided a much-needed second wind and I screamed as I forced the blade away from my chin.

'Keep hold of his hands,' cried Denzil.

'I'm trying,' I shouted as we pulled our adversary to the floor. We were like two unstoppable tag team wrestlers, without the muscles, the moves or the millions.

The manservant let out a muffled, 'No!' as the tide of our intimate battle turned. He toppled backwards and Denzil planted a knee on his chest. Now, while Mr Reid may not be the fittest guy in town, he's pretty big, which enabled him to hold Fish-fiddler down long enough by the throat for me to deliver the hardest kick possible to his crotch. I even took a bit of a run-up. And it must have been a real doozy, because it made him scream like a dog whistle and drop the knife like a piece of hot lava.

Denzil maintained his chokehold while I went to free Ziggy from the cage. The second I opened the door, the crazy mutt ploughed into me with such force that I was thrown backwards. I lay on my back as he licked my hands and wagged his tail like a lunatic. At least he didn't try to hump me. Denzil came to my rescue for the second time in thirty seconds and grabbed Ziggy's collar, thus allowing me to get back to my feet.

They say things come in threes. Well, first I was attacked by Fishman, then by Ziggy and finally by a wave of fatigue that made me feel like I hadn't slept for a year. I was still smiling inside, though. I was alive and Ziggy was alive and it felt amazing.

I watched Denzil reach down to check Fishman's pulse. 'Is he dead?'

'No,' he replied. 'Unfortunately.'

I touched the underside of my chin and winced. There was a respectable amount of blood and I knew the weasel had got me good.

'Are you okay?' Denzil sounded legitimately worried.

I put my arms around him, giving the guy a big old man hug.

'Ah mate, don't get blood all over my fancy new clothes.'

But I wasn't listening. 'I love you, man,' I said. 'Another second and I would have been cult food.' Tears pricked the corners of my eyes as I stepped away.

Denzil burst out laughing. 'You do realise that I own you now? You're basically my bitch.'

'Hardly. Who rushed the stage and tried to save you during the ceremony?'

'Bullshit.'

'On my life.'

Denzil's eyes narrowed. 'You charged the stage?'

'Yes.'

'With those army dudes?'

'No. I did it on my own.'

'On your own?' He sounded dubious.

'Yes.'

'Just you?'

'Just me.'

For a fleeting moment Denzil looked seriously impressed, then he smiled. 'Well, I didn't see it, so it doesn't count.'

I threw him the bird.

Ziggy started growling and I turned to be confronted with the reason why. In the doorway was Lady Ashbury's plus sized black snake, which I had to admit was significantly bigger in real life than anything I'd seen on the television. Easily five hundred pounds of pure killing machine watched us with eyes far too intelligent for my liking. The scary serpent slipped around the kitchen door with a grace to match Lady Ashbury.

'You must leave now,' it hissed, before slithering over to the manservant, who was starting to regain consciousness. Now don't get me wrong, I'd seen a lot of crazy things since leaving the hotel, but a talking snake was way too much to compute. So I just sort of stood there, with my mouth open. Fishman had just enough time to scream before the beast wrapped him in a corpse cuddle.

I exchanged glances with an equally freaked out looking Denzil, who motioned towards the door with his head. If ever there was a good time to get the hell out of somewhere, this was it. I scooped Ziggy up in my arms and made a swift exit. Sadly, it was a case of out of the frying pan and into the fire.

Stepping into the corridor we bumped into everyone's favourite servant, Sarah. She was dressed in a long black habit and was pointing an equally black hand gun at our heads.

'Turn around,' she said coldly.

'Your friend Fishman's in there,' said Denzil, 'and he needs your help.'

Sarah's expression didn't flicker. 'I said turn around and get down on your knees.'

'He's being eaten by a snake,' I added.

'Turn around and get on your knees,' she repeated.

Now I'm no expert in dealing with armed people, but those instructions didn't sound particularly promising.

'Please?' I begged, as I clutched a confused Ziggy to my chest.

She raised the gun into the air and fired a shot. 'I said turn around and get down on your knees!'

Out of options and afraid of being penetrated at high velocity by a bullet, we turned around and got down on our knees as instructed. The noise had freaked Ziggy out and he was wriggling and growling.

When I heard Sarah say, 'Goddess Hyrattanti, I, your humble servant…' I really started to worry.

'Oh my God,' I said. 'Please don't do this.'

'…have served you well these past years,' she continued. 'And now I give you this offering.'

There was an almighty bang as the gun went off and I squeezed my eyes shut and braced for the end.

'If you two have quite finished trying to get yourselves killed,' said Antony, 'then perhaps it wouldn't be too much trouble for you to follow me?'

I turned to see Sarah lying on the floor, staring vacantly at the ceiling. Antony looked pissed off, but I didn't care. I had both my dog and my brains, which were still tucked safely away inside my skull.

Antony kept his rifle raised in front of his face as we jogged back down the corridor. I'm guessing we were around the halfway mark when I heard a host of weird barking and squeaking sounds. Ziggy growled in response, bless him, but that turned out to be like bringing a knife to a nuclear war. As I turned my head I saw a group of angry pandas waddling along behind us. And I knew they were angry, because they were calling us some rather unpleasant names. I decided that if animals could talk, Doctor Doolittle would need to find a new revenue stream. Now, if they'd continued at that pace it would have been Sunday, Monday Happy Days, but then they charged. Okay, waddled a bit faster.

'Run!' I shouted, although it really didn't need to be said. I mean, we were hardly going to hang around to be eaten.

You know the feeling you get as a kid when you're being chased? Well times that by a thousand and you have some idea of what it's like to be on a panda's dinner menu. Antony fired behind him without looking back and I saw at least three bears fall under the shower of bullets. What a show-off. I was pleased to see that Ziggy had overcome his earlier bouts of bravado though, and had concluded that the best course of action was to make a run for it. Maybe my inherent cowardice was starting to rub off on him.

By the time we re-joined Antony's crack troops, they had cleared the entrance hall of armed guards. As we came charging through the doorway, Hager set about dispatching a number of the pandas that seemed so keen to use us as human chew toys. However, as the largest beast, which I assumed was Sebastien, burst into the room it avoided the bullets and leapt onto Antony from behind. The pair went crashing to the floor. Through some miracle Antony twisted his body, landing on his back with the giant animal falling down on top of him. The panda struck at his head, but the soldier blocked it, grabbed its jaws and they began to wrestle. I couldn't believe the strength of the man; it was unnatural. With one great pull he ripped the panda's jaws apart, produced a blade and ran it through. After the struggle, Antony simply got to his feet and acted like nothing had happened.

'Are you chaps okay?' he asked.

I couldn't believe what I'd just seen. 'Are you?'

'Never better,' he said with a grin. 'Now follow me.'

Denzil looked at me wide-eyed and mouthed, 'What the hell?'

We ran out of the vast doors and into the cold night air. At the side of the house we came upon a car park with an incredible range of high-end motorcars.

'Jack's with me,' called Antony as he stepped into the driver's side of a black Bentley Turbo. I wondered if it belonged to the war hero from the party. The others clambered into a large Mercedes. I put Ziggy on the back seat and was about to jump in when I heard someone calling for help. I paused, one foot in the car, listening over the hum of the impressive engines. 'Get in,' cried Antony, but I ignored him and continued listening for the faint noise. It sounded like a woman.

Spurred on by my questionable success saving Ziggy and Denzil, I disobeyed Antony for a second time and set off to find the mystery woman. I snaked through the parked cars and found her sitting on the cold ground with her back against the side of a limousine. It was Lady Ashbury. She was clutching her left side, which looked in the darkness to be soaked with blood. I could see more of the liquid at the corners of her mouth.

When she spoke to me her voice was strained. 'Jack? Dear, sweet Jack.'

I stood over her, unsure of what to say.

'I tried to protect you, Jack. Because you're…special.' As she started to cough, it was clear she wasn't in great shape. 'You're more important than you know,' she continued. 'I sent my Nahash to protect you. They want to control you. You can trust me, Jack.'

Was this crazy bint actually for real? Earlier in the evening she had wanted me dead. Now she was trying to convince me I could trust her.

'What happened to you?'

'Lord Ashbury was reluctant to grant me a divorce.' She coughed several more times. 'And so was his army of pandas.'

Before I could answer I realised Antony was standing at my shoulder.

'Get in the car,' he growled, helping me on my way with a generous shove.

This time I did as I was told. I heard the gunshot as I sat down in the car. Lady Ashbury was dead.

We drove through the animal-infested grounds at frightening speed while poor Ziggy skidded about on the shiny leather seats in the back. We'd made it about a quarter of a mile before we realised the exotic zoo animals were security and not scenery. It started with a lone rhino trying to block the road. We swerved to the left when it charged, only to find ourselves being shot at by a troop of screeching baboons now sporting handguns. I ducked down as the side of the car was peppered with bullets. Fortunately, the rich owner appeared to have made the vehicle bulletproof. Unfortunately, the designer had clearly overlooked the risk of elephant attacks. We left the tarmac and bumped along on the grass as a mighty bull elephant clutching a huge club in its truck gave chase. It caught the rear of the car three times, each strike sending horrendous shockwaves through the vehicle and making the roof a little closer to my head. Yet still the tank of a car remained intact. We careened back onto the road and accelerated away from the roaring beast, as a herd of random animals began throwing themselves against the Bentley in a kamikaze-style attempt to stop us. Luckily, machine guns and expert driving trumped angry animals, just, and by winding down the windows the soldiers were able to dispatch enough of the genetically modified menaces for us to escape.

When the iron gates came into view, I could see that they were closed. However, there was no need for me to be concerned. The Mercedes simply overtook us and one of the soldiers casually leant out of the window and fired a rocket at it. And that was the end of the ornate antique structure, demonic symbols and all.

We tore along the winding country roads in the pitch black. When I enquired about the headlights, Antony just smiled. Lady Ashbury's words were starting to play on my mind. Who were the people she'd mentioned? Why would they want to control me? And how did she know anything about me when we'd only just met? The whole thing gave me the creeps and I pushed all thoughts of the conversation from my brain.

I had far more immediate concerns that I needed to deal with, like Antony not crashing into a sodding tree.

CHAPTER 13

Antony could sense my concern over the lack of headlights. Maybe it was the screaming and swearing that gave it away? The lunatic still didn't switch them on, though.

'How are you feeling?' he asked in what I guessed was an attempt to distract me.

'Like I'm about to be involved in a serious road accident,' I replied.

'I mean physically?' He glanced at me in the darkness.

'Jesus Christ,' I said, 'keep your eyes on the road.'

'I'm being serious.'

'So am I!'

I prised my white-knuckled hand from the side of the seat and tentatively touched my chest. I was amazed that despite being carved up like a Christmas turkey I couldn't feel any pain, only newly formed scars. I also felt a lot more relaxed about everything that had happened to us and nowhere near as concerned about calling my parents. Intellectually, I knew that was a little off, but at the same time I wasn't concerned.

'What did you inject me with?' I asked.

'No headache?' Antony replied, answering a question with a question.

'My head feels fine.'

He seemed satisfied by the response.

I spent the next few minutes providing a rundown of the events that led us to our satanic Golgotha. I had to lead into a few parts by swearing on both mine and an array of family members' lives that it was all true. I could have left stuff out but I was too tired to bother. The weirdest thing about my insane story was that none of it appeared to surprise him. Even the part about octopuses swinging from trees didn't warrant a reaction. This made me highly suspicious. Who were these people? And more importantly, what the hell was going on?

I decided to go about things the old-fashioned way and ask the man.

'What were you doing at Ashbury Hall? And how did you know my name?'

Antony smiled. 'Well, that's straight to the point.'

I waited several seconds for him to respond.

'We've been tracking you since your car accident.'

'How?'

'We got your name from your car registration.' He said it like it was the most obvious thing in the world.

'Why were you at the crash site?'

'We were following political undesirables.'

'So, what do you want with me?' I asked, as we took another turn insanely fast.

'Don't worry, Jack, I work for the government. And lucky for you we arrived when we did, because there's a terrorist organisation that would kill to get their hands on you.'

I felt a mild panic. 'What terrorist organisation?'

'You have something they want. But I won't let them take it.'

I immediately thought of the blue light and fired off a series of questions. But try as I might, getting any more information out of Antony proved as challenging as a kid building a Stradivarius from a rubber band and a couple of socks.

We raced around a bend in the road and found our path blocked by a fallen tree. Antony slammed the brakes on so hard that Ziggy went crashing into the back of the seat, yelping in the process.

'Wait here.'

Antony grabbed his gun and stepped out of the car. Ziggy made a desperate scramble onto my lap. I could hardly blame him for not wanting to stay in the back. There was a screeching sound followed by a bang as the source of the noise slammed into the back of us, propelling the Bentley into the tree trunk. I had my arms around Ziggy, which prevented him hitting the dashboard, but unfortunately this meant that my arms did, which bloody hurt. I froze when I heard the crack of two gun shots and decided that the best option was to hide in the car like a total hero.

Shortly afterwards, Denzil appeared by my head and started banging on the passenger window. He looked distressed.

'There was a toilet bug in the car,' he cried, as I wound down my window. 'It was running about everywhere.' The guy was panting like a dehydrated dog.

'No way.' I rubbed my still painful right elbow and forearm.

'The nasty little thing must have been hiding under the front seats or something. It actually ran across the back of my neck at one point.'

I shivered, despite not being cold. I'd hoped we'd seen the last of those nightmarish creatures.

'You should have seen Jabari,' Denzil continued.

'Who?'

'The big bloke with the beard. He caught it in one hand, removed it from the car and shot it. It made that copper back at the Naysmere look like a right wussy.'

With no useable vehicles, Antony announced we'd be walking to the nearest village to acquire a suitable form of transport, by which he clearly meant stealing something. We trudged along under the stars in silence, crossing fields and hedgerows. When I wasn't worrying about nasty creatures waiting for us in the darkness, or wondering why Lord Ashbury's blade had melted away, my mind drifted to Lucy. It generated a now familiar sense of emptiness, guilt and loss. I'm ashamed to say that a tiny part of me almost hoped to forget about her, just to take the pain away.

I was cold and tired by the time we reached the village of Little Rissington. Its perimeter was marked by a signpost, underneath which lay an ornamental flowerbed punctuated by a mangled head and torso.

'Jesus!' Denzil appeared at my shoulder. 'The local tourist board needs to rethink their advertising campaign.'

'It's not ideal,' I replied.

'Don't British villages have the weirdest names?' Denzil was clearly not overly bothered by the gruesome sight. 'Did you know that there's a Bellend near Worcester?'

'There's a bellend near me.'

'And a Fanny Barks in Durham and a Scratchy Bottom in Dorset.'

'Nice.'

'Oh yeah, and a Twatt in Orkney.'

'Enlightening,' I replied with no small amount of sarcasm.

'I wonder if Jenny Hanson went there?' said Denzil with a snigger.

'Piss off,' I replied, at which point Antony told us to, 'Stay Alert!', which I translated as, 'Shut up, you idiots.'

The picture postcard village of stone houses and narrow winding lanes lay quiet and still. Well, right up until the big guy with the beard and the funny name used his fist to smash a car window. This caused the alarm to start shrieking and my heart to leap about inside my chest like a drunken student on a trampoline. The security system was quickly disabled and we piled into the seven-seater, seemingly without any of the local residents noticing. The car's engine surged into life shortly before something large and dark threw itself against the side of the car with tremendous force. I looked out of the window to find myself eyeball to eyeball with a cat that must have been the size of a horse. And if that wasn't enough, this one had four heads and four sets of huge kitty fangs. The forecast wasn't looking all that sunny.

The striped monstrosity began attacking the vehicle with its giant claws. To be honest with you, if it wasn't for the multiple heads, the freaky red eyes and the fact that it clearly wanted us dead, it would have been cute.

'Drive!' shouted Denzil, and myself and Ziggy joined in enthusiastically with his programme of panicking.

The soldiers, however, appeared unphased by the attack. Antony guided the car out of the parking spot like a man taking his family on a shopping trip, then accelerated up the narrow high street, past the tea room and antique shop as if the beast wasn't there. The freaky feline gave chase for a couple of minutes, but like cats so often do, it lost interest, and gave up the chase.

'What the bloody hell was that?' asked Denzil.

'The worst pet ever?' I replied.

'Imagine having that as a pet,' he said. 'Just think of the litter tray.'

'You'd definitely have to get it neutered.'

'We need to find a petrol station,' said Antony, frowning at the fuel gauge.

'Tight bastards,' said Denzil. 'They live in a ridiculously expensive house in a posh village and the stingy so and so's can't even be bothered to put petrol in their car.'

'You do realise we stole it?' I replied.

'Same difference,' said Denzil.

'There's a petrol station two clicks along this road,' Jabari announced.

Denzil clicked his fingers twice but no one laughed. I was left pondering how Jabari could even know that. He hadn't looked at a phone, satellite navigation device or anything for that matter. But sure enough, after about two kilometres we arrived at a petrol station that was reassuringly full of vehicles. I was also happy to see signs for a coffee shop and convenience store. I was starving and the thought of a sandwich and a flat white filled me with an unexpected degree of excitement.

'Jeez! These petrol prices are a bit steep,' said Denzil as we pulled up.

'Don't worry,' said Antony with a smile. 'I won't be expecting you to pay for it.'

'Maybe they've got a phone?' asked Denzil.

'The networks are down,' replied Antony. 'We're on our own, I'm afraid, so, it's critical we get you to safety as soon as possible.'

As we parked next to Pump 14 I could see the head of a woman in her late fifties moving about behind the counter in the shop.

'This will do nicely,' said Denzil. 'I could murder a blueberry muffin and a sausage roll.'

The soldiers jumped out and stood there with their guns on full show. So much for trying to blend in.

'Can we go and get some food, please?' I asked.

'We'll get something for you,' replied Antony, but never one to do as he's told, Denzil was already out the door and walking towards the shop.

'Get back in the car,' demanded Hager.

'But I'm hungry,' said Denzil, without stopping.

'Just tell us what you want and we'll get it,' said Antony.

'But I'm not sure what I want yet,' said Denzil, momentarily walking backwards. 'I'll go and have a quick look, yeah?'

'No, you won't,' called Hager.

'But I'm not sure what I want.' Denzil now had his back to them.

'Go with them, Seth,' said Antony to the other soldier while nodding at me. 'You'll need to pay.'

'Yes!' I jumped out of the car like a kid being told he was allowed to buy the chocolate bar he'd been craving.

I caught up with Denzil by the glass double doors, which glided open. With Seth in hot pursuit, we stepped inside and I reached for a metal shopping basket from the stack by the door. Two of the baskets lifted up together and Denzil laughed and called me a dipstick as I struggled to prise them apart. Baskets successfully separated, we took one each and turned our attention to the food and drink. There was so much great stuff on the shelves. They say you shouldn't go shopping when you're hungry and our selections reflected this. Once satisfied with our produce, we headed to the tills while Seth grabbed some extra bottles of water.

'Jesus,' said Denzil with a smile. We both stopped and stared.

'I'm seeing it,' I said. 'At least I think I'm seeing it.'

The woman behind the counter was stark naked. 'Hello,' she said in a high-pitched voice.

Denzil sniggered and I responded with a swift elbow to his ribs. There was clearly something wrong here.

'Well, she's not shy,' he mumbled.

'Don't be a dick.' I said, 'She must be in shock.'

'Hello,' she said again with a smile.

'She looks like your Auntie Debra,' said Denzil as he strolled towards the tills. I hoped he was referring to her face. The woman beamed at him as he approached. 'Are you a bit hot?' he asked her.

'You know you're a real arsehole sometimes,' I said.

'Alright, keep your knickers on.' He let out a sigh. 'Are you okay?' he asked the woman.

'Hello,' she repeated politely.

Denzil turned to me and shrugged.

Her eyes held a vacant expression that reminded me of an old war veteran. I felt sorry for her. Our rubbish world was sliding into the bin of hell and people were suffering. I felt like we needed to help this woman and bring the universe back into line ever so slightly.

'Hello,' she said again.

'Are you alright?' I replied.

As I stepped towards her I felt something brush against my cheek. Instinctively, I lifted my hand to wipe it away and realised something white was stuck to my skin. I glanced up at the ceiling and immediately felt sick. Every last inch of it was covered in spiders' webs. But that wasn't the horrific part. In amongst the mass of tangled and twisted white cord, people's faces were sticking out.

I gasped and backed away, managing to trip over my shaking legs in the process. I swore as I landed hard on my backside and the food from my basket spilled out across the floor. 'We need to get out of here right now.'

In one surging motion the shop assistant rose up into the air and I watched in horror as a mass of red and black spiders' legs appeared on the counter. The top half was definitely a woman, but from the waist down she was all spider. There was a secondary mouth: a large and unpleasant affair, filled with razor-sharp teeth, eight fierce red eyes and a long black flickering tongue.

The creature was fast, but so was Seth, firing almost immediately. 'Get back!' he shouted as the hideous arachnid launched itself at us. Bullets pummelled her stomach and face, causing black blood to splatter all over the confectionary. The bullets did just enough to slow the creature down, which gave Denzil time to grab my collar and drag me towards the automatic doors.

Seth took a few more shots at the beast as we ran out onto the forecourt with the screeching spider monster hot on our heels. Antony, Jabari and Hager were all standing in a line with their rifles pointed straight at us.

'Get down,' shouted Antony, and we threw ourselves to the floor as the sliding doors closed behind us. The monster smashed through the doors, and emerged amidst a halo of flying glass and bullets, landing on top of me.

I looked up at the fang-filled fiend straddling me on the forecourt and screamed as the screeching black orifice descended towards me. Three of its horrendous hairy legs pinned my arms down while the stinger on its tail probed and groped its way towards me.

'Help!' I screamed in a blind panic. 'It's trying to bum-sting me!'

Time elapsed in slow motion as the monster tried to impale me. I kneed it in the abdomen several times as hard as I could. Why was no one firing at it? Had the bastards all run off and left me? Then I heard a barking sound to my right.

Ziggy!

I saw a flash of white as my furry hero bit into one of the beast's disgusting legs. I think that was the moment I really fell in love with that stocky little pooch. I was caught up in the fight of my life, moments from death and completely alone, and who was it that came to my rescue? Who was it that stood by my side against this monstrous creature? Who was it that risked his fuzzy little life to try and save mine? It was Ziggy. Well, up until he was tossed unceremoniously through the air by the spider lady and landed in a yelping heap somewhere behind my head. But it's the thought that counts.

The creature reared up onto its back legs and the soldiers engaged in a bit of carpe diem, filling it with lead. If demons in hell have a soundtrack, then the screams it made were definitely the title track from that album. As the force of the soldiers' attack pushed it backwards, the spider released me from its grip, and I rolled away to the left. I looked up and saw bullets slicing through the still smiling face that rested on top of its bloated belly like the figurehead of a grotesque ship. The four soldiers approached us as they fired, reloading whenever needed. The monster's legs began scrabbling for purchase on the smooth concrete floor and then it twitched several times and died. Ziggy decided to make a valiant second charge and spent some quality time skipping about on the spot and barking defiantly at the corpse. Although he did jump back when the monster's leg twitched.

I got unsteadily to my feet and gave the dog a stroke. 'Good boy.'

'Are you okay?' asked Denzil.

'I think so. Although I'm probably still in shock.'

'From now on you will both do as you're told,' said Antony. 'That was far too close for comfort.'

I walked over to the creature, which lay twitching on the ground, and watched the smelly black goo ooze from its ruined body.

'Let's grab some supplies and get out of here,' said Seth.

I followed them in a daze as we headed back inside the petrol station. Ziggy was trotting at my heels with the pride of a mythical Greek hero.

We gathered up the shopping baskets and the food that had spilled out across the shop floor. I shivered and looked up at the ceiling again. The people hung there in silent stasis. I began to well up when I noticed that two of them were young children.

'We have to help them,' I said.

'They're dead, mate,' said Denzil, patting me on the shoulder. 'There's nothing we can do.' He turned and started grabbing more food from the shelves. I looked at one of the woman's faces and guessed that she must have been in her mid-to-late forties. I was trying to decide whether she'd suffered, when the woman opened her eyes and stared right at me.

'Help me,' she mumbled.

'Seth!' I shouted. 'Quick! She's still alive. We have to help her.'

'It's too late,' he said, striding towards me with two baskets of supplies. 'Come on.'

I glanced up into that pale, frightened face and saw she was crying. 'There must be a stepladder or something out the back.'

'We need to leave.' Seth marched past me and out of the shop.

The woman made an unpleasant gagging motion and then from out of her mouth poured hundreds of miniature spider people. They were fully formed but no more than three inches in length. The other victims started to gag and the whole ceiling began to fill with the tiny abominations. With frightening speed they began making their way down the walls.

I turned and ran out of the door, well, I jumped out through the smashed glass. Unfortunately, while this allowed me to exit post-haste, it also meant the spider babies could too. And out they poured in their thousands, like a hideous moving carpet. I raced towards the now fully fuelled car and leapt in through the open rear door.

'Come on,' I shouted to Ziggy and Denzil.

Ziggy dutifully followed, but Denzil ran to the pump and started emptying the contents onto the forecourt.

'Leave it,' ordered Antony, at which point Denzil dropped the fuel dispenser and ran back to the car. He pulled out the Zippo lighter that he'd picked up back at the caves and with one fluid motion struck the flint. An orange flame sprung into existence and Denzil tossed the lighter into the slick liquid that was now coating the floor, before jumping back into the car. It was a genius idea from Denzil, but the wazzock missed the bloody great patch of petrol and the lighter hit the floor and the flame petered out. Fortunately, the soldiers were better trained and equipped than us, and Hager rolled a small silver ball across the forecourt before returning to the safety of the car. We were about thirty metres from the petrol station when an explosion I'm guessing you could see from the moon occurred.

I turned to Denzil. 'Are you okay, mate?'

'Not really,' he replied. 'I bloody loved that lighter.'

CHAPTER 14

We pushed that seven-seater to its absolute limit. Well, Antony did. The rest of us just sat there and swayed from side to side. We screeched, revved and skidded up and down hills, over bumps, around corners and along the winding Cotswolds roads, all once again without the headlights on. Talk about a bloody death wish. I spent the time peering out of the rear passenger window thinking about everything that had happened.

There was a loud bang as something hit the front of the car and my butt was lifted off the seat as we bounced over it. I guess that was my own fault for not wearing a seatbelt. The impact reminded me of when my dad hit a deer in Shropshire, except this time Brenda wasn't busy shouting at him for being a 'stupid blind sod'. Anyway, Antony slammed on the brakes and for a family car, it came to a surprisingly robust halt.

'What the hell was that?' asked Denzil.

I looked out of the back window and saw a dark shape lying in the road. 'Oh God. We hit something.'

Antony glanced in the rear-view mirror. 'We need to keep moving,' he said.

'Shouldn't we stop to take a look?'

He ignored me and started pulling away. I looked at Jabari.

'There's nothing we can do,' he said, sounding neutral. 'Even if she survived the initial impact, what then?'

I wondered if 'she' was a slip of the tongue and, meeting Denzil's eyes, I knew I wasn't alone. I mean, how could he even know the shape was female?

'We should probably take "her" to a hospital then,' recommended Denzil.

Antony glanced at us in the rear-view mirror. He knew we'd clocked Jabari's slip of the tongue.

'I guess you've not been watching the news,' said Seth. 'But while you two were busy partying, the whole world has turned to shit.'

'Stop the car,' said Denzil.

'We can't,' said Antony.

But Denzil wasn't buying it. 'Stop the car or I'll smack you in the bloody mouth.'

At that I opened the door as if planning to make a swift exit. Not that I would have jumped; I'm not a compete imbecile. But it appeared to work, because Antony stopped.

'Alright,' he said, sounding seriously pissed. 'We'll go back. But it's a waste of time.'

We reversed back to where the alleged female lay motionless in the road. As I stepped down from the car I began to shake. I had no idea what I was about to see. Did police officers or firefighters feel like this? It wasn't the first road accident I'd encountered since we left the Naysmere Hotel, but I was still deeply unsettled. I pushed Ziggy back inside the car despite his irritated barking and approached the murky shape in the road.

It was, indeed, a woman. My mind would have been filled with questions about how Jabari could have known, if it weren't for the tiny person crouched down beside her. A girl of no more than seven or eight was sitting on the cold, hard ground, stroking the woman's hair. When she looked up at me with fear in her eyes, I wanted to reach out to her, to comfort her. I wanted to say it was going to be okay, help was here. Instead, I settled for, 'Hello.'

I guess the sight of strange men with guns was too much for the child to cope with, because she took off like a whippet up the tree-lined track to my left.

'I'll go,' called Antony. 'You wait here.' And off he went in pursuit of the kid.

I looked down at the woman's body lying in a crumpled heap on the road. There was something synthetic about the hue of her skin bathed in the moonlight. If I'd have stumbled across her on a late-night stroll, I might have thought she was a mannequin.

Denzil appeared next to me. 'Of all the things that could have killed her,' he said quietly, 'it was us.'

'It was an accident,' said Jabari from behind him, with the emotion of a broken toaster.

'That doesn't make me feel any better,' I replied.

'We need to help that child,' said Denzil.

'No,' said Jabari. 'We should leave her behind.'

'Now that is a genius idea,' replied Denzil. 'Oh no, wait a minute. We're in the middle of nowhere with no one around for miles, you heartless prick.' It was nice to have my friend back after his shameful performance during titty-gate at the petrol station.

A gunshot reverberated and my heart nearly jumped out of my chest. Denzil and I glanced at each other before running up the track. As we hunted for its source, Antony came charging out of the darkness.

'Monsters,' he cried. 'Run!'

I was immediately filled with panic.

'I killed two,' he yelled as he ran past us, 'but there's more coming.'

We didn't need to be told twice. Turning on a very small coin, we ran back towards the car.

'Where's the girl?' shouted Denzil as we raced along.

'Dead,' Antony shouted back.

We piled into the car, ignoring the loud protests from an affronted Ziggy, and Antony hit the gas. I glanced back towards the track, expecting to see a hoard of ungodly beasts streaming towards us. But all I saw was darkness.

'I can't see any monsters,' said Denzil as we disappeared around a bend in the road.

'What happened to the girl?' I asked.

'A beast,' replied Antony, sounding totally calm.

'What beast?'

'Does it matter? She's dead.'

'But what happened?'

'I've just told you,' said Antony.

'Sorry, Antony,' I said, 'we're not trying to be annoying. We just want to know what happened.'

'Have you not experienced enough horror already?'

'She's definitely dead, though?' asked Denzil.

'If her head being separated from her body qualifies as dead,' he snapped, 'then yes, I'd say she was probably dead.'

'But what happened?' I asked him.

Antony let out a sigh. 'Very well. There's a small wooded area at the top of the hill. As she ran past the trees, a large creature emerged from the darkness and tore her apart. I raised my rifle and fired off a shot. The bullet entered its head and it fell to the ground.' He paused. 'Sadly, it was too late for the girl.' But he didn't sound sad. In fact, he sounded like he didn't give two shits. 'Another creature rushed me from the trees, and I turned and fled.'

'You watched her die?' asked Denzil.

'I watched it tear her to shreds.'

'And you're sure she was dead?' I asked.

'Yes,' Antony replied curtly.

I knew by this point that he was getting pissed off with us, but a nagging feeling spurred me on. 'What did it look like?'

'How do you think a decapitated child would look?' he said. 'What's wrong with you?'

'Not the girl,' I replied. 'The monster. I meant the monster.'

'I've already told you.'

'She wasn't just hurt?' asked Denzil.

Antony was on the verge of losing his patience. 'I don't like where this is going,' he said through gritted teeth.

'I'm sorry,' I replied. 'I didn't mean…The whole thing is just so messed up.'

Antony appeared to soften. 'I'm sorry too,' he said, before letting out an exaggerated sigh. 'It's been a long couple of days and we all want to get out of this mess, but we can only do that if we all work together.'

'You're right.'

'The death of that poor little girl and her mother doesn't make any sense. None of this does. But we can't blame ourselves for the abominations that lie outside of our control. We need to be strong and we need to favour logic over emotion. There will be a time and a place to mourn for her, but it's not today. Today is about surviving. We must do what we can and leave all else to the gods.'

'I'm sorry,' I said.

'It's fine, Jack. We've been thrust into a terrible situation and each of us needs to make sense of it.'

'I'm not sure what's going on with me at the moment,' I replied.

'You're in shock,' said Seth. 'It's normal. Eat one of the chocolate bars we got from the petrol station. It will make you feel better.'

'You mentioned two,' said Denzil.

I turned to look at him.

'Antony, you mentioned two creatures.' Denzil was staring at the back of Antony's head. 'You said you killed two when you were running down the hill. And now you said you killed one and ran away from the other.'

'You must have misheard. It was a high-stress situation and the human mind can play tricks on us.'

'No,' replied Denzil. 'You definitely said you killed two of them.' He looked to me for support. 'He definitely said two, didn't he, Gibby?'

I tried to remember what Antony had actually said, but without any luck. 'I don't remember, mate,' I replied honestly. 'Sorry.'

Denzil looked at me like I'd betrayed him.

'You're in shock,' Seth repeated.

'I'll give you a shock in a minute,' snapped Denzil. 'I'm not stupid. I know what I heard and I also know that I didn't see any frigging monsters.'

'Watch it,' said Hager, which translated as, 'If you carry on with this line of questioning I'm going to rip your bloody throat out.'

Ziggy started to growl and I stroked his head, trying to settle him down.

'Or what?' replied Denzil, pushing his luck.

'I think everyone needs to calm down,' I said, trying to be the voice of reason.

'I am calm,' replied Denzil in the most sarcastic tone he could muster.

'I think that's sensible advice,' said Antony.

'I know what I heard.' Denzil turned to me. 'Or perhaps you think I'm a liar?'

'Of course I don't,' I replied. 'But you've been drugged, tortured, caught up in a knife fight, chased by killer pandas and just seen a corpse.' I paused before continuing in a softer tone. 'So, all I'm saying, mate, is that maybe you misheard, or maybe it was a slip of the tongue on Antony's part.'

Denzil gave me a filthy look, but at least he kept his mouth shut.

Despite what I'd just said, Denzil's doubts raced around my head like a motorbike on a wall of death. What if he was right? What if the girl wasn't dead? Or what if Antony had killed her? Surely not? He didn't seem like a monster.

The sound of explosions saved me from further musings. The stress of this unwanted road trip to Shitsville, Nowhere was never ending. Ziggy jumped up and trampled over everyone's laps to look out of the window.

'Ouch,' said Denzil. 'That's my nuts.'

'Fireworks or gunfire?' I asked no one in particular.

'SA80 rifles, L7A2 machine guns and AT4 anti-tank weapons,' said Seth.

'Plus, mortars and a Challenger tank,' added Hager.

'They must be hunting something big,' said Jabari.

'Maybe we should turn back?' said Denzil, pushing Ziggy away.

But Antony kept driving and the soldiers remained stoic. I tried to do the same, but when you're essentially a coward there's only so much you can do.

'I don't think this is a good idea,' I announced when I spotted the shape of a tank up ahead.

The huge death machine was surrounded by other vehicles and soldiers. They were all firing at an assortment of monsters that was bearing down on them like some sort of mutant cavalry. There were hundreds of the things, coming at them in waves from across the fields. The noise of the battle was atrocious. A soldier stepped in front of our car, forcing Antony to make an abrupt stop. She waved and five of her companions that had been sheltering behind a stone wall ran over and surrounded us. Antony wound his window down as his companions tried to hide their weapons by their feet.

'You can't be here,' shouted the woman.

'General Antony, 22 SAS,' he replied over the piercing sound of gunfire and explosions.

Denzil looked at me and mouthed, 'Bugger me.'

'This is my team,' he continued. 'We're transporting persons of interest to Station Zulu.'

'Step out of the car,' ordered the woman.

Antony spoke to her while the rest of us sat there under the watchful gaze of the machine gun massive. After a few minutes, Antony opened the driver's door and told us to get out. We were catching a lift.

Stepping from the car onto the edge of what was basically a battlefield got my adrenaline pumping. A soldier dragged me by the arm to a large armoured vehicle. I picked up Ziggy as she pushed me aboard. There were benches down either side and I found myself sitting opposite Denzil. We waited there until the firing ceased, at which point tired-looking soldiers started filling up the vehicle. The doors were slammed shut and then we pulled away.

The soldier sitting next to me started stroking Ziggy. 'Nice dog,' he said. 'Smiffy used to have a pit bull.'

'Thanks,' I replied. 'He's an English bull terrier.'

'Oi! Smiffy,' shouted the man.

'What?' replied another soldier.

'Didn't you have a pit bull?'

'A staffy,' he replied.

'I thought pit bulls were illegal?' asked the soldier.

'I believe they are,' I replied and the man looked confused.

'Do you know what's happening?' Denzil asked one of the soldiers.

'The world's gone to hell is what's happening,' replied the woman.

'Supposedly a terrorist attack,' answered another scornfully, 'because, as everyone knows, terrorists have armies of monsters in their back pockets, right?'

'Is it just in the Cotswolds?' I asked.

'Is it hell,' said Smiffy. 'These things are everywhere.'

'Everywhere?' asked Denzil.

'They're all over Europe, Asia, Africa, North America, South America. Literally everywhere.'

I felt a sinking feeling inside my chest. I'd always taken my world of relative peace and economic stability for granted. A blissfully unaware existence, focussed on consumerism and hedonism. Now terror and uncertainty were storming my shores. Was this how people felt during World War II?

'Sometime Thursday evening,' said a soldier, 'these creatures just began pouring out of sewers and toilets.'

'We saw them,' I replied, 'back at the hotel we were staying at.'

Another woman spoke up. 'People were innocently laying some cable and then wham! A bug would scramble right up their corn bomber.'

'The emergency services couldn't cope,' said one guy. 'I mean, they struggle when we get an inch of snow, right? So they had no chance. The government was forced to declare martial law.'

'How many are there?' asked Denzil.

'Bloody millions,' said Smiffy. 'But they're evolving.'

'Evolving?' asked Denzil.

'You never see the same type twice,' said another soldier.

'The deformed people are the worst,' said the guy stroking Ziggy. 'They're like walking nightmares.'

'It's their blood-red eyes that really freak me out,' said the woman.

Less than seventy-two hours ago, Denzil and I had been laughing and joking in a hotel bar. My biggest fear then was waking up with a nasty hangover. Now monsters were roaming the countryside and Lucy was dead.

I wondered if there was a place where everything was still normal, because I really wanted to be there, away from this nightmare.

I was exhausted and it was warm in the back of the vehicle. The hypnotic rise and fall of Ziggy's chest pressed up against me, and I closed my eyes and slept.

CHAPTER 15

The driver hit the brakes, causing Ziggy to headbutt me in the face. It wasn't the most pleasant alarm call, but it did the job. The doors were pulled open and we filed out of the vehicle. Looking to my right I saw a hangar the size of two football fields. Thirty-metre high walls with watchtowers surrounded both the hangar and the glorified car park alive with the sound and movement of people and machines. A Royal Marine with a big gun and a green beret shouted at us in the way you'd engage people who struggle to understand the English language.

'Follow the yellow line! Do not speak! Do not stop! Keep moving!' he yelled, while pointing to the hangar.

So, we followed the yellow line, kept quiet and kept moving, until we reached a door in a corner of the building. We lined up in silence with a mixture of civilians that looked unwashed, lost and bone weary. Denzil and I fitted in perfectly. We were subjected to an upsettingly thorough body search, before queueing up again to be registered by a friendly soldier who made a fuss of all the children. I started to relax, but Denzil looked concerned.

'Are you alright?' I asked.

'I'm just thinking about those soldiers we met,' he said.

'Antony?'

'No, not Antony. I mean the Grand Master woman and that terrifying beast man.'

'Those psychopaths? What about them?'

'Well, what if they're here?'

'Why would they be here?'

'Don't be a div,' he said. 'Did you see the weapons they were carrying?'

'The silver disks?'

'The silver disks, the SUVs, the assault rifles. That's no random group of thugs. I'm thinking they're probably government-related and we should be using false names while we're here. Just to be on the safe side.'

I recounted the conversation with Antony about the group being part of a terrorist organisation. Denzil frowned. He no longer trusted our rescuer.

Even if he was being overly paranoid, I agreed it wouldn't hurt to err on the side of caution. 'Okay. What should we call ourselves?'

'I'll be Jesus Ferrari and you can be Bobby Boston,' he announced with a worryingly straight face.

'Are you mental?'

'What?'

'How many people in the south of England have you met called Jesus bloody Ferrari?'

'Alright, keep your pubes on,' replied Denzil. 'I'll be Duke Smith, then, and you can be Harry Jones.'

'Duke?' I raised an eyebrow.

A soldier shouted at us to keep moving and we duly obliged.

'Why can't I have a cool name?' said Denzil.

'Fine.' I shook my head. 'Duke Smith and Harry Jones it is.'

'Nice one, Harry,' said Denzil.

'Don't say it like that,' I replied. 'I'm not a bloody wizard.'

Denzil was the first to be efficiently registered and then it was my turn.

'Identification?' said the soldier in a friendly tone.

'I'm really sorry,' I lied. 'I've lost it.'

They'd clearly missed a trick with their security because all she did was ask me to look at the camera.

I stared at the small green light as my photo was taken.

'Name please?'

My mind went completely blank.

'I need your name to register you,' she said patiently.

I blurted out the first thing that popped into my empty head. 'Jesus Ferrari!'

She looked at me properly for the first time and the blood drained from my face. Then she smiled. 'You must have had a fun time at school with that name.'

'It wasn't ideal.'

'Actually, I think it's pretty cool.' She handed me a photo ID on a lanyard.

I couldn't work out if she was being sarcastic or not.

'Grazie, Mr Ferrari,' she continued. 'The dog will need to be kennelled. If you follow the blue line through the door at the back, you'll be given further instructions.'

I thanked her rather too enthusiastically before encouraging Ziggy to follow me, and by encouraging, I mean dragging his big old lazy backside along behind me.

I followed the procession of people until a soldier pulled me out of line.

'The dog needs to come with me,' he said, scanning my pass.

'Where are you taking him?'

'The kennels. He'll be looked after until you're free to go.' The man snatched the lead from out of my hand and dragged a now barking Ziggy away. He hadn't even asked for the poor mite's name. Fortunately it was on his collar.

Feeling vulnerable without my little buddy and irritated by the method of his departure, I followed everyone else towards a huge lift. Inside it was crowded and unpleasant. A woman was comforting her screaming child and I ended up pressed against the back of some weird-looking, sweaty bloke with a world-class combination of rancid breath and excessive body odour. Of course, the lift took ages to reach its destination, which meant it was either a crappy old elevator, or we were descending a seriously long way. By the time we reached our destination I was flustered and fed up with trying to hold my breath. When we finally shuffled out of its oppressive metal walls, my senses were overwhelmed by the world before me. Large screens suspended from the ceiling blasted out instructions like an aircraft safety video. It was loud, it was busy and the smell left a hell of a lot to be desired.

'Harry!' came a shout from behind me and I turned to see Denzil pushing through the crowds. 'You alright?'

'Yeah,' I replied. 'You?'

He looked around. 'Well, this is all rather charming, isn't it?'

We moved through a series of corridors and bunkers as we searched for our assigned beds. The place was laid out in a grid format with each bunker being named after a British town and the corridors after famous London streets.

'It looks like a refugee camp,' I said.

'Funny that,' replied Denzil.

'You see them on TV, but I never thought I'd actually be in one.'

'Does anybody? Anyway, I think it looks more like one of those South American hellhole prisons. You know, the ones where the inmates are in charge, and they go around beating and torturing each other.'

'How about we say it's like being at an underground music festival so I don't completely crap my pants?'

'Word to the wise.' Denzil winked at me. 'Don't go dropping your soap in the showers round here. Burt Reynolds isn't going to be popping up with a bow and arrow to save your little muckhole.'

'Aw, that's really sweet of you.'

'Just saying it like it is, Gibby.'

'*Dein atem stinkt*,' I said.

'You what?'

'Just saying it like it is, Denzil,' I replied. 'Just saying it like it is.'

As we walked down Regent Street, Denzil announced that with all this security the monsters didn't have a hope in hell of getting in.

I looked around. 'Or anyone getting out.'

'Why would you want to be outside? It's nice not having to worry about being killed every few seconds.'

'I don't want to be out there, but at the same time this place doesn't give me a warm, fuzzy feeling.'

'Well, of course it doesn't, you muppet. It's a bloody refugee camp.'

'It's not that.'

'What then?'

'I'm not sure.'

'You need to chill out, mate.'

I didn't respond.

'You do know Antony was lying earlier?' he said as we walked past a guy I swear used to present the weather on the TV.

'Did you honestly hear him say that?' I replied.

'On my life. I just don't trust the bloke, Gibby.'

'You don't trust the man who saved our lives?'

Denzil frowned and said nothing.

'He said he wants to protect us.'

'Lenin said he wanted to give the proletariat peace, land and bread,' said Denzil, 'and look how that turned out.'

'Yeah, but his 'Imagine' song was really good.'

Denzil gave me a filthy look. 'You do know that during the Russian famine the government had to print posters telling people that eating their children was a barbarian act?'

'Are you serious?'

'Yes, mate. Catastrophe comes calling for all societies eventually and right now the outlook for ours isn't particularly rosy. There's a global agenda to wipe out mankind unfolding before our eyes, and something tells me your new BFF is involved.'

I knew Denzil had my back and I knew he wouldn't be pushing the point unless he believed something was wrong. But it wasn't a viewpoint I shared. The guy saw conspiracy theories in empty fish bowls. The truth was Antony had saved our lives. Blaming him for not getting his facts straight under pressure seemed ungrateful.

According to the camp clocks it took us forty-three minutes to locate our designated beds. Our bunker was named Dundee. Denzil said we could have walked to the real one in the time it took us to navigate the crowded camp. I checked the numbers on the sides of the beds against those printed on our passes. It was a bit like hunting for cinema seats. The cots were uninspiring, single residency affairs that came with a pillow, a sheet and a blanket. I sat on mine and bounced up and down appraisingly.

'I've never been to prison,' I said. 'But I imagine the beds are similar.'

'Probably covered in more fluids though,' said Denzil. 'Just like on the A level Biology trip.'

'Oh, shut up,' I said with a groan.

'You lying on the top bunk and Pete the Penis Rimmington rubbing one out below.' He started laughing.

'I said, shut it.'

'Puffing and panting…' Denzil made a bunch of sex sounds and hand gestures.

'You're obsessed with Pete Rimmington.'

'Pete *the Penis* Rimmington,' he replied. 'Please, Gibby, he worked hard for that title. Let's not do the gentleman a disservice.'

'I want to see if I can find these kennels,' I said, changing the subject. 'You coming?'

'No, I was just pretending,' he said with a stupid smile.

'Ha ha.' I concluded I must have done something bad in a previous life to be exposed to this.

We wandered about until we saw a map of the camp fixed to a wall.

'This place looks pretty decent,' said Denzil. 'There's toilets, showers, a medical centre, mess hall and even an information desk.'

'Nothing about a phone or a kennel though, is there?'

'Well then, let's go and ask one of those friendly soldiers.'

I asked the first armed guard we encountered. It turned out there weren't any telephones, but we were right next door to the kennels.

'That's good then,' I said to Denzil. 'We won't be too far from Ziggy.'

'Yeah, or the smell of piss.'

We soon found a door with a sign saying, *Royal Army Veterinary Corp.* Unfortunately, we also found an armed guard who wouldn't let us enter.

'Visitors aren't allowed,' he announced with all the sympathy of a robot. He followed this up with a moody, 'Move along.'

After the third 'Move along' we decided to heed his advice and headed to the showers, which by this point were most definitely in order. Just like elections where some people's logic dictates that if you don't vote you can't complain about future policies, I felt that if we didn't wash ourselves we couldn't bitch and moan about the smell of our fellow refugees. And to be fair, there was a lot to bitch and moan about.

We arrived back at our beds post an ice-cold shower to find a married couple in their early thirties with a child sitting on the cots next to ours. Their names were Ryan and Steve, and their inquisitive two-year-old was Mary. They were warm and friendly and I liked them immediately.

'We live in South East London,' said Ryan. 'We were on the way back from Steve's parents near Gloucester when it started.'

'The road was blocked by three overturned cars,' said Steve. 'So, Ryan got out to see if he could help.'

'The cars were empty,' said Ryan. 'But there was blood, and lots of it.'

Mary came and sat on Steve's lap. 'We decided to turn around and start driving back along the road,' he said, cuddling her, 'which is when these horrific creatures came racing out of the woods.'

'We managed to outrun them,' said Ryan. 'But it was a damn close call. By the time we'd reached the next village, the things were everywhere.'

'We hit one of them,' said Steve. 'The car's a total write-off.' He looked at Ryan. 'I have no idea what we're going to tell the insurance company.'

'I think that's the least of our concerns.'

'We hid in the car for about an hour,' he continued, 'ducking down as low as we could. But it's a nightmare when you've got a two-year-old with you.'

'We had to turn it into a game,' said Ryan as Steve stroked Mary's hair.

'In the evening we saw lights on in the local church and hammered on the door until the vicar let us in. It's a miracle we didn't attract the attention of any monsters.'

'Tony the vicar was amazing,' said Steve. 'They all were.'

'The old ladies made a real fuss of Mary,' said Ryan. 'We basically drank tea, ate biscuits and prayed.'

'We're not religious,' said Steve, 'but it's amazing how much you're willing to believe when your life's in danger. Hypocritical, I know.'

'Sensible, I'd say,' said Denzil with a warm smile.

'Better to be safe than sorry.'

'So how did you end up here?' I asked.

'Well, we were there for two nights,' said Ryan.

'The night time was the worst,' added Steve. 'That's when the monsters would come out. You could hear them fighting with each other and one even tried to get inside the church.'

'The doors were rock solid, though. Thank God, if you'll excuse the pun. On the third day a convoy of soldiers passed through the village and the vicar ran outside and flagged them down.'

'It was frightfully brave,' said Steve.

'It was such a huge stroke of luck that the soldiers were passing by,' said Ryan.

We shared our story, well, most of it, because it seemed prudent to leave out some of the more fantastical details. But the conversation inevitably took a sadder turn as we spoke about Lucy and the family and friends we hadn't been able to contact. Being in almost constant fear of death had a way of focussing the mind on a single purpose. So, as terrible as it sounds, I had only periodically thought about my parents. But now it hit me and I felt it in the pit of my stomach. As Denzil shared how we lost Lucy, I felt an overwhelming sense of shame and guilt.

'It was my fault,' I said to no one in particular. 'I shouldn't have made her go with them.'

Steve looked at me. 'It's not your fault, Jack,' he said gently. 'You were trying to do the right thing.'

Denzil gave me a much-needed pat on the shoulder. 'Don't blame your-self, mate. No one else does.'

'Lucy might.'

'No, she wouldn't. She was injured and needed medical attention. Trying to help her was the right thing to do. Don't ever forget that.'

'I fear we'll all have lost people we love by the time this nightmare's over,' said Steve.

Ryan put his arm around him and looked at their daughter. 'We've still got Mary,' he said quietly.

'Yes. We've still got Mary.'

While Ryan and Steve took their daughter to find provisions, Denzil and I lay on our beds discussing our greatest albums of all time. We didn't man-age to agree on the top spot, but it was between Hendrix, the Stones and The Beatles. I did have to spend a couple of minutes batting away Denzil's per-sistent attempts to include a greatest hits album. This was in the form of Bob Marley's *Legend*. He only shut up when I said we could do a list of greatest hits albums as a separate category. Man, we knew how to have a good time. We were halfway through a murderous a cappella rendition of Marvin Gaye's 'What's Going On' when Denzil sat up.

'Heads up,' he said. 'Fit alert.'

I turned my head to see two women walking towards us.

'Look at that blonde,' said Denzil. 'If I got my hands on her she wouldn't be walking for a week.'

'Only a week? You must be losing your touch.'

'Please be next to us. Please be next to us. Please be next to us,' said Den-zil, followed by, 'Try not to fuck this one up, Gibby. We all remember Ibiza.'

Irritatingly, there wasn't enough time for me to tell him to piss off with-out the women hearing.

'Hi ladies,' he said with a big smile. 'My name's Duke Smith. Welcome to Dundee.'

'The words I've always longed to hear,' said the Asian woman sarcastically.

The blonde looked him up and down and laughed. 'So, you're the local tour guide, then?'

'Well, Dundee is the city of discovery. So maybe we can "discover" some things together.'

'I think I can live without discovering herpes,' she replied with a smile.

Denzil laughed and grabbed his chest as if wounded. 'Ouch! Burn!'

'And what's your name?' she asked, turning her attention to me.

'Jesus,' I replied, pretending not to notice Denzil's reaction to the name.

'Of course it is.' She laughed. 'So, we have royalty and the son of God for neighbours. I never knew Dundee was so prestigious.'

'Well, it is the home of marmalade and a number of video games, plus it's built on a volcano,' said the Asian woman. We all turned to look at her. 'My uncle used to live there,' she said with a shrug.

'And what are your names?' asked Denzil.

'I'm Francesca,' said the blonde woman, 'but do call me Fran. And this is Riya.'

Fran and Riya were students in their final year of a history and philosophy degree at Magdalen College, known as Oxford University to the intellectual peasants among us.

'We were in the middle of a seminar about epistemology,' said Fran.

'No way,' said Denzil and Fran stopped to look at him. 'We were too,' he said and Fran started to laugh like a goat before hitting him on the arm.

'We could hear people screaming from somewhere in the college,' continued Riya more seriously. 'Our professor opened the door and these monstrous creatures ran up his clothes and started attacking his face. I don't know what would have happened if Tarquin, who's captain of the rowing team and built like an ox, hadn't given the professor a jolly good shove in the back with his foot. That sent the poor fellow flying into the corridor and then Tarquin was able to slam the door shut.'

'We had to break a window and jump down from the first floor,' said Fran. 'Christina hurt her ankle and, er…' She started welling up and Denzil didn't miss a beat, placing an arm around her shoulder.

'Shh. It's okay, Fran, you're safe now,' he said, giving me a sly wink. Thankfully her friend didn't see it.

'What Fran is trying to say,' said Riya, 'is that not everyone was as lucky as we were.'

'How did you get here?' I asked.

'We were picked up by a chap from RAF Brize Norton. He'd driven to Oxford to collect his sister and bring her to the camp. They saw us running along the side of the road and picked us up.'

'That was lucky,' I said.

'It was jolly lucky,' said a tearful Fran.

'Have you heard from your boyfriends?' asked Denzil.

'We don't have boyfriends,' answered Fran earnestly and I could see the smile twitch at the sides of Denzil's mouth.

Despite our social and educational differences, we shared the same sense of humour. The four of us must have hung out together for a good hour, chatting and laughing. Riya was smart, posh and pretty, and I was embarrassed when Denzil decided to lend me some unwanted assistance.

'You need to watch this bloke, Riya,' he said, smiling. 'He's a right player.'

'Is that so?' she replied in her perfect Queen's English.

'Seriously,' he continued, 'he's a total womaniser.'

I rolled my eyes. The guy was killing me.

'So, what do you chaps do for a living?' asked Fran.

'Well,' said Denzil. 'You know the Red Arrows display team?'

'Yes?'

'Well, we're the guys that train them.'

Fran did another goat laugh. 'I'm being serious, silly.'

'Okay, okay,' said Denzil. 'You got me. No, actually we design racing yachts.'

'That's marvellous.' Fran sounded impressed. 'Daddy's just bought a cabin cruiser. It's fifty-nine feet.'

'They're lying, Fran,' said Riya.

Fran looked at Denzil.

'Busted,' he said with a smile.

Riya smirked. 'I think you both do thoroughly boring office work.'

'If you can refer to what Duke does as work,' I said, 'then you're in the right ball park.'

'Charming,' replied Denzil.

Riya looked at me and raised her eyebrow. 'It seems that I can read you like a book, Jesus,' she said.

'I wouldn't be so sure,' I said with a grin.

Riya looked amused.

We spent the next two weeks in the relative safety of the camp, hanging out with our new group of friends. And while we did hear about fights breaking out and a few people having things stolen, we were fortunate never to encounter any trouble directly. Mary was a super cute kid and a constant source of entertainment. She took a particular shine to Denzil, who seemed to have a never-ending supply of patience, enthusiasm and ways of keeping her occupied. Steve turned out to be a massive music fan, so we were able to pull him into our nerdy discussions. There was much heated debate over the ultimate greatest hits album, which resulted in Steve choosing Madonna, me going for Queen and Denzil arguing passionately for his hero, Bob Marley.

Despite the closeness of our new little community, I began spending more and more time alone with Riya. She told me all about her childhood in Sunningdale, her school years at Wellington College and her trips to see family in India. She talked for hours about her love of food, classical music, Bollywood, physics, Jane Austen, drinking fancy gin in even fancier London hotel bars and Oxford University. What impressed me the most was that when I told her about my dull existence she seemed legitimately interested. Perhaps it is the way you tell it, after all.

As time passed, my feelings for Riya grew. Our refugee camp romance finally blossomed with a late-night kiss on Carnaby Street. The encounter sparked a few days of excessive PDAs and Denzil and Fran telling us more than once to 'Get a room.'

Thoughts of Lucy would drift into my brain from time to time and leave me feeling guilty, as if somehow I was betraying her memory. But each time they appeared, I would wrestle them aside. If the last few days had taught me one thing, it was that life was both short and precious, and I needed to enjoy it whenever and wherever I had the chance.

It was nearly a week after our first kiss that I awoke to see the outline of Riya's face peering down at me in the darkness.

'Follow me,' she whispered.

I was still fully clothed, so I slipped out of bed and put on my trainers. Riya took my hand and led me silently through the sleeping camp.

'Where are we going?' I asked, but all I got by way of a response was, 'Shh!'

As we reached the women's toilets, Riya giggled and dragged me through the door.

'What are you doing?' I asked, freaking out. 'I'll get arrested.'

'Live a little, Jesus,' she said, pulling me into one of the cubicles. Riya locked the door and we stared at each other for a moment under the harsh lights. 'Would you like to?' she asked suggestively.

I regarded the grubby toilet behind her. 'I prefer to go alone,' I replied.

She laughed. 'No, silly billy, I mean would you like to have sex with me?'

'Oh,' I said, as the memory of the bathroom incident at Ashbury Hall popped into my head. 'That sounds amazing, but I don't have a condom.'

Riya smiled. 'Don't worry, Jesus. I've got one we can put on your little Ferrari.' She took my head in her hands and started kissing me. When I didn't reciprocate, she pulled away. 'What's wrong?' she asked, as a woman gave birth to a Kraken a few stalls down.

'Nothing,' I lied.

'Don't you find me attractive?'

'Of course I do.'

Riya tried kissing me again, but I gently pulled away.

'Are you serious?' she said.

'I'm sorry.'

Riya glared at me as the Kraken master muttered 'Oh dear,' and, 'Not on my jeans.'

'It's not you,' I said.

'I know it's not. Do you know how many men want to sleep with me?'

I had no idea how to articulate the loss of Lucy. But I liked Riya and I didn't want to hurt her. So, I opted to tell her how I wanted our first time to be special.

Riya softened as the compliments flowed, until she was smiling again. We ambled back through the camp with our arms around one another and squeezed into my tiny single bed. We then spent some quality time making out. Despite the awkwardness of our conversation in the toilet and her surprisingly fiery response, at least Riya liked me. And along with her warm body that felt good. As I drifted off to sleep I felt a happiness and relief that I'd not experienced for a long time.

Sadly, nothing ever lasts.

CHAPTER 16

I felt it as I was falling asleep but decided it could wait. Unfortunately, 'it' didn't agree with me.

I was so horrendously tired and so wonderfully happy pressed up against Riya's warm body that I couldn't be bothered walking all the way back to the toilets. However, the last thing the modern man about town needs while lying in bed next to a woman he's trying to impress, is to do a big old plop in his undies. So, I decided to take care of the situation.

As I slid out of bed, Riya woke up. 'Are you okay?' she asked.

'Yeah,' I whispered. 'Go back to sleep.'

'Where are you going?'

'I'm just off to spend a penny.'

'Oh.'

More like blow the national budget I thought, as I slipped on my trainers and set off across the base.

Soldiers were patrolling with machine guns hugged to their chests, but there were almost no civilians. A woman walked past in a long coat, with her arms crossed and her shoulders hunched. Her body looked strange, like it was too wide for her small head. It reminded me of NFL players in their winter capes. I smiled, receiving an icy glare for my trouble. So much for British people coming together in a crisis. I wondered if they really had been more united during the Blitz. But as my brain clicked into gear I realised she may just have lost her entire family and friends. The last thing she'd want was some random guy smiling at her after she'd just finished a tricky poo.

The lights in the gents were so bright that they hurt my eyes. I decided that I needed to be quick to reduce the chance of Riya thinking I'd gone to pinch a loaf. A week into the relationship was too early to be sharing that kind of information. I walked into the first cubicle, soundproofed the toilet bowl with a layer of tissue, whipped down my jeans and boxers and placed my pasty-white bottom onto the ice-cold seat. Leaning forwards with elbows on knees, I pondered life to a soundtrack of my own flatulence. I missed my old world. The dull, boring, ordinary life I used to resent but which I now realised was pretty damn good. Straining hard to give nature a helping hand, I suddenly felt light headed. One moment I was sitting on the toilet and the next I was flying through space.

Unhindered by anything as mundane as a rocket ship or space suit, I glided at godlike speed past planets, stars and meteors. I traversed galaxies in the blink of an eye, seeing every atom and every subatomic particle. Losing speed, I moved purposefully towards an area of the cosmos where light and matter fell into nothing. I crossed the black hole's event horizon without spaghettification and dropped down through a tunnel of light, shooting past the elongated ghosts of stars and planets shimmering from ages past. The noise was incredible, increasing with the momentum and causing my vision to blur and shift. I traversed space and time, moving through it, passing beyond it, warping it like an infinite clay to my own ends. Then everything stopped and I was floating in silent space. Before me lay a giant golden planet orbited by six great moons. The specks of light marking the celestial bodies that hung in eternity started to blink out one by one, until I was enveloped in darkness.

I woke up on the toilet floor with my boxers and jeans around my ankles and pins and needles in both of my legs. I climbed unceremoniously back onto the pan and hoped Riya hadn't been waiting up. Wiping as fast as I could while maintaining the appropriate standards of hygiene, I flushed the toilet and cursed a number of times as the blood rushed painfully back into my legs. As soon as I was able, I hobbled out of the cubicle. Deciding that because I'd been gone so long speed was no longer a concern, I took my time washing my hands. A man in his forties wearing a long coat finished up at a urinal and joined me at the sinks. As I took one last glance at my tired face in the mirror and rubbed some sleep from my still unfamiliar blue eyes, the chap spoke to me.

'I don't suppose you've got the time, have you?'

'Sorry,' I replied, 'I don't have a watch.'

'Me neither,' he said. 'My wife bought me one for my birthday. Not much use wrapped up in her bedside drawer at home though, is it?'

'That is annoying.' I yawned and walked past him to reach the hand dryer.

'I'm Brian,' he said, offering a smile and a hand for me to shake.

'I think I'll wait for you to wash that first,' I said with a smile of my own.

Brian barked out a laugh. 'Quite right.'

The air dryer roared into life and I stared at my hands as I half-heartedly rubbed them together. I felt so tired that I could have fallen asleep on the spot.

The attack came from behind. Something dark was placed over my head and I received a firm thump in the solar plexus. This knocked the wind out of me and caused my legs to fold like a piece of pissy paper. Once on the ground, I was struck several times in the ribs, head and back. The hood was lifted momentarily so a cloth could be rammed into my mouth with a force that left me thinking I might be about to lose some teeth. I was carried face down through the camp at speed and into what I guessed was a lift. I received another couple of kicks at that point, presumably to keep me docile. Then we began moving again and I heard the sound of various doors opening and closing. Finally, I was forced down into a chair and had my wrists tied behind my back. I heard another door closing followed by nothing but a deathly silence. As I sat there waiting for God knows what, I realised I'd not even tried to fight back, a thought that only added to the sense of complete helplessness.

I was breathing so hard that I must have been on the verge of hyper-ventilating. Images flashed through my mind of surgical tools, car batteries, chainsaws and waterboarding. I began to shiver uncontrollably despite the warmth of the room. My body hurt like hell and I could feel blood running down the side of my face. I wanted to scream for help, but I knew instinctively that was a bad idea.

As I attempted to get my breathing back under control, I remembered a film I'd once seen about a South African police officer and a writer. The writer used her imagination to escape the cruel torture to which she was subjected. I tried to focus my mind on anything other than my current situation. 'Too Much Too Young' by The Specials popped into my head. I'm not sure how much it helped, but I was still hearing Terry Hall's vocals looping around my throbbing skull like a broken record when someone entered the room.

A chair scraped along the floor and the hood was lifted from my head. I screwed up my eyes to protect them from the blinding light that was being projected right at my face. As my vision adjusted I looked down and saw a shiny metal table. A large mirror I assumed was two-way glass dominated the wall to my right and there were cameras in the corners. If you've ever imagined an interrogation room, this was probably it. I glanced around, searching for a table holding nightmarish implements of torture, and was relieved not to see one.

My attention was drawn to the woman sitting on the other side of the table. It was the Grand Master from the car crash. She was wearing a big coat like the lady I'd smiled at on the way to the toilet. Except hers was wide open and I could see she was wearing thick body armour underneath.

She gave a sharp intake of breath. 'The eyes,' she whispered. 'It can't be.' She looked legitimately confused, like someone had just told her the only part of your reflection you can lick is your tongue.

I stared at her for several seconds like a piece of roadkill right before it gets squished. Drops of blood fell from the cut on my head, making pattering sounds on the table. I really wasn't in optimal condition.

'Who did this to him?' she asked.

Turning my head to look in the mirror, I saw the Scottish man from the crash site standing behind me.

'We may have dropped him en route.'

'Where did you drop him? Down the entire lift shaft? I know you're angry, but this is not the way.' She stared at him and her next words came out like ice. 'And if I find so much as another hair out of place on his head, then you'll answer to me. Do I make myself clear?'

'Yes Grand Master,' he replied. I was concerned to note the hint of defiance in his voice.

The woman turned her attention to me and adopted a calm, business-like manner. 'Hello Jack,' she said.

My confusion kept me silent.

The Grand Master smiled. 'I'd like to ask you some questions,' she said. 'Would that be okay?'

'Yes,' I said tentatively. I was hardly in a position to say no, was I?

'Thank you. There's really no need for this to be an unpleasant experience.'

'It's already pretty unpleasant,' I replied, tasting the blood in my mouth.

She nodded. 'I'd like to know a little more about the car accident. There was a road crash and you hit a black SUV. Travelling in the SUV was a strange-looking man with pale blue skin. The man died, but you spoke with him.'

I stared at her with my eyes half closed and tried not to pass out. Where the hell was Antony when I needed him? Maybe Denzil was right: perhaps he was part of some evil global conspiracy.

'What did he say to you?' she asked.

My head drooped. I could hear loud noises coming from somewhere in the distance, although I wasn't sure from exactly where.

'Go and investigate,' ordered the Grand Master and the man left.

The woman stood and walked around to my side of the table, before untying my hands. Then she smiled. 'It's okay, Jack, I'm a friend.'

I stared at her in disbelief, which is quite tricky to pull off when your head's wobbling about on your neck like a melon on a pipe cleaner. First Lady Ashbury had wanted to be my friend and now this lunatic. God knows what my car had crashed into back in the Cotswolds, but it sure had made me popular.

'We don't have much time. I need to know what happened.' There was an urgency to her voice as she gently took my head in her hands to stop me from keeling over.

'There was a blue light.'

'Did it touch you?'

'Yes,' I said, as what sounded disturbingly like an explosion occurred off in the distance.

Her eyes went wide. 'Where did it touch you?'

'I…I swallowed it. It felt cold.'

'And then?'

'I don't know.'

The sounds in the distance grew progressively louder and the Grand Master took me by the shoulders. 'Are you seeing things?' she asked. 'Are you having visions?'

I thought about the strange dreams but didn't reply.

'I need to know!' Her voice was taking on an increasingly urgent tone.

The noises continued to get louder.

'Tell me what you've seen,' she demanded.

I could hear gunfire.

'We don't have any time,' she said as she lifted me to my feet like I was made of feathers. Pain shot through my body. 'The blue light is an ancient psychic energy called the Ternion.'

The explosions and gunfire were getting closer.

'It wasn't coincidence that brought you and the Ternion together. I think it was searching for you.'

The idea of light having conscious thought was bloody ridiculous.

She glanced at the door and then at me. 'You are the last of your kind, Jack. Born with incredible abilities for which they will try to kill you. I can help you, but you need to come with me, right now.'

The Scottish man burst through the door. 'We have to go,' he shouted.

'You need to come with us, Jack. I can help you.'

I quickly concluded it probably wasn't in my best interests to go gallivanting off with these nut jobs. I decided to keep it polite. 'I can't,' I said.

'Time's up,' said the man as he marched out of the door, his long coat trailing behind him. I noticed he was also wearing heavy body armour underneath.

'Wait here, Jack,' the Grand Master said. 'Once my forces have taken control of the facility, I'll come back for you.'

'What about all the soldiers?' I mumbled.

'You're talking to the woman that infiltrated Gandareen.'

I had no idea what Gandareen was, but she sounded pleased with herself, so I assumed it must be impressive.

The Grand Master sat me back down in the chair, leaving me to ponder my fate. I placed my head onto my folded arms. Incredible abilities? Was she high? That's certainly not how anyone I'd ever met would describe me. However, even if she'd spent the past few hours in a meth den, I knew the blue light had been real. My musings ended when the door burst open.

'It's okay, Jack,' said Antony. 'This will make you feel better.' There was a sharp sensation in my neck and then the pain and fatigue were replaced by an intense energy. I felt amazing. As soon as the cuffs were off I was up and following him out of the door, wiping blood from my face as I went.

Stepping into a corridor, I was confronted by a group of soldiers sporting futuristic body armour and clutching insane-looking guns.

'On me,' said Antony as we marched down a complex series of pipe-lined tunnels. The sounds of gunfire echoed around the base as we stepped into a lift. En route back to the surface I asked about my friends. 'Don't worry, they're being extracted as we speak.'

Once again Antony was saving our sorry behinds. That's when I decided Denzil needed to drop his mad conspiracy theories. Antony was on our side. The Grand Master on the other hand, was to be avoided at all costs.

We stepped from the lift and passed through several heavy doors until we reached the outside world. After more than two weeks in that smelly camp the morning air was like fresh water in the desert. I sucked in great lungfuls as we passed the hustle and bustle of vehicles, machinery and armed soldiers running towards the battle raging somewhere in the base. Fortunately, they didn't seem interested in us. I looked up once more at the thirty-metre-high concrete walls peppered with watchtowers, and tried to imagine the original purpose of such a place.

Sitting in one corner was a huge helicopter. It was hard to say what colour it was, because it blended in perfectly with its surroundings. I could have easily walked past it without giving it a second glance. The strangest thing of all was that it made no sound. As we approached the machine, I bent double. This was something I'd always assumed was to prevent cranial amputation from the whirling rotors. I now realised its main benefit was to stop you from being blown bum over brains by the downdraught.

As we climbed in through the open door I saw that it was filled with more of the sci-fi soldiers. I was herded like a rogue sheep up a flight of stairs to a smaller room directly behind the two pilots. Strapped to each wall like tourists on a theme park ride were Denzil, Riya and Francesca. My heart surged when I saw them. I sat down next to Denzil and metal straps appeared from nowhere like robotic snakes, sliding around my body to hold me in place. I looked around at the interior but there was no sign of Ziggy.

Denzil's eyes widened when he saw me and he mouthed, 'Are you alright?' I nodded, but he looked a long way from convinced. When I mouthed 'Ziggy?' he just shook his head. I felt a pang of sadness. After all we'd been through, I didn't even get to say goodbye.

Silently we bade farewell to terra firma and my furry little friend and began our ascent. Thoughts swirled inside my brain like a tornado. Who was the Grand Master and her Scottish pal? Why was I having such weird dreams? What did they mean? Why was she so bloody desperate to know about them? And where was my dog? Only one thing was clear: Antony was on our side. I sat and watched the dead-eyed soldiers sitting opposite. It was a bit like being on the Tube, minus the dirty windows, the drunks and the rancid seats. With their body armour and guns, the soldiers looked cool as shit.

A series of loud thuds wrenched me from my daydream and the helicopter banked sharply, causing my stomach to spin. The soldiers' suits sprouted helmets like Transformers and they were up and moving towards a door in the side of the craft. As they slid it open a giant red-eyed bat the size of a tiger flew at the doorway. The soldiers opened fire and it dropped out of the sky. Unfortunately, the thing wasn't alone. Through the gaps between the troopers I could see hundreds more racing across the sky towards us.

The thuds and bumps increased in number and intensity and I realised we were under attack. The soldiers shot bats out of the sky with seemingly little effort, but the beasts had one big advantage: numbers. At one point a mass of creatures ploughed into the soldiers and I watched in horror as a man was pulled out of the door. He was immediately covered in a swarm of the beasts and pulled down to his death. But what was most shocking about that whole incident was when the soldier came flying back in through the window. I would have spent more time on that one, but there was a terrible bang and the helicopter began to spin. At the mercy of some pretty severe physics, I hung on for dear life. Fortunately, the straps held me securely in place. Denzil, Fran and Riya were screaming like banshees, which was impressive because I was too afraid to make a sound.

The soldiers started jumping out of the helicopter and I honestly believed they were leaving us behind to die. Then my harness released and one of the faceless warriors carried me like a sack of scared potatoes towards the door. Rows of small houses lay below me like a model village. I only had a moment to notice this before I was involuntarily ejected from the helicopter. However, instead of falling out of the sky like a pair of stones, we were travelling horizontally. My overloaded nervous system couldn't process it at the time, but we were actually flying! It was hard to enjoy it though, when the sky was filled with a swirling melee of soldiers and bats locked in mortal combat. We raced between them, the wind pummelling me in the face as we dodged from left to right and up and down. Leaving the carnage behind, we descended towards a vast sports stadium that I guessed was a mile or so to our left. The speed at which we travelled caused my head to wobble on my neck like a newborn baby. Although, unlike an infant I managed to avoid peeing my pants.

We glided into the stadium, landing smoothly near the centre of the pitch. As soon as the soldier let go my legs gave way and I stumbled sideways like a drunk, landing unceremoniously on my face. Looking up from my pile of jittery limbs, I knew exactly where I was. I was slap bang in the middle of Twickenham Stadium. I knew this because my Uncle Barry was a massive rugby union fan and after Thomas died, he started taking me to games with him and my cousin, Daniel. I thought about Daniel then. He had Down's Syndrome and it broke my heart thinking about how he might be processing the nightmare unfolding around him.

Antony lifted me to my feet. 'Can you walk?'

'I think so,' I replied tentatively.

'Then walk.'

I looked up at the stands and my heart sank. Hanging from the underside of the roof like a bad David Attenborough documentary were hundreds of the giant bats.

'Oh, my good God.' Riya appeared beside me.

'Maybe now's not the best time to be upsetting him with blasphemy,' I said.

'Head for the players' tunnel,' said one of the soldiers, and I ran like an overly sensitive bottom after a slice of salmonella pie. I was only a quarter of the way there when horrific screams erupted from the stands. They'd seen us!

The flying monsters dropped from the roof and swarmed up into the great big blue, turning in unison and arcing back down towards the stadium. I heard random shouts as we raced across the pitch like Australia's Trae Williams, except slower and less likely to survive. I sprinted past the soldiers, who were busy firing skywards at the entrance to the tunnel, and continued through a set of doors. Bats and soldiers poured in behind me, clambering over the floor, walls and each other as they tried to reach their prey, which sadly in this case was us. There was a spine-chilling scream and Francesca was attacked by one of the red-eyed monsters.

'Help!' she cried in hopeless desperation.

A soldier opened fire, but not before the bat had ripped out her insides. I watched with a kind of detached shock as she crumpled to the ground. Her mouth filled with blood and her eyes scanned the ceiling until they glazed over and she went still.

Riya screamed and tried to reach her friend, but a soldier dragged her away by the arm. We were ushered further and further into the building and as we moved through each new door, the number of monstrous pursuers diminished until we finally escaped. The predators' bestial screams were now replaced by Riya's. She was hitting the soldier with her free hand. He released her and I grabbed her and pulled her away. Riya's rage evaporated and she clung to me and began to sob. I tried to comfort her, but it was a token gesture. I knew nothing could soothe the pain of her loss. At least, I thought nothing could, as I watched a soldier jab her in the neck with a black pen and the subsequent expression of confusion on her face.

'The pain's diminished, Jack,' she said slowly.

'Over here,' said Antony, throwing a large black bag onto the floor.

The soldiers began retracting their Transformer helmets like a Mexican wave. What surprised me about them was the diversity of the fighting force. Men and women of every ethnicity were represented. Whoever these warriors were, they were certainly equal opportunities employers.

'Suit up,' said Antony, as he pulled clothing like his from the bag, throwing items unceremoniously at our feet. 'You need to put them on naked or they won't work.'

'I'm not getting changed in here,' said Riya.

Brilliant. So I'd have to wop it out in public.

We each grabbed a suit, gloves and boots, all of which looked far too big. Denzil was clearly relieved to be getting rid of his fashion faux pas. I turned my back on the group of soldiers, deciding it was better to flash the ring than the ding-a-ling, and stripped down to my birthday suit. I put the heavy garment on as quickly as I could, not wishing to expose my bottom for any longer than was strictly necessary. The outfit immediately shrank to fit my body. Despite how heavy it felt when I was holding it, once it was on it was weightless. Hell, I felt weightless. I tapped the rock-hard chest plates. I looked ripped, like a superhero. A soldier snatched my phone from my hand and slapped it against the outside of my thigh. I watched as the suit absorbed the handset.

'Pretty cool, huh?' she said with a smile.

I grinned back at her. 'You're telling me.'

'We can't stay here,' said Hager. 'Look at the claret on the walls. It's a tomb.'

I took in my surroundings for the first time.

'Whatever made this mess could come back,' added another soldier.

'Quite right,' said Antony. 'Let's keep moving.'

Riya had been touched by melancholy again, which considering what she'd just witnessed was understandable, so I put one of my newly buff arms around her shoulder and tried not to stare at how cool it looked as I comforted her.

'It's so unfair,' she said.

'It's certainly a big old shit sandwich,' said one of the soldiers who'd been listening. 'You just need to shut up and choke it down.' She shrugged. 'Or bitch and die. It's up to you.'

Riya hugged me. 'Francesca's gone,' she whispered. 'My sweet friend is gone.'

I gave her a gentle squeeze. 'I'm so sorry, Riya.'

Antony fell in step beside us as we were shoved onwards through the stadium's interior. 'Bit of bad news I'm afraid,' he said. 'There's reports of enemy troops in the area.'

'Which enemy?' asked Riya.

Antony ignored the question. 'Your suits will help you with what we're about to face,' he continued. 'Now please listen carefully. These are top secret prototypes. With the mask down, you can survive under water or even in space for up to ten minutes. After that point you'll need a source of oxygen such as the air around you for it to replenish.'

'Wow,' said Denzil.

'Wow indeed,' said Antony. 'They can absorb both extremely high pressures and temperatures and, due to an advanced exoskeleton, they will support your bodies and reduce fatigue by up to five hundred per cent. Oh yes, and the masks are equipped with night vision and infrared with enough magnification to see most targets.'

'How do you control them?' asked Riya.

'It's all powered by thought.'

'By thought?' He'd most definitely lost the plot.

'Yes,' said Antony, as if it was the most logical thing in the world. 'Have you not seen mind-controlled prosthetics? It's a similar principle, only infinitely more advanced.'

'What about relieving yourself?' asked Denzil.

'Just go right ahead and the suit will take care of the rest,' said Antony.

Riya looked appalled.

Antony pulled me to one side. 'Are you okay?' he asked, his eyes sweeping over my face.

'Thank you for bringing my friends.'

'Well, I didn't think you'd be very happy if I left Denzil behind, and he seemed adamant he wouldn't leave the others.'

I thought about poor Ziggy and hoped he'd find a good home. 'I can't believe what happened to Fran,' I said, as the reality of the situation dawned on me.

Antony peered at me closely. 'What did the woman say when she interrogated you?'

I wondered how he knew it was a woman. 'Oh god, all sorts of crazy stuff about energy and abilities. I think she might have been on something.'

'Well, she's certainly insane. Unfortunately for you, she's also very dangerous.'

'She said she wanted to help me.'

'She would hardly admit to wanting to kill you.'

My heart skipped a beat. 'Kill me? Why?'

Antony ignored the question. 'As soon as I heard they'd infiltrated the base I came looking for you. And it's lucky we arrived when we did. They're highly skilled at extracting information. You wouldn't have lasted long.'

I thought about the exchange with the Grand Master and the beating I'd received. But somehow she didn't seem inherently evil. But then I guess toxic people don't come with a warning sign. I desperately wanted answers to the questions swirling around my brain. What did Antony, the Grand Master or the late Lady Ashbury want with me? And what about the blue light? Was it really an ancient energy source, as she had said? All I knew was Antony was a master at avoiding my questions and it was becoming rather irritating.

A few minutes after receiving further instructions about operating the suits, and assuring Denzil that despite the state of my face I was okay, we stood in a deserted entrance hall, staring at a coach parked outside. Several creatures perched on top of it resembled the green parakeets you get in the area, only significantly bigger and more demonic.

'Engage masks,' said Antony, and his face disappeared from view.

Despite feeling marginally confident that the man was talking a load of bollocks, I willed the mask to cover my face. And guess what? It only bloody did. It was such a shock that I panicked and willed it straight back off again.

Antony glanced over and laughed. 'They do take a bit of getting used to,' he said.

I looked at Denzil and Riya who appeared to have had no such issues. Show-offs! We followed the soldiers towards the door and I re-engaged the mask. This time I knew what to expect and despite the strange sensation, I was able to breathe normally.

'The key here is speed and aggression,' said Antony as we reached the glass doors. 'No matter what happens, just keep moving towards the coach. Understood?'

We said yes, which appeared to be satisfactory enough, despite Riya sounding like she was thoroughly unsure about the whole endeavour.

We burst through the doors and ran towards the large vehicle. The birds screeched and threw themselves at us, slamming some soldiers along with Denzil and my good self into the ground. The soldiers made quick work of killing them and then we were manhandled onto the coach. I raced to the centre of the vehicle and was relieved to see the last of our party clambering onto the bus. We were safe. At least, I thought we were. The engine rumbled into life and the driver pulled away. I guess we made it about a quarter of a mile from the stadium when our party bus began drawing unwanted attention from the local wildlife. It started with a number of foxes the size of bears with missing fur and flesh. You could see the exposed jaw bone and huge fangs on one of them, which was particularly disgusting. These were then joined by an assortment of what might once have been cats, rats and even a giant bloody chinchilla.

The driver joined the A316 so fast I thought the coach was going to flip over. But no matter how hard he pushed the lumbering vehicle, it wasn't quick enough to shake off the disastrous menagerie in hot pursuit. As we raced along the road I glanced out of the rear window and my heart sank. The land-based predators were growing in number and worst of all, they were now being joined by more of those appalling bats and parakeets.

It was going to take a miracle to outrun them.

CHAPTER 17

Even at full speed the coach was horribly slow. It didn't help matters that the driver was forced to swing from side to side to avoid the abandoned vehicles littering the road. There were so many that he had to drive straight through some of them, and all the while the monsters were getting progressively closer. I was told to keep my head down as the soldiers took up defensive positions against the descending cloud of death. I opted to park my backside on the floor and hold on to the nearest seat with the superhuman grip you can only achieve when you are absolutely bricking it. About a millisecond after my butt eagle had landed, the fight began.

The beasts crashed into the sides of the coach in horror-inducing waves, triggering a response from the soldiers akin to the finale of a New Year's Eve fireworks display. Windows evaporated under the barrage and I heard thumping sounds as worryingly large dents started to appear in the roof. The soldiers spoke calmly to one another as they directed their defence. I marvelled at how the helmets allowed me to hear their voices despite the fight unfolding around me. The volume of animals started to become almost overwhelming, but every time a monster made it into the coach it was blasted right back out again. Well, right up until the explosion, that was.

A flash of biblically white light illuminated the world, before the back end of the coach lifted off the ground. Soldiers were thrown to the floor and out of windows, while animal parts splattered across the coach's interior, as if launched from a sawn-off shotgun. The vehicle spun ninety degrees and tipped onto its side, sliding along the road in a shower of sparks before screeching to a halt. There was a moment of ear-ringing silence, offering a harsh counterpoint to the explosion. Then, from my crumpled heap on the floor, I heard the sound of gunfire.

'The Fallen,' shouted a soldier.

Another warrior stood up and something hit them in the neck. The great lump fell on top of me and lay perfectly still. Panic gave me a cuff around the back of head as I realised the supersuit hadn't saved them. A firefight exploded into existence and I felt myself being pulled out from under the corpse by my leg.

'Get up!' Denzil's words cleared away the gloopy fog filling the Victorian streets of my mind.

'There's too many of them,' said a soldier.

'Go on ahead,' said Antony, 'we'll hold them off.'

'What about you?' I asked.

'I can track your suits. Now go.' He turned and leapt from the vehicle, weapons blazing.

Denzil dragged me along the side of the bus that was currently serving as the floor, while pushing a crying Riya ahead of him. He looked a bit like those overwhelmed parents you see out shopping on Saturday afternoons with an entourage of badly behaved kids. The noise from the battle was terrifying and I could only watch as Denzil kicked a hole in the cracked windscreen. 'Come on!' he shouted.

As we crawled out of the ruined coach I realised luck had kindly positioned a large red car to our left, affording us limited protection from the battle.

'Hurry up!' cried Denzil, as he and Riya sprinted along the road. Glancing back, I saw the soldiers engaging an enemy who looked as well kitted out as themselves. I knew I couldn't stay where I was, so I took a deep breath, kept as low as I physically could and ran like a jacked-up cheetah.

'What the hell just happened?' I shouted to no one in particular, as more explosions echoed behind us.

'How the hell should I know?'

We snaked as fast as we could between the abandoned vehicles while Denzil handed out useful advice such as, 'Run, then!' and, 'Hurry up, you pair of pricks!' What can I say? The guy was a real motivator.

Then I saw them, or at least I thought I did. So, despite the bullets zipping and pinging all around me, I turned and ran back towards the white van we had just passed. The passenger door was wide open and my mask zoomed in on the set of keys I'd noticed moments before in the ignition.

'Denzil?' I shouted.

'Keep moving,' he replied without looking back.

Riya was sobbing by this point and I wondered if the suits could also process tears and snot. Ignoring Denzil, which I did on a regular basis anyway, I jumped into the vehicle and turned the key. The van's engine started immediately and I set about chasing them down the road. Once alongside my friends I shouted, 'Get in', which I'm pleased to say they did. Well, Denzil threw Riya in, but it's the same difference. Then I floored it as fast as I could away from the battle.

There were so many abandoned cars that I was forced to utilise the foot and cycle paths. This didn't lend itself to speed or comfort, but we had no other choice. I noted absentmindedly that the interior of the van was filthy. There were bits of plumbing detritus scattered everywhere and a dirty old mug containing the dregs of cold tea was sitting in the cup holder. Most surprising of all was the extensive collage of lewd furry pictures decorating the inside of the sun visor. The owner was clearly a connoisseur.

We must have stuck out like a tortoise tit in a trifle driving along that abandoned road, and we only made it about six hundred metres before a group of bats attacked. They swarmed over the roof like a horde of oversized wasps. At one point a baby bat slid slowly down the windscreen with a confused look on its face. Upon seeing our masked kissers, its rage returned and it began screeching and displaying a set of fangs of which Bram Stoker's Dracula would have been proud.

My helmet zoomed in on the road up ahead and my heart sank like the Mary Rose. Twickenham Bridge was completely blocked by cars. Out of options and motivated by a keen desire not to stop and get eaten by monsters, I took the last turning before the bridge on the left, a street known as The Avenue. It was around this time that a much larger creature appeared on the windscreen and the two monstrosities began fighting with one another. Thanks to those selfish pricks I could barely see where I was going. Fortunately, this area of Middlesex was home turf for me and Denzil, and into the frontier town of my wild brain rode a proud sheriff of a plan. Well, more like an embarrassed deputy trainee.

'Watch out for the sharp turn,' shouted Denzil. However, in light of my terrible idea this didn't overly concern me.

'We need to get into the water,' I shouted back.

'You what?'

'The suits will protect us.'

'I'm not getting out of the van,' shouted Riya.

'We don't need to,' I replied.

'Well, how else are we going to jump over the railings?' asked Denzil.

I glanced at him and despite the masks he knew exactly what I was thinking.

'Oh, dear God. Please tell me you're not,' he said.

'Not what?' asked a concerned-sounding Riya.

I ignored them both and focused on the plan at hand. I was gambling that those railings were old and decrepit enough that a van travelling at a suitable speed would be able to plough right on through. I kept my foot flat to the floor, willing the functional automobile ever faster. As the van topped eighty miles an hour, the grotty mug rattled in the cup holder. I wondered if this was how Evel Knievel had felt when he was about to undertake one of his jumps.

In my head I went down the life-coaching route and visualised the van bursting through the railings and landing in the water. In the imaginary landscape of my head it all seemed so simple. Despite the bats crawling all over us, I wound the window down a couple of inches to aid our escape once we were in the river. I'd seen something about that in a movie once. By this point Denzil and Riya were screaming at me to stop, but with a lot more expletives and references to my wavering sanity, but I had my pretend life coach willing me on inside my head and no desire whatsoever to let him down.

My plan was hit by a minor setback when I discovered the railings were significantly stronger than those in my visualisation. The van crashed headlong into the metal bars amidst the cacophony of our screams. Unfortunately, the vintage safety measure that had guarded the riverbank since the late 1800s rose to our challenge magnificently and buckled but somehow held firm. Bloody British engineering! Thus, while the back wheels of the vehicle lifted an impressive distance off the ground, the machine remained safely on dry land. All was not lost, as right at that moment Mr Momentum swooped in to save the day. We were propelled like rag dolls through the windscreen and out over the water, collecting some rather surprised-looking bats en route. Which is why, kids, you should always wear a seatbelt. After travelling a number of somewhat frightening feet, we arced downwards and splashed inelegantly into the murky water of the River Thames, landing amidst a jumble of bats and limbs.

The impact with the water absorbed our velocity and we came to an abrupt stop no more than a couple of metres below its previously smooth surface. The humans and the bat monsters, neither of which were in their natural habitats, set about panicking and splashing. I couldn't tell if I was upside down or downside up, so I waved my arms like a lunatic to fend off the bats and kicked hard several times with my legs. Then I was free.

It took me a couple of seconds to get my bearings, but I soon realised I couldn't hold my breath any longer. I had an exploratory attempt to see if I could breathe underwater in the supersuit. The first couple of inhalations were nervous, stuttering affairs, but it worked. I spent a few seconds floating underwater while I adjusted to the strange sensation. Thanks to the suit, my visibility was good and I quickly spotted Denzil engaging in a deranged synchronized swim with one of the bats. I swam towards him, which was surprisingly easy in the strange outfit. Grabbing an arm, I pulled him out of the melee.

'Can you breathe?' I asked.

'Yes,' he replied as I felt something touch my shoulder and spun around to see the murky figure of Riya in front of me. I reached out and grabbed her with my left hand. The bats' frantic splashing began to slow as one by one they surrendered to an eternity in the embrace of Mother Thames.

'We've got ten minutes of air,' said Denzil, 'so what's your plan?'

'Can you swim?' I asked them.

'So that was your master plan, was it?' replied Denzil, sounding irritated. 'Brilliant.'

'We need to get as far along the river as possible before we climb out,' I replied. Like he had any better ideas.

'We're not going to get far in ten minutes,' said Denzil.

'We will if we use our feet,' said Riya.

'Oh well, thanks for that, Einstein,' replied Denzil. 'Really useful. Did you buy your way into Oxford University?'

'Not helpful, mate,' I said.

'Maybe if you'd let me finish, you ignorant oaf,' said Riya, 'I could explain.'

'What's your idea?' I asked her, and felt Riya squeeze my hand.

'We're wearing antigravity boots,' she continued. 'And if the soldiers can use them to fly through the air, then surely we can use them to propel us along under water?'

'That's actually not all that bad,' replied Denzil. 'In fact, it's pretty clever.'

'You're welcome, you utter plonker,' said Riya.

'But we don't know how to use them,' I said.

'We do,' said Riya in the tone of a teacher. 'Antony explained it to us. We just haven't used them yet. That's the difference.'

She was right, of course.

'Remind me,' I said.

'Let's grab hold of each other and try it.'

'We're already holding on to each other,' replied Denzil sarcastically.

'It's not against the law to stop being an ignorant arse once in a while.'

I laughed.

'Shut up, Mr Under the Thumb,' he said, as a dark shadow appeared to my left. 'Bro's before—' Denzil stopped.

'Bro's before what?' asked Riya with a sharp edge to her voice. In some ways she and Lucy were similar. Neither of them took any shit.

Denzil let out a shrill scream as I was hit in the side by what felt like a speeding car. As I looked down I saw my waist residing in the mouth of a truly huge river monster. The grip I had on my companions was surprisingly firm however, and as such, when I was pushed through the water at a confusingly fast speed, my colleagues came along with me.

They say that when you're in the midst of a crisis it's important not to panic. But then, 'they' are never bloody there, are they? In that moment I felt like I had no other option. My mind went as blank as a blank sheet of paper as we raced along the riverbed in a hail of bubbles and flailing limbs. I prayed the suit would afford me better protection than the soldier back at the bus. I also hoped I could get free of this creature before the ten minutes of oxygen ran out. Then it hit me. The boots!

I tried to clear my mind. Quite a feat when a giant fish monster was trying to eat me at high speed. But I focused on the antigravity boots and used the imaginary lever in my head, just like Antony had told us. Taking a firm grip on the sticks with my pretend hands, I edged the controls forwards. Then, just as suddenly as this shitshow had begun it was 'Bye bye, fish face' and off we went. I'd clearly overcooked it because the force was incredible! The beast let go as the three of us were instantaneously propelled up and out of the water. We flew through the air for about thirty metres, then skimmed along the river's surface like some strange-shaped stones.

When I saw Kew Bridge up ahead I started freaking out. We were on course to crash right into it. Despite my fear I managed to move the levers forwards and we rose skyward, flying up and over the structure. A momentary slip in my concentration and we were crashing back down into the water on the other side. We must have struck, hit, collided, smashed, snapped and bounced off every bit of junk in that water. Our chaotic journey along and often in the River Thames continued as we shot past islands, under and over bridges and around bends. We spent time both above and below the water, but the suit was affording me superhuman grip, so there was no way I was going to let go of my friends any time soon.

The river run lasted for what felt like a lifetime, but was in reality more like a couple of minutes at the most. Without warning, the adrenaline stopped and rational thought returned to my brain. After a couple of seconds, I was able to imagine the levers in my mind again and I gradually lowered the output of my boots until we were travelling at a far more manageable speed. I visualised flying a couple of metres above the water surface, which caused us to level out. This was a point worth noting: not only could I control the suit with the mental levers, I could also control it by imagining the desired state.

'Hold on,' I said with some degree of confidence. 'It's time to slow this crazy train down.'

Denzil and Riya responded by flapping around in the wind on either side of me.

I slowly reduced both speed and height and braced for impact. But I was starting to get the hang of it by this point and executed a classy finish, like waterskiers gently losing speed. We came to a halt and bobbed up and down with our masked heads poking out of the water.

'Now that's what you call an adrenaline rush,' said Denzil, laughing.

'Now that's what you call bloody awful,' replied Riya.

'This looks like it might be Chelsea Harbour,' I said.

'That's because it is, Jack,' she replied.

My heart skipped a beat, just like when you get caught in the act of doing something naughty as a child. 'How do you know my real name?'

'Denzil told me everything.'

'And you're not mad?' I asked, embarrassed.

'Why would I be mad? I think it sounds jolly sensible. Besides, I really like the name Jack.'

I felt like I was starting to get the hang of the antigravity boots by this point and used them to propel us towards the bank. I got a bit showy-offy after that and lifted us out of the water and up onto dry land. We retracted our helmets and sat down on the ground, and I lay back and gazed up at the clear blue sky. I smiled at the universe in general. I was just so damn happy to be alive.

It was Riya who broke the silence. 'I want a go,' she said. Even dishevelled she looked pretty. I wondered if we were officially an item now, but couldn't make my mind up. The rules of dating had always confused the life out of me.

'A go of what exactly?' asked Denzil.

'The antigravity boots, of course. It's important that we all learn how to use them. You never know when they'll come in handy.'

'I can talk you through it if you like,' I replied.

Riya laughed. 'Because you did so well. We only came close to meeting our maker fifty times.'

'Better to be close than dead.'

'Now's not the best time though, is it?' asked Denzil.

'Why not?' Riya placed her hands on her hips.

'Because, Jerome K Jerome, we don't have time to be messing about on the bloody river.'

'Er, I think you'll find that we're not three men, you idiot,' Riya retorted.

'You're telling me,' said Denzil. 'If we were, then this would be a lot more fun. Besides, women are terrible drivers.'

Riya looked like she was about to hit him. 'Actually, the stats clearly show women are better drivers than men.'

'Not in my experience.'

'Okay then, Mr Cretin, what evidence do you have?'

'Well, how many doughnuts have you done in Asda car park in Twicken-ham?'

Riya looked at him like he'd just stripped naked and started dancing about humming Christmas songs. 'Give me strength.'

'Thought not.'

'You really are chronically dumb.'

'Well, I may be dumb, but I'm still a far better driver than you'll ever be.'

'To be fair, you have written off two cars,' I interjected.

'Hey, the second one wasn't my fault. Have you tried eating a double whopper while driving around central London on a Saturday night on your phone? It's actually bloody difficult.'

'You're such a moron,' said Riya.

'Oh, pipe down. Anyway, I'm just stating a fact.'

'Well, you're a cock,' snapped Riya. 'How about that for a fact?'

I decided to wade in and break it up. Tensions were high and arguing wasn't going to get us anywhere, particularly when it was as unnecessary and unhelpful as this. I was ready to give a big presidential speech about how we needed to cast our differences aside and only through unity could we prevail, but Riya had other ideas and grabbed our wrists. Then, and not for the last time in my life, I was glad the suit could process wee.

We shot up towards the clouds at a sickening speed, while an angry Riya ensured that she most definitely did have 'a go'. The wind blinded me until I managed to re-engage my helmet. I looked down and to my utter dismay realised that we'd exchanged the relative safety of having a river below us for solid roads. Soaring over buildings, I felt my feet clip a number of roofs and chimneys. Then we made a stomach-spinning dive towards the streets of London town.

It was around the time that Riya shouted, 'Oh shit!' that I knew we were probably in some, and it was likely to be deep.

CHAPTER 18

I was a metre away from the mother of all face plants when I managed to engage my boots. It took every ounce of brain power to alter our trajectory. Unfortunately, I still wasn't fast enough to stop my chest and stomach from making contact with the road.

'Turn them off,' I shouted as we shot back into the air, holding on to each other for dear life. We twisted and spun through the deserted streets of the capital, bumping into an assortment of abandoned cars, signposts, bus stops and bins. It was a miracle we weren't decapitated. At one point we shattered the large window of a passing shop. Well, Denzil did: Riya and I were helpfully cushioned from the impact by his body. What a thoroughly decent chap.

After the broken window incident Denzil joined in with my new favourite pastime of shouting at Riya to turn her boots off. He wasn't as kind as I was, referring to her at one point as 'Dickhead Biggles.'

Desperate to slow down and born from my selfish desire to stay alive—I know, I'm a bad person—I switched off my boots and wrapped myself around Riya's lower half. I hoped that by humping her leg like a flying dog I could steer us in the right direction. However, it was right then that Riya got the hang of things and managed to cease her footwear-based propulsion. The event occurred so suddenly that we dropped out of the air like three futuristic-looking lead balloons and skidded and rolled for two hundred metres. By some miracle the supersuits cushioned our fall, yet afterwards they didn't have a single mark on them.

Once again I lay on my back and stared up at the peaceful blue sky between the buildings, and assessed whether I was about to crap, cry or create a pavement pizza.

'I'm sorry,' said a sheepish-sounding Riya.

Denzil ignored her. 'Are you okay, Gibby?'

'Well, I've not broken anything, if that counts.'

'You've not broken anything besides the window, the bus stop, the lamp-post and the roof of that taxi, you mean? Oh, and the statue.'

'Exactly,' I replied. 'Besides that.'

'I really am very sorry,' said Riya.

'How about you?' I asked. 'Are you okay?'

'Define okay,' replied Denzil.

'Look guys,' Riya insisted. 'I'm truly sorry.'

I sat up gingerly and retracted my mask. There was a strange smell in the air that I couldn't quite put my finger on.

'If I'd known what a pickle we'd be in,' she continued, 'I can honestly say with my hand on my heart that I would never—'

Denzil coughed, looking distinctly unimpressed.

'And I mean never, ever…Not for one single second. Not even for a single teeny, tiny second. And I mean a single—' Riya went quiet, her eyes widened and she sat up, looking around like a meerkat. A smile appeared on her face.

My heart sank like a stone life jacket. 'What is it?'

'Oh goody,' she said, pointing. 'We're outside Harrods!' You wouldn't think that moments before she had been rocketing through the air and screaming about not wanting to die. 'Come on, you two. Chop chop! It's time to go shopping.'

Annoyingly, Denzil looked just as excited. 'I bloody love this place,' he announced, scrambling to his feet.

I executed a confused shake of the head and a WTF facial expression by way of response.

'Oh do come on, Jack, you miserable so and so,' said Riya. 'It'll be fun.'

Denzil looked down at me. 'Yeah, cheer up mate, it's the sickest store in London.'

'Wouldn't that be a pharmacy?' I replied, reluctantly getting to my feet. But the two shopaholics weren't listening.

I followed them to the main entrance and watched as they pressed their faces up against the glass like kids staring through the window of a sweet shop.

'I think we should be careful.' I looked around at a deserted Brompton Road. 'We don't know who or what might be hiding in there.'

'I can't see anyone,' replied Riya.

'Nor can I,' I said without looking, 'but that doesn't mean they aren't in there.'

Being in central London when it was deserted like this gave me the willies. It was reminiscent of a dystopian nightmare. Riya seemed to have no such reservations, however, as she pulled the door open and gestured for us to enter with an elaborate bow.

'This way please, gentlemen,' she announced grandly.

I was the first to take a few valiant steps into what I prayed was an empty building. Looking around I could see no immediate damage to the interior, apart from a few luxury accessories lying on the floor, which seemed both comforting and suspicious in equal measure.

'Talk about the perfect place to hide while we wait for Antony.' Riya clapped her hands together in glee. 'What more does one need?'

'Keep your voice down,' said Denzil warily.

Riya shot him an irritated look, but did as she was asked.

'Why is it still in one piece?' Denzil seemed to be thinking along the same lines as I was. 'Surely, this would be the first place to get looted.'

'Perhaps Londoners were given a warning,' I said, 'and they all managed to escape.'

'But where to?'

'Well, I don't know. Maybe to the countryside in boats along the River.'

'All nine million of them?' Denzil wasn't buying it. 'That would take a hell of a lot of boats. I'd say people are more likely to try the underground or buses or even cars to flee. But I saw those abandoned in the streets when we flew over. If you can call that nightmare flying.'

'So where did they go, then?' I asked.

'Now that is a good question.' Denzil frowned. 'A very good question indeed.'

We walked further into the department store, which had an entirely different vibe to the busy Saturday afternoon when I'd last visited. It was actually rather pleasant not having to shuffle around, bumping into the crowds of toffs and tourists.

'Hello?' shouted Riya.

The sound sent a surge of adrenaline through my body and I froze, butt cheeks clenched.

'What are you doing?' whispered Denzil. 'Are you mental?'

We watched Riya listening for sounds with a smile on her face, and waited to be attacked. Several seconds passed and nothing happened, but my senses were still on a state of high alert.

'See?' she said. 'There are no monsters in here.'

'Did you bang your head when we crash landed?' snapped Denzil.

'Er, excuse me,' she said. 'Who's the one reading history and philosophy at Oxford?'

'So you're going to graduate and be qualified for absolutely nothing, then?' replied Denzil. 'Well done you.'

'Someone's bitter that they were born with the IQ of a lamp,' she said. 'A really ugly one.'

'I guess that's why I'm such a bright spark with an electric personality, unlike you, you librarian.'

'Ooh, cutting. What are you going to do about it? Slap me about with your—'

'For God's sake,' I interrupted. 'Will you two shut the hell up.' I felt a sudden pang for Lucy, who'd always adopted the role of parent. If only she was with us.

Riya and Denzil decided to take my advice. For all of two seconds.

'She started it,' said Denzil.

'Actually, I proved there's no one in here,' replied Riya.

They looked at me expectantly like I was some sort of referee.

'Yes, but we didn't know that when you announced our arrival so loudly,' I said. 'We could have been killed.'

Riya walked over to me, took my chin in her left hand, kissed me and smiled. 'It's okay, Jack Gibson. I'll protect you from the invisible monsters.'

'Hmm,' I said in response.

Drawing back, she stroked my battered face in concern. 'You got beaten up quite badly, didn't you? You still look really handsome, though.'

'I think I might puke,' mumbled Denzil.

Riya slipped her arm around my waist and I reciprocated.

'Denzil, I'm sorry for shouting,' said Riya, almost sounding sincere. 'It was reckless of me and I should never have done it. But you have to admit that's it's not a bad spot to hold up in a crisis.'

Denzil sighed. 'I suppose there are worse places to spend a couple of days in London. Hopefully, there's still enough supplies left in the food halls though, because I could eat a bloody horse.'

'There should be some good places to hide,' I added.

'Of course there will be,' said a jubilant Riya.

'But going forwards, let's agree to conduct our investigations with a little more discretion,' I said.

'Fine by me,' said Riya. 'Right. First things first, we're going to need new clothes. I don't want to keep this ghastly suit on forever.'

'You're seriously not saying you want to go shopping, are you?'

'Yes, Jack. That's exactly what I'm saying I want to do.'

'Now don't get me wrong,' said Denzil, 'Jack will vouch for how much I love shopping for sick new duds, but I'm not sure we should be taking these protective suits off. They're the best defence we've got.'

'Not right now, of course,' replied Riya, as if she was the sensible one in the conversation. 'But we should grab something for when the opportunity presents itself. I for one don't want to be wandering about au naturel.'

'Alright,' said Denzil with a smile, 'I'm in.'

A flicker of movement to my right caught my eye and I spun around. I scanned the store, but couldn't see anything.

'What's wrong?' asked Riya.

I looked about again, but there was nothing. I was so tired, stressed and on edge that I guessed I was starting to see things that weren't there. I wondered if this was how soldiers felt after spending time in a warzone.

'How do you know if you've got PTSD?' I asked.

'A sore helmet and smelly discharge,' replied Denzil.

'If you were any dumber you'd be a sponge.'

'Are you sure you're okay?' Riya started stroking the small of my back and staring at me intently.

'Yeah, forget it. I just need to get some sleep.'

I stared at the Egyptian-themed décor as we rode the central escalators. They'd come a long from the woven leather version that became England's first moving staircase way back in 1898. I'd always loved the design, but now it gave me unpleasant flashbacks to the dead blue bloke from the Cotswolds. Once upstairs, we spent the best part of an hour traipsing around the ladies' clothing departments, which contained the most insane evening gowns I'd ever seen. As I stared at a nasty £2,000 gold coat, I wondered at what price point fashion started to look cheap.

By now I'd survived monsters, a satanic cult and an interrogation, but I'd not been so close to laying down and dying as when I was listening to

Riya and Denzil discussing different types of jackets. It took me five minutes to pick my items out from the men's section. Then, with our new designer clothes in our new designer backpacks, we followed Denzil back downstairs to the wristwatch department, which was actually a series of small, individual stores, although today they weren't populated by a host of staff and security guards trying to guess our bank balances.

I was both worried and impressed by the speed at which Denzil walked out the back and found the keys for the display cases. Apparently, a guy he knew used to work in this very department and had seen fit to share some of the security measures while shoving coke up his nose at a house party.

'You do realise this is theft?' I said, as he began perusing the obscenely expensive timepieces.

'Don't be soft. Look around, Gibby. In case you hadn't noticed, we appear to be living through the season finale of *The End of Days* show.'

'Hopefully not, Mr Positive.'

'Besides, you didn't look very bothered when you helped yourself to a £700 outfit.'

'Taking clothes for survival purposes is hardly the same as taking a diamond-encrusted watch,' I said, knowing I was on a slippery slope.

Riya smirked.

'Yeah, but £700 worth?' Denzil replied.

'But that jacket looked wicked with those jeans,' I said sheepishly and Denzil laughed.

It turned out that not purchasing an expensive watch is a rather time-consuming affair. So, I updated them both on my personal interrogation party with the Grand Master, along with my series of strange visions born from the absorption of a supposedly ancient psychic energy. Riya seemed more interested in the ladies' watches, but Denzil made up for it by ranting about wanting to knock them out, as he wrapped a £25k timepiece around his wrist. The supersuit absorbed the new watch and it disappeared from view. 'Energy sources contained within gold chests sounds like something out of an *Indiana Jones* movie. Maybe she's the granddaughter of a Nazi scumbag that escaped to South America after the war? I don't suppose she mentioned where this energy came from?'

'Nope.'

'What it does?'

'Sadly not.'

'Anything helpful?'

'Not much.'

'Well, she was about as useful as a tissue tarpaulin. The visions have to mean something, though,' he said, 'something important. Perhaps they're a clue?'

'But I'm just seeing planets and space and stuff. They feel more like random dreams than anything meaningful.'

'Yeah, but that Grand Master seems to think they're important. And it's a bit of a coincidence you're having visions after absorbing a psychic energy, especially when she thinks you have some freaky abilities.' He paused. 'Maybe one of those planets is important somehow?'

'Like how?

'Buggered if I know.'

'Thanks, Denzil,' I replied. 'Enlightening as always.'

'Well, when you have a better idea, let me know.'

I decided to keep quiet, because I really didn't.

We were starving by this point and concluded with no small amount of excitement that it was time to visit the food hall, although we opted for the Brasserie on the lower-ground floor as we felt it would be less exposed. As we approached the lift, I heard a noise coming from somewhere behind us.

'What was that?' asked Riya.

'Probably Gibby's smelly discharge.'

Riya squealed and I turned to see a woman scrabbling towards us on all fours. I guess the main difference between her and your run-of-the-mill lady was the two small horns protruding from her mousy brown hair. Oh yes, and the long thin tail flowing behind her. I started running before I'd even turned back around and as such ploughed straight into Denzil. We landed in a heap outside the lift. Riya screamed and hit the button. Unfortunately, the door wasn't ready to open and the female monster was getting closer and closer with her evil red eyes. The look they contained was pure predator. When the beast was ten metres away, I accepted my fate. When she was eight metres from us, Denzil and I were hugging each other and babbling like lunatics. Six metres and I remembered I was wearing the suit. Four metres and I shouted, 'Masks!' Two metres and I braced for impact.

Then she leapt.

I closed my eyes as the beast made contact, and placed all of my trust, slightly lacking by this point, into the supersuit. After the initial impact, which involved a hard body blow, a hand in the face for me and a scream from Denzil, I found myself trapped, waiting for the barrage of death-inducing blows to begin. But the violence I was expecting didn't come and I held my breath as the monster shifted around on top of us. Then, after several tense seconds I opened my eyes.

Now that I observed the creature up close and personal, she looked surprisingly attractive. Well, besides the two little brown goat horns and the tail protruding from her back end. But then beauty is in the eye of the beholder. Her outfit, however, left a heck of a lot to be desired, comprising an assortment of men's and women's clothing that looked like a wardrobe had vomited all over her. But the creature had zero interest in me. Her sole focus was on Denzil. Unfortunately for him, she didn't look happy. She moved her head in fast jerking motions while touching Denzil's mask. Then something truly bizarre happened. The monster that had charged at us with such finality folded her arms across her chest like a petulant child and made a 'Hhmph' sound. It was a bizarre sight to behold.

'What does it want?' whispered a petrified Denzil.

'I think she wants you to take your mask off,' said Riya, although she didn't sound convinced.

'Are you taking the piss? Have you seen the claws on it?'

The beast placed a hand on either side of his head, eliciting a squeal from my best mate. Then she sniffed his helmet and started shaking her head.

'She definitely wants you to take your mask off.'

'I'm not taking my bloody mask off!'

The more I observed the creature, the less afraid I became. Now don't get me wrong, the red eyes were a bit of a horror show and the sharp teeth weren't ideal, but she seemed more inquisitive than dangerous. It was obvious that she wanted Denzil to remove his mask, but for the life of me I couldn't understand why. I mean, who'd want to see his dopey mug?

I decided that if Denzil wasn't going to grow a proverbial pair, then I'd have to. I had no idea how quickly I could re-engage my mask once it was removed, but hopefully a bit quicker than the time it would take the she devil to rip my face off. So, despite being filled with a healthy dose of doubt, I removed the mask and promptly started crapping myself. The creature whipped her head around to look at me with her demonic red eyes and it was like staring at the personification of death. Then, she gave me one of the sweetest and most disarming smiles I'd ever seen before turning back to Denzil with a look of pure excitement. And I'm talking like a child on Christmas morning.

Riya removed her mask too. The monster started leaping up and down on the spot like a chimp. Unfortunately, the spot was Denzil and me, so it wasn't the most comfortable of situations. Finally, Doctor Denzil prescribed himself an intensive course of courage and his mask retracted into his suit.

I cried out as the beast lunged at his face. The speed at which she moved was terrifying. In a heartbeat she had wrapped herself around his neck and struck like a rabid vampire. Denzil screamed and Riya and I immediately re-engaged our helmets. Hey, I'm not proud of it, but you would have done the same in our situation. Yes, you would.

'Denzil?' I cried.

I heard Denzil's muffled voice. 'Jack?'

'Are you okay?'

'Well…' He sounded both frightened and confused. 'This may sound a bit on the weird side.'

'Tell me?'

'I think she might be kissing me.'

The creature lifted her head and beamed at Denzil.

'Oh my God, she likes you,' said Riya, in awe.

'You've got to be kidding me.'

The monster was pecking him all over the face and head at super-fast speed and despite the danger, it looked almost comical. After several seconds Denzil took her wrists and gently pushed her away, although this didn't prevent the creature from shooting her head forwards to land a quick peck on his forehead. Then she laughed and leapt backwards. I stood up slowly because I didn't want to startle whatever the hell the thing was, and looked down at her, if indeed it was a she.

'What do we do now?' asked Denzil as he got up.

'What do you mean, we?' I asked. 'She's your missus.'

'Piss off. I don't want that thing following me around like a bad smell.'

The monster skipped up to Denzil, stroked his face and leapt backwards again. The whole time her tail whipped from side to side like an excited puppy.

'Oh bless,' said Riya. 'Denzil's got a girlfriend.'

I laughed.

'She's not my sodding girlfriend,' he snapped.

'I'm not sure she'd agree with that.' I watched the creature approach Riya and have a brief sniff. Riya smiled while carefully extricating her hands. She pointed to herself and said, 'Riya' in the kind of sweet tone you usually reserve for small children.

'R'a,' said the creature experimentally.

'That's right. Riya,' Riya repeated with a smile.

'R'a,' said the creature, as she watched her with innocent, adoring eyes.

'She's so sweet,' said Riya.

'What do you mean, sweet?' said Denzil. 'It's not you she keeps trying to snog.'

'Well, it's not her fault she's got a ghastly taste in men.' Riya giggled.

The monster laughed. 'R'a,' she said again.

'What is she?' I asked.

'A pain in the sodding arse,' replied Denzil.

'Don't be horrible,' I said. 'She's like a child.'

'I've no idea what she is, Jack.' Riya reached up slowly and touched the horns, eliciting a high-pitched coo from the thing. 'She's clearly not human. Not with those. She's like no monster we've encountered so far. I mean, look at her, she's so sweet natured and my God, she's beautiful.'

'Beautiful?' snapped Denzil. 'She's got a bloody tail.'

'Do you think she might have been human at some point?' I asked.

'I've no idea,' answered Riya. 'But she's certainly got a humanity the other creatures don't.'

'And horns,' added Denzil. 'She looks like that guy in the original *Clash of the Titans*.'

'You've done worse,' I ventured.

'I've never done an animal.'

'Debatable.'

Riya took a step back and looked at the creature appraisingly. 'The poor thing can't go around looking like this, though, can she?'

'Can't she?'

'No, she can't, Jack. There's nothing else for it, we need to do some more shopping.'

So, despite the fact the whole goddamn world was falling apart, I was subjected to yet another shopping trip. It took well over an hour to get the creature dressed due to all of the wriggling and laughing that she engaged in. We also had to hunt down some scissors to cut a slit in the back of some ludicrously expensive stretchy jeans, so that she could poke her tail through them. Finally, our creation was complete and we stood back to admire our handiwork.

'She still needs a hat, coat and sunglasses,' said Riya, almost to herself.

'What the hell for?' replied Denzil.

'To hide her horns, eyes and tail,' I said.

'But there's no one here to see her,' Denzil protested.

Riya barked out a laugh and pointed at my best friend. 'Denzil,' she said.

'D'zl,' repeated the monster with a big smile.

Denzil looked at the creature like she'd just shat in his lasagne.

'Well, I very much doubt that your new admirer will want to stay behind when you leave,' said Riya.

I could see the cogs spinning inside Denzil's head. 'Oh no. There's no way that thing is coming with us.'

Riya sighed. 'Oh, Denzil, Denzil, Denzil.'

'D'zl,' repeated the creature.

'You really don't understand women at all, do you?'

By this point in proceedings I was so hungry I could have eaten a fried ferret, so we headed to the Brasserie via the Food Hall. This time we managed to successfully use the lift without being attacked by any more of Denzil's admirers. The only challenge was that the creature insisted on pressing all of the lift buttons, so it took a little longer than expected to get there. But once we did, we were confronted by an embarrassment of culinary riches. We must have spent well over an hour feasting on the amazing food.

As we ate, Denzil tried lecturing me about the dangers of Antony and how the monsters were probably part of a secret government experiment gone awry. But I was getting more than a little sick of his paranoia by this stage and while I knew he was only trying to help, it just irritated me. He gave up when I pretended to yawn.

We also made the most of the fine wines and spirits. Denzil was swigging from a gold champagne bottle at one point, and the more we drank, the more we relaxed. Eventually, we started to feel safe again, caught up in our own little bubble, tucked away from the horrors of the outside world. No one got up to use the toilet, so either my friends had developed huge bladders, or, like me, they were discovering that the supersuits really were handy.

As daytime surrendered to evening and then to night, I could feel my head start to nod. While still in a sitting position, I drifted off into a dreamless sleep.

I awoke sometime later with a head that was already pounding from the booze. Riya and Denzil were fast asleep, but the creature was standing a couple of metres away to my right and appeared to be listening to something. I closed my eyes and tried to do the same. A few seconds later I heard what sounded like voices and worryingly there appeared to be quite a few of them. The noise level increased as the intruders grew closer and the creature started hissing like an angry cat. I gave Denzil a firm nudge.

'In my mucky bum bum,' he mumbled, as he awoke with a long trail of drool hanging from his chin.

I tapped Riya on the shoulder and she re-joined the world with far more grace and dignity than Mr Reid. I placed a finger to my lips, signalling for them to keep quiet, before engaging my helmet. My friends followed suit if you'll excuse another pun, and once we were all safely sealed up inside I spoke to them.

'Someone's in here.'

'Who?' Denzil sounded half asleep.

I was about to answer when several people came strolling into the Brasserie dressed in dirty tracksuits, baseball caps and trainers. Scarves and bandanas covered their faces and they were carrying an assortment of home-made weapons. I shivered, counting at least twelve as they walked with the confident struts of complete arseholes.

'Well, well, well,' said one of them. 'Looks like we've found ourselves some perverts.' The others laughed and sneered. 'Nice gimp suits!'

'Oh, for God's sake,' said Denzil, 'We look like wrong'uns.'

'They're just trying to intimidate us,' said Riya.

'Then they're doing a pretty good job of it.'

'And what have we got here?' said another, much larger man with a tattoo on his neck. He was sporting a large, fresh-looking scar under his right eye. The man leered at the creature. 'I can definitely give you a good time, darling. Do you fancy having a bit of fun with me?' He grabbed his crotch. Then he noticed her horns and his eyes went as wide as buckets. 'Monsters!' he shouted and the entire gang charged at us. The game was afoot.

Now, I've never seen a skinny-arsed supermodel in a real-world fight and I'm guessing that I probably never will, but I reckon they'd be pretty damn useless. Those little emaciated arms against a big burly guy is never going to end well. Not so Denzil's new squeeze. The creature moved so fast she was quite literally a blur. The man nearest her swung a cricket bat towards her head, which she brushed aside with little to no effort, before tearing his throat out with her claws.

Seeing this, I was immediately up and running towards the fight. I've never been what you'd call brave, in fact I'm hardly brave at all, but whether it was due to being desensitised by all of our previous experiences, or whether I was subconsciously bolstered by the protection of the suit, I threw myself into the melee.

The beast lady was doing pretty damn well on her own, but despite who she was, or more to the point, what she was, I felt like she was part of our team now and we needed to help her. A woman slashed at me with a meat clever and I instinctively put up my left arm, causing the blade to bounce harmlessly off the protective garment. I followed this with a punch to the nose, then one to the stomach, and she dropped like a Led Zeppelin. My euphoria at being able to beat up a woman half my size while wearing a prototype military suit was short-lived, however, as I took a heavy blow to the back. I turned to see another woman swinging a vicious-looking baseball bat covered in nails at my cranium. As it made contact with my body for a second time, I lost my balance and collapsed face first onto the floor.

Now I was really screwed.

CHAPTER 19

I confess that seeing the souped-up baseball bat swinging towards my head was a sobering moment. Instinct made me roll to the left and my attacker screamed with rage as her bat struck the floor. I leapt to my feet just as a man swung a crowbar at me. It caught me square in the side of the head and, despite the suit, the force sent me stumbling sideways towards the woman like a human tennis ball. She raised her weapon to continue with the cranial rally and I found myself facing a potential knock-out blow, but then Riya appeared behind her and brained her with a champagne bottle. The woman fell to the ground and Riya struck her again, leaving blood smeared all over the bottle and a sizeable dent in the woman's skull.

Crowbar man screamed and flew at Riya, to which she responded by throwing the champagne bottle at his face. This was enough to divert his swing and he must have missed her head by an inch. I panicked when I saw the attack and charged headlong at the man, slamming him to the floor with the hardest rugby tackle I could muster. He was considerably bigger than me and on a normal day would have been far stronger. But this wasn't a normal day, because I had the supersuit. I grabbed the crowbar and we rolled on the floor in a desperate fight to the death. At one stage he got the upper hand with me on my back with the metal implement being pushed down onto my throat. There was pure violence in his eyes as the pressure increased. If it wasn't for the suit I would have ended up like Marie Antoinette, but with less cake. I kicked my legs, kneeing him repeatedly in the back, but no matter how hard I tried, I couldn't dislodge him. Then, in a moment of warped inspiration, I remembered the suit moulding itself around both my phone and Denzil's watch. If it could do that, could it be manipulated in other ways?

I tried to imagine the front of it turning into a bed of nails. I then watched with horrified interest as the man's eyes widened and blood appeared at the

185

corners of his mouth. I witnessed the light leave his eyes before rolling onto my side and pushing the guy off my suit, which was already returning to its original shape. I scrambled to my feet as the girl with the meat cleaver screamed like a banshee and swung wildly at Riya.

'Fucking die!' she shouted over and over, as Riya tried to defend herself against the baseball bat. But it was painfully obvious who knew how to fight out of the two of them. I immediately warped the suit into fist blades like Wolverine's. What can I say? I'm a fan. Then I punched the psycho as hard as I could in the side of the head. She died instantly and I was left staring in morbid fascination at the blades as they blended back into the suit. Turning to my left, I saw Denzil wrestling with two men at once on the floor, as his admirer grabbed a man twice her size and thrust her clawed hand into his stomach. His mouth flopped open and he gawped as she pulled out a bloody mass of organs, before stuffing them back inside via this alternative route.

As I watched the remainder of the gang turn and run from the food hall, I knew we'd won the greatest fight of our lives. After throwing the doomed man aside like a piece of rubbish, the creature's whole demeanour changed and she smiled and helped Denzil back to his feet, fussing over him like an over-protective mother. This time he let her get on with it. I looked around and saw complete carnage. Blood and body parts were everywhere. But hey, they started it.

I removed my mask and wrapped my arms around Riya. I could feel myself shaking from the adrenaline. 'Are you okay?'

'Yes,' she replied, sounding a little shocked.

'You were amazing,' I told her.

She smiled. 'Amazing at getting hit a lot.'

'Actually, Riya, you saved my life.'

'And you saved mine.'

We kissed and Denzil began making loud puking noises. 'Yeah, I'm fine too guys,' he said. 'Thanks for asking.'

I turned to see Denzil having his head being petted like a dog, and couldn't stop myself from bursting out laughing.

'Oh piss off,' he said.

'We need to give your girlfriend a name,' said Riya.

'No, we bloody don't,' said Denzil, trying to move her hands away. 'And she's not my sodding girlfriend.'

'But then what's the vicar going to call her at the wedding?' I asked.

Riya giggled.

'You'll be listening to a vicar soon,' said Denzil. 'At your funeral.'

'She needs something fitting, though,' I continued more seriously. 'Ordinary just isn't going to cut it.'

'How about Atalanta?' said Riya.

'You can't name her after a city,' replied Denzil.

'I didn't say Atlanta, you lamp.'

'Oh shut up, you librarian.'

'Atalanta was a mortal heroine from Greek mythology,' said Riya.

'Never heard of her.'

'Oh my God, Jack,' said Riya. 'She was so cool. She was left on a mountain to die as a child by her parents.'

'Oh yeah, that's cool,' said Denzil sarcastically.

'She was seriously cool, you buffoon. Her parents abandoned her as they wanted a boy and she was raised by a she-bear and then later by a group of hunters. But she grew up to be this beautiful and formidable warrior. Her name came from the Greek word *atalanta*, meaning 'equal in weight' because she could kick most men's butts.'

'Well, Mrs Reid sure can fight,' I said.

Denzil flipped me the bird.

'She was an amazing wrestler and runner,' Riya continued, 'and I think she might have gone on the Argonaut expedition with Jason and his chums and won a wrestling match against a hero called Peleus.'

'I bet she didn't have a lion's tail, though,' said Denzil.

'Well, it's funny you should mention that, lamp boy,' said Riya, 'because I think Zeus may have turned her and her hubby into lions because they had sex in his temple.'

Denzil looked at the creature. 'How do you fancy being called Atalanta?' he said.

'L'nta,' she replied.

'She can't even say it,' said Denzil.

'L'nta,' repeated the creature.

'Very well, then,' said Riya with a beaming smile. 'We shall call you Lanta.'

Looking around the room, I started to feel uncomfortable. 'I think it's time we got out of here. These scumbags could have friends.'

'Shouldn't we wait for Antony?' asked Riya.

'Absolutely not,' said Denzil.

I chose to ignore him. 'It's okay, he can track the suits.'

'Where are we going to go?' asked Denzil, as he fought to keep Lanta's hands away from his hair.

'My parents have a house just around the corner in Chelsea,' said Riya. 'It'll be empty. We could lock ourselves inside and barricade the doors and windows with furniture. My parents have got some awfully big pieces.'

'Is that a euphemism?' asked Denzil.

'Your whole face is a euphemism,' replied Riya.

'F'ism,' said Lanta.

I considered Riya's plan. 'Well, it's got to be safer that trying to defend an entire department store with a ton of unlockable entrances.'

'Fine,' said Denzil. 'Let's go to Chelsea.'

Riya added the coat, hat and sunglasses to Lanta's now rather blood-stained outfit and we headed for the main entrance on Brompton Road.

'We need a backup plan,' said Denzil as we left the shop. 'We've no idea who or what might be waiting for us in the streets.'

But we didn't make it to Riya's house in Chelsea. Hell, we didn't even make it to the next corner. As soon as we stepped outside, eight robotic figures descended from the sky like avenging angels, looking identical to the Iron Man character that had ripped off our van roof in the Cotswolds.

'You move, you die,' said one of the robots.

We put our hands up and tried to remain still. Well, Denzil, Riya and I did; Lanta just skipped about and hissed a lot.

'Be quiet,' whispered Denzil, but he clearly had as much authority as a cat herder, because she ignored him. Then they shot us.

I saw a flash of green light and then I don't remember a whole heap until I woke up in a small white box with a bench down one side and a shimmering, transparent wall of blue light on the other. Sitting up made me feel like I had serious motion sickness, so I placed my head in my hands. Keeping my eyes closed, I prayed for the feeling to pass. When the sensation had subsided enough for me to open them again, I noticed I was wearing plain white clothes.

'The nausea will wear off soon,' said a familiar voice.

I looked up. The psychotic woman who'd been my interrogator back at the camp smiled at me. I opened and closed my mouth as if trying to catch invisible flies.

'I understand how you must be feeling, Jack. And I'm sorry for how you were treated. But we are on the same side.'

How could this lunatic think we were on the same side after her soldiers served me a portion of kidnap cake with extra deep-fried kickin'?

'I have something important to tell you,' she continued. 'And I need you to listen to me. Will you do that, please?'

'Piss off.' I rested my head back on my hands. It wasn't the most mature or eloquent of responses, but it served a purpose.

'If you won't listen to me, then perhaps you'll listen to her,' said the woman, before turning and walking away. The shimmering blue light evaporated and another female walked into my cell. My jaw almost hit the floor and my heart started racing like Secretariat in the Belmont Stakes.

'Hello Jack,' said Lucy.

'Lucy?' I leapt to my feet. 'I thought you were dead!'

We hugged each other tightly and Lucy started to cry. The woman I loved was alive! She was alive and standing there in my arms. We started kissing, long, passionate, desperate and it was honestly one of the most incredible kisses I've ever had in my life. All the pent-up chemistry that had been bubbling away between us for almost two years exploded into existence like flowers on the first days of spring.

At some point we stopped kissing and just held one another. I don't know what she'd been using to keep clean, but her hair smelt wonderful. A surge of guilt hit me in the face like a speeding freight train.

'I'm sorry that I told you to go with them,' I blurted out. 'I should never have said that. It's all my fault.'

'It's okay, Jack.' Lucy held my head in her hands and kissed my bruised face. 'It's not your fault. You were trying to save me.'

We sat down on the bench, arms wrapped around each other. Being this close to her was amazing.

'Did they hurt you?' I asked, afraid of what the answer might be.

'No, not like that,' she said, kissing me again. 'Do you remember the soldier that shot at us?'

'He's hard to forget.'

'He was part of Charles's regiment, and a complete pig. He kept making jokes about torturing his parents and parties on their family yacht. He was a total nut job.'

I thought about the stomach-churning photos strewn across the floor in the cottage. Then about the beating in the toilets at Station Zulu. 'Where have you been?'

'I doubt you'd believe me if I told you,' she said. 'The woman you just spoke to is called Cleo. She rescued me from the soldiers.'

'That psycho rescued you?'

'Charles lied to us. They had a radio. Cleo heard them talking about us over the airways. Next thing I knew, robots were descending from the skies and all hell broke loose. Then they brought me here.'

'And where exactly is here?' I asked, looking around.

Lucy laughed. 'You wouldn't believe me if I told you.'

'Try me.'

She took a breath. 'We're in a secret base underneath the Levantine Sea.'

'The what?'

'The Levantine Sea.'

'Where's that?'

'Somewhere in between Beirut, Tel Aviv and Cyprus.'

'Bullshit.'

Lucy smiled. 'That's not the best part. It was built more than a hundred and fifty thousand years ago.'

'And Cleo told you this?'

'Yes.'

'Then it's definitely bullshit.'

'Cleo's going to explain everything,' she said.

'Cleo can go screw herself.'

'She told me what happened to you, Jack.'

'She bloody happened to me,' I said. 'Her and her friends.'

'That was really awful, but she told me she didn't ask them to hurt you and I believe her. I know you're angry, but she's on our side. You should listen to what she has to say.' Lucy stroked my face, then kissed me on the lips. 'Will you listen to what she has to say, Jack?' She kissed me again. 'Will you do that for me?' She gave me another one of her smiles.

I knew exactly what she was doing and it was working like a charm. 'Okay. I'll listen to her.'

Lucy grinned. 'Thank you, sweetie.'

At that moment Cleo miraculously reappeared. 'Come with me, Jack,' she said. 'I'll explain everything.'

I decided that while I may have just agreed to listen to the psycho, I sure as Sherlock didn't have to like her.

I held Lucy's hand as we followed Cleo and her armed guards through the unusual-looking building. The place appeared strange to my eyes and I tried to work out what it might have been made from. The floor and ceiling were a dull silver and the walls a pristine white. The style was utilitarian and I suspected military, but there also appeared to be a dash of psychiatric ward thrown in for good measure.

I asked one of the guards if they had a phone, but he said all the networks were down. As we walked through the strange building, Cleo fell in step beside me. 'We didn't get off to the best of starts,' she said, 'and I want to apologise.'

I was still angry, so decided not to respond in case I said something I might regret.

'I only asked them to bring you to me. I know it's no excuse, but the fate of the universe is at stake and sometimes the quickest route isn't the easiest. But for what it's worth, I'm sorry.'

Lucy squeezed my hand, but I remained silent. I didn't trust this woman. Despite the irritation that must have been written all over my face, Cleo forged ahead. 'Have you felt it yet?'

'Felt what?' I sounded like a petulant child.

'You must know you have a great talent.'

'Well, I can do a decent karaoke version of "Sex Bomb".'

'Before you lies an ocean of power. And if you let me, it would be my honour to teach you how to swim.'

We arrived at a door marked with hieroglyphs that disappeared then reappeared as we passed through it, and I found myself in a long oval room. An equally long table stood at its centre, surrounded by high-backed chairs. Everything was white and it all looked like some sort of science-fiction cliché.

There were people sitting around the table, wearing the same white clothes I'd just woken up in. I froze as I noticed my Scottish attacker smiling at me. Then, to my relief, I also saw my friends. Denzil and Riya jumped up and I dropped Lucy's hand like it was hotter than the desert sun in the height of a particularly fiery summer. I gave Denzil one of those awkward man hugs that guys like to do, as Riya used the time to fire daggers at Lucy. She followed this visual assault with an elaborate show of hugging me and enquiring if I was okay. Riya was glued to my side like a limpet when she asked far too sweetly, 'So who's this then, Jack?'

Lucy looked at me, looked at Riya and then looked like she was about to pee hot sauce. 'I'm Lucy,' she said, offering a hand.

Riya eyed it like it had been smeared in bubonic plague.

What on earth had I done? I'd never felt so awkward in my life. Well, apart from the time Jimmy Higgins's mum tried hitting on me in the kitchen at his twenty-first. She'd consumed a ton of wine and even more garlic, so her dog breath was off the charts. She spat in my face as she grabbed at my crotch and mumbled something about being 'Mrs Robinson', whatever that meant.

I had no idea how I was going to get out of the mess I'd just birthed. I was most definitely in love with Lucy and now I knew she liked me too. I was living the dream. And the kiss! Oh my God, that kiss. It was as if our bodies had been made for each other. But now there was Riya. Okay, so we hadn't slept together, but we'd been falling for each other, or at least I thought we had. We'd been through so much together in such a short space of time, and while we hadn't put a name to it, we were as good as an item. I liked her a lot. But now Lucy was alive and available. I'd thought I'd lost her. Pondering it left me feeling torn up inside. I didn't know what to do. However, there was one thing that I did know with cast-iron certainty. If Riya found out what had just happened with Lucy, I'd be a dead man.

My best mate had clearly read the situation, and like so many other times in my life he stepped in to save my sorry ass. 'Come and sit down, buddy,' he said, guiding me towards two empty chairs. I really do love that man sometimes.

Cleo stood at the head of the table and waited for the room to fall silent before she spoke. 'What you are about to hear will be hard to believe.' She paused for dramatic effect. 'But every word of it is true.'

I desperately wished in that moment to be safely back with Antony and his soldiers. In fact, anywhere was preferable to hanging out with this bunch of maniacs.

'Where's Lanta?' asked Denzil.

'The parasite,' replied Cleo with a look of mild disgust, 'is undergoing tests.'

'Don't call her that,' said Riya.

'You'd better not hurt her,' added Denzil.

Cleo's Scottish pit bull started to bark. 'Shut up and listen to the Grand Master!' The guy clearly had anger issues.

'Dickheads say what?' muttered Denzil.

'What did you just say to me?' replied the hipster beefcake.

'I rest my case.'

Lucy and I laughed, but Riya still looked like she was sucking a lemon, which I knew was all my fault.

'I'm going to kill you, you wee shite.' The man leapt to his feet, slamming his huge hands down on the table.

'Guardian,' cried Cleo in a tone that left no doubt about who was the boss. She waited for him to sit. 'Everybody needs to remain calm,' she continued. 'It's critical that you hear what we have to say.'

'Why should we,' asked Denzil, 'after what you did to Jack?'

'I wish certain things could have been avoided. But difficult times call for difficult actions. I have spoken to Jack and that incident is in the past.'

'Oh well, that's alright then,' said Denzil sarcastically.

'I'm your friend, Denzil,' she said. 'I'm on your side.'

'On my side?' He was unconvinced.

'Just relax, mate,' I said, trying to calm him down a bit. 'It's fine.'

'It's not sodding fine, Jack. These *Star Trek* rejects are a bunch of arse-holes, and this bloke,' Denzil pointed at the Guardian, 'is a total cu—'

The Guardian struck like a cobra. One moment he was sitting on his side of the table looking like he wanted to tear Denzil a new ring piece, and the next he'd leapt over said table, slammed Denzil to the floor and attempted to do so. I was on my feet immediately, guided by raw instinct and a dash of panic. I drew my leg back and gave him a Pelé-esque kick to the side of the head. Unfortunately, the footwear I'd been given had the rigidity of a slipper. So, while the Guardian was sent sprawling onto his side, I was forced to hop up and down, holding my toes and shouting, 'Bugger me' a lot. Clearly more used to combat than a junior project manager from Richmond, the Guard-ian jumped back up and punched me in the stomach. I buckled as memories of the refugee camp came flooding back. This time, however, I knew that Antony wasn't coming to save me.

I realised that I hated this guy more than I'd ever hated anyone, which is why once he was restrained and I was able to get back to my feet, despite the intense pain, I ran over and kicked him as hard as I could in the boy bits. And just like Fishman, his legs buckled and his face went a satisfying shade of red. His bulging eyes reminded me of one of those googly-eyed goldfish. Several people grabbed me, thus preventing any further attacks, although I did manage to throw in a choice 'Nob head' and a highbrow 'Come on, tit face!' I remember Cleo shouting at me to calm down, along with something about needing to listen.

'Why?' I shouted as I struggled to break free.

'Because everything you've been told about the world is a lie.'

There was a passion and sincerity in her voice that stopped me dead in my tracks. I stood there, restrained and panting. She finally had my attention.

It must have taken a good five minutes to calm the situation down properly. Denzil and I were told to sit at one end of the room and the Guardian was positioned at the other, in the way teachers separate naughty schoolchildren. Riya looked like she wanted to kill someone and I'm guessing that someone was probably me. When we were quiet, Cleo waved an arm and 3D holographic images appeared above the centre of the table.

'Brother Martin,' she said as a tall man with a thick grey beard and ponytail stood up. He looked like an aging seventies rocker.

'What I'm about to tell you is important,' he said. 'The Grand Master is right. Everything you've been told about the world is a lie and now you will learn the truth.'

'Talk about milking it,' whispered Denzil, as 3D footage of the earth's evolution appeared above the table.

Brother Martin continued. 'Most humans believe they evolved from single-celled organisms into the anatomically modern people of today. But what if I told you that you didn't evolve, you were created?'

'I'd say Billy bullshit.' Denzil sat back in his chair with arms folded like a stroppy teenager.

Cleo looked at him with an expression that was difficult to read, but probably meant she was trying hard not to murder him.

'Firstly,' said Brother Martin, 'human beings are not alone in the universe.' He paused and let that hang in the air for a moment like a smug professor. 'There are quadrillions of humanoids scattered across trillions of worlds. But there is one race who are quite literally the masters of the universe.' He paused for a moment. 'They are known by many names, but in the ancient tongue they are called the Hu.'

'Like the band?' Denzil looked at me and mouthed, '*Wankers.*'

'They are divine beings, and direct descendants of the creator Goddess, Hyrattanti.'

I shook my head. This made Lucy's claims about an ancient underwater base seem pretty pedestrian.

'Did they create us?' asked Lucy. 'Is that why we're called humans?'

Brother Martin smiled. 'They possess psychic abilities, magnified through the manipulation of gold. Their thirst for this precious metal led them to conquer most of the known universe. It's what brought them to earth and Mars four hundred and forty-three thousand years ago.'

'Are you high?' asked Denzil.

'No,' replied Brother Martin. 'Why?'

'Fair enough,' said Denzil. 'It's just that you're talking a complete load of bollocks, so I was just wondering.' He sniffed. 'Carry on.'

Brother Martin gave him a blank look and turned to Cleo.

'If you can't remain quiet, you will be returned to your cell,' said Cleo.

Denzil gave her his best 'I really couldn't give a toss' look.

Brother Martin continued. 'The Hu grew weary of mining, so they created a laboratory, called Edin. Here they spliced their DNA with what they viewed as the simple psychic hominids populating the planets, generating a new slave species. They were careful to deactivate the most advanced psychic abilities within the genome to ensure they could exercise control over their creations. They called the males Ademu and the females Evu, and collectively they became known as humans.'

I glanced at my conspiracy-loving friend, who despite his irritation now looked truly fascinated. I, on the other hand, was a little more sceptical.

'The Hu found their creations beautiful and against the wishes of the High Council started to breed with them. But for all of the Hu's genius, mother nature can be an unpredictable mistress, and their illegitimate offspring were psychic giants, born with a fully functioning genome. A combination of the most potent elements of both species, making them even more powerful than their Hu masters. Hyrattanti sent her elite troops, the Seraphim, to earth around thirteen thousand years ago to eradicate this new species. And for forty days and forty nights the skies rained blood and the land was flooded with the bodies of the fallen.'

Something about the story seemed vaguely familiar, but I couldn't quite put my finger on it.

Cleo walked to the head of the table. 'Thank you, Brother Martin,' she said. 'One of the High Council went rogue when he fell in love with the most gifted of the Evu, and she bore him two sons. When the slaughter began, a father's love forced him to betray the Creator Goddess and he gave them to a trusted friend, who hid them in a stasis chamber at the bottom of the ocean until such time that they could emerge in safety. And there they remained, first lost to memory, then history and finally legend, or so it was thought.'

An alarm burst into existence from nowhere. It was so loud and unpleasant that it made me jump halfway out of my seat. I prayed no one had noticed me do it.

A woman leapt to her feet. 'They've found us,' she shouted.

'Everyone to your posts,' cried Cleo.

I looked around like a surprised tortoise as our captors were up and running out of the door. Cleo grabbed the Guardian by the arm and said something to him. He nodded and left.

Cleo turned to face us. 'We're under attack,' she shouted over the alarm. 'Follow me.'

CHAPTER 20

My friends and I—assuming Riya and Lucy still wanted to be my friends after recent events—followed Cleo along a crowded corridor. People and aliens scattered in all directions as the underwater base suffered from a violent case of the shakes.

'Where's Lanta?' shouted Denzil.

Cleo ignored him.

'*Where's Lanta?*' he repeated with more gusto.

'There's no time,' cried Cleo.

'Where is she?' he shouted again and we came to a halt almost in unison.

Cleo spun around, grabbed him by the front of his shirt and slammed him against the wall. 'We're under attack,' she screamed. 'If we don't get to the fly-pods we're dead!'

'Who's attacking us?' demanded Lucy above the noise.

There was the sound of an explosion and the whole structure shook. Sparks rained down on us from the ceiling.

'Follow me to the upper level.' Cleo turned and continued along the corridor without so much as a glance in our direction. She was clearly used to people doing exactly what she said when she said it. But then she'd never met Denzil Reid.

Without a word, Denzil charged off into the depths of the underwater base.

'For God's sake,' I shouted.

'Go with him,' Lucy urged. 'We'll make sure they don't leave without you.'

I smiled at her, which won me a death glare from Riya, before taking a deep breath and setting off in hot or at least lukewarm pursuit.

We ducked, weaved and bumped into an assortment of people clogging up the corridors. Each time the base was struck by God knows what we were thrown to the floor or against the nearest wall. Some areas we ran through were pitch black and I almost lost my footing a couple of times. Periodically, small fires would burst into life, triggering the fire-suppression system to shoot targeted streams of gas at them. It was loud and it was frightening, and I knew the situation was quickly going south. I tried to avoid thinking about being trapped underwater in a glorified tin can. It made me think about how my parents would cope with never knowing what had happened to me. The outcome of that was anything but good. By now I'd also completely lost my bearings, although I decided that not having any clue where I was headed wasn't critical, because I was following Denzil. I just hoped he had some semblance of an idea.

We reached another large door that appeared to be without any handles or discernible way of opening it.

'Bollocks,' shouted Denzil, as he banged on it frantically.

'Why in there?' I asked.

'The cells,' he replied. 'That must be where they're keeping Lanta.' Denzil took a run up and charged shoulder-first into the door like a SWAT team creating a breach. Unlike a SWAT team, he bounced right back off it and landed on his bottom. I had to haul his stunned self back to his feet.

'Are you okay?'

He ignored me and continued banging on the door and yelling, 'Lanta?' at the top of his lungs.

My attention was drawn to an old skinny guy running towards us like he'd just crapped his pants. He must have been out of shape because he was puffing and panting like a necrophile in a morgue. Sadly, his portfolio of effort investments wasn't yielding good returns in the way of speed. I concluded that getting old really does suck. He was in uniform, which I guessed meant he was some sort of senior officer. As he was passing by, I lunged out and pushed him against the wall as hard as I could.

Usually I'm all about being kind to the elderly. Well, the nice ones. Some old people are downright mean. Mr Stephens from Number 42 was horrible to us as kids. He was always shouting and moaning. Every time we stepped outside the nosy tosspot seemed to be hanging about like a bad smell, checking to see we weren't up to no good. He burst Thomas's new football when it went into his garden once. The miserable old sod brought one to the funeral when he came to pay his respects. It was too late by then. You need to be nice to people when they're alive; it's no good to anyone once they're dead and gone. I told him as much a couple of years ago when he tried speaking to me in the street. I'm sure you can imagine how that went down with Harold and Brenda. I stand by my comments, though. He *was* a mean old dick with a face like a pigeon.

In this case, this old soldier was clearly part of Cleo's AI (Arseholes Incorporated), so I didn't feel much in the way of guilt about manhandling him. I grabbed the tops of his arms and he struggled to break free. Gills on the side of his neck opened and closed.

'Open that door,' I shouted in his face. I was trying to be intimidating and despite my relatively unassuming appearance, it worked like a charm. He stared at me with wild eyes then over at the door. 'Open it!'

The soldier took something from his pocket, waved it in the air and the door opened. Denzil snatched whatever it was from the chap's webbed hand. After that I let the old guy return to his incontinence workout. Difficult times called for difficult actions.

We entered a long room containing rows of white cells. As we ran past the strange selection of incarcerated creatures, the occupants implored us to set them free. Well, the ones that could speak English did, the others just made random noises. This presented a moral dilemma. If the base was going to flood, surely it wasn't right to leave them here to die. But at the same time, I had no idea why they were here. If I set the wrong inmate free, then I could quickly end up being best buddies with Casper the Friendly Ghost. I stopped next to one of the cells and gawped for a couple of seconds at what looked like a cross between a woman and a lizard. The creature stared back at me with emerald-green eyes and then threw itself against the bars of light and roared. This instantaneously caused my legs to resume their running motion. I decided that the decision to release the prisoners required more thought: a choice that would haunt me for some time afterwards.

At the end of the row of cells was a large white door that vanished when Denzil approached, allowing him to sprint right on through. I caught a fleeting glimpse of an operating theatre and two figures in surgical gowns standing with their backs to us. Just as I reached the doorway it closed again and I ran headfirst into the flipping thing. I have to say that for something that moments before hadn't existed, it was now really bloody solid and really bloody painful.

I didn't have time to worry about my bruised forehead and ego though, as I was distracted by the screaming emanating from inside the locked room. I pushed as hard as I could against that door, but I may as well have been trying to bench press the Empire State Building for all the good it did me.

'Denzil?' I yelled in desperation. 'Let me in.'

I banged on that strange door over and over in a state of panic.

'Denzil?'

'That won't open it,' came a familiar voice from behind me. I turned to see the nine-times winner of the Global Mr Prick Contest himself: the Guardian.

The door vanished as he approached, revealing an operating theatre in which Denzil was engaged in a stand-off with a man and a woman in futuristic surgical attire. They were brandishing nasty-looking silver implements while Denzil was wielding what looked like a pedal bin, although it might not have been to be fair, as we were on an ancient underwater base after all. Surely, they'd have a more high-tech solution than that? Denzil was using the bin like a Victorian lion tamer's chair to fend off the vicious beasts. Behind him on the operating table lay a sedated Lanta. At least, I hoped she was sedated.

'Guardian,' cried the woman. 'Thank the unspoken that you're here. This man broke in and attacked us!' She pointed at Denzil with no small amount of disgust.

The Guardian's expression remained implacable. 'What did you learn about the parasite?'

The medical staff looked a little surprised by the question, but quickly pulled themselves together.

'It's quite remarkable,' said the man, glancing nervously at Denzil and his weaponised waste disposal unit. 'Something has gone wrong with the process. The human DNA has dominated its development.'

'Meaning?'

'Meaning the parasite shouldn't develop with more than twenty per cent of the host's DNA. But this has more than eighty.'

The Guardian stared at Lanta. 'How is that possible?'

'Well, it's not,' said the woman. 'At least it shouldn't be. Something unique has happened here.'

'How unique?'

She considered the question for a moment and I used the distraction to edge closer towards the operating table. 'Somewhere in the ball park of impossible.'

The Guardian frowned. 'Will there be more of them?'

'That depends,' replied the man.

'On what?'

'Well, how often do you believe that miracles happen?' replied the guy with a smug smile.

'We've done what you asked,' said the woman, watching me touch Lanta's neck. I was relieved to feel a strong pulse. 'Now let us go.'

The Guardian maintained his frown as he pulled out a laser gun and shot the man in the head. The guy's brains went everywhere, with some of them spattering against my face and a respectable amount even landing on my lips. I opened one eye and saw him execute the woman. She, however, was kind enough to utilise the floor to store her exploded brains. Denzil pointed his pedal bin at the Guardian, while I wiped my face and gagged.

'Looks like it's your monster's lucky day,' said the Guardian. 'Get it on its feet or I'll terminate it.'

Denzil threw down his bin and turned to look at Lanta. 'Help me, Jack,' he said, and I tapped a series of random buttons on the side of the bed until the plethora of restraints vanished.

'Lanta?' I said, shaking her. 'Lanta, wake up.'

'Move out of the way.' The Guardian placed a mask with a canister attached to it over Lanta's mouth. There was a strange whooshing sound and her eyes snapped open. The Guardian immediately backed away and pointed his gun at her. 'Keep it under control or it dies,' he said.

We both agreed to the demand. Like we had a choice in the matter.

'Time to go.' The Guardian grabbed my upper arm and dragged me out of the room like a naughty child.

The base was in a terrible state by this point and the occupants had long since left. We exited via a different door and splashed through the water that now rather alarmingly covered the floor.

The Guardian seemed cold and unaffected by the chaos unfolding around us.

'Who were the doctors you killed?' I asked him.

'Hu genealogists. We captured them at Station Zulu.'

'Station Zulu?'

'That was no regular base.'

'But why shoot them?'

The Guardian looked even angrier than normal. 'My brother died in that raid.'

His words took me by surprise and I didn't know what to say.

'So you'd better be worth it, Jack Gibson.'

No pressure, then. What made it worse was that I had no idea what they wanted me to do.

'During the Gandareen invasion we discovered an ancient temple, resting sixteen miles above the planet's surface on the slopes of Mount Olyran.'

I frowned, recalling Cleo's comment that she had infiltrated Gandareen.

The Guardian broke into a jog. 'There we discovered a powerful ancient psychic energy that had the potential to destroy the Empire of the Gods.'

'The what?' I said, increasing my pace to keep up.

'The Hu's Empire.'

'No egos there, then.'

'We battled our way into the Temple at great personal cost. There we found a golden ark containing an energy source, known to the Gandareens as the Ternion.'

We arrived at a lift, which creaked as we climbed inside. There were strange hieroglyphics on the wall and the Guardian hit one that looked like a triangle with three dots below it. Denzil and Lanta only just made it inside before the doors closed. The elevator shook horribly in response to another huge explosion, and I was relieved when I felt us moving upwards. I have to be honest: throughout that lift ride I was bloody petrified.

'It requires an individual of immense psychic power to absorb it. The Gandareens were too afraid to even try.' The Guardian looked at me pointedly.

The bottom fell out of my stomach as I realised his implication. The blue light. 'So how the hell did I manage it?'

'Look inside yourself, Jack.'

An image of my internal organs popped into my mind's eye, closely followed by a voice saying, 'You're a moron.'

The lift stopped and the doors whooshed opened. The Guardian shoved us out into a hangar, which must have been close to a hundred metres in length. I wondered how big this base was. On one side of the room was a large window that appeared to be made of shimmering blue light.

'Suits are over there,' came Cleo's voice.

I turned and saw Lucy and Riya talking to one another. The thought of them conversing filled me with even more fear than being trapped in the disintegrating base.

Next to Cleo stood a small yellow alien in a smart uniform. It looked like a frog. 'So, let me get this right,' I shouted above the throng, while putting on my supersuit. 'You lot are part of the Hu army that conquered the Universe?'

'We are the enlightened, for which we are hunted by the Hu's secret police force, the Illuminati.'

'Bullshit,' cried Denzil. 'Everyone knows the Illuminati are just rich old perverts that wear robes and wank into jam jars.'

Bits of the roof started to collapse around us and I instinctively ducked.

'Isn't that the Bilderberg Group?' I asked as Lanta's suit adjusted to the shape of her body.

'No,' replied Denzil like I was stupid. 'They shove wooden owls up their bums.'

'And he's off,' said Lucy as she and Riya joined us.

'Follow me,' instructed Cleo.

'It's true,' continued Denzil as if we weren't under the immediate threat of being squashed to death. 'They shove them up their arses and film the newbies sniffing them while saying how much they love it.'

'Jesus Christ, Denzil,' said Lucy.

'If anyone breaks the code of silence, bam! The video appears on the internet.'

'Come on,' shouted Cleo as we jogged along next to her, the Guardian and Mr Frog.

'So, you see a lot of videos of world leaders on the internet waxing lyrical about their love of sniffing poopy wooden owls then?' asked Lucy sarcastically.

'Well, no one's going to talk with that threat hanging over them, are they?' Denzil cried, as if it was the most obvious thing in the world.

Cleo stopped and a number of small crafts drifted down from the ceiling. They looked like stubby, mechanical stingrays. The rear ends curved into tails and they sported stumpy barrels on each side, just above the short rounded wings. Two propulsion engines were sculpted into the rears.

Cleo shouted at the frog chap. 'Sergeant, take Riya and Lucy,' which as you can imagine went down like a pube in a fondue. 'Guardian, take Denzil and the parasite, and Jack, you're with me.'

Riya and Lucy looked at each other and then at me. Both had a 'You must be kidding' expression plastered across their faces, although at least they no longer looked like they wanted to kill each other. But there was nothing I could do to help my friends in that moment. So, I turned and climbed in through the opening in the side of my allotted vehicle and sat down next to Cleo. The door closed and everything went silent.

We lifted into the air in formation and moved towards the shimmering blue window. Huge parts of the roof were now collapsing around us and my heart was thumping in my chest like a chipmunk on charlie. We had to get out of here in the next few seconds or we'd be fish food. Just as the other pods neared the window, they accelerated and shot out of the hangar.

'Hold on, Jack,' said Cleo. 'This is going to get a little bumpy.'

'How bumpy?'

'Engage your helmet, please. It will stop you from blacking out.'

I decided that would probably be preferable, and activated it as we sped through the light and into the sea.

An underwater dogfight of bubbles, lights and acrobatic vehicles raged all around us. We were instantly under attack from a range of craft. My senses went into overload as we ducked, weaved and bobbed, both firing and being fired upon. I heard voices including Cleo's directing the battle. One moment, we were on the tail of a craft and firing on it with our weapons, the next we were trying to shake it off. It was kill or be killed and I prayed Cleo was a good enough pilot to keep us alive.

'What's happening?' I asked as we rocketed through the damaged hull of a sunken oil tanker.

'It's the Illuminati,' she replied.

'What do they want?' But I already knew the answer as I was pushed back into my seat.

'You.'

Cleo shot at a large black vehicle, which exploded in a halo of bubbles and flames. Then she accelerated towards it and we flew right through the debris.

'Who the hell are you?' I asked.

'I am Grand Master Cleopatra Thea Philopator.'

'You're a chess player?'

She laughed. 'Not quite. I was once the head of the Hu's most elite fighting force, and a devout servant of the Goddess Hyrattanti. But now I'm a truth seeker.'

'Where are you from?'

'I was born in Egypt.'

'So, were you named after the famous Cleopatra?'

She laughed again. 'She was named after me.'

'Piss off,' I replied. The woman had clearly lost touch with reality.

We rolled left then right, as balls of light raced past us. We turned at a right angle and dived towards the sea floor as more alien fire came raining down.

'You're no more than thirty,' I said.

'I am,' she replied, 'if you add three hundred thousand years to that.'

'You're insane,' I told her.

'The universe is at war, Jack. And you're right at the heart of it.'

As I looked to my left I saw the geriatric officer from the base swimming through the water at incredible speed. His body was covered in scales and he had a large flowing tail protruding from his rear. I watched in awe as he ripped pieces off an enemy vessel, while concluding you really shouldn't judge a book by its cover.

We took a hit. The pod shook and I was thrown about in my seat like a workman holding a runaway pneumatic drill. Cleo remained calm as she regained control and dodged several more attackers.

'You are the lost piece of the puzzle. The missing link.'

'I'm not a bloody ape.'

We barrel rolled several times, causing my tummy to turn with the craft and making me feel nauseous.

'The Hu Empire wants you,' said Cleo. 'Or more importantly, what you have.'

'The psychic energy?'

'Exactly,' she said as we were struck again. 'The shields won't hold much longer. We need to find an exit.'

'But why?'

'You are the last of an ancient race.'

I thought about Harold and Brenda as we did a loop the loop. They hardly seemed ancient. Well, besides their fashion sense.

'You alone besides the creator Goddess may have the power to wield the Ternion.'

'May?'

'Well, it could kill you.'

We barrel rolled again before racing through a large school of surprised-looking fish.

'We turned our back on the Empire and stole the Ternion, hiding it here on earth.'

'But what is it?'

'The blue light is a source of great power.' Cleo fired a volley of shots at an enemy craft and then banked sharply as another fired at us.

A realisation dawned on me. 'Don't tell me you betrayed this creator Goddess and you don't even know what this Ternion thing does?'

'The writings in the Temple were taken by the Illuminati before we had a chance to read them in their entirety.'

'So you *are* traitors and terrorists?'

Cleo laughed as we swung violently from left to right. 'Who told you that?'

'Antony. He said you can't be trusted.'

'That's rich coming from the head of the Illuminati. We're not the ones trying to wipe out the population of an entire planet.'

We careened headlong towards an enemy craft in a terrible game of chicken as each ship fired at the other. Cleo achieved two direct hits, cutting a hole right through the centre of her opponent. They broke up amidst a storm of bubbles.

'What do you mean?' I asked.

'Look around you, Jack,' she said. 'Where do you think all these creatures came from?' We were hit once more and Cleo cursed.

I managed to ask 'Why monsters?' as we spun around and she fired on another craft, sending the pilot to heaven or to hell or to absolutely nowhere, depending on your viewpoint.

'Other methods have left planets uninhabitable,' she said through gritted teeth.'

A craft raced towards us, firing. I thought we'd had it until one of Cleo's friends blasted it into a million pieces.

'So, they released monsters into the toilets?' I asked. It seemed ridiculous.

'First they release microscopic organisms into the water system, yes. They consume the creatures around them, evolving and growing each time.' Cleo destroyed another ship. 'Once the planet's animals and in this case, humans, are gone, the remaining obscenities feed on one another. When the food runs out, the last of them will die and decompose back into the earth, leaving the Illuminati free to search the earth unhindered for the Ternion. The added bonus is that no humans are left standing. It's a new process and the earth has the pleasure of being the guinea pig. But it backfired, because you now possess the Ternion.'

'But if the Hu are Gods, why can't they wipe out planets and find the Ternion with their super powers?'

'In the mortal realm the Gods have to play by mortal rules. Plus, in this solar system they created crystal rings around Saturn that block much of the psychic activity. It was an extra security method to keep their slave species under control. Only the strongest psychics are able to use a fraction of their power. The average human is virtually blind to the psychic world.'

I watched two escape pods explode nearby and prayed my friends weren't on them.

'Saturn's rings aren't natural?'

'Of course not. While gold enhances psychic abilities, the crystals in the rings diminish it.'

I couldn't think of a suitable response to that. So I kept quiet.

'The rings of power made the Hu's invasion of the earth thirteen thousand years ago far easier. Without their full abilities the Children of the Watchers were forced into a more physical fight. A fight they could never hope to win. Although they had a dam good try.'

'I don't want this Ternion,' I said. 'Can we get another one of those golden boxes to put it in?'

'I have no idea how to remove it,' she said, while ramming another craft into the sea bed.

'Where did you hide it?'

'Good question,' she replied. 'It was hidden inside a long forgotten city underneath the Great Pyramid of Giza. Many such places were built. I discovered it during the deluge. Sadly, it also contained information about someone I now believe to be you.'

'Me?' I squeaked. 'That's ridiculous.'

'We couldn't let the Illuminati get their hands on the information.'

I felt sick. 'It was you that destroyed the Pyramids?'

'We had to, Jack,' she said. 'The information was too important to fall into the wrong hands.'

'But all those people?' I said. 'Children were killed in that attack.'

'This war is for the lives of quadrillions,' said Cleo as she destroyed another ship. 'The suffering of a small group of people that were destined to be exterminated anyway is of no consequence. The needs of the many outweigh the needs of the few. It's basic utilitarianism.'

'Not necessarily,' I replied. 'It depends on the people involved.'

Cleo turned to look at me and despite the face covering I could sense her raised eyebrow.

'I'm not sure the lives of innocent children are worth less than a bunch of space-hopping psychopathic murderers. However many there are.'

'This is war, Jack. No decisions are simple and no actions can be undertaken without collateral damage. But the end always justifies the means.'

Her cynical approach to killing people sickened me. I knew Antony would never do anything so abhorrent. I had to get away from this mass-murdering traitor and fast.

We took another two direct hits and started spinning out of control. Balls of light flew all around us.

'We need to bail,' shouted Cleo. 'Stay close to me!'

She pressed something on the control panel and I was blasted out of the craft and up into the open water. As I looked down I saw the pod explode. I decided to engage my antigravity boots and make a break for the surface. I felt exposed outside of the craft and desperately needed to get the hell out of there. Looking around, I could see pods like ours running from the battle in every direction. What was strange was that the opposition didn't appear to be giving chase. To my right I could make out the outline of a huge pyramid protruding from the sea bed. Could it really be an ancient base? And more importantly, could I be part of some long-lost race of hybrids? The whole thing made my head spin.

I flew up and out of the sea, rising higher and higher into the air, spurred on by an intense fear. Looking down, I was relieved that I couldn't see any pursuers, although I also couldn't see Cleo. Being alone over the water made me nervous as hell. I had no idea how long the suit would keep me airborne. Damn, I didn't even know how it was powered. I thought about Flight 19, where the crew had probably been disorientated in the Bermuda Triangle and run out of fuel over the sea, to be lost forever more. If this was the Levantine Sea, however, then it followed that I wasn't too far from dry land. I continued my ascent up above the patchy layer of pristine white cloud until I could finally make out a body of land in the distance. I changed my trajectory and headed towards it, hoping it wasn't a trick of the light.

I'd been flying for several seconds when I noticed a large black triangular craft pulling up alongside me. I tried to fly faster, but the propulsion on my boots was no match for its vast engines. It was a bit like an ant trying to out-run an F1 racing car. My initial fear soon turned to confusion. Why weren't they attacking me? Just then a door opened, and I saw Antony casually hold-ing on by one arm and grinning from ear to ear.

I felt a sudden and incredible sense of relief. Antony had come to save me yet again. So, Denzil had been wrong about him. Antony truly was on our side. I'm ashamed to admit it but I felt a pang of irritation at my best friend. His unwarranted suspicion of Antony could have got us killed. He waved me towards him and I duly responded with an enthusiastic and rather nerdy thumbs up, before steering myself alongside the ship. When I was close enough I reached out an arm and Antony grabbed my hand and hauled me into the craft. The door closed, shutting out the screaming wind, and I removed my mask.

'Are you okay?' he said, looking concerned.

'I think so,' I replied, although my head was spinning and I was breathing hard.

'Good man.' He clapped me on the shoulder and smiled. 'You've just survived twenty-four hours with the world's most dangerous terrorist group. I think you deserve a drink.'

'What about my friends?' I asked.

'They fled with the other insurgents. But don't worry, I've sent teams to hunt them down.'

'Thank you,' I said.

'Try to relax. We'll have them soon enough. Come on, follow me.'

The inside of the craft was far more luxurious than the plain black exterior suggested. It felt like the interior of an extravagant motor vehicle. I followed Antony into a large room containing a huge floating desk and two matching floating chairs. One wall contained a window, which I stared out of in dis-belief. We had risen so high that I could actually see the curvature of the earth.

'It's not a real window, of course,' said Antony as he came to stand next to me. 'It's projecting external images onto the wall.'

'But what about the frame?'

'It's all just a 3D projection,' he replied with a smile.

I was shocked by how real it appeared and realised I must have looked like a medieval country bumpkin that had just landed in present-day New York. 'Where are we going?' I asked.

'Edin,' he replied.

'Where's Edin?'

'More important than the where is the what.' He grinned.

'Okay, what's Edin then?' I asked, unable to peel my eyes away from the stunning images that lay before me.

'Why, it's the moon, dear boy,' said Antony, slapping me on the back. 'It's the moon.'

Despite all the strange things I'd seen and done, my brain couldn't cope with that concept and I started to feel faint.

Antony took me by the arm and guided me to the nearest chair. 'Yes, I suppose it is a lot to take in.'

I gazed at the projection as we passed the International Space Station. 'Can they see us?' I asked.

'Not at all,' said Antony. 'We're currently cloaked.'

It was like being in a movie.

The soldier placed a strange black receptacle in my hand. 'Drink this,' he said. 'It'll steady the nerves.'

I took a sip of what looked like liquid, but felt more like breathing in a type of gas. But it was sweet and warm and after a few seconds I began to feel relaxed. I kept my focus on the images of the earth as we moved away from it.

'Better?' asked Antony.

'Better,' I replied as my mind started to become a little foggy. I realised then I was no longer concerned for the safety of my friends. I now knew without question that Antony's soldiers would be able to rescue them. I also no longer cared about contacting my parents. A strange thought drifted into my cloudy head. 'Why are we going to the moon, sorry, Edin?' I asked, as if that was a perfectly reasonable thing to be doing.

'Great question. That's what I've always admired about you, Jack. Your brains and your initiative.'

'Thanks.'

He peered at me in earnest. 'We've been through a lot together. I'd like to think that during that time we've become friends.'

It was true, we had faced numerous dangers together. The thought that this virtual superman wanted to be friends with me was beyond flattering. It may sound pathetic, but I was buzzing and I couldn't help but smile. 'I guess we have,' I replied.

'Good,' he continued affably. 'That's why I feel I can trust you. I can trust you, can't I, Jack?'

'Yes.' I was starting to feel sleepy, like I'd just eaten a big meal, and the floating chair began to recline as if it could read my mind. 'Of course you can trust me.'

'I'm glad to hear that. I was worried you may have heard things from the insurgents, things about me and my soldiers.'

'What things?'

'Who knows what web of lies and false truths Cleo and her despicable order would weave.'

'She didn't tell me anything,' I replied.

'She must have told you something,' he said with one eyebrow raised.

'Well, not about you, only about Gandareen and the Illuminati. Oh, and about the universe being at war. Yes, and something about an ancient energy and Gods wanting to wipe out mankind.' My eyelids were starting to get heavy. 'And that she destroyed the Pyramids and murdered all of those innocent people.'

'She did indeed murder those innocent men, women and children,' said Antony. 'Life to her kind is worthless. That woman is the personification of evil. There's a lot of innocent blood on her hands.' He sighed. 'What did she say about the Illuminati?'

'They work for…They work for…' My head was starting to wobble about on top of my neck. 'They walk for the Empire of the Dogs.'

The door to the room slid open and in swept a woman.

'Did she say what they do?' Antony persisted.

'I'm, well, I'm not really sure. Something with owls, perhaps,' I said. 'Or wanking off jam jars…' I was confused and found it almost impossible to stay awake. 'The police. They're the police.'

'That's right,' he said. 'The Illuminati are like the police. We keep people safe. Like you, Jack.'

'Yes,' I said, although I no longer understood what I was agreeing with.

My eyes were half closed when the woman came and stood over me. 'Hello Jack,' she said in a super-posh English accent.

Just as I was drifting off to sleep, I heard Antony say, 'I'd like to introduce you to a friend of mine. Her name's Namah, but you know her as Lady Ashbury.'

CHAPTER 21

I opened my eyes. I was lying on a bed in what looked like a medical bay. The room was filled with strange machines and a small grey alien was standing over me, running a wand up and down my body. I shut my eyes for a few seconds and yawned. I still felt sleepy. In fact, my whole body felt like lead. My mind flicked back to the alien standing over me and my eyes popped open like a champagne cork. The strange creature was examining the wand along with a machine that was positioned next to the bed. I tried getting up but found I was unable to move. Looking down, I saw restraints of red light holding me firmly in place.

'What the hell?' I said in a panic.

The alien turned around and looked at me passively. Every alien abduction horror story I'd ever heard came rushing into my brain like a tidal bore.

'Please don't probe me,' I begged.

The thing's eyes widened. 'Welcome to Edin,' it said in what sounded like a German accent. 'I am happy to report that you are quite well, young man. Quite well indeed. You will be feeling a little sleepy, of course, but this is a natural side effect of the Elatorin that you have ingested.'

'Who are you?' I asked.

'My name is Doctor Hans Friedrich Adelsberger.'

A male alien, then. I wondered what experiments the twisted little freak had been performing on me. 'Oh my God! You didn't?'

'Didn't what?' he replied.

'You know.'

'It may surprise you,' he said loftily, 'but I have more important things to be doing than rooting around inside some disgusting human's bung hole.'

'Are you German?' I asked.

Even though he had no eyebrows, when his big oval eyes widened the skin above them went all wrinkly, which provided a similar effect. 'Do I look German?' he asked, sounding irritated. Then he laughed and his mouth became a smile.

Was I being wound up by an alien?

'Our accents do sound German to you new humans,' Doctor Hans Friedrich Adelsberger said. 'However, our accents predate yours by nearly a hundred thousand years.'

'But your name does sound German.'

'No, it most certainly does not. You copied us,' he snapped. 'Now please try to keep up. You will find that most German names are Zeta Reticulan in origin.'

I wondered whether he was wearing a skin suit, or if little grey aliens just liked to walk about like new-age naturists. Annoyingly, as I was strapped down I couldn't check to see if he had any tackle hanging between his weedy alien legs.

'And you are from Albian, correct?' he asked.

'I'm from Britain,' I replied.

'Exactly.'

'No, Britain,' I repeated.

'You humans with your fashionable new words like "Britain". Whatever next?'

'I'm sorry?' It was all getting rather confusing.

'Some names for towns and cities used by the settlers in America and Australia are based upon the names from Albian, no?'

'I guess,' I replied.

'Then why couldn't names for your things on earth come from other worlds?'

'Well, I suppose they could…'

'I must say that you are an arrogant species for one so new. It's like babies telling adults how to perform alior on a Greet.'

I had no idea what to say to that, so I just nodded and said, 'Hmm.'

'The creator Goddess, praise be her holiness on high, created you. All human civilisations were based on Hu culture, back in the days when the Hu still walked openly among you. When they took a more hands-off approach, Edin became an observatory and gateway to the stars. Did you know this? Of course not. You new humans are too stupid.'

The door opened and in walked Lady Ashbury—no, what was it? *Namah.* She glided across the room and over to the bed, looking far younger and even more beautiful than I'd remembered.

'How is he, Doctor?' she asked, stroking my face with her soft, silky hand.

I felt myself shiver involuntarily.

The alien bowed his head. 'Quite well, your Highness, quite well indeed.' He looked down at the wand and frowned as best he could without eyebrows. 'Only, he has some quite remarkable DNA. I've not seen its kind before.'

My heart skipped a beat. Was I really a hybrid?

'Get dressed, Jack.' Namah winked and touched the end of my nose with her finger.

'But you're…you're dead,' I spluttered. 'They shot you.'

'Oh really?' she asked theatrically. 'How was my funeral? I trust it was suitably fabulous?' She laughed and then glided out of the room.

The restraints vanished from my body and Doctor Adelsberger took his leave. I noticed a blue uniform of some description had been placed next to the bed and I quickly got dressed. As soon as I'd finished, the door opened and two masked soldiers entered. Their prompt arrival freaked me out, as clearly the sickos must have been watching me getting dressed. It wasn't the greatest thought in human history, but still preferable to having your rectum probed in the interests of alien research.

'Follow me,' said the smaller of the two soldiers in a deadpan tone.

I followed them out of the room and into a corridor. There were doors along each wall but no signage to give any indication of what lay inside. I decided that the people who worked here probably got lost frequently. At the end of the corridor was a rather dull-looking door. However, what waited on the other side was anything but ordinary.

As we passed through it and entered a chamber, my mouth dropped open. I'm terrible at guessing the distances of things, but it must have been nearly two hundred metres high. It was also several times wider than it was tall and easily a mile in length. Along one side was an architectural mix of buildings and walkways, but what left me awestruck was the single continuous window that ran from floor to ceiling along the entire length of the room. It was a truly epic feat of engineering and something I'd never expected to see in my lifetime. Hell, I didn't even know that kind of thing was possible.

On the other side of the vast window loomed Edin's grey, pitted surface and beyond that, the blackness of space. Instinctively I knew this was the far side of the moon. I was struck by the fact that no stars were visible. It looked weird. The place was teeming with a plethora of humanoid creatures hurrying about in all directions. Some walked, some slithered, some rode on vehicles and others were flying through the air on antigravity boots. I watched as a large silver train came to a halt on the window side of the chamber. Various people and aliens alighted and new passengers clambered on.

'Keep moving,' said one of the soldiers and we shuffled through the crowds towards the busy platform. Despite their large guns and combat suits, our fellow travellers weren't particularly keen to move out of the way and I was repeatedly pushed and jostled. It was all a bit too much like the London Underground in rush hour for my liking. I just hoped I wouldn't need to stand about with someone's stinky armpit in my face. I had a sudden flashback to the lift at the refugee camp. I wondered whether aliens had armpits and concluded that they must do, but I should do some casual research when the opportunity arose.

One moment I was happily walking along and the next I started to feel really cold. Everything around me slowed as a strange blanket of silence descended upon the world. Well, upon Edin. Through the motionless crowds I noticed a momentary flicker of faint white light, and then I saw a slender figure watching me. The figure was dressed in black and wearing a strange helmet that shielded their face.

'Keep moving!' commanded the larger soldier, grabbing my arm and hauling me through the crowd. The world snapped back into motion.

I glanced around as I was dragged away, searching for the mystery figure. But they were already gone. Assuming they'd been there in the first place. Man, the whole incident was just plain creepy.

One of the soldiers took the lead and forced people out of our way, which is the only reason we made it to the front of the platform. Where I'd expected to see a space-age train track was only a recessed area of the floor. After a short wait, the next train pulled up and the doors opened to let passengers on and off. The soldiers pushed me down into a seat and stood beside me, alert and ready for action. However, judging by how disinterested the people sitting around us looked, I doubted they were going to see much.

The seat afforded a great view out of the window and I sat mesmerised by the show that unfolded before me. The ride was smooth, with zero noise and no sense of motion. If there hadn't been windows I would have sworn blind that we weren't even moving. I watched the strange landscape passing by and had to pinch myself. I was on Edin. The moon! That huge grey ball I'd seen in the sky on so many nights and even on some days. It had always been unfathomably far away and unreachable, a vision of impossibility gracing my existence.

Now I was actually here, I had the feeling you get when you visit an iconic country or famous city halfway across the world. Except I'd have to say that this experience was far more surreal. The most incredible environment now stretched out before my eyes. I never knew something so grey and so devoid of colour could be so utterly beautiful.

The train made a couple of stops as we passed through a series of underground tunnels and stations. The further we went, the more passengers alighted from the train, until eventually we were the only ones that remained. My mind wandered back to the figure in the mask. It seemed so real at the time and yet how could it have been? Maybe it was a new type of vision, but it was one that I really didn't like.

I was so lost in the maze of my own thoughts that I hadn't even noticed that the train had exited the tunnel. I grabbed onto the chair as we lifted up into Edin's pitch-black sky. The train swept over the barren landscape for several miles before snaking down towards a blue portal in the side of a cliff. We passed effortlessly through the shield before coming to a smooth and silent stop.

'Get up,' said the smaller soldier.

I did as I was told and we exited the train. I'd thought that the last place was big, but this was ridiculous. I was standing in the largest indoor space I'd ever seen. You could have placed a skyscraper inside it and there still would have been room to spare. Immense gun-metal grey platforms protruded from the walls, each supporting a range of spaceships. As I gazed around, I saw a host of other craft parked at ground level. At one end was a vast shimmering blue window leading to the outside world, or should I say the outside moon, and ships were using this portal to enter and exit the hangar. A small open-topped vehicle flown by a strange three-armed woman with lumpy green skin and wild jet-black hair came hovering towards us. Her eyes looked exactly like Riya's. I thought of my friends then for all of a second, but weirdly I still felt no concern for their safety or even a desire to know where they were.

We climbed into the vehicle, which lifted us into the air before traversing the vast interior. We floated over a large black triangular craft that was coming in to land and I thought about the Octopuses swinging through the trees in the Cotswolds. Were they connected to Antony in some way? After all the crazy stuff I was now seeing, anything was possible.

We came to rest on one of the grey landing pads high up on the right-hand side of the hangar. The smaller soldier instructed me to follow and I stepped down onto the platform. It was so high that it made me feel dizzy and my legs started to shake.

'Thank you,' I said to the driver, who turned and gave me a friendly smile before lifting back up into the air and disappearing from view.

We walked through a pair of colossal sliding metal doors and were confronted by humanoid soldiers moving about in every direction. Aliens passed by on contraptions that looked like hoverboards and floating Segways. After a few minutes of walking I started to feel aggrieved that we didn't have any transport ourselves. My thoughts returned to the alien armpit question, which I was still pondering when I was told to stop next to another big door.

The entrance slid open and I was presented with a large room that resembled a high-tech mission control centre. There were soldiers of all shapes, colours and sizes sitting in front of floating desks and strange-looking screens. Before them lay a vast window overlooking the earth. I gawped at the view before me and knew in that moment that our planet was truly a thing of wonder. I thought about all of the damage human beings did to the environment and to one another, and standing there in that moment, it all just seemed so pointless.

'Quite a sight, isn't she?' said Namah, placing a hand on my shoulder.

'Yes,' I murmured without turning around. 'She really is.'

'Earth and Mars used to be called "The Sapphire Sisters".'

'You mean Mars used to look like that?' I asked, sounding like I didn't believe a word she was saying.

'Mars was one of the most beautiful planets in creation,' she said wistfully.

'What happened to it?'

'Its atmosphere was compromised and the planet lost. Cleopatra left many to die there when she fled.'

'But Cleo told me it's the Illuminati that want to wipe out the world?'

'And you believed her?'

I sensed something behind me and turned around to see Namah's giant snake watching me passively. There's nothing like feeling at ease during a conversation, is there? It took a great deal of willpower to turn my back on the killing machine. 'What is this place?'

'It was built by the Hu as a laboratory to genetically engineer humans. It was here that they were given life, and later, knowledge.'

I turned then to look at the woman standing beside me. 'Who are you?'

She smiled and ran a finger down the side of my neck, before taking her hand away. It sent an electric tingle down my spine and I swallowed hard.

'I'm a Psychogenial.'

'A what-a-genital?'

'A Psychogenial,' she said with a laugh. 'Our order does many things, but we are part of the Illuminati. We keep planetary leaders under close supervision.'

'Why?'

She laughed once again. 'Because they are children that cannot take care of themselves. We bind the global elites to secret societies, so we can manipulate their thoughts and actions.'

Perhaps Denzil's conspiracy theories weren't totally crazy after all. 'So, you're a spy?'

She looked at me and smiled. 'I suppose I am.' She followed this with a conspiratorial wink. It made my heart beat a little faster.

'So that's what you were doing at Ashbury Hall,' I said, more to myself than her.

'Why, of course.'

'And then we knocked on your door.' I sighed. 'It's a funny old world.'

'Your arrival was no coincidence. I drew you towards me.' She gazed at me seductively. 'You don't mind being drawn to me, do you, Jack Gibson?' I guess my nerves showed on my face, because she laughed. 'Your absorption of the Ternion was like a psychic atom bomb exploding. There's an incredible power inside of you. But you must reach out and take it.'

'How?'

Namah frowned. 'Imagine an energy that flows throughout the entire universe, permeating all things. You will have touched it at times during your life. What is it you say in Britain? Someone walked over your grave.'

I thought back to all the times I'd felt that sensation. Surely that wasn't me touching some weird universal energy? It all seemed a bit hippyish for my liking.

'Our strength depends on how much energy we can manipulate. It's harder in this solar system than elsewhere, but for those of true power, much can still be achieved.'

I looked around the control room. 'Well, if it's everywhere, I can't see it.'

'Oh, sweet Jack. That's because you're looking with the eyes in your head. You must open yourself to it, relax and let it flow. Controlling it is a little trickier, but the first step is to open yourself to it.'

'What about the Ternion? How does that work?'

'Now that is something we must figure out together.'

I was started to get freaked out so decided to change the subject.

'Why did you let me think you'd been killed at Ashbury Hall?'

'We knew Cleopatra was after you. If you were captured, Antony felt it would have been advantageous for her to believe I might be deceased.'

'Welcome to the Eyes of Edin, Jack,' came a familiar voice from somewhere behind me. I turned to see Antony sweeping into the room.

'What's the Eyes of Edin?'

'It's an ultra-secure control centre from where we monitor the earth in great detail,' he said. 'All level five planets and above have one these days.'

I felt both honoured and awkward. 'I'm grateful that you've let me see it,' I said, sounding like a right flipping dweeb.

'Not at all. It's actually part of a shameless sales pitch.' Antony laughed.

'What are you trying to sell?' I asked, confused.

'I'm trying to sell us, Jack,' he said with a broad smile. 'The Illuminati. Would you like to join?'

CHAPTER 22

I didn't know what to say. I mean, it's not every day you get asked to join an intergalactic special operations force, agency, group, whatever it was. It was definitely an ego boost. I've never been headhunted by a recruitment agency for a job, but I'm guessing it would feel pretty similar. There was just one tiny issue, a small thing, really. This being my complete lack of any formal training in espionage, martial arts, weaponry, tactics, interrogation, surveillance, or anything else vaguely useful for such a role. This should have been the first point to raise. However, what actually came out of my mouth was, 'Do I get a spaceship?'

Antony laughed. 'Not quite.'

'Do I get a gun?'

'No.'

'Do I get a badge?'

'No badge.'

'Do I get a code name, though?'

'We could make one up?'

'Hmm. Will there be any foreign travel?'

'Not a huge amount.'

'I've got to be honest.' I screwed up my face. 'This job sounds rubbish.'

Antony and Namah laughed.

'We need you to do something infinitely more important than that,' said Antony.

'Like what?' I asked, disappointed I wasn't being recruited as a planet-hopping super spy.

'Before I answer that,' said Antony. 'There's someone you need to meet.'

'Who?'

'Follow me and I'll show you.'

Namah left us with a coquettish wink, followed by that monstrosity Nahash, and I followed Antony to a side door. The woman was so alluring it was starting to bother me. A vague notion that I was being manipulated entered my brain, but it vanished as we walked into a white room with a raised platform at its centre. Next to it sat a young man who reminded me of Crazy Legs Crane and a tall blue alien with three identical heads. Both were wearing smart white uniforms and looked thoroughly official as they stood behind their sleek terminals.

The blue alien gave us two smiles and a pout as we entered. 'Greetings General,' said two of the mouths in chipper-sounding voices not unlike a doorbell.

'Hello Genevieve,' replied Antony cheerily.

The alien may have been rather strange-looking, but at least it had manners. The young man didn't even smile. He looked like a moody dental hygienist.

'I'll go first, Jack,' said Antony. 'There really is nothing to worry about. Just step onto the platform and you're off.' He could clearly read the look of concern on my face. 'It's as normal for us on Edin as an elevator would be on earth.' Antony stepped onto the platform and turned to face Ms Heads and Mr Moody. 'The temple, if you'd be so kind.'

A cylinder of white light came down from the ceiling and surrounded Antony. He winked at me, which was nowhere near as enjoyable as Namah's, and vanished. One second the man was standing there sporting his cheesy grin and the next he wasn't. It was so sudden that I flinched. Which wasn't embarrassing at all.

'Step onto the platform, please,' said Genevieve's mouths in concert.

I'm ashamed to say I was so busy gawping at the alien's multiple heads that I tripped over the platform. It served me right, because you shouldn't stare at someone like that, it's rude. I stumbled and did a little involuntary run to prevent myself from falling flat on my face. Why is it when you see someone trip over their own feet in the street it's hilarious, but when you do it, it's mortifying?

'What just happened?' I asked.

'You tripped,' said Mr Moody with all the emotion of a table.

The words 'You're a cock' sprang to mind, but in the end, I settled on, 'I meant with the light?'

The man looked at me like I was a complete simpleton and gave a huffy sigh.

'Please step onto the platform,' said one of Genevieve's heads, leading me to conclude she was the only one who'd actually attended any customer service training.

'Where did Antony go?' I asked.

'The Tubes are the fastest method of travel on Edin,' replied Genevieve. 'They're temporary tunnels allowing you to travel close to the speed of light.'

Something troubling from a documentary I'd seen popped into my head. 'Doesn't your mass increase the closer you get to the speed of light?'

'Please stand in the middle of the Celestisus, the General will be waiting,' said grumpy guts.

I laughed out loud. 'What's it called?'

'A Celestisus,' he replied in his delightfully disinterested tone.

I laughed again. 'That sounds like an STI.'

They both stared at me like I was a massive twat. Although to be fair, I didn't look at all of Genevieve's heads, so maybe one of them found me amusing. Anyway, I shut up pronto and stepped into the centre of the Celestisus. I could feel my heart racing with anticipation. Who am I trying to kid? It was from fear. Could a human being really survive travelling at close to the speed of light? I looked up and saw nothing but a flat white ceiling. So, where the hell was the light going to come from? And more importantly, where the hell was I going to go? I wondered momentarily if this was how the Mayans felt when the conquistadors rocked up on their shores, decked out in futuristic-looking clothes. With their big puffy pants and technologically advanced weapons, they must have seemed strange indeed. I was hoping this situation would turn out a little better for me, however.

'This is definitely safe, right?' I asked as the cylinder of light surrounded me. They both chose to ignore me. Charming. The bright light felt strange, almost as if it had physical properties. There was the briefest moment of panic, then I was travelling through a tunnel in a world of utter blackness. I felt so heavy, it was like being crushed, as time in the tube stretched on for an eternity, but paradoxically took no time at all.

I emerged standing inside an immense cave next to Antony with a confused look on my face. Two rows of mighty golden columns stretched out before us, ascending into the blackness far above. Hundreds of metres away I saw a large, wide staircase with gigantic serpentine statues guarding each side. At the top of the stairs stood a vast golden temple, easily a hundred metres high. The place was simply jaw dropping.

I felt a strange sensation filling my body, but decided it was probably a reaction to the Elatorin.

'Where are we?' I asked Antony in little more than a whisper.

'We stand before the holy temple of Hyrattanti,' he said.

'What's that?' I was unable to pull my eyes away from the strange construction.

'Before you lies one of the most sacred and powerful places in the Galaxias Kyklos,' he said, placing a hand onto my shoulder.

'The Galaxias what?'

'The Milky Way.'

'Wow,' I said. 'So how many planets are there in the Milky Way, then?'

'One hundred and nine billion, seventeen million, three hundred and sixteen thousand, six hundred and sixty-six.'

'Bloody hell. And this is one of the most sacred?'

'It most certainly is. And there's close to a hundred billion moons on top of that.'

The numbers were getting so big that my mind couldn't comprehend them. 'What are we doing here?' I asked.

'We are here to converse with Hyrattanti.'

'In there?' I pointed towards the distant temple.

Antony nodded.

'It's bloody miles away. Could we not have been dropped off a bit closer?'

'Be patient,' he replied calmly.

'Why's it so special?' I stared in awe at the massive structure.

'Because it's one of the sacred seats of power. It contains the statue of Hyrattanti.' He could see from my face that I had zero clue what he was going on about. 'It's one of the seats of divine power that Hyrattanti occupies while answering the prayers of her subjects in this galaxy.'

I looked at him blankly. I still had no idea.

Just then, a row of people emerged from the temple's large entrance. I was shocked to see by just how much the structure dwarfed them. When they reached the top of those great stairs, they didn't simply walk down them, because that would have been too normal for Edin. Oh no, this bunch chose to float towards us through the air. It was seriously weird.

'They're flying,' I said.

'It's a little more complex than that,' Antony replied, sounding amused.

'Well, it looks like flying.'

'It's not flying, Jack.'

'What is it then?'

'It's complicated.'

'Well, who is this group of complicated people, anyway?' I asked.

'They're not people, they're the Priestesses of Hyrattanti. And they are coming to greet us.'

'Why are they floating through the air, though?'

Antony smiled. 'Because as you say, it's bloody miles away.'

'Fair point.' I said. 'So, let me get this straight. Hyrattanti is the creator Goddess, right?'

'That is correct.'

'And this is where people come to pray?'

'They come here to converse with their Goddess.'

'I don't want to offend you,' I said, feeling awkward, 'but I don't really believe in Gods and Goddesses.'

Antony smiled. 'Two days ago, I suspect you didn't believe in life on the moon.'

He had a point.

'So, what exactly did Hyrattanti create?' I asked.

'Everything,' said Antony.

'Rubbish,' I replied, sounding highly dubious.

Antony didn't look overly impressed. 'She created everything,' he repeated.

'This place?' I asked.

'Yes.'

'Me?'

'Yes.'

'You?'

'Of course.'

'My shoes?'

'Correct.'

'The little toothbrushes you get on planes?'

'Yes.'

'Sharting?'

'What's that?'

'Nothing.'

As the priestesses drew closer I saw that their skin was the colour of red poppies and their hair was as white as virgin snow. The weirdest thing though, was their six arms and the excessive number of fingers. Their overabundance of limbs undulated rhythmically as if they were trying to re-create Dead Or Alive's video for 'You Spin Me Round'.

'But Hyrattanti can't have created everything,' I said. 'It's not possible.'

'Why not?' asked Antony.

'Well, if I make a cup of tea, Hyrattanti didn't make it, I did.'

'Actually, she did,' he said.

'No, she didn't,' I replied. 'I made it.'

'Ah yes, but she made it indirectly.'

'You sound like a politician,' I said.

Antony smiled. 'I did dabble in a previous life. Now, leave the talking to me, please.'

The priestesses floated down, landing gently all around us. Their red arms were covered in strange white runes and their pupil-less eyes were the colour of milk.

Antony bowed his head, touched his heart with his right hand and then raised it with his palm facing the being standing before him. 'Greetings High Priestess.' He spoke with great reverence. 'May Hyrattanti grace you with eternity.'

The Priestess copied the hand gesture. 'Greetings my lord,' she answered in a deep, booming voice. May Hyrattanti grace you with eternity.' She turned to look at me. 'So, this is he?'

'Yes, High Priestess,' replied Antony.

As she looked me up and down I remembered going to a village fete as a kid. They had a vegetable-growing competition, which apparently passed for entertainment in rural communities. Mum and Dad made us watch the local mayor judge the winners. It was seriously bloody boring. But the Priestess now appraised me in the same way that the mayor had appraised those over-sized vegetables. I was being judged. I just hoped I wouldn't be found wanting.

Then, as if it was just a normal day at the office, we lifted up into the air and floated towards the temple. I could feel something solid beneath my feet, as if I was still standing on the ground. But when I looked down, there was nothing but empty air. I felt dizzy and immediately looked up again, deciding it would be better to focus on the temple. I concluded that, like Antony had said, it probably was a bit more complicated than just flying.

I tried striking up a conversation at one point to take my mind off of 'not' flying. I asked Antony if we could visit the site of the Moon Landing.

He replied rather dismissively that he didn't have time to stand around gawping at a flag. At least that confirmed it wasn't a hoax. I desperately wanted to ask what part the Hu played, but decided it would be better to bide my time.

My feet restarted their relationship with the floor at the top of the stairs.

'This is as far as I go,' said Antony.

'Why?' I asked.

'You,' said the High Priestess, 'and you alone are permitted to enter the holy temple.'

'Why me?'

The wavy-arms woman ignored my question. 'You will enter with your eyes focussed upon the ground and with your head bowed low. You will not dishonour her divine excellency.'

It all sounded a bit on the dramatic side to be honest. I mean, really? No statue was going to give a monkey's if I looked at it or not. It's a statue, for God's sake. I decided, not for the first time in my life, that religious people were basically mental.

'What happens if I accidentally look up?' I asked.

'You will accidentally be killed,' she said, without a microgram of humour.

So, I decided to shut up and do as I was told.

I stood in the entrance and bowed my head as low as I could without licking the floor. It looked like it was made from marble and I wondered if I was going to see a white piano or Siberian tiger. I snuck the odd glance to my left and right as I walked down the long, well-lit corridor. The walls appeared to be covered in gold and there were a number of enormous matching urns. Hyrattanti clearly wasn't a proponent of keeping it low key.

The further I walked, the more the strange sensation began filling my body, as if some invisible weight was being lifted from my soul. Despite that my back was starting to ache as I entered a large chamber, but the threat of being killed kept me focussed. I was forced to stop when I nearly walked into a big gold platform. Standing there like a lemon and trying to decide what to do next, I heard a voice as smooth as silk and as old as time.

'Arise,' it said.

I slowly lifted my head and got my first look at a Goddess.

Hyrattanti was tall, very tall. I guessed around ten feet. She was skinny as a rake with long, slender limbs. Her face looked humanoid, but with only nostrils in place of a nose, and no mouth. Her eyes were like two shining black pools of forever. With her elongated head she looked more alien than god. But then what the hell did I know about the immortal realm? She sat majestically on an imposing golden throne atop the equally imposing golden platform that I'd almost walked into seconds before. All around her danced strange blue light. The effect was intimidating, but then I'm guessing that was the idea.

What was even more intimidating however, was when invisible hands hauled me into the air. And I found myself eyeball to eyeball with the creator Goddess.

Hyrattanti looked at me with a mesmeric gaze and I became lost in those dark, endless pools. They reached down inside of me, and I don't mean like when Doctor Papadakis checked my prostate. He had a strong Greek accent and a husky voice. When he stuffed his tubby digit inside, he tried to comfort me by saying, 'I'm sorry, my friend, I'm sorry.' I knew he was trying to be nice, but it was like being interfered with by a Greek mob boss.

No, this was like Hyrattanti could reach down into my soul, read my past, present and future. She was inside my brain, sifting through my thoughts like a blade slicing through warm, soft flesh. Memories and images from my past flickered in my mind: being comforted as a baby, the day Thomas died, kissing Anna from Heidelberg, being strapped to the crucifix at Ashbury Hall, Ziggy sitting on my lap in the van. A lifetime of being the chess piece and never the player.

I felt excruciating pain flood my body and knew instinctively that Hyrattanti was extracting the Ternion. I opened my mouth to scream, but no noise escaped from my frozen prison. In that moment I was more alone than any point in my entire life. I'd been a fool not to listen to Denzil. My best friend had tried to warn me, tried to show me the signs. But all I'd done was resent him for it. I hated myself. I was a useless and pathetic husk of a person, the lone audience member in my own failing play.

But the loathing went deeper. I felt ashamed that I'd been using the loss of my brother as a reason not to try. I'd been drifting on life's tides, always expecting someone or something to sail right on up to my shores. I'd placed ego, entitlement and fear on an alter above truth, action and purpose. But that's not how life works, is it? You have to take that mean ugly old bull by the horns and wrestle it through the pain and the fear. You have to wrestle it through the hurt and the grief and you have to keep wrestling it, no matter how much your muscles scream or how huge the odds you face.

Alone in that moment, I finally understood something. Everything in life started with me. Remembering Namah's words, I screamed as I opened myself up to the energy of the universe. Sensing this, Hyrattanti turned to face me and we crashed together like two roaring elephant seals on the shores of eternity. We fought and wrestled inside my mind. Her power was immense and several times it almost engulfed me, but still I fought on. I was like the lonely Viking standing against the hordes of King Harrold's troops on that narrow bridge. I battled through the pain, I battled through the fear and I battled through the hopelessness. I knew I was doomed, yet something raw and fundamental understood that the nobility of the defiance transcended any victory. Righteousness meant more than glory. But then something strange happened. Not that the rest of that shit show was exactly normal, but as I battled against my tormentor I found my mind slipping and slithering down a long, dark tunnel, on the other side of which lay Hyrattanti.

I watched the birth and the destruction of galaxies, stars and planets. I saw the joy, the sorrow, the hope and the desperation of trillions. Despite everything I witnessed, I felt only a sense of neutrality. No sympathy or empathy. Just a detached, clinical interest. But the same passivity wasn't displayed towards me. In the eyes of Hyrattanti I was no more than a mongrel abomination. A filth needing to be wiped from the universe. She was searching for something inside of me. Some truth that lay just beyond our reach.

Then a vision hit me like a freight train. I was kneeling before Hyrattanti, in a pool of perfect red blood. My friends and family lay all around me, their pale faces wearing the expressions of the dead.

The link was broken and I dropped to the floor like a fossilised feather. Hyrattanti rose to a pair of big old feet that would put Shaquille O'Neal's to shame, and despite not having a cake hole at her disposal, let out a massive roar of anger. The Goddess glared at me with such deep and heartfelt animosity that I almost peed myself.

But there was no time to invest in worrying about my fate, because from somewhere off in the distance came the sound of a huge explosion.

CHAPTER 23

I found myself staring at a lifeless statue of the Goddess as my head throbbed and blood poured from my nose. Hyrattanti had vanished so damn fast that for a moment I wondered if I'd imagined her. But then my skin began to crawl. I registered the echo of her creeping like a tarantula around the inside of my brain and felt violated, but also confused. How did she almost extract the Ternion? Did she understand what it was? And what did the vision of the dead mean?

There was another terrifying bang and the ground shook. I bent my knees and threw my arms out like a surfer. While riding the aftershocks I considered whether moonquakes were a thing. But not for long, because as soon as the wobbling stopped I took the opportunity to turn and run like a cheetah on steroids.

No longer bent double, I noticed elaborate golden screens adorning the top half of the walls. I guessed they told a story like the Bayeux Tapestry, or the Boring Tapestry as Denzil had called it on our French exchange trip. Now that was one crazy, fun holiday. I kissed my first girl there. Her name was Melanie Bernard and I tell you what, that mademoiselle touched me in places I'd never been touched before. Meanwhile, Denzil got flashed by some old fat bloke at Mont-Saint-Michel. Don't ask. Anyway, I wanted to stop and analyse the pictures on the walls, convinced they could provide some context for the brave new world I was now inhabiting. But while my world was brave, I was not. So, unlike Monsieur Voltaire, I opted to shun enlightenment and wave goodbye to answers. Proverbially that is, because actually waving at walls while running past them is a successful application for funny-farm membership.

I sprinted down the golden corridor towards the exit and then came screeching to a stop. Standing before me against a backdrop of moon rock, which was raining down like the cave was in the midst of monsoon season, was a lone figure in black. At their feet lay a mass of dead priestesses. I realised then it had been more than just a vision I'd seen before boarding the moon train. I froze, waiting to meet my fate. The figure's visor vanished and Cleo stood before me, looking irritated.

'Don't just stand there like a limp lizard,' she shouted. 'Hurry up.'

I must have been in shock, because my feet stayed right where they were. 'What are you doing here?'

'Saving you.'

'How?'

'It seems you have a fan. Namah gave us the codes to get past Edin's security, just like she did for Station Zulu.'

'Why?'

'I don't know. Although I doubt it's because of your winning personality. But as there's currently a battle raging, maybe you could do us both a favour and hurry the hell up.'

I didn't have time to reply, because Cleo decided she didn't have time to wait for me. Scooping me up like a baby, which wasn't damaging to my pride in any way, shape or form, she carried me out of the cave. The speed at which she took off was unbelievable. And when I say unbelievable, I mean like coming home to see a koala in pyjamas smoking a spliff on your sofa, while it looks at you like you're the odd one out in that equation.

The staircase was so vast that the temple was basically on top of a hill. We tore down the first of the steps, leaping maybe ten or twenty at a time. Well, I say we. It was all Cleo. I utilised the time by grunting as each jarring impact knocked the air out of my lungs. The initial pace was so great that I lost control of my body. No, not like that you sicko, I meant my limbs wobbled about like a rag doll. I also found myself staring up at the disintegrating roof as Cleo ducked and weaved between both fallen and falling projectiles. She actually leapt on and off some of them as they fell, the flash so-and-so. She never looked up once though, like she could sense them coming. It was beyond weird.

We were two-thirds of the way through our descent and I was thanking the universe for preventing me from puking everywhere, when the far end of the cave collapsed. It was the loudest and most terrifying thing I'd ever heard. But despite the noise, Cleo didn't miss a beat. She just raced onwards towards the advancing cloud of impenetrable rock dust.

That's when I really panicked. I remembered hearing that the smallest piece of moon dust can cut through Kevlar. Surely, we were about to be shredded into oblivion. I underwent an internal battle to accept my fate. The issue, however, was that I didn't want to. So, sue me. I mean, come on, I hadn't even had the chance to tell Lucy I loved her. Although after the sunken spaceship and Riya, maybe now I never would.

I noticed something moving out of the corner of my eye and turned my head to see a small silver craft racing towards us. Its roof disappeared, revealing a pilot with sparkly silver skin and eyes on stalks like a snail. She raced down towards the steps, turning sideways at the last second. Then, with one epic leap, Cleo jumped a distance of at least twenty metres into the seats at the rear of the moving vehicle. It was such a badass move that it left me stunned. Slightly less badass was when Cleo threw me down next to her like a bag of balls and leapt into the front seat. The roof reappeared over our heads and we were off.

The craft lifted rapidly into the air. Despite the sudden vertical acceleration, I wasn't thrown around in my seat. Just like with the train, it felt like we were hardly moving. What was horrific, however, was that the whole interior vanished. With the exception of its outer frame, I could see everything outside the vehicle in all directions. Up, down, left, right and everything in between. It looked like we were floating in mid-air. However, I wasn't fully sold on the enhanced visibility, because I flinched every time a rock appeared to be striking and bouncing off an invisible surface above our heads. The craft shook as we took more and more hits and the dust cloud enveloped us. I'm not too proud to say there were a couple of times I had to shut my eyes.

We veered to the left before dropping and speeding through the grey mist of death, towards what I guessed was the cave wall. I saw a small entrance to a tunnel right before we shot into the pitch-black tube. The narrow passage provided momentary shelter from the collapsing cave. I estimated it at five metres top to bottom and about the same from left to right. With the amount of twisting turns we had to make it was a miracle we didn't crash in a big fat fireball. Then we were outside. We shot up into the air, or lack thereof, what with Edin being the moon and all that, banked and levelled out.

The aftermath of the explosions confronted us. Streams of debris floated silently upwards from the surface into the nothingness above. Under transparent domes I saw buildings burning and inhabitants running around like ants.

We flew around the outside of one of the columns of detritus.

'Corporal,' said Cleo in her neutral tone, 'I can't contact anyone on the ship. I'm being blocked.' It confused me as I hadn't even seen her try. I guessed she'd attempted it while waiting for me to finish my appointment with Hyratithead.

'Something's been blocking us since your distress call, Grand Master,' replied the pilot.

'Damn it,' she said, sounding angry for the first time.

'What's happening?' I asked.

'A coordinated attack,' she replied. 'Think of it as a prison break but on a much larger scale. We've managed to hit the power stations, air filtration plants and communications posts at the same time. Most of Edin's emergency functionality is out too.'

I wondered how she could know all that.

'Edin's network will have triggered lockdown protocol,' she continued. 'So we can't get back inside and now we can't reach the ship. We're sitting ducks.'

'What's lockdown protocol?' I asked.

'Each compartment will be sealed off like hundreds of small life rafts. That way, if one fails, the remaining sections will be safe.'

'So, what happens if you're in the one that fails?'

'Use your imagination.'

'We can't stay out here,' said the Corporal, 'we're sitting ducks.'

I thought back to my battle with Hyrattanti and felt emboldened. 'What if I help you?' I asked.

'Be quiet, Jack,' snapped Cleo. 'I'm trying to think.'

Her response irritated me, but I couldn't be bothered to argue, as we clearly needed to get the hell out of here. So, not for the first time that day, I followed Namah's advice. Closing my eyes, I opened myself up again to the universe. The sensation was diminished compared to inside the golden temple and I felt a tremendous sense of fatigue from my battle with the Creator Goddess. I was about to give up when I saw it. Even with my eyes closed I could sense the power flowing through everyone and everything around me. With no clue what I was doing I climbed the energy like a psychic ladder, up into the blackness above. There, cloaked from view was a mighty spaceship. My mind raced towards it at infinite speed and passed right through the hull and into the control deck.

Standing there was the bull-faced beast from the crash site in the Cotswolds. I could feel a tremendous pressure growing, as if my mind might burst into a billion pieces. In a last-ditch attempt I projected the image of us into the soldier's mind, and sensed his surprise, right before I blacked out.

I came to with a headache and Cleo slapping my face while shouting at me to wake up. Over her shoulder I could see a vast silver disc descending towards us. It was so much like the quintessential style of flying saucer you see in movies, that it almost looked fake.

'Bugger,' said the Corporal. 'Well, this isn't good.'

'What is it?' I asked, wiping yet more blood from my nose.

Before I got an answer, three small spaceships came racing towards us through the ascending clouds of debris and opened fire. I don't know how I knew, but know I did, that one of them was Antony.

'Go!' shouted Cleo.

We veered towards the lunar surface as a number of small objects peppered the front and rear of the vehicle. We immediately lost power, but continued our descent towards the ground. The interior of the craft reappeared around me and the sensation of momentum came rushing back. Then I found myself struggling to breathe.

'Hold on!' shouted the Corporal.

I shut my eyes as the panic started to flow. This was going to seriously bloody hurt.

I tried to adopt the brace position you see on the safety cards on aeroplanes, which was a tricky manoeuvre as I'm quite tall and had to angle myself sideways. Then we stopped. I froze for a couple of seconds as my brain attempted to catch up with what was happening. I was now able to breathe again. I opened one eye, then two, before sitting up to look around. As the craft ascended towards the underside of the UFO, which was firing on the small spaceships, I could only assume that we had been caught in some sort of tractor beam.

'He's found us,' said Cleo, before telling me to lie down. But like a car crash on a motorway, I couldn't look away from the impending doom. One of the small ships exploded under superior fire as the large ship got progressively bigger. It must have been as wide as a football field. A piercing green light appeared at its centre, growing in intensity, and I closed my eyes in an attempt to shield them. Placing my arm across my face, I buried my head in the seat. There was shouting, followed by yet more shouting. Then some cursing followed by even more shouting. It took a moment to realise the random voices were shouting at me and it appeared like they wanted me to get up.

I sat up slowly, deciding it was best not to piss anyone off. At least not any more than they already were. However, judging by their tone it would be pretty damn hard to do that.

The room looked like a flight bay and was peppered with other small craft. A number of militant-looking aliens were pointing their weapons at me and I have to say that it wasn't the warmest or fuzziest of welcomes. While disembarking I was thrown around a bit before being forced to the floor. Someone called, 'Clear,' and I was hauled to my feet.

'Come,' said a huge grey-skinned creature with a head like an octopus and thousands of long, skinny tentacles protruding from all over its body. It looked as rough as rotten rats. Some of the tentacles held weapons, but it still had more than enough left to wrap around my arms and push me forwards. The writhing limbs felt disgusting, causing me to shudder. I considered what a pain it must be for it to find clothes and guessed that was why it wasn't wearing any.

I was speed-marched through the ship like an errant cadet. My journey culminated in being shoved through a door that led onto a *Star Trek*-style bridge. Just like the craft that I'd arrived in, the floor, walls and ceiling were transparent. Entering the room felt like stepping outside. The sensation was frankly horrible.

Cleo went and stood authoritatively in the middle of some floating desks. The crew stood behind them, focussed on a multitude of screens. The huge creature from the crash site eyed me with interest as I entered.

'The ships are destroyed,' said a weird-looking alien. 'But one pilot ejected.'

Cleo stared intently at the lunar surface. 'There,' she said, pointing to a rocky area below. 'Fire!'

I followed her gaze and saw a figure dive behind some of the rocks, which were blown to buggery by the blast. It was Antony.

'Again,' shouted Cleo as the ship spun around to the other side of his hiding place and fired. The craft kept circling and I watched with bated breath as the person who'd happily sent me to my death fled for his life.

Dust and debris poured outwards and upwards in all directions.

There was no sign of Antony.

'Fire,' she said again.

If he hadn't been dead before, I knew he sure as heck would be after that.

The man, or Hu that had saved me so many times was now gone. He'd promised so much and delivered only misery.

'Good work,' said Cleo to her crew with a smile. But the grin was wiped from her face as a figure appeared from amidst the debris, crossed some serious distance in a couple of bounds and lifted what looked like a hatch in the floor, before disappearing from view.

'Damn it,' shouted Cleo in frustration. 'Helmsman, get us out of here.' We began to ascend.

A number of triangular black craft started to ascend from Edin's surface.

'Let them go,' ordered Cleo and we stood and watched them racing away into the blackness of space. Looking down, I saw Edin becoming consumed by millions of small explosions. Grand Master Cleopatra Thea Philopator turned to look at me and she didn't look happy. Although with a name that complicated, who would be.

'We found your friends,' she said in a neutral tone. 'They were down on their knees in the dirt, about to have lasers blasted into their brains at high velocity when we intervened. It's a miracle we found them in time.'

'Are they okay?'

'They are.'

'Thank you,' I replied. 'And thank you for saving me.'

Cleo smiled and nodded.

I looked down at the exploding moon as it grew progressively smaller and my gaze followed an object as it flashed up from the surface and hit us. The whole spaceship shook from the impact.

I stumbled sideways and fell onto my bum just as an alarm started screaming.

'Get up!' Cleo pulled me to my feet. 'Or we're both dead.'

CHAPTER 24

'It came from the second sister,' cried a woman on the bridge.

'Send a distress signal to Cyta-Alpha 54,' replied Cleo.

Now that's a mouthful in an emergency.

'And tell them we have the Ternion.'

We ran out of the door and along a curved corridor, turning sharply to the right before passing through a number of crossways. Everyone else appeared to have the same idea, so it was a complete free-for-all. I was pushed, shoved and elbowed by everyone and their mums. Their alien mums. With lots of limbs and messed-up faces.

The crowds parted as we entered a vast room peppered with vertical silver cylinders. Each had shiny doors that the crew members were racing to open. Inside the tubes were vertical red leather loungers and I knew that these must be escape pods. Cleo pulled rank on three aliens fighting to get into one of them, touched a button on the side and the front whooshed open. I stepped inside and turned to face her.

'Press this,' she said, 'and good luck.'

Then I was alone.

I tried to follow Cleo's instructions, but before I could press anything, some total dickhead ran into me. We bumped heads, which I have to say hurt like hell. I swore at the interloper, but he ignored me and whacked the button. A clear screen covered us and we were away. My stomach almost leapt out of my mouth as we shot out of the UFO and into the blackness of space. Then, with an almighty rush, our tiny craft arced away from Edin and thrust earthwards. I watched helplessly as luminous green lights began flashing towards us. To my left and right I saw pods exploding silently upon contact.

'Incoming fire detected,' said a soothing voice. 'Evasive manoeuvres engaged.'

I was pushed back against the seat as we accelerated. The pod ducked and weaved between the ghoulish lights emanating from the earth's surface as I clenched my bum flaps and started to pray.

Unless you've been living under a rock, you'll have seen images of the earth. But trust me when I say that none of them do it justice. It is utterly magnificent. Below us lay oceans and continents in high definition, obscured in places by swirling weather patterns. Somewhere amongst the fear I marvelled at people who thought the world was flat. Mind you, they weren't the only ones with odd ideas. Colin from the mail room had some strange theories indeed. He was convinced that foreign governments sent agents to the UK to create traffic jams, increase supermarket queueing times and walk about being generally rude and annoying to anyone they met. This he said increased the nation's depression and anxiety, thus decreasing productivity. But then he also picked the sleep from his eyes and ate it. So, I tended to take what he said with a pinch of salt. Denzil 'Conspiracy' Reid on the other hand, had always been a big fan.

Sadly, the most beautiful view of my life was ruined by incoming fire. Oh, and having some chap lying on top of me. I mean, really. The escape pod was clearly designed for one. I managed an awkward, 'Are you alright?' but the cuckoo gate crasher dude just gurgled a bit and went limp. In fact, disturbingly so. I therefore gave him a slightly more robust shake to try and elicit a response. 'Excuse me?' I asked, 'are you alright?' I opted to wait a couple more seconds before my next attempt. 'Seriously mate, are you alright?'

Still no response. It was all rather irritating.

The pod continued to dodge the incoming lights and I placed a hand on the gentleman's side to try and push him off. He felt wet. I hoped the idiot hadn't pissed himself; that was the last thing I needed. As I lifted my hand away I saw it was covered in blood. I developed several additional chins while trying to get a better look at the gate crasher. Sadly, that was when I realised that the selfish prick had only gone and died on me. As if being in mortal danger and racing towards the earth in an escape pod wasn't enough, I was being pressed up against a corpse. At least it was a fresh one, I guess.

As you can probably imagine, I was freaking out a bit by this stage and the physical contact was making my skin crawl. Every time I pushed him away his head would flop back against my neck. It was as if he was trying to give me a hickey from beyond the grave. I'm sure Buzz Aldrin never had to put up with this crap.

The only saving grace, and I have to be honest with you, it was literally the only one, was the speed at which we rocketed towards the earth. Although technically it was an anti-gravity propulsion system rather than a rocket, but whatever. I saw my tiny little island homeland somewhere south of my feet and longed to be safely on the ground. Then a worrying thought strutted into my head like a pimp on an evening stroll. I was about to re-enter the earth's atmosphere in a transparent fronted craft. Now, I'm not a scientist as you know, nor a spaceship designer, but even an idiot like me could see this was a recipe for clusterfuck fondue.

During re-entry the nose of a spaceship glows like Rudolph at a reindeer orgy. I won't get too techy, mainly because I lack the neurons, but it goes something like this. When an object enters the atmosphere, it slams into the air, the air gets compressed, compression heats the air, hence the need for a heat shield. The re-entry is hypersonic, so more than five times the speed of sound, and the speed creates shockwaves. This is right where the heating takes place. In order for the shockwaves and therefore the heat to form away from the capsule, the capsules are usually blunt in shape. Unfortunately, my escape pod was pointed like a witch's tit in an ice storm. It also had a bloody great see-through window slapped on the front.

As me and Sir Dead-A-Lot started our re-entry, the front of the escape pod began to glow. The glow rapidly transitioned to totally bloody blinding and it wasn't long before the light had obscured my view of the earth. I used the man's body as a human shield. Not that a hunk of meat was going to hold back the tide of physics, but self-preservation had set in and at least he was making himself useful. It didn't matter that I wasn't actually getting any hotter and it didn't matter that the screen automatically darkened to stop most of the light coming in. My whole being was obsessed, and in my opinion rightfully so, with the flimsy-fronted screen and needle-like nose.

A beeping sound entered the cockpit and I opened my eyes to see the glow had vanished. We'd descended so far that we were passing through a scattering of white clouds. Once on the other side of the white, fluffy gas, London loomed larger and larger in the pod window. I saw the origin of the green lights as they continued to fire at us from the top of the Shard. No wonder the tip didn't look finished: it had a sodding great laser canon strapped to it. London began to look like a model city as we got progressively closer. The Palace of Westminster, St Paul's Cathedral, the Tower of London,

Buckingham Palace and Tower Bridge were all there in miniature. After my off-world travels I was comforted by their iconic familiarity.

Unfortunately, my brief moment of relief was violated by the sight of monsters, some the size of houses, marauding about in the streets. And they weren't the only problem waiting for us on the ground. The day's main event was the hundreds, if not thousands of soldiers and their hardware, which included tanks and heavy artillery, dotted around London. They were literally positioned everywhere. I knew that as soon as we landed, wherever we landed, we'd be surrounded.

Many of the escape pods were already on the ground. Their crews had taken cover wherever they could, battling the hordes of descending troops. To say I wasn't looking forward to landing would be an understatement. Although Cleo's soldiers had better tech, modern, cutting-edge weapons were still magnificently efficient killing tools. Because of that and the sheer force of numbers, it meant we were most likely arriving back in Blighty to meet our makers. My immediate concern, however, was that I was about to crash. I started to shout at the computer to slow us down, but it didn't respond. So, I braced myself for impact. Then, right before being splatted horribly on the road, the escape pod made a perfect landing. A weapon appeared from somewhere by my leg and the transparent screen disappeared. I shoved the lifeless body aside, grabbed the gun and leapt from the witch's tit like a man with a pound of party poppers in his pants.

The noise of the battle was horrific as the enemy soldiers unleashed hell. Bullets whizzed, whooshed and cracked with terminal aggression all around me.

Above my head a black triangular craft was being attacked by a number of flying Iron Men.

'Over here,' shouted the big bull-faced beast. Up close and personal he was damn right frightening, but hey, he was on my team, whatever that team may be. I fired off several shots with what turned out to be a high-velocity laser canon, and managed to separate a couple of enemy soldiers from their heads. A volley of bullets bounced off the pod next to my skull, motivating me to break cover and head for the minotaur man.

I can't have taken more than two steps when I was hit in the back by what felt like a London bus. It wasn't a bus though, or even an enemy soldier, it was a leaping demon the size of a large horse. Lucky old me! I was forced to the floor like a feather colliding with a fighter plane, and it bit into my shoulder with razor-sharp teeth. The pressure was so extreme that I felt it split flesh and crunch bone. It removed its teeth along with my left arm, which it then rather offensively spat out. I obviously wasn't the kind of taste sensation its usual victims provided and it screamed with rage before going in for the kill.

There's a sense of weakness mixed with fear that's unique to being attacked by a force of nature. It's at these moments the universe really puts you in your place. Mankind may conquer the globe, cure illness, create epic monuments, even build inventions of utter wonderment to make us feel superior, but it's a facade. I knew my time was up and I was going to be torn to shreds. It was debatable whether I'd be swallowed, but if I was, I'd be crapped out as a pile of monster dung somewhere in the metropolitan London area. I've got to be honest, it wasn't how I'd expected to go.

The thing reared up, but before it could strike its killer blow, the beast was hit several times by weapon fire. Its guts then made a rather dramatic entrance onto the world stage, before the stinking monstrosity fell down dead.

Cleo hauled me to my feet.

'Move!' she shouted, although it was quite unnecessary as she was already dragging me along by my remaining arm. 'We're a mile from the church.'

I had no idea what she was going on about. 'I can't,' I moaned.

'These are Illuminati soldiers attacking us,' she said. 'We absolutely cannot stay here.'

A giant winged beast swept down from on high and Cleo shot it out of the sky without a backward glance. If I hadn't been in the process of dying, I would have given the woman more kudos. Lasers from a Black Triangular craft tore through the rubbish and junk that covered the roads, and hit Cleo in the side. She turned and peppered the responsible craft with laser fire. Before it could fire on her again, it was attacked by flying Iron Men.

Despite her body armour she started to bleed a hell of a lot. 'We stop,' she screamed, 'we die!'

I remember thinking I was probably done for either way.

If I was to be honest with you, I'd have to say that being injured and in mortal danger is one of the worst feelings in the world. You just want to sit down and sort your shit out. Sadly, you can't. You have to keep going. So, you find yourself obsessing with needle-like focus on the pain. I wanted to give up so badly and collapse on the floor, hell, I wanted my bloody mum, but Cleo kept me upright and moving. What was most impressive was how little effort it seemed to take for her to do it. A creature the size of a van leapt down from a rooftop and landed on my rescuer, sending us both sprawling to the floor. Now, if the creature had attacked me at that point I would have been screwed, but the dumb animal went for Cleo. She repaid its selection process by shooting a massive great hole through its stomach. I got splattered with some of its body parts, which was nice, although to be fair, I was too far gone to care. Cleo pushed its carcass to one side and crouched down next to me as if nothing had happened. I forced myself to sit up with my back against the rusty car, panting like a dog in the desert. The pain was unbearable and it felt like my heart was going to beat right out of my chest. The minotaur came and crouched down next to us and started shooting at the enemy soldiers.

Cleo pulled out a knife and cut strips from the clothing of a fallen soldier. She bound them around my shoulder and I screamed as she tightened them. 'It'll stop the bleeding,' she said, although I thought it was a bit like putting toilet paper over a hole in the Hoover Dam. She then grabbed me by the back of the neck and pushed our foreheads together. 'Jack?'

There was a frightening intensity in her eyes, like she was trying to force her strength into my failing body through will alone. I confess I did feel slightly better as a result.

'We've got to get to the Temple Church,' she said. 'Below it lies a secret city. There's a weapon there.'

'What weapon?' I whispered. Just speaking sent shockwaves of pain through my body.

'It will stop the heartbeat of any living thing within a ten-mile radius. We will be safe underground.'

On a normal day I'd have been like, 'Wow! Ten miles? That's amazing! What on earth is it? How does it work? Blah, blah, blah,' but instead I just felt my eyes starting to close. A wrecked car lying next to us was hit by a shell and lifted into the air. Those of Cleo's troops who'd been next to it died where they crouched. I felt something hit my leg and cried out in agony. It was only a bit of bloody shrapnel! The intergalactic soldiers wasted no time returning fire. Considering how outnumbered they were and the speed at which the enemy forces were amassing, they were literally superhuman.

'I'll hold them here,' said the minotaur man. Cleo put a hand on his shoulder. There was an exchange between them I couldn't hear, although right then I confess I couldn't really be arsed to listen. Then she grabbed me and we continued up the street under a hail of fire.

We were moving slower than I would have liked thanks to our injuries and being attacked from multiple angles. Cleo had my arm wrapped around her shoulder and was holding me around the waist. With the combination of blood loss and the newly acquired shrapnel wound in my leg, she was basically carrying me. We moved along the street, dodging the rubbish and detritus blocking our path. Jet planes roared overhead and missiles rained down on the soldiers. No one could survive what was being thrown at them, yet somehow, they fought on. My foggy brain noted the sign for Fleet Street, shortly after which we arrived at a timber-framed Jacobean town house resting on a stone archway. The arch contained a heavy black door that looked ancient.

A volley of bullets hit the stone archway directly above our heads, the velocity, noise and force of which were terrifying. My face was peppered by flying shards of stone. Like I hadn't been through enough crap for one day. Cleo pushed me through the archway while turning and firing. A round caught her straight in the chest and sent her flying backwards through the air. She lay motionless on the ground a couple of metres away from me. In response to this latest attack I decided rather heroically to lie on the ground and bleed a lot.

Cleo wasn't moving. Despite being seriously out of it, I still knew that by lying here we were booking a one-way trip to destination dead. Yet despite that realisation, I couldn't move. I was injured and I was tired and there was nothing left in the tank. All thoughts of self-preservation had long since evaporated, so I lay there in a crumpled heap and watched Edin breaking apart in the bright blue sky above. That sight alone should have caused a certain degree of alarm, but right then I confess I was a little preoccupied with dying.

It's true what they say. Your life really does flash before your eyes when you're about to go. What surprised me was that it didn't come in chronological order. Instead it arrived in random Technicolor bursts. One moment I was laughing and drinking with friends. Next, I was playing rugby on the school field. I went from losing my virginity in Stacy Derwent's sister's bed, to observing a rescued hedgehog in my grandad's greenhouse. I nervously held Brenda's hand on the first morning of school and I sat in the car watching the ocean during a family picnic in the rain. Then the beautiful Lucy Chong smiled at me from across the office, lighting up my bland world like a hazy summer's day. I saw dreams that would never be, observed moments of joy, the tears, the laughter, the sunsets and the storms.

Then, I saw Thomas.

He looked worried.

'Get up, Jack,' he said, shaking me. His small hands looked tiny against my adult arm. 'You have to get up.'

I wanted to speak, I wanted to talk to my brother, but no words would come out.

'They're coming, Jack,' he said, as his shaking became more desperate. 'You have to get up. Jack, get up!'

I opened my eyes and saw that Cleo was shaking me.

'Get up, Jack,' she shouted. Her teeth were covered in blood and I knew she was in seriously bad shape. 'Get up!'

Despite having nothing left, some basic survival instinct rose up inside me and I heard my internal voice screaming, 'Get up, Gibson!' Using my remaining arm, I began pushing myself to my feet. It hurt like hell and I cried out from the strain.

Cleo dragged me between the buildings and past a stone church and its ornate entrance to our left. We reached a courtyard, surrounded by a number of buildings and containing a large stone column, upon which sat a horse carrying two knights, one of which was holding a banner. I remember feeling sorry for the pretend horse having to carry two heavy-arsed armoured riders on its back. Somehow it didn't seem fair.

While I was busy daydreaming, Cleo was firing back at our pursuers like an Amazonian warrior, except she had both breasts. Or maybe not, I can't confess to seeing them. As the last of the soldiers fell, she screamed at me to 'Come on,' but it was more likely to keep herself moving than to elicit a response from my dead weight of a body. We moved towards a door in the side of the church and if I had to guess, I'd say we were probably about three metres away when the horror show to end all horror shows decided to make an appearance.

Clinging onto the wall of the church above our heads was the most disgusting, spine-tingling beast I'd seen so far on my messed-up road trip around Southern England, the Levantine Sea and beyond. Its body was a blobby, fleshy mess covered in tons of eyes, and at its centre was a vicious and repugnant mouth full of giant pin-like fangs. It had ten long, multi-jointed arms ending in a range of unpleasant accoutrements, such as claws, deformed human hands and pincers. And its legs looked like they were taken from a giant frog, each ending with grotesque clawed hands, rather than the more pedestrian option of actual feet. It really was like a nightmare made flesh.

'Damn,' muttered Cleo, which I thought was pretty restrained, all things considered.

Now you're probably thinking that this was the point at which I laid down to die. God knows I'd been on the verge of it for long enough. However, dying right then would have meant being eaten by that thing, and there was no way this side of interfering with the pope with a popsicle that I was going to let that happen. However, the nightmare had other ideas and it leapt through the air with a surprising amount of grace, hinting at the perfect killing machine it no doubt was. Cleo pushed me away from her with such force that my feet left the ground and she began blasting it with her laser gun. The Grand Master and the laser fire were impossibly fast, yet the beast was faster. She swung her weapon, firing in an arc as the creature raced along the side of the church wall and fled back up and over the roof.

Cleo had just turned around to pick my dying arse back up when the monster reappeared and launched itself at her.

'Look out!' I shouted.

It caught her from behind, forcing Cleo to the ground. Her gun went flying out of her hand and struck me square on the forehead. Talk about hitting a man when he's down. The force of the beast's attack would have killed any normal person, but then Cleo wasn't a normal person. Before it could pin her down with its overabundance of limbs, she'd hooked a few of its eyes out with her fingers.

The monster screeched and reared up on its frog's legs to deliver the killing blow. After thousands of years traversing the stars, Cleo was about to be ripped apart by the ugliest thing I'd ever seen. As I looked skyward from my crumpled mess on the floor, I saw the statue of the knights on horseback once more. Now it reminded me of knights on a chess board. Always a chess piece, but never a player. My body was almost broken, but my mind was still functioning, well, just about. Virtually using will alone I rolled my wrecked body towards the gun, picked it up and opened fire. The volley of shots tore into its flesh, causing its innards to be splattered across the courtyard. It let out a chilling scream and then the monstrosity fell down dead. That was the moment my mind joined my body and gave up the fight.

My memory is sketchy from that point onwards. I think people may have been shouting and there was definitely a ton of gunfire. I do have a hazy memory of being inside and Cleo shouting, 'Now!'

Then the consciousness that I'd been fighting so hard to hold on to, slipped through my fingers like water.

CHAPTER 25

I opened my eyes to see Denzil's delightful little face staring down at me.

'Watch out, gene pool,' he said with a huge smile, 'Gibby's manky semen is back in the game.'

'Denzil!' Lucy hit him on the arm. 'Don't be so gross.'

'What?' he replied. 'He's lost his arm and a leg, not his sense of humour.'

'For God's sake, Denzil, could you be any more insensitive?'

'Probably,' he replied.

'You're unbelievable.'

'What?' he said. 'They fixed them!'

An image of my ruined arm passed through my brain, overshadowing my relief at seeing my friends. I don't think I'd ever given my limbs the appreciation they deserved up until that moment. But all thoughts of lost appendages were put on hold as Riya leant in and kissed me on the lips.

'Welcome back, gorgeous,' she said.

It was a little over the top and clearly not just for my benefit. My eyes wandered to Lucy, who looked like she was trying not to appear bothered by it. Denzil, on the other hand, was trying not to laugh.

'My arm?' My throat was as dry as a cracker-eating challenge and I felt totally spaced, so it came out as little more than a whisper.

'Just wait until you see what they've done,' said Denzil. 'It's fricking awesome.'

Lucy gave him a stern look.

'What have I done now?'

'Do you remember what happened to you?' Lucy asked me delicately.

'You had an accident,' added Riya, as if engaged in a sympathy contest. 'And injured your arm and your leg, remember?'

I was donkey-punched by a wave of emotion and clearly didn't do a good job of hiding it.

'It's okay, Jack,' said Riya. 'I'm here for you.'

'I lost my arm and leg.' I was on the verge of tears. I was exhausted and the enormity of it was too much to handle.

'Don't worry, mate,' said Denzil, sounding surprisingly chipper, but then he hadn't just lost any limbs, had he? He threw back the pristine white sheet covering my body. 'They've only gone and given you new ones!'

I looked down at my arm and leg, except they weren't mine. I mean, they were the right shape, the right length and in the right places, but what aroused my suspicion that something was afoot was the fact that they were shiny, metallic black.

'Wiggle your fingers and toes,' said Denzil.

My fingers and toes moved instinctively. I touched the bedsheets and felt everything.

'They're going to cover them in synthetic skin,' said Riya. 'So, they're going to look and feel just like the real ones.'

I stared at the alien attachments for a while. It was so surreal. Eventually, I closed my eyes and drifted back to sleep.

I spent the next couple of days isolated from my friends with the steady stream of medical staff being my only companions. Once the limbs were finished and looking unsettlingly realistic, I was summoned to a meeting with a fully recovered Cleo. Her office was an obscenely grand affair, but then I guess she was the boss. Behind her stood a large window containing one of the most beautiful landscapes I'd ever seen. I thought back to Antony's office on the spaceship.

'It's Lake Iri on the planet Aladorn,' she explained with a smile.

I stood transfixed, watching the pink water lapping against the stunning white shoreline. The most impressive elements were the huge mountain and the two vast planets that hung in the sky, appearing to be almost within touching distance.

She stood up from behind the enormous desk. 'Sit with me, Jack,' she said, beckoning to a pair of chairs. We sat down on them and the room instantly vanished and I found myself surrounded by what looked like rolling Tuscan fields. We were gently gliding over them with the wind ruffling my hair. Cleo laughed at the look of shock on my face.

'Where are we?' I asked.

'Ten kilometres below the earth's surface,' she said. 'It's one of the lesser-known underground cities built on earth. The Illuminati don't even know it's here.'

'But this looks so real.'

Cleo laughed again.

'What happened to the Illuminati?' I asked.

'You don't need to worry about them,' she said as we passed a field of grazing sheep. 'Edin was destroyed in our coordinated attack. The Eyes of Edin are blinded.'

'Did your friends respond to the distress signal?'

'Not yet,' she replied. 'But as soon as they receive it they'll send a fleet of ships to begin evacuating earth.'

'Is there anyone left to evacuate?' I asked.

'Of course,' she said. 'The Hu didn't succeed, Jack. Their weapon didn't fulfil its purpose.'

We passed over a familiar-looking walled town filled with a jumble of small buildings. I recognised Monteriggioni immediately.

Cleo smiled as we flew up and over the town. 'I hope you like the scenery. Denzil said it was one of your best holidays.'

'It was,' I mumbled, thinking back to those two happy weeks when I was still a twin brother. 'I need to contact my family. Check they're okay.'

When I looked at Cleo's expression I knew whatever she had to say wasn't good.

'You need to accept who you are. The last of the demi-gods.'

I laughed. 'Which one's the god, Harold or Brenda?'

'They aren't your real parents.'

'Of course they're my real parents.' Our eyes locked and I knew deep down in my soul that she was right, even if I wasn't ready to accept it.

'They raised you, but you are half human, half Hu, as was your brother, Thomas. You're the last of your kind.'

'That can't be true.'

'Why not?'

'Because it's ridiculous!'

'Ethylene glycol may look like water, but it won't make flowers bloom.'

'You what?'

'You have to face up to who you are, Jack Gibson.'

I shook my head. 'I have to find my parents.'

'We've already located them.'

The world spun as my insides went into free fall. 'You found them? Are they okay? Are they hurt? Have you spoken to them?'

'They're in a military base on the edge of London.'

'That's amazing,' I almost shouted. 'Can I see them?'

'I will reunite you as soon as I can.'

Waves of relief swept over me. 'I can't thank you enough.'

'Please, there really is no need. What's important is that you accept the reality of who you are and you become the person you were born to be.'

Despite all of the crazy shit I'd been through, this was a bridge too far for now. And weirdly, now I knew my parents were safe, it somehow seemed less important. So, I opted to change the subject.

'So best guess, how long until your friends arrive?'

'Soon,' said Cleo. 'They won't want to give the High Council another chance to get to you.'

'Who was the blue man that died in the Cotswolds?'

'His name was Anattai. He was one of my best and most loyal soldiers.'

As we passed over a herd of cows, they turned and started to run.

'Why did you turn on your people?'

Cleo looked troubled. 'Some of us grew tired of the constant slaughter, becoming ever more critical of the Goddess's methods. When we found the Ternion on Gandareen, we knew it had the potential to make Hyrattanti invincible. So, we chose to steal it before it reached our home world. It was hidden on earth until we could decide what to do with it. But we had a traitor in our midst. Once compromised, we had to move it. Then you came along.'

'But what does it actually do?'

'All we know is that the bearer is imparted with the ability to see all, know all and be all. However, the Illuminati are in possession of the ancient scriptures found on Gandareen. I curse myself for handing them over after the battle. It was a terrible error.'

'So, as I managed to absorb it, does that mean I'm quite powerful, then?'

Cleo smiled. 'You could be incredible.'

'And you think it was searching for me?'

'I confess I had my doubts, but now I do, yes.'

'So, I'm basically like the chosen one?'

'More like the last bruised apple on the shelf.'

'Charming.'

Cleo laughed. 'But when you need to make an apple pie, what choice do you have.'

'But the Ternion isn't working. I'm just having a load of random visions.'

Cleo looked thoughtful. 'Then we will have to discover its power together.'

It wasn't the first time I had heard that. 'What if your friends don't come?' I asked.

'They will come,' she said with a smile. 'Trust me on that. But while we wait for them you must begin your training. It was a miracle you survived your encounter with the Goddess, but it's one she won't forget. She knows what you are now and will stop at nothing to get her hands on the Ternion and destroy you. When she makes her move, we must be ready.'

'One final question.'

Cleo raised an eyebrow.

'If you and Antony and Namah are all Hu, why don't you look like Hyrattanti?'

Cleo smiled. 'We're psychic shapeshifters. This is not my natural form. But while on earth I prefer to blend in. So I project a human image into the minds of those around me. I can hardly walk down Oxford Street on a Saturday afternoon looking like a blue reptilian. Tongues would wag.'

'So you're a goddess, then?'

'No, only the High Council are of divine origin. But we are their direct descendants. We are the children of the twelve.'

'So you're related?'

'Created. Gods don't breed, they build. But enough of this. I have some news that might cheer you up a little.'

'More than my parents?'

'We rescued Ziggy from the military base. He's here now.'

I shook my head, confused. 'Really?'

'Really.'

'That's amazing.'

'But first you have more pressing matters to deal with.' A light danced in her eyes.

'Like what?' I asked as the room reappeared around us.

'You have two women who both appear to care about you very much. So, you need to make a choice.'

I pulled a face.

Cleo laughed. 'Well, go on then. You can't cower in here all day.'

I needed time to process what Cleo had told me. So, I explored the underground city for a couple of hours, which turned out to be far bigger than I'd expected. It looked magnificent, with obelisk-lined streets and Egyptian-styled buildings, the tallest of which was a pyramid, stretching high up into the darkness above. Most chilling were the statues of what I assumed to be Hyrattanti arrogantly watching over me as I explored. Somehow it made her appear more like a dictator than a goddess. I walked through a maze of lanes, up and down steps, over bridges, and past strange-looking people who all appeared to be in a great rush. But then I guess they were conducting a rebellion. Despite that it truly was a beautiful place. It would have been even nicer if I didn't have two armed guards following me about like overly loyal hounds. It kind of killed the ambiance.

What I loved best about the underground city was that like all good urban spaces it had a centre, which contained a bar. Thanks to the strange mix of patrons and tech, inside it looked like something out of *Star Wars*. As soon as I entered, I saw Denzil and Lanta sitting at a table in one corner.

'Here comes Darth Vader,' announced Denzil from across the room, causing everyone to turn and stare at me.

'Piss off,' I replied when I reached the table.

'Did you ask them to give you a new willy as well?' He laughed. 'That little thing's no good to man or beast.'

'It's a good job I don't plan to use it on either, then,' I replied.

'Sit down, Gibby,' Denzil said. 'You've got to try the drinks in this place.'

'I thought we'd quit the hard stuff?'

'We have, but that's drugs: alcohol's totally fine. Anyway, stop being such a monk. The Sugar Beer is off the charts and the Purple Pistons will blow your head off.'

'I guess a couple won't hurt.'

Lanta gave me one of her radiant smiles. 'H'll J'ck,' she said sweetly.

'Hello Lanta,' I said, smiling back.

'H'w yh?'

I looked at Denzil.

He shrugged and grinned. 'Her English is getting better by the hour. It's unbelievable.'

I turned back to Lanta. 'I'm good, thank you. You?'

'W'll, th'nk.'

She laughed and gave Denzil an enthusiastic hug. Lanta was clearly still smitten with him, although for the life of me, I had no idea why. But instead of pushing her away, he smiled warmly. It was the first time I'd seen him look happy in a long time. It suited him.

'How's the new limbs?' Denzil asked me. 'You could probably crush a snooker ball with that arm. Best not get too carried away when you're rubbing one out.'

'It's fine,' I replied. 'I'm right-handed.'

Denzil laughed and I took a deep breath. 'I owe you an apology.'

Denzil's expression became solemn. 'You're right. Your face is really offensive.'

'I'm being serious.'

'So am I, bum face.'

'L'st'n,' said Lanta, and by some miracle Denzil actually did.

'I'm so sorry I didn't listen to you about Antony. You were looking out for me and I threw it back in your face. I feel terrible about it. It was a shitty thing to do and I'm so sorry.'

Denzil looked uncomfortable during my apology. 'It's fine,' he replied when I'd finished. 'It just means you have to buy the drinks for the rest of our lives.'

I smiled. 'In your dreams.'

'I take it you've not seen Lucy or Riya yet?'

'Not yet.'

He laughed again. The guy must have downed a few Purple Pistons already. 'Well, they're both looking for you.'

'So Cleo tells me.'

'Just pick one and move on. They'll both be annoying once you get into a relationship with them anyway, so it's irrelevant.'

'Thanks,' I replied. 'That was truly insightful.'

'Just pick the one you want to sleep with the most. I assume it's going to be Lucy?'

'Why?'

'Er, how about because you're in love with her, you idiot?'

'Chz wth hrt,' said Lanta.

'Chaz will hurt?' I said, confused.

Lanta frowned and tried again. 'Chz wth hrt.' She said whilst tapping herself on the chest.

'Mate, she's telling you to choose with your heart,' said Denzil.

'Ys! Chz wth hrt.' Lanta beamed.

'Maybe you can take the lucky lady on a date to John O'Groats to catch a ferry,' said Denzil with a grin. 'Say hi to Jenny Hanson if you do.'

'Piss off.'

'Have you seen Ziggy yet?'

'I'm going to visit him later.'

Denzil laughed. 'Well, when you see the hairy little freak, say hi from me.'

We sat together for a couple of hours, talking, drinking and laughing. It felt just like the good old days. But as much as I was enjoying myself, I knew there was something I had to do.

I downed the last of my drink, said goodbye and walked out with my bodyguards in tow. Twenty minutes later I found myself standing outside an apartment in one of the tallest buildings in the city. I paused and took a deep breath. It had been a long time coming, but I was finally ready to grow a pair.

'Time to play chess,' I whispered, before knocking on Lucy's door.

ACKNOWLEDGEMENTS

A huge thank you to the writer James Nash who has the permanent misfortune of being my uncle. Your continuous encouragement and support along with reading the first fifty thousand iterations with such enthusiasm made a universe of difference.

I'd like to give a big shout out to the main woman Bryony Sutherland. You edit like a boss. Thank you for your skill, professionalism and for putting up with my humour. Please send my love to Katie when you see her.

Finally a massive thank you to all the friends, family members, colleagues, acquaintances and random strangers that have shown even a modicum of interest in my writing. You know who you are and you know you rock. Peace and love.

Printed in Great Britain
by Amazon